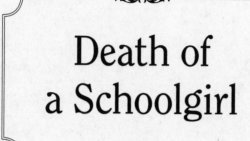

Death of
a Schoolgirl

Death of a Schoolgirl

The Jane Eyre Chronicles

Joanna Campbell Slan

BERKLEY PRIME CRIME, NEW YORK

THE BERKLEY PUBLISHING GROUP
Published by the Penguin Group
Penguin Group (USA) Inc.
375 Hudson Street, New York, New York 10014, USA

Penguin Group (Canada), 90 Eglinton Avenue East, Suite 700, Toronto, Ontario M4P 2Y3, Canada (a division of Pearson Penguin Canada Inc.) • Penguin Books Ltd., 80 Strand, London WC2R 0RL, England • Penguin Group Ireland, 25 St. Stephen's Green, Dublin 2, Ireland (a division of Penguin Books Ltd.) • Penguin Group (Australia), 250 Camberwell Road, Camberwell, Victoria 3124, Australia (a division of Pearson Australia Group Pty. Ltd.) • Penguin Books India Pvt. Ltd., 11 Community Centre, Panchsheel Park, New Delhi—110 017, India • Penguin Group (NZ), 67 Apollo Drive, Rosedale, Auckland 0632, New Zealand (a division of Pearson New Zealand Ltd.) • Penguin Books (South Africa) (Pty.) Ltd., 24 Sturdee Avenue, Rosebank, Johannesburg 2196, South Africa

Penguin Books Ltd., Registered Offices: 80 Strand, London WC2R 0RL, England

This book is an original publication of The Berkley Publishing Group.

Copyright © 2012 by Joanna Campbell Slan.
The Edgar® name is a registered service mark of the Mystery Writers of America, Inc.
Cover art by Alan Ayers. Cover design by George Long. Logo devices by Shutterstock.
Interior text design by Laura K. Corless.

ISBN 978-1-62090-417-6

PRINTED IN THE UNITED STATES OF AMERICA

For my sister, Jane Ransome Campbell

Acknowledgments

As a young girl growing up in an abusive home, I discovered Charlotte Brontë's classic *Jane Eyre: An Autobiography*—and it saved my life. Since then, I've met countless women who also heeded Jane's example by getting the best education they could. So I would be remiss if I did not start my acknowledgments with a grateful nod to that supreme muse, Charlotte Brontë.

This book would not have been possible without the dedication, professionalism, and support of my wonderful agent, Paige Wheeler of Folio Literary Management, LLC, and my superlative editor, Shannon Jamieson Vazquez. I cannot thank either woman enough. Copyeditor Marianne Grace brought a wealth of knowledge to this project, and I am enormously in her debt. Early encouragement for this project was also given by Louis Bayard, and early readers included my longtime friend Theresa Kaminski, professor of history at the University of Wisconsin–Stevens Point; Nancy LoPatin-Lummis, professor of history and chair of the History department at the University of Wisconsin–Stevens Point; Becky Hutchison; and Allyson Faith McGill. Novelist Shirl Henke and William Burgan both suggested marvelous historical resources. David R. Beech, FRPSL, head of the Philatelic Collections at the British Library, kindly answered my questions, as did Francine Matthews. Any errors are my own.

Hank Phillippi Ryan supplied my mantra, "You can do it if you want to do it."

My husband, David Slan, provided me with the perfect spot for writing, our lovely home on Jupiter Island. He has always been my greatest supporter and asset. My son, Michael Slan, urged me to "think big." My aunt Shirley Helmly served as a wonderful assistant and nurturing friend. Most of all, the one "Jane" in my life, my fabulous sister, Jane Ransome Campbell, provided love, encouragement, and faith in me, for which I shall always be deeply indebted.

And the King shall answer and say unto them, Verily I say unto you, Inasmuch as ye have done it unto one of the least of these my brethren, ye have done it unto me.

—Matthew 25:40, King James Version of the Bible

Women feel just as men feel . . . It is thoughtless to condemn them, or laugh at them, if they seek to do more or learn more than custom has pronounced necessary for their sex.

—*Jane Eyre: An Autobiography*

When Jane Eyre first wrote her autobiography, it was intended as a multivolume work, for she'd lived a rich and varied life despite her harsh beginnings. But after publication of the first volume of her early life, from her birth to her marriage in 1819, the book received such an overwhelming amount of attention—some positive, but much negative—that it quite turned her against publishing the rest of the story she'd written.

A young woman well acquainted with that timeless classic purchased a stack of papers at one of the bimonthly Sunbury Antiques Markets held on the grounds of the Kempton Park Racecourse. Among the pages, this reader discovered a handwritten manuscript. On closer inspection, the papers told a tale, the ongoing saga of one Jane Eyre Rochester.

And so, dear reader, her story continues . . .

Preface

Ferndean Manor, Yorkshire
April 1, 1820

Reader, I am delivered of a son.

What a noble burden it is to be entrusted with the life of another!

The midwife settled the little stranger in my arms, and with a bit of adjustment I became comfortable. That is, *we* became comfortable, young master Edward Rivers Rochester and his mother. My baby relaxed in my arms, and I sighed with happiness.

Everything about this moment seemed right. Satisfyingly so.

"Jane, my darling. My brave, brave girl. We have a son. Shall we call him Ned?" My husband, Edward Fairfax Rochester, planted a tender kiss on my lips and another on the top of our baby's downy head. "Welcome, little man."

I unfurled our son's tightly clenched hand and counted all the fingers. Five, I assured myself. I repeated my investigation with his other hand. From there I moved to his budlike feet—pink and fresh and new—and examined his curled toes. How could he be so impossibly small? So tiny? So vulnerable?

Mrs. Alice Fairfax, our housekeeper and Edward's second cousin on his mother's side, hurried into the room. "He is perfect. What a blessing! I shall go tell the others. They will be over the moon with joy." In short order, I heard happy voices from the other side of the bedroom door.

Inwardly, I laughed. My son was less than five minutes old and already he had set the household aflutter.

Spent with the exhaustion and emotion of a long labor, I adjusted the unaccustomed bundle. I stared down at Ned's wrinkled, red face and wondered, *Who is this?*

With a yawn, Ned blinked up at me. Long lashes framed eyes the same color as his father's. At that moment, I fell unreservedly, irrevocably in love with my baby. I knew I would do anything to safeguard my child. Anything! A lump formed in my throat, a pain squeezed my chest, and I burst into tears.

"Are you all right?" Edward stroked my hair and gestured frantically for the midwife, a quiet grandmother from Millcote, our nearest town. A woman much recommended for her experience, but whom I valued for her manner. Her reddened hands were rough to the touch, but gentle when assisting me.

"'Tis to be expected, sir." The midwife peered over Edward's shoulder as she sipped her well-earned cup of tea with three lumps of sugar. "Tears are part of the package. A body's heart overflows wi' joy."

Oh, my little one! my heart sang. *Sum of my heart's desires! Forgive me for I am new to this business of being a mother. I pledge to you all that I am, and all that I have, to safeguard you. You lie here trustingly, but the world is vast and I am so weak right now.*

As I wept, with joy and fear and frustration, my husband put his arm around me and our son. "It will be all right, Jane," he promised me. "We will be enough. I promise you, we will be."

But it takes more than a promise to protect a child.

I have reason to know.

Chapter 1

Ferndean Manor, Yorkshire
October 13, 1820

In the months and days that followed Ned's birth, my thoughts often reverted to my own orphan childhood. When I was but a year old, I lost both my parents to typhus and was taken in by my mother's brother, who, upon his own deathbed soon thereafter, entreated his wife, Mrs. Reed, to care for me. She did so in the barest sense—she did not, after all, send me directly to the workhouse—but extended to me, a blameless infant, none of the affection and indulgence she lavished upon my three cousins, her own children, who tormented me mercilessly. I was alone in the world without protectors, without a guiding hand or kind heart to ease my journey.

I shuddered to imagine such a fate befalling my son. Tucking his blanket around him, I was struck anew by how wholly dependent he was at six months of age.

These days Ned was not the only one who relied on me. His father saw the world through my eyes. When fire destroyed Thornfield Hall, the Rochester family home—a conflagration set by my husband's first wife, Bertha Mason, and in which she also perished—it not only burned the mansion to the ground; it nearly cost my husband his life. A beam fell on Edward, partially crushing him, partially protecting him. His right eye was knocked out, and his left hand was damaged so badly that amputation was done directly. The other eye, in sympathy to its twin, alternated inflammation with good health, severely limiting his vision. Recently, I feared his sight had gotten worse.

Most cruelly, his injuries took from him his ability to ride horseback alone, an activity previously perfectly suited to his personality and love of the outdoors. Nowadays, my husband often visits the stable, standing with his forehead pressed against the slats of his horse Mesrour's stall, the old comrades communing and remembering happier days. Robbed of his ability to ride, Edward finds it difficult to get out among his tenants and talk to them as he should. Reading is impossible, and writing is nearly so.

"Mr. Carter has arrived to examine Mr. Rochester," Mrs. Fairfax said as she stood in the doorway. "Your husband waits for you. Hester can watch after the baby." This was a gentle rebuke. Our housekeeper worries that I will spoil our son with too much attention.

I planned to.

Hester Muttoone, my son's wet nurse, had had much experience in the nursery, certainly more than either the childless widow Mrs. Fairfax or myself. Watching Hester's deft movements with Ned, I realized how awkward I was, how tentative, a beginner at motherhood. Yet I was determined to do many of the chores often relegated to a baby's minder. These small tasks brought me pleasure; I admit that I was in awe of my son. But Hester held him, cleaned him, and offered him her breast as though my child was wholly unremarkable.

"The girl is fully capable. You will spoil him." Mrs. Fairfax made a clucking sound with her tongue, a weak attempt to scold me.

"But he is my own, my firstborn child."

"Ah, and we would all give our lives for our young master. Be assured of that," Mrs. Fairfax said. "But Ned's father relies on you to help him. Master and Mr. Carter are in the garden." She paused and cocked her head toward the window. "Perhaps you will still have time to stroll the lane together. Mayhap you can pick the last of the rose hips before the birds get them all."

If we could hurry through Mr. Carter's visit, I had every intention of taking a walk that afternoon with Edward. Indecisive weather marred our autumn. The scent of rain and change was on the air. A storm moved in from the coast. The yellow tassels of the furze nodded winningly, as the fern fronds waved sleepy heads in the woods surrounding our home. Leaves had begun to turn, a prelude to their drifting down and leaving bare branches in their place.

We lived far from human society. Ferndean Manor lay half buried, deep in a thick stand of trees. Millcote, the closest town, was thirty miles away. To reach the main road into town, one must travel a lumpy, uneven grass path, a trial to passengers in carriages.

"Tell Mr. Rochester that I am coming." I ran a fingertip along the crown of my son's head and down his plump cheek. In response, his lips pursed and he suckled the air.

"As you wish." Retreating footsteps and the squeak of door hinges signaled that Mrs. Fairfax had at last left me alone. I studied my little boy, committing every inch of his form to memory. He was already growing so quickly!

In truth, I needed a few moments of privacy to gather courage to face what lay ahead. Mr. Carter visited Ferndean regularly to check on Edward, my darling husband, once a strong and mighty man, now my sightless Samson. With each examination our hopes soared, only to be dashed and come crashing down, as a pheasant falls from the sky when felled by a percussive gun.

"What if he pronounces my improvement beyond his

skills?" Edward had asked me only last evening as we sat together companionably beside the hearth, basking in the dying embers. His stern brow, interrupted with a scar from the conflagration, creased with concern. "What if I can never see more than the haze of light as it pours through the window? Or the dancing red tongue of a candle's flame?"

"Then I shall have to be your eyes. Such deficiency matters little. I am here for you. All my heart is yours, sir. Always and forever."

I relived this poignant moment as Hester entered the nursery and executed a sloppy partial curtsy. Keeping her protruding eyes downcast, she took her accustomed place on a chair near Ned's crib. I gave my son one last kiss and started toward what we euphemistically called "our garden."

I passed by Mrs. Fairfax, who struggled mightily to keep a slight expression of disapproval on her face. She aims to make me a more conventional lady of the manor and endeavors to mold me into her ideal of a country squire's wife. It is a challenge—because I care little for outward appearances—but one she approaches with tact and persistence.

Alice Fairfax had known my husband since he was a lad. She worked as Mr. Rochester's housekeeper for many years, but after the fire, he settled an annuity on her. How fortunate we were that when she heard of our marriage and Ned's impending arrival, she had written inquiring if we might have need of her!

At first, however, our new roles caused friction.

Mrs. Fairfax was accustomed to running the master's household. But now I—who had once been hired by her to serve as a governess for Mr. Rochester's ward, Adèle—was her mistress. She would tell Cook to make lamb chops, and I would ask for veal. Cook would take advantage of our confusion and serve up leftover pigeon pie. Mrs. Fairfax demanded that we eat on good china and drink from crystal glasses. I would have been content with an old chipped plate and a tin mug. She would suggest that we inventory all the bed linens to determine what needed mending, and I would think that could wait until the bluebells finished blooming. What did I know of fine living? I was, after all, little more than a grown-up orphan girl. The shift from governess to mistress was still fresh with me, and my new role proved an awkward fit. Mrs. Fairfax frequently reminded me, "One can't converse with servants on terms of equality. One must keep them at due distance, for fear of losing one's authority."

Over my more than twenty years on this earth, I have found that most of the kindness I have enjoyed was delivered from the hands of servants, not masters! I think I can be excused if I parted company with our servants reluctantly.

But I knew the good widow was right. I looked to her for guidance in a multitude of matters, including the art of entertaining, although currently our situation was complicated by our cramped quarters here at Ferndean.

This house was built as a hunting lodge for the Rochester men. Gradually, nature had encroached upon the property, seeking to reclaim that which was rightfully hers. The location was both out-of-the-way and unhealthy. In addition, it had been long ignored, thus rendering the main building almost uninhabitable, with the exception of a few rooms that had been done up to accommodate my husband's late father when he used to visit during hunting season. Therefore, we made do with limited space, living a cramped existence, especially considering our growing family.

So far, we had not had any visitors who wished to come and stay, but that might change. I have a handful of cousins. On my father's side are my cousins Diana, Mary, and St. John Rivers, delightful people whose companionship I enjoy. On the Reed side, I have been less fortunate. No doubt they feel the same about me.

I am no great beauty, nor even passing pretty; indeed, I am possessed of a pale coloring and a small stature that renders me quite ordinary. I have heard myself compared, not inaccurately, to a house sparrow. Certainly, like that ubiquitous bird, I tend to blend into my surroundings. Although my features are irregular, I compensate for that by keeping my person neat.

In addition, I have two talents I might reasonably claim. First, given a pencil and paper, I can reproduce anything I've seen with reasonable accuracy. Second, if people were to look beyond my unassuming façade and their own prejudices, they would notice my curious and analytical mind, a faculty that gives me a talent for quiet observation.

I also have another dependable virtue: my compassion for those in reduced circumstances. After all, I know what it feels like to be alone and without resources.

As I walked down the hallway, my heart caught in my throat. A tingle ran up my arm. Someone or something begged my attention.

I whirled around, expecting to face an intruder or the source of my unease.

I was alone, but I thought I had heard a voice, calling out to me.

I entered the parlor and found it empty, except for the lingering scent of pipe tobacco. I moved to the window, disturbing Pilot, my husband's Newfoundland.

No one was there.

Sensing my alarm, Pilot rose from his bed and nudged me with his cold, wet nose.

"Do you see someone or something, old friend?" I traced the gray in his muzzle. "No, I imagine not."

It could only be my imagination. Lately an unsettled feeling had gathered strength within me. At present, it was vague, but insistent. I shook my head to clear it. There had been no reason for alarm. None. Ned was in his crib. Hester was there with him. Leah, our maid of all work, and Cook clattered about in the kitchen. I could see Edward and Mr. Carter through the window from where I stood. Turning the other way, I watched Mrs. Fairfax struggle with the front door, which was heavy to open and harder yet to close. The recent wet weather had warped its frame.

I went to her, and by adding my weight to that of hers, we managed closure. She stepped aside. "Mr. Carter gave me these as he got out of his carriage. Bless him for remembering our mail."

"Yes, he always does," I said with a smile.

Our housekeeper waved a rather large bundle of letters at me, which the good doctor had fetched from the Millcote shop designated as a dropping-off point for the post. My name— "Jane Eyre Rochester"—had been scrawled across a few of the pieces.

"These will take up much of your day. I could handle them for you. Or help you decide how to answer." The scent of lily-of-the-valley toilet water enveloped me as Mrs. Fairfax put a gentle hand on my arm.

"Thank you, but you have other work to do. I shall tend to these. I'll go over them with Mr. Rochester. It will give us a task to complete." I tucked the mail firmly under my arm. "And now to face the doctor."

Mrs. Fairfax gave me her kindly smile. "Whatever the good doctor's prognosis, I am certain that you and Master will face it together. His burden is halved because he shares it with you."

"Yes." But my feet refused to move. As much as I knew I had to go and greet Mr. Carter, I found my courage waning. Still, I had to hear his prognosis. I had to know the status of my husband's health.

"Shall I instruct Leah to bring tea so you can pour?" Mrs. Fairfax's suggestion softly reminded me of my responsibilities. All of our visitors traveled far to find us. As a consequence, good manners dictated that we serve them refreshments.

"Yes, of course. Tea. That will help if . . . if there's bad news." I did not worry for myself. I worried for my husband, who keenly felt the restrictions of his infirmity.

"Jane." Mrs. Fairfax interrupted my thoughts. "Listen to me. You love Mr. Rochester, and he loves you. Nothing the doctor says can alter that. You will bring the world to him if you must, dear girl."

Seeing that I seemed unconvinced, she took me by the shoulders. "You are stronger than I guessed when I first met you. Then you were a mere girl, untouched by love, unsure of her place in the world. Since then you have both won and opened the Master's heart. Edward Fairfax Rochester is no longer the brooding, unhappy man I once knew. No matter what the doctor predicts, you have accomplished a miracle. Why would you doubt yourself now?"

I hugged the older woman, and she responded by patting my shoulder. "Go to your husband. I shall be along directly."

She was right. He, who was once my master, now loved me as my husband. Should I not take joy in that? Is it not the expressed desire of every living soul to be loved?

I loved Edward, deeply. As part of our wedding vows, I pledged that we would face any obstacles together. This was but one more challenge. I paused to gather my thoughts. Whatever happened, I would make the road ahead more bearable for Edward. I would manage. No. *We* would manage, together.

I was not alone in my desire to help him. I could count on Mrs. Fairfax to assist us. Though I could not always count on her to hold her tongue. Recently, over our evening meal, Edward had announced plans to rebuild Thornfield Hall, on Ned's behalf.

"Rebuild Thornfield?" Mrs. Fairfax had thrown her hands up in alarm. "The place is in ruins. It is nothing but a charred wreckage. The rooks and owls inhabit the carcass."

True, but cruelly said. I swallowed a sigh. Sometimes Mrs. Fairfax went too far. When we lived at Thornfield, she took her meals in her own small dining room. But at Ferndean we invited her to sup at our table. This offered both benefits and deficits. On occasions like this, her opinion was both unwarranted and unnecessary.

"You will have to run off the vermin, clear the wreckage, and start from the ground up."

"I intend to." Edward kept eating his cold pigeon pie.

"It will take you years." She wouldn't leave it alone.

"I believe you are right."

Later she took me aside. "He will waste his fortune on that house."

"Perhaps. But it is his to waste."

Now it was her turn to sigh. "You support him in this?"

"I support him in whatever makes him happy. Did you notice how animated his face grew? How excited his voice was? If rebuilding Thornfield restores a sense of mastery to him, I personally will drive carts to transport stones from the quarry."

At that image, she laughed. "You are his other half. I swear that I've never known two people with such harmonious desires. Bless you both with many, many happy years together."

Ours was a marriage of true equals. We valued each other's opinion, even when we disagreed. Our discourse gave us many hours of pleasure. In fact, it was our intellectual equality, in part, that had convinced Edward we should marry. He had grown tired of vapid women who parroted his views, or who suggested none of their own. As for my own opinion of Thornfield Hall, I missed it as a landmark, and I owed it a bit of sentimentality since it was there that I met Edward. More importantly, my husband wanted a project to ignite his passions and give him purpose. Rebuilding the family manor could do both, and assure my husband that he would leave to his son a tangible legacy.

Although I support my husband's rebuilding plans, I must admit: I am happy here at Ferndean. The isolation suits me, and my mood is decidedly more lighthearted than ever. Both Mrs. Fairfax and Edward have remarked upon how cheerful I am. Marriage and motherhood have changed me, for the better. Certainly, I am more confident. That boldness that was always within me now finds expression almost daily.

Despite my new sense of self-possession, I have had no wish to leave this secluded, half-hidden spot. Our distance from Millcote sets us apart from our neighbors. That is fine by me. Edward has vowed that our honeymoon will shine our whole lives long. "As long as we have each other, we have little need for company," he proclaimed.

But Ned's arrival changed everything.

While I'd never been appreciative of society, I began to see its value. Ned would want the fellowship of other children as he grew older. On occasion, I realized I could benefit from conversing with other mothers. And although he claimed his interactions with me were quite enough, I sensed that Edward missed the society of others, particularly other men who were active in the county and its politics.

"Being closer to Millcote offers several advantages, Jane," Edward had said. "For one thing, there's a larger pool from which to hire servants."

Presently, Leah juggles the duties of my personal maid, parlor maid, and kitchen help. Mary and her husband, John, have been with Edward since he was young, but time has caught up with the old couple, and they have slowed down noticeably since the harsh winter. On Mondays, a woman from two farms away comes to do our laundry. The nursemaid, Hester Muttoone, grew up on these lands, and her family has farmed the Rochester acreage for three generations. One of her brothers, Nehemiah, works part-time as our stable hand. Another brother, Josiah, whom I have seen only in passing, is said to be one of the finest judges of horseflesh in the parish. On occasion, he, too, helps with the horses.

Even though neither of us admitted it, there was a larger, more ominous reason for us to live closer to town: Our location made it difficult for Mr. Carter, the doctor, to examine Edward without making a special visit.

Due to his injuries, Edward needed examination regularly.

Outside the window, my husband sat stiffly on a wooden bench while Mr. Carter ran knowing fingers along his patient's temple and brow, tracing and probing the angry scar. The doctor held up a series of cards and asked questions. Each of Edward's responses struck the physician a visible blow of disappointment. The light bent around them, hopeful patient and frustrated healer, freezing the two old friends in a painful tableau.

I blinked back tears and struggled to compose myself. It would never do to let Edward know how worried I was on his behalf. To me, the loss of his sight was an inconvenience, nothing more. To him, it was a prison sentence. No jail cell in Newgate could be more confining. Increasingly, Edward's poor vision curtailed his activities in ways that rendered him dependent.

How different my husband was from the man I first met! The troubles we have weathered have worn down his rough edges, the way nature works to soften the sharp features of a rocky outgrowth.

The Edward Fairfax Rochester who first welcomed me as his ward's governess may have been physically intact, but he bore the unhappy imprint of a man who had suffered many injustices.

His own father had not borne the thought of dividing his estate and leaving a fair portion to Edward, the younger of his two sons. Neither, however, could old Mr. Rochester endure the thought of an impoverished heir, so he and his elder son, Rowland, had tricked Edward into marrying a Jamaican heiress, a woman whose family bore a strain of madness. As her character ripened, Bertha Mason Rochester exhibited all the grossest aspects of lunacy. Her violent outbreaks drove the then twenty-one-year-old Edward to the brink of despair. He even considered ending his own misery, but hope stayed his hand and revived his will to live. Instead of death, he escaped to Europe, where for ten long years he traipsed from one capital to another, seeking a soul mate, but never finding her.

One of his many mistresses, a French opera dancer known as Céline Varens, affirmed him as the father of her child. Although simple math disproved Adèle's patronage, the little girl's plight sufficiently moved Edward that when her mother abandoned her, he brought Adèle home with him to England. Both old Mr. Rochester and Rowland had since died, leaving Thornfield Hall to Edward, so it was there he installed little Adèle and Mrs. Fairfax, as well as his faithful manservant John and John's wife, Mary. He also locked Bertha Mason in the attic, as much for her safety as his, and hired a nurse to watch over the madwoman. This, of course, was Thornfield's secret—none except he and the nurse knew Bertha was there. It was also Edward's cross to bear, a pain he felt every day of his life.

Wanting to do right by Adèle, he instructed Mrs. Fairfax to hire a governess for the girl.

Thus I came to Thornfield Hall, and into the life of the man who was once my master and is now my mate. He swears that my affection has changed his soul from a charnel house to a sanctuary. With me by his side, he is free to show the world a more kindly nature.

My love has helped him.

We have arrived at a happy ending to our journey, but we paid heavy tolls along the roadway here. I do not believe that most people, even as they envy us our good fortune—our healthy son, our loving marriage, our monetary wealth—would choose to endure all that we have. Nor would they survive such deprivations as I did in the harsh environment of my boarding school, or as Edward did when trapped in a first marriage to a madwoman. Perhaps they might even look upon our current situation—our isolation, the scandal that tainted us, and Edward's injuries, including his near-blindness and the loss of one hand—and see only a future devoid of light or hope.

But I saw glorious possibilities. I saw a brilliant beginning that rendered me both thankful and joyful when I contemplated our future, a future we shall traverse together.

"This child is God's blessing upon our union," Edward said when he first held our son in his arms. "You, my wife, are the instrument of my redemption. Where once I questioned, now I believe. The Universe is governed by a benevolent spirit, call it what you may. What a miracle it has manifested from the wreckage that was my life!"

Yes, my son and husband were the sun and the earth, and I the happy moon suspended between.

"Jane? Is that you?" asked Edward now as I walked down the hallway. Although his vision was uncertain, there had been compensations. His sense of hearing had become exceedingly sharp.

"Yes, sir."

I stepped out of the gloomy manor into the sunlit garden. The sun-warm fragrance of fading wild roses floated over the garden wall. A playful breeze ruffled Edward's dark, unruly hair. He was never a handsome man, but still my heart melted at the sight of him.

"Come join us, Jane. Carter, am I not a lucky man? How wonderful she is! Is that sunshine I feel on my face or the glow of my well-loved wife?" Edward's hand reached out and grabbed mine tightly. Edward does not care who sees his affection for me. In fact, I rather think he revels in showing to all and sundry that at last we are wed.

I was, I admit, a well-loved wife. Edward took seriously his duties as my tutor in the art of lovemaking. His tender ministrations could not help but inflame my passions. "You must turn me loose, dear husband. Free me so I can pour you another cup of tea. Good day, Mr. Carter. Tea for you, too?

Thank you for bringing along our mail." I held up the packet Mrs. Fairfax had given me.

Mr. Carter laughed. "Rural delivery will come one day, Mrs. Rochester, and you will get your mail right to your door daily. See if you don't!"

I set the batch of letters to one side. They could wait, but Mr. Carter could not. His services were much in demand. "How are we today, sir?"

"I wish I had better news for you. But Mr. Rochester's vision continues to decline." The doctor pointedly stared into his teacup rather than engage me. It is a game he plays. Mr. Carter tries to keep the worst from me, and I respond by working harder to pry it out of him. He thinks me too young and delicate to bear up under this adversity. I think he underestimates me. In fact, I know he does. It is a common mistake.

"Are you certain? Is there nothing you can do?"

"I have done all I can, but I encourage you not to give up hope. I suggest that Mr. Rochester visit an oculist in London. I have located one who has an astonishing success rate."

"We shall pack our bags immediately!"

"Not just yet, my darling. Carter thinks we should wait," said Edward, putting a staying hand on my knee. "He thinks that if I rest properly, some healing might occur. The oculist would be a last resort."

"More to the point," Carter interjected, "I prescribe hot compresses twice daily. And no strenuous activity. For several days at least."

I put on my best smile and tried to sound cheery. Instead, I heard myself prattle on and on. "So, my husband, you must let me devote myself entirely to you and your comfort. I shall start by warming your tea and serving you scones. Mr. Carter, may I offer you more refreshments, too?"

"That would be most welcome. But I cannot stay long. I need to hurry back in the direction of Millcote. The Farrows' youngest son has a touch of the croup. It makes the rounds of the countryside faster than I do. I promised I would stop in on my way home." He frowned at the sky. "Perhaps I will be forced to spend the night with them. A storm appears to be moving in. When the clouds cover the moon, the roads are too dark for a lone traveler to journey safely. Especially with highwaymen about."

The talk then drifted from the weather to politics. Eventually that led to a discussion of the ongoing adultery trial of Queen Caroline, wife of King George IV, who had ascended the throne when his father died that past January.

"The masses are supportive of her. After all, our King was the most dissolute of all princes," Mr. Carter said with a disapproving shake of his head.

Few thought Queen Caroline innocent, but since her husband publicly cavorted with his mistresses, many found it difficult to blame her for seeking comfort in the arms of another man. Even at this distance from London, we had heard how her daily processionals to the trial aroused sympathy.

"It is shameful," my husband said, "how the King has lived a life of pleasure and excess while many of his subjects starve because of the low price of corn. The common folks identify with her and repudiate him—and with good reason."

The subject of crops changed the course of conversation. I sorted the mail and listened carefully as Mr. Carter reported sadly on the general condition of farmers in the area. Pauperism in the counties was a very real problem. The local landowners feared a revolt, much like the French had suffered, so they met regularly to share their views and to try to find methods for reducing unemployment and the more general discontent.

"Is there a letter from Adèle?" Edward asked me after a while, likely seeking a break from such dismal news.

"I am looking. Surely this bundle will include a note from her."

For a short time before our marriage, unhappy circumstances had caused me to take my leave of Edward. My absence had left then eight-year-old Adèle without a governess. Considering the girl's overly dramatic nature and her chaotic early upbringing, Edward decided she would benefit from a traditional English education. He asked his friends for recommendations. Mrs. Lucy Brayton, the wife of Edward's dearest friend, Captain Augustus Brayton, suggested the Alderton House School for Girls, in London.

Once Edward and I were reunited, we did not have time to fetch her back from London before the wedding, which we conducted hastily before a parson and a clerk, not even telling John and Mary until it was done. I did not like to be fussed over—it suited me to have been married in that way. Afterward, Edward and I sent out notice of our marriage. We received back several polite letters of congratulations from his business associates, a letter expressing happy surprise from my cousins Diana and Mary Rivers—and an exuberant missive from Lucy Brayton petitioning us newlyweds to come to London to visit her "for the whole of the Season."

We took extra care with our letter to Adèle, explaining our new situation and assuring her of Edward's affection and mine. We planned to visit her as soon as possible.

We also sent a letter to the school's superintendent, Mrs. Webster, and that kind soul replied that she wished us many long years of happiness.

Although it had been our intention to visit Adèle immediately after our wedding, I became enceinte within days. Complications of my condition, punctuated by frequent upheavals in the basin, rendered travel impossible, at least in those early months. Before we knew it, a brutal winter was upon us. Snowdrifts piled high against our doorway. The road to Ferndean, always a challenge, became impassable. We were housebound for the duration of the winter, spending the long, dark days huddled in front of the fire. In the uncertain light of the coals, I would read to Edward and sometimes to Mrs. Fairfax while her knitting needles provided a steady clicking accompaniment to my voice. The tangy smoke from the logs on the hearth hallowed our evenings with a pleasant haze, putting me in mind of incense at church.

This period of enforced solitude proved a blessing, as Edward still suffered the aftermath of the conflagration, his damaged but noble presence reminding me of that majestic oak tree at Thornfield that had been rendered nearly in two by a bolt of lightning. Despite the damage, the tree survived, tentatively putting out one sprout and then the next as if testing its vitality, until finally it succeeded in producing a verdant canopy of sheltering leaves, a wholly pleasing result. The oak was never the same, but its new form still struck me with admiration at its tenacity and virility.

Through the long winter nights, my belly grew, and Edward's spirit flourished, imbued with expectation and anticipation. Slowly, his maimed stump healed, as did his remaining eye, but his vision never quite recovered.

Thankfully, the last of the winter's snow melted and the lane was passable in time for the midwife to attend me when I delivered Ned. He arrived hale and pink with plump and perfect little limbs, but the birth was arduous, and afterward, I was slow to regain my former vitality. Still, the months passed with Ned growing and thriving, and over the summer the color came back to my cheeks. By the first chill of autumn, my clothes no longer hung loosely on me and a shine returned to my hair. In my husband's presence, Mr. Carter pronounced me fit, but the good doctor warned me in private that I needed to gain back several pounds. "You are far too thin, ma'am," he said as he shook his finger at me. "You need to eat more and take meals with regularity."

Throughout my convalescence, I sent letters to Adèle, signing them with my name and guiding Edward to sign his. But since Ned's birth, her responses have proved confounding! She made no mention of congratulations, nor did she seem excited about the arrival of our baby.

"I fear the girl has mastered the fine art of a Gallic pout.

She learned it at her mother's knee," was Edward's summation. Although we pretended otherwise, we were both hurt.

Many weeks had passed since her last letter. All of her correspondence left us disappointed. We wanted news of how she was getting along, letters that evoked her sense of gaiety and drama. Instead, we received nothing more than a scribbled sentence or two, usually a weather report and a bland recitation of what she was studying. It lacked every evidence of Adèle's usual ebullience. In fact, each letter so strongly resembled the one before that I began to suspect the child was copying a lesson from a blackboard rather than penning her own missive to us.

Fortunately, Mrs. Brayton had visited Adèle often, and her amusing letters brimmed over with how the child looked, what new songs she favored, and so on.

Every fresh batch of letters brought hope that Adèle would congratulate us on Ned's arrival, and each left my heart aching with disappointment. I didn't care about the new poem she memorized or the psalm she could recite by heart. I wanted to hear about Adèle's feelings. I loved the little French girl— how could I not, seeing how her situation was so much like mine had been—and the time I spent out of contact with her had been one of the most painful of my life.

I shuffled through the stack, searching for her familiar scrawl.

"It is here!" I opened it quickly and read the letter out loud, heedless of Mr. Carter's presence:

Dearest Mr. and Mrs. Rochester,

I study very hard. I say my prayers every night and day. I am learning simple mathematics. My Latin and Italian have improved. I hope to master German as we are to have a new teacher.

Yours faithfully,
Adèle Varens

"Is that all?" Edward asked.

I stared hard at the careless script before turning the letter on its side. Using my finger as a pointer, I traced the letters, hoping to discern the word written crosswise over her short message, a method of communication I myself had often used to save money on postage.

By careful examination I was able to make out one phrase in French repeated three times:

Au secours! Au secours! Au secours!

"She begs for help!" I translated.

"She has always been a fanciful child," Edward spoke slowly.

"That is true." But the excuse sounded weak, even to my own ears. However, I persisted with it. "Do you recall how she would feign illness when I assigned Latin translations to her? She is quite the scamp."

"I had hoped this school would encourage her to be more . . . British. But even so, this is unlike her," my husband mused.

"The message does seem quite desperate," agreed Mr. Carter.

"There is more," I said. A scrap of watercolor paper fluttered to the ground as I unfolded her note. "Perhaps this will offer an explanation."

But that wretched scrap only made the situation worse. On it was scrawled: *God rot your filthy soul. You will die! I will see to it! Avec plaisir!*

The three of us sat in stunned silence.

I turned to my husband. "We must go to her at once!"

Chapter 2

"Someone has threatened Adèle? No more harmless will-o'-the-wisp ever graced this good earth. This is hard to credit, and we cannot let it go." My husband pounded the tea table with his fist. The cups danced and a jostled spoon flew off the tray and onto the ground. "What child could have written that vile note? That dastardly threat?"

A moment's reflection set me wondering. "Mr. Rochester, I am not sure it *was* written by another person. The handwriting is unfamiliar, but it is unsigned. It could be an intrigue. Perhaps this is a bid for attention. Such a scheme would not be beyond Adèle's contrivance."

What I did not admit to was the possibility that it was not another child at all, but someone in authority. I knew the school environment; I knew it well, both as student and as teacher. I had seen the petty cruelties inflicted on schoolchildren, and I knew them to spring from twin fountainheads of preening self-righteousness and unearned moral superiority. Those in authority justified false economies and capricious acts of discipline all in the name of "saving souls." They acted as judge and jury, pushing God off his throne so they could sit there in His stead. At their hands, and according to their whims, children with no one to speak on their behalf could suffer.

I also knew, however, that Lucy Brayton had recommended the Alderton House School for Girls to Edward, so I trusted it was well run. She knew of the superintendent, Mrs. Webster, and vouched for the woman's character. However, these messages from Adèle set me wondering.

"I suppose it is possible this is all some sort of an intrigue . . ." Edward began.

Mr. Carter nodded vigorously. "I have two daughters myself. The whispering, the fights, the making up. Well, it keeps Mrs. Carter and me quite busy. Perhaps the girl is lonely, and the second note is but a bid to force you to pay her attention."

"Is there any other mail? Perhaps a letter from Mrs. Webster, the superintendent? Something that might explain Adèle's plea?" Edward leaned toward me, straining to see.

"Here's one from Lucy Brayton. We haven't heard from her in a while." I unfolded the paper quickly and started to read:

Dear Edward and Jane,

I returned from Bombay last Monday to discover the letter I'd written the two of you still sitting on my dresser! It appears that I forgot to mail it! Oh heavens, I would misplace my head if it were not melded to my body! Could it be that six months have gone by without us corresponding?

Well, it was a short note, so I shall recap its contents. Augie had sent me an urgent message requesting that I go to him in Bombay. Seems he'd contracted malaria, and he wanted me for a nurse. (I can imagine you laughing at the absurdity of that, Edward! However, since he rarely asks for my presence, I felt much obliged to hasten to his side.) So I threw my clothes into trunks and took the next ship bound for India.

By the time I disembarked, he was much improved, although the fever came and went, leaving him quite spent. Despite Augie's illness (or possibly because of it, since I—like the fever!—was free to come and go as I pleased) I enjoyed my time there. I bought your new bride a beautiful gift!

To make amends and work my way back into your good books—for I truly meant to mail that letter so you would know I was out of the country!—I decided to visit Alderton House immediately. My intention was to send you a full report on Adèle.

Well, you will scarcely credit this, but when I arrived, I was turned away at the door by a large woman with a face like curdled milk. She introduced herself as one Maude Thurston, the new superintendent. It seems that Mrs. Webster has retired!

I was told that the girls were in their lessons. I replied to Mrs. Thurston that I was confident Adèle could miss a few minutes of her lesson without incurring a great disaster to her education, but the woman would not budge. Finally, I retreated. I came again on the next day at a different time. I was told that Adèle couldn't see me because she was being disciplined. Again, this sour-faced harridan and I argued. I even invoked the name of Lady Kingsley, the founder of that institution. To no avail.

You know me well, Edward. Augie once likened me to a mad dog. Once I sink my teeth in, I absolutely refuse to let go. I waited two days and traveled again to Alderton House.

Mrs. Thurston told me quite coolly that my visits were ill timed. I told her that if she did not produce Adèle on the spot I would take myself to the local constabulary and complain. You can imagine how unhappy my threat made her!

At length, she fetched Adèle.

I tell you, the child's appearance shocked me. She has always been slight, but now her shoulders stick out at sharp angles. Her pale skin shows no hint of good health. I asked her how she fared, and she answered, "I am fine. I am happy here. I work hard to be a good student." Of course, Mrs. Thurston glared at both of us during this exchange.

Recognizing I could learn little more, I took my leave, but before I went, Adèle threw her arms around me and whispered in my ear, "I am unhappy! Where is mon bon ami? Ask him to come rescue me!"

I suggest you come visit me sooner rather than later. Bring your lovely bride. I shall take her to all the best places in London!

Yours sincerely,
Lucy Brayton

"Jane, after this letter, I agree with you wholeheartedly. We must see this for ourselves. If Adèle is unhappy, we need to know why. If the school is rigorous, then her discomfort is part of her education. However, if she is being mistreated, I shall not abide it." Edward's face transformed into a mask of anger. "I remember the way the upper form treated us new boys at Eton."

I knew of these memories. He had shared them with me. His days at school were nearly as bleak and lonely as mine, except for the friendship he had formed with Augustus Brayton. As both were second sons, the two boys had been cast adrift, left to their own devices. They endured all sorts of indignities, chief among these being unreasonable punishments designed to assault the spirit as well as leave bloody markings on the body.

"We meant to visit Adèle," I said, when I regained control of myself. "And to see Lucy Brayton in London. This only adds urgency to our plans." With that, I tucked the two letters into my pocket.

Adèle's misery could not be ignored, but as for the threat, it might be a simple schoolgirl quarrel taken to an extreme. Perhaps Adèle had written the second threatening note herself, as a way of insuring our immediate response. If so, I would endeavor to uncover what caused her to sink so low as to perform that odious vice. If not, I could take appropriate actions to see that the true author received a reprimand.

Mr. Carter had been quietly sipping his tea and nibbling at one of the spicy gingerbread biscuits that Mary baked for us weekly. "Allow me to assist you. I would be happy to take Mrs. Rochester to the Farrows' house this evening, where we can spend the night. The next morning, I will drive to Millcote, where you can be a guest at my own home until you can secure passage at the coaching inn. I believe their carriages leave for London daily, but I am unfamiliar with their schedule." He checked his pocket watch. "If we leave directly, we should make it to the Farrows' in time for supper."

"I shall go pack our things, Edward." I jumped to my feet.

"Pardon me, Mrs. Rochester? Perhaps you misheard," said Mr. Carter. "If one of you must travel immediately, then I offer to take you, Mrs. Rochester, but you alone. As I have warned, Mr. Rochester cannot travel at this moment. If you do not rest your eye, sir, at least for a few days, you will go blind."

There followed a disturbing silence. Mr. Carter had put our situation in stark relief. I believe he surprised himself as well by being so bold. But he had no other option. Barring such an unhappy prognosis, Edward would of course have made the trip with me.

"Listen, my old friend." Mr. Carter pitched his voice low and filled it with authority. "I, too, am a father. Your child will love you whether you can see him or not. However, if you miss the chance to behold your son, you will miss one of life's great joys. I urge you, still that restless nature. A few days of enforced leisure sounds like an eternity, but I promise you, it is not. Besides, the specialist will not be available for another month."

I watched my husband react to this advice. At first, Edward's features contorted with emotion that betrayed the full measure of his helplessness. But slowly, the sensibility of Mr. Carter's remarks moved him to acceptance. Mr. Carter did not speak out of pettiness. He spoke as a healer and a friend. Edward knew this. I did, too.

"Leah can go with you," suggested Edward, turning toward me.

"No," I reminded him, "she cannot. Her sister is having a baby this week or the next. I promised she could travel to Headley to assist."

"You cannot make the trip alone." My husband was not commanding me, but merely stating what to him seemed obvious.

"Of course I can. Remember that I was only ten when my aunt put me in a carriage bound for Lowood Institution, and that was a trip of fifty miles."

"Lowood!" said Mr. Carter. "You must be grown from hearty stock to have survived such a miserable place!"

True. When I was sent to Lowood Institution, a "charitable" boarding school for girls, it was a blessing to be away from my cold aunt and cruel cousins. But the school was a dismal place, one that used the pretense of Christian charity as an excuse for deprivation. The Reverend Robert Brocklehurst, the supervisor of the school, attempted to explain away our starvation, poor living conditions, and harsh treatment by pronouncing such measures necessary for the sake of our characters. Yet while we starved, while we shivered in the cold, while we darned threadbare stockings to make them last, money intended for our care dressed the Brocklehurst family in fine clothes, fed them lavish meals, and decorated their home to their expensive tastes.

An epidemic of deadly typhus ran rampant through the school my first winter there—made all the more virulent, sadly, because the living conditions were dire and the occupants were weak—and though I escaped without contracting the foul disease, many others at Lowood were taken. Without those human sacrifices, we would have suffered even longer from the stern deprivations impressed upon us by Reverend Brocklehurst—for the resulting discoveries so horrified other wealthy and benevolent individuals that they paid to build us a new school in a better location, improved our diet and clothing allowances, and removed Reverend Brocklehurst from a position of authority.

"I can accompany you, Jane." Mrs. Fairfax stood in the shadows of the portico into the hallway, her quiet intrusion startling all of us. Tendrils of ivy climbed up the lattice and wove their way down the other side. New leaves of soft green blended with the older, darker ones.

"Thank you," I said to her, "but no. That is kind of you, but you are too dearly needed here. Earlier today you offered your help with our correspondence. There will be requests regarding Thornfield. They should be answered without delay. Master will appreciate your secretarial skills, and I know that no one would watch over Ned more closely than you. With you here, I can leave my son without worrying."

This was a lie, and we all knew it. Of course I would worry. How could I not? My heart fluttered and my mouth went dry. I did not want to leave my son. I hated to leave my husband. But I could not accept Mrs. Fairfax's offer. The gentle housekeeper was beyond middle age when I met her, and over the past year, she had moved more slowly and with more effort. A trip to London would be arduous, and I had no desire to see her suffer. Besides, she was accustomed to running a household and to Edward's ways. With her here, I knew that neither of my boys would lack for anything.

"It is a long way," Mrs. Fairfax said. "Are you sure you want to travel alone?"

For a tick, I nearly gave in. I nearly said that the visit would need to wait.

But as I stood there in the garden, torn between worry over Adèle and concern for my son and husband, Mr. Carter provided an answer to my dilemma. "My wife has been wanting to visit London. She could accompany Mrs. Rochester from Millcote. They can leave either Saturday or Sunday evening, depending on whether Mrs. Rochester would like to accompany us to church."

Edward's shoulders relaxed. Mrs. Fairfax let go of the breath she had been holding and with her gnarled hands smoothed the snowy muslin apron she always wore. My insides untwisted, slowly.

So it was settled.

I would check on Adèle.

I would go to London.

Once I made my decision, a frisson of excitement stirred within me.

London! I was bound for London!

In his youth, Edward had traveled to the capitals of Europe and farther, to the island of Jamaica. Oh, such wondrous sights he'd seen! But I had never visited beyond the local counties.

In my childhood, books of adventure had been my constant companions. I spent many solitary hours weaving fantasies about the great wide world. Of course, I had heard much of London and its various sights. I supposed that Mrs. Brayton would want to promenade in Hyde Park where all the ton, the high society, went to be seen. Perhaps we would visit Fortnum and Mason and shop for spices. Certainly, a grand lady like her would take me to visit a milliner so I could replace my much worn hat.

As I considered these options, there came the happy realization my trip would also permit me to visit Hatchards bookshop on Piccadilly. I could replenish our library and replace many of the volumes lost in the fire at Thornfield Hall! The prospect delighted me beyond words.

The library that had served Adèle and me as our schoolroom at Thornfield was now nothing more than a feathery pile of ashes. Gone were the floor-to-ceiling glass-fronted bookcases with their volumes of light literature, poetry, biography, travels, and romances. How I missed them! Especially at night when I read to Edward and Mrs. Fairfax, who often fell asleep to the sound of my voice with her knitting still in her hands.

This was a trip long overdue.

We could procrastinate no longer.

I was eager to see my former student—and London. But I hated to leave Ned and Edward!

My emotions warred against each other. I fought to keep my face from exposing my dilemma. This was a time for duty, not for indulgent sentiment.

"I will guard Ned as if he were my own son," Mrs. Fairfax assured me, trembling with emotion.

I knew she meant it.

She inclined her head and added, "But Master is correct. You are not accustomed to the city. How will you cope without a chaperone?"

I nearly said, "Quite well," but stopped my tongue lest she think me impertinent. "I shall have Mrs. Carter for companionship to London, and I will be in Mrs. Captain Brayton's capable hands thereafter."

Or so I hoped. I couldn't imagine a society lady having any long-lasting interest in me. However, based on our husbands' friendship, perhaps we would find common ground.

"This might work well. Lucy has been insisting you come for a visit. She is lonely in that big house." With this, Edward laughed softly. "What a pair you will make."

"Do you not think we shall get along?"

"On the contrary. I know you will. You are genuinely kind-hearted. That's one of the qualities I love about you. Lucy is also. Both of you are highly intelligent, although at first meeting one might be so dazzled by her finery that one might fail to see her wit."

"Then it is settled." Mr. Carter rose to his feet. "How long will it take you to pack, Mrs. Rochester?"

"I shall start preparations," said Mrs. Fairfax. Over the next

Mrs. Jane Eyre Rochester
c/o Captain Augustus Brayton
#24 Grosvenor Square
London

"You want a good bonnet," said Mrs. Fairfax, lowering the trunk's lid and nodding toward my well-worn chapeau.

"I do not own a more fashionable bonnet. My old one must do."

"Jane, I know you prefer simplicity, but you now reflect on the Rochester name and fortune. Things are different in London. Appearances are everything! You won't want to appear at Mrs. Brayton's dinner table dressed too simply. Such a presentation might prove awkward. Why not take the Rochester diamonds with you? The pieces will add interest to your dresses and go a long way toward making up for any deficiencies of style."

"I suppose you are right."

After I had first agreed to marry Edward, he wanted to have his mother's jewelry sent to us by courier from the bank in London, but I declined the offer. When described, the pieces sounded far too grand for me. Typically, I wore no jewelry except my gold wedding band, a recent gift from Edward, or the brooch from Miss Temple. That was enough for me.

Shortly after Ned was born, however, Edward revisited the subject of the Rochester diamonds. "Please, Jane, do not disappoint me. Allow me to properly thank you for giving me a son."

The pieces had arrived a few days ago. Mrs. Fairfax had brought them to me as I sat rocking little Ned in the nursery. We opened the parcel together. The necklace, earrings, and circlet sparkled like dewdrops on the morning grass against the green velvet lining of the rosewood jewelry box. The sight of such opulence stunned me. "They are magnificent. Just as I remember them." Mrs. Fairfax sighed.

hour, she bustled with activity, overseeing my efforts. she stared down into my portmanteau, a soft "tsk" escaped her.

"Pity your wardrobe is so plain," the housekeeper said least there are the newer dresses made from fabric you orde from the warehouse in Millcote. They will have to do."

I nodded. One frock was an amethyst that flattered n green eyes. The other, my favorite and the most recent, per fectly copied the jewel-like color of a glass of claret.

I tucked a well-worn copy of *Waverley* in my portmanteau, one of the few books at Ferndean—left behind, I presumed, by one of the Rochester men while on a hunting trip.

Reflecting again on the treasures I might find at Hatchards, I turned back to my packing. I added two pencils, a charcoal stub, and a vegetable gum rubber for removing stray pencil marks, along with my sketch pad, to my bag.

"You should pack one serviceable dress, too," Mrs. Fairfax said. "Your black silk would be useful. Black always travels well."

Finally, to the pile in the trunk, I added a gown of silver gray silk that I had worn only once. The frock featured a mod- est neckline that I could fill in with a frothy white fichu. Rather than waste time, I chose to continue wearing my gray corded muslin, an everyday dress that would withstand the rigors of travel and not show too much soil. As a final touch, I pinned on my pearl brooch, a token given to me by a beloved teacher, Maria Temple Nasmyth.

Mindful of the changeable autumn weather, I also carried over my arm a soft wool shawl that my cousins Diana and Mary had woven for me. The blanket of brown, maroon, gold, and orange provided a tangible expression of their love.

I twisted a golden key in the lock of the portmanteau, then pinned the key to the inside of my waistband.

On my dresser rested a card that would be hammered to the trunk lid.

I handed Ned to Hester and held the necklace up to the sunlight to see the multitude of prisms dance around the room. The pieces might be excessive for my tastes, but I could still admire their beauty and craftsmanship.

"Yes," I said as I fought a lump in my throat. "They are dazzling."

But Edward cannot see them, so what use are they? I thought.

With my portmanteau packed and ready to go, I retrieved the jewels and pondered how best to carry them.

"Why not put the jewels in your reticule?" Mrs. Fairfax handed me my purse. "That way they will stay close at hand."

Following her suggestion, I tucked the velvet bag with the diamonds into my reticule with my wallet.

"I shall tell John to fetch your trunk."

I thanked her and turned to Hester, who was holding Ned on one hip.

"Come here, little boy," I said as I took my baby from the nursemaid's arms. "My darling," I cooed to him as I walked him around the nursery. He was nearly asleep, and I kissed him repeatedly before settling him down in his crib. "Save them up, little man. I shall be home before you know it, but I hope to deposit enough kisses that you won't want for any until I return."

For as long as I dared, I stood beside his bed, gazing in wonder at my sleeping child and stroking the peach fuzz of his hair. A quivering bubble of spit rested on his rosebud lips, and I wiped it away with my linen handkerchief. "Good-bye, my darling. I promise I shall come home soon."

My breath caught and the room swam before my eyes. Had my mother whispered these selfsame words in my ear before she went to nurse my father? He had been the curate in a large manufacturing town and had caught typhus while ministering to the poor. My mother caught the fever from him. They died within a month of each other.

"I promise I shall come back to you," I told Ned again with

more feeling. I pressed a last kiss onto his rosy cheek and stood up, ignoring the growing pang in my chest.

Mrs. Fairfax accompanied Edward and me down the path leading to the grassy lane. Pausing there, I kissed my husband a tearful good-bye. Withdrawing from his embrace was nearly impossible, but I did it. Mr. Carter offered me his hand as I mounted the stone step and climbed into the doctor's Stanhope Phaeton.

"I sent one of the stable hands on ahead to Millcote with a letter for Lucy," my husband said. "A rider can outpace you in that carriage, easily. I told him that if he missed the mail pickup in Millcote, he was to hurry on to the next posting inn. The letter should arrive before you and alert her that you are coming. I shall tell her to expect you either Sunday or Monday."

"Thank you." My heart raced; my pulse thrummed loudly. Edward's gaze reflected stoicism, but I detected a tension along his jawline.

He smiled at me, with effort. "Godspeed, my darling."

"Are you ready, Mrs. Rochester?"

"I am."

With a clap of the reins, Mr. Carter urged the horses forward.

Chapter 3

Dear Lucy,

I have dictated this letter to Mrs. Fairfax, who sends along her best regards. Although the hand is hers, rest assured the words are mine alone! She has become a tremendously helpful amanuensis, serving me whenever Jane is unavailable.

Your requests have not fallen on deaf ears! I send to you my greatest treasure—my bride, Jane Eyre. Care for her as you would any object of great value! I swear to you, Lucy, she is the world to me—her love has brought me such joy and contentment that you will scarce recognize me.

As you might guess, I am over the moon with joy at becoming a father. Our union has been truly blessed. We welcomed Edward Rivers Rochester into our lives six months ago. (We sent you a letter then to let you know of our son's birth. Did you receive it? I ask because it is not like you to overlook a chance to celebrate.)

Young Ned is thriving. He is plump and active, rolling from here to there, and sitting up with some assistance. He babbles like a mockingbird. Jane tells me he has my own eyes, so dark they seem almost black.

I know it pains my darling girl to leave her son behind. However, a week or so under your watchful eye should do her good. She has always been slight, but Ned's birth proved difficult, and she needs to regain the weight she lost. I remember what a wonderful cook you have. Please make sure to tempt my wife to eat!

I shall follow before the week is out. I cannot come straight-away because that tyrant doctor Mr. Carter has forbidden me from immediately undertaking the strains of travel. He fears I shall go blind. The specter of that disability haunts me, and hangs over my head as precipitously as the sword that threatened Damocles. But as long as I am assured of Jane's love, I can man-age, although I wonder that a young and vital woman could happily play nurse to a blind stump of a man like me.

You are probably wondering why Jane did not wait until we could travel together. Your letter proved most persuasive. Thank you, Lucy, for checking on Adèle. Her recent letters to us have been less than helpful. Jane cares for the girl as if she were her own flesh and blood—so my darling wife declared there was nothing for it but to see to Adèle's welfare immediately.

Like you, my wife is a woman of strong intentions. When fixated on an outcome, Jane will give it no quarter! The timbre of her voice warns me of her determination; she will visit the school and she will be apprised of Adèle's well-being. As you will see, Jane is as tenderhearted as she is intelligent. Perhaps she is also responding to the new impulses common with mothers, that sense of attachment that allows a woman to sense when her child needs her. I do not know, but I believe this to be so. We trust that Adèle is merely petulant, as is her wont to be, but concern speeds Jane on her way (and no little guilt that we have been slow to visit before now).

You might ask yourself, who is this stranger who dictates such a fawning letter to the wife of his best friend? I imagine you laughing in wonder, as you ask yourself, who is this man I once knew to be so proud—so stern, so angry, so disgusted with life— who now writes like a mewling youth about his loved one?

I tell you, it is I—and I am Jane Eyre's husband.

Yours truly,
Edward F. Rochester

Chapter 4

On the road to Millcote, Yorkshire

The clouds parted, only to regroup and grow darker. Mr. Carter and I hurried along to make the best of the dying sun. The wheels of the carriage crushed the sparse fallen leaves, forcing them to release their spicy dying fragrance. The horse pulled the two-wheeled carriage down the country road with ease.

"I hope you will not misjudge me," said Mr. Carter with a nod at his phaeton. "I bought this secondhand from a young man in London, who lost his allowance playing cards. It is both light and fast, which makes it perfect for traveling from one needy patient to another."

While I admit the bright yellow wheels had rather surprised me, I found no reason to complain. The phaeton took the bumps better than most carriages I had ridden in. Since rain threatened, the doctor lifted the roof and secured it over us. Luckily the bad weather held off. Our progress was steady, but by no means fast.

Mr. Carter proved an interesting conversationalist, quite knowledgeable about the area tenants. He pointed out this farm and that, telling me about the inhabitants. "The past few years have been hard on them, Mrs. Rochester. The charity baskets from the church keep most of them going. But that is not enough for the families with young ones. Their children present with hollow eyes, thin limbs, and enormous bellies. Their eyes stare out into an uncertain future."

I remembered the incessant pang of hunger, how a lack of food could bring lethargy to one's limbs and render clear thinking difficult, if not impossible. Thinking of the children and their needs, their helplessness in the face of such misery, caused tears to prickle my eyes. I knew full well how hard it could be to sustain hope, much less to believe in a brighter future. Poverty for me was synonymous with degradation. In the pursuit of survival, dignity was the first virtue to be cast aside.

My own wealth was of such a recent vintage that I did not dare take it for granted. Since God above had blessed me so richly, I could not ignore the urge to give back.

I resolved then and there that I would assist the church with its good works, and I would endeavor to sponsor a small school in the nearby hamlet, as my cousin St. John Rivers had done for peasant girls in his parish outside of Morton. Such efforts were easily within my reach. They would make me more useful to Edward and to our tenants.

When we arrived at the Farrow house, Mr. Carter saw to not one but two Farrow children with the croup. Mrs. Farrow proved a good hostess, if an overly curious one, feeding us and asking nonstop questions. I sidestepped most of them as best I could without being rude. Her husband had his own queries. They both wanted to know more about Edward Rochester's girl bride, but I feared their interest was unwholesome, especially when they asked our wedding date and the date of Ned's birth in an obvious attempt to calculate his legitimacy.

As I crawled under the down coverlet that night, I worried about Adèle before moving on to missing little Ned and

Edward. I wondered if I would get along with Lucy Brayton. I hoped I would not embarrass myself with my lack of social polish. Again and again, I wondered about Adèle. What would I find? How was she? Why hadn't she written to us, a real letter, an honest communication, in so long?

A dream awakened me rudely. No, not a dream. A nightmare. A pillow was pressed against my face, suffocating me. My lungs struggled for air. When at last I came to my senses, I sat up fighting to take a breath, and my throat hurt. The bedclothes lay strewn around me and half on the floor.

Unable to return to sleep, I dressed at the first hint of dawn. Bypassing Mrs. Farrow's generous offer of fresh eggs, rashers, and blood sausages, Mr. Carter and I made do quickly with tea and bread before setting out again.

We stopped at several households before arriving in Millcote. At each, I did my best to assist Mr. Carter in small ways, handing him items from his walrus-hide doctor's bag and so forth. At the Biddles', he helped a grandfather with arthritis. At the Morris home, he dispensed medicine for a lingering cough. The Hobson child needed a splinter removed. In each case, there were the telltale signs of hunger: hollow eyes, bulging bellies, and listless demeanor. The womenfolk bustled about and offered us thin tea at every stop. Knowing the sacrifice it represented, I had trouble choking the brew down.

With each mile, an urgency within me grew more demanding, like an itch I could not reach to scratch. I needed to get to London, to visit Alderton House, and to see Adèle with my own eyes. Then I could be at ease.

At long last, we stopped at Mr. Carter's home. My arrival surprised his wife, and she did not hide her dismay well. The atmosphere grew distinctly icy. The couple excused themselves to discuss my visit.

I waited in their vestibule, trying not to overhear their conversation but unable to help myself. I had thought I overheard the name "Blanche Ingram" as Mrs. Carter spoke. I moved closer to the parlor door. Yes, there was "Blanche Ingram" and "upstart" and "indecent" and . . . my name. Now I knew for certain what had happened.

Miss Ingram, a member of the local gentry, was a lovely and accomplished—if also vapid and cruel—young woman who had hoped to become Mrs. Rochester, not for any love of Edward but out of a vigorous affection for his purse. Edward had tested her by setting forth a rumor that his fortune was only one-third of what was supposed. Once that falsehood took root, he visited her, only to be received coldly by both Blanche and her mother, the Dowager Lady. By now they would have learned that his fortune was indeed vast, and that he had married another. As to the improbability of Edward Rochester, a member of the landed gentry, marrying a governess—well, Dowager Lady Ingram spoke for herself and her daughter both when she said of my former profession: "I have just one word to say of the whole tribe; they are a nuisance," as if we were a subhuman, monstrous breed of insect that spoiled their Sunday picnic.

So, Blanche Ingram had been talking about me—and worse, she had cast me as a conniving, grasping fortune hunter. A cold anger nipped at me, but I am no shrinking flower. Let her talk! I had done nothing wrong! Gritting my teeth, I vowed again to leave my seclusion and become an active presence in this community, if for no other reason than to irk my detractors!

I bethought myself to leave this place, especially since Mrs. Carter had shown the sort of irrational prejudice I could not abide. I spent the first ten years of my life as an intruder; I had no desire to spend another night under anyone's roof as an unwanted guest.

When Mr. Carter returned, twin spots of red on his cheeks betrayed that the conversation had not gone well. "Seems my youngest daughter has a touch of the croup. I regret to say this, but it appears you will have to travel to London alone after all. I can deliver you to the coaching inn right after church tomorrow."

"I do not wish to further inconvenience you, but perhaps you could take me to the coaching inn directly? That would free you to spend your Sunday with your family in prayer."

"Of course," he said, rather too quickly. (And of course, his daughter's croup was already remedied!)

At the inn, we surveyed the waybill. According to the posted timetable, I could wait until the next day and take a stagecoach for five pence, but the rate of travel would be exceedingly slow. The mail coach, on the other hand, would leave at eight P.M., one hour away, and although the cost to ride inside was twice that of the stagecoach, the trip to London would take only eighteen hours.

"The mail coaches travel at night when the roads are clearer," Mr. Carter explained. "The guard sounds his horn at the tollgates, signaling the keeper to open them in advance, and because the mail does not pay tolls, they fairly fly through. However, the stops at posting inns are less frequent, and much abbreviated. For a lady, that might be troublesome."

Regardless, I chose the mail coach. After directing the transference of my portmanteau, Mr. Carter shook my gloved hand solemnly.

"I wish you well, Mrs. Rochester. Let me say I have found your company most stimulating. I think Mr. Rochester quite a fortunate man. Perhaps I am being forward, but I hope you will make yourself better known to the inhabitants of the parish. You have good sense and a good heart. They would benefit from knowing you."

His approbation cheered me immensely.

I purchased a cup of tea and a light meal of cold sliced mutton, bread, and hard cheese from the innkeeper. The blare of the coach's tin horn at 250 yards sent the hostler into a flurry of action, readying fresh horses, while the innkeeper and his wife scurried about preparing food for hungry travelers disembarking. The changing of the horses took less than five minutes. The guard opened the door to the maroon and black coach with the royal coat of arms on the door. But before I could climb in, one of the four seated passengers started to complain most violently. "We are full up. No room. You must tell her to wait!" spat out a florid-faced man with a balding pate.

"There is no room here," said the woman sitting across from him, her knitting in her lap and her yarn covering the rest of the seat.

The guard swung the door open farther and gestured down at me. "She's nowt but a mite of a thing. Won't take up any room at all."

The passengers stared down at me. "Confound it!" said a man, dressed like a dandy in ruffles, lace, and velvet with a brocade vest straining over his bloated belly.

I stepped forward, presenting myself. The guard pushed me toward the seat. "Go on, miss."

"Is she a child?" said an old woman who held up her quizzing glass to get a better view of me.

Another passenger, a well-dressed young woman, glanced at me, her fashionable bonnet framing a smug face. "We are too crowded here already."

I said nothing, deciding to let them make of me what they wished, and mounted the wooden step the guard had set out. On closer inspection of me, the older woman's face softened as she pulled her fur-trimmed cape close. "Going to London, dearie?"

"I have a young friend who needs me." A partial disclosure can be useful when employed judiciously.

"If you must, you can sit by me," she said, sliding her yarn over. I climbed in. Before I had finished adjusting my shawl, we set off for London.

After a while, I closed my eyes, expecting only to doze lightly, but I must have fallen fast asleep, for the crack of thunder awakened me. Soon rain pounded against the carriage in a percussive rhythm. The horses slowed, struggling a little as the roadway turned slick and treacherous. We had traveled for another hour when the blare of the yard-long tin horn warned we were coming upon the Hardwicke Arms along the Great North Road.

The other passengers stirred. The old woman searched for her ball of yarn, which had rolled under my feet. The "gentleman"— at least that was how he styled himself—sneezed repeatedly and wiped his nose on his sleeve. We rolled to a stop, and I heard the passengers on the top of the carriage scramble down, hitting the ground hard and running through the rain, heading toward the inn where food and a fire waited.

The guard opened our door and the men pushed past us ladies. I was the last one out, and the full impact of the rain surprised me. My feet tingled from inaction, causing me to move tentatively, unbalanced by the unfamiliar muddy terrain, and with the fog of sleep still clouding my thoughts. The guard warned that we had but fifteen minutes to refresh ourselves. Ignoring the drops beating hard against my face, I followed along a winding walkway of half-broken, half-erupted paving stones.

Finding a seat in the inn's crowded parlor, I requested from the innkeeper's wife a strong cup of tea and any foodstuffs that might travel well. She brought a steaming mug, but no milk, and a hot pasty tucked in a muslin bag.

"Grew up in Cornwall. Pa worked the mines there," she said, her voice rising over the din of the men in the adjoining taproom.

I paid the good woman and took one quick bite, savoring the flaky crust, the peppery blend of minced beef, onions, swedes, and carrots. That was all I had time to eat before the tin horn sounded a warning blast. Time to get back to the carriage. I tucked my pasty back into its muslin bag, grabbed my reticule, pulled my shawl over my head, and walked out into the night and the wet.

The uneven pathway demanded concentration, as exhaustion claimed me and the downpour made each step tricky. Since my departure from Ferndean, I had been traveling for the better portion of two days, and had rested only fitfully the night before at the Farrows. The wet had soaked through my shawl and invaded my dress, chilling me to the bones. Alone, cold, wet, and hungry, my brave talk back at home seemed to mock me. My fellow travelers rushed past, their shapes flickering in the unsteady light of the inn's lanterns.

Out of the darkness, a figure hurtled along, coming parallel with me. A man. Young, slight.

I ducked my head down, trying to keep my face dry.

Without warning, he changed course and slammed into me. My body absorbed the blow. I landed hard on my left side.

The wind was knocked out of me. I clambered to my knees, but the mud gave no traction. Using my unbalance to his advantage, my assailant shoved me to the ground, and I slammed into the stones hard. A rough hand clapped over my mouth, bursting the skin inside my lip.

He tugged on the ribbons of my reticule.

The diamonds! I cannot let them go!

The ribbons bit deeply into the flesh above my gloves, burning and stinging. I shrank back, and he kept coming, filling my nose with the scent of hay and horses. Instinctively, I yanked my hand in the opposite direction he was pulling. Back and forth, we fought for possession. The man set to cursing under his breath.

The thief pushed my head down, banging me into the uneven stones once more. I still grasped the reticule. He struggled against me. I would not let go of my reticule. He pulled and I resisted, both of us writhing in the mud. His grip loosened. I gave a mighty wrench, trying to get free, and he twisted the other way.

Our heads knocked together. His crown slammed into the

right side of my face. My eye stung with tears. The pain stunned me nearly into submission.

I must protect the diamonds!

More than my own safety, I feared losing them, for Edward's sake. So few of the Rochester heirlooms remained after the fire. I wrestled free and staggered to my feet. The thief jumped to his as well. One of his hands flew out and grasped me by the collar, using this grip to shake me hard. I smelled fear and exertion and the wet richness of mud—and something more. Horseflesh, and the stink of a saddle leather.

A crescent of silver flashed above my head.

He had a knife!

I thought of Edward and Ned. And Adèle! How foolish I'd been to travel alone!

Ah, I thought. *He plans to kill me!*

The blade swooped down—and cut my purse strings!

I lost my balance, tumbling backward and landing flat in the mud. But as I fell, I grabbed at the thief's cap, which had been pulled low. In the half light from the lanterns, I caught a glimpse of him, but only a quick glance, and made note of his face, in particular his large, globe-shaped eyes.

"Hey!" the guard yelled from a distance. "What?"

"I've been robbed!" I cried.

With a grunt of victory, the assailant ran off with my reticule.

"Stop, thief!" yelled a voice behind me, as a horse galloped off into the night.

"You all right, miss?" The guard squatted down to look at me. "My name is Glebe. Are you hurt?"

"He . . . he took my reticule." With great effort, I clambered to my knees and tried to stand. The pain astounded me. I staggered to one side and Glebe grabbed my arm to steady me.

"Will you be needing a surgeon?" asked Glebe.

"No, no. I am all right."

"You sure? The coach is leaving. You must get on board. We have to keep on schedule!"

"But my reticule! It is gone."

"Aye," said Glebe. "You can't be missing that much. Maybe a few shillings. Might have seemed like a king's ransom to you, but that ain't so much. Not really."

"If only that were true. If only! In my purse I carried a diamond necklace, earrings, and matching circlet! They were worth a fortune!"

Chapter 5

The guard's lantern shed light on my appearance as he helped me climb the stair into the carriage. My fellow passengers expressed shock at my appearance.

"I was knocked down and robbed," I said.

"Oh my!" The old lady offered me her handkerchief. "A thief, you say?"

I tried to nod, but the pain in my head shrieked in protest and a moan escaped my lips.

"That mud on you?" asked the self-styled gentleman. "Keep it to yourself."

The other passengers edged away from me.

The rest of the ride passed slowly. Without my reticule, I could not read, or buy tea or food. The thief had even taken my Cornish pasty, although the fragrance of it lingered just to spite me. Twice more when we stopped, I tried to talk to Glebe about my losses. His indifferent attitude left me feeling furious and impotent. But there was nothing to be done at the moment. I amused myself by parting the curtains and watching the scenery. As we neared London, the roads grew more crowded, and the verdant hills gave way to clusters of houses. A low cloud hung over the rooftops, its dark belly dragging along the tiles and chimney pots. Slowly, the air changed, thickened, and became too dense to breathe. Several of the passengers started to cough. I picked out the twin scents of burning coal and horse droppings.

By the time we arrived at our destination, my injuries had blossomed fully, swelling around my eye and covering my legs over with scabs. Getting out of the carriage proved painful. The guard handed me down and walked me to where my trunk sat on the pavement under the dripping eaves of the porte cochere.

"Will you lodge a report with the constable about my loss?" I asked him. We stood in a puddle. My mud-laden dress clung to my legs. Hunger assailed me, and my poor shawl was sodden to the point of being a burden.

Glebe's watery eyes squinted as he looked me up and down. "Been thinking about that. How can it be that the thief targeted you, miss? You ain't dressed like quality. Why did he bother you and not them that was dressed fine?"

"Sir?"

"You claim you was carrying precious jewels. That don't seem sensible, does it? You're dressed like a lady's maid. Mayhap those diamonds didn't rightly belong to you. I been wondering, what if she stole them? And now she hopes to blame it on a robber. But what if they was working together?"

His accusations shocked me mute. I stood there, my head aching and my knees burning with the tightness of fresh scabs. Was it possible this foolish man thought I had rolled in the wet dirt and punched myself in the eye for sport? His lack of intelligence lit a brush fire in my hurting skull.

I pulled myself up to my full height to respond, but before I could, a tall man in livery tapped me on the shoulder. I turned toward him and he bowed, causing the gold buttons on his maroon greatcoat to sway. His broad shoulders were covered with a huge cape that dripped water on me and on the ground. "The name is Williams, ma'am. Mrs. Captain Brayton sent me." He gestured, "The driver over there said you was Mrs. Rochester. Is that right?"

Although stylishly attired, the coachman twitched and yanked at his jacket as if the costume did not fit properly. In his buttonhole a fresh nosegay nodded, and the fragrance of Sweet William and sweet pea seemed incongruous next to the man's rough face. His leathered skin betrayed the years he'd spent in the sun. One leg stuck out at a rather awkward angle. His entire person struck me as peculiar, as though he'd once been reduced to pieces and stuck back together, badly.

If he thought my bruised face surprising, he showed no sign.

But there was a flicker in his eyes. Yes, he'd noted my injuries. He simply refrained from remarking on them. I had the impression he'd likely seen worse.

"Yes, I am. Thank you for meeting me."

He nodded gravely. "Guard? What has happened? Mrs. Rochester here is a guest of Mrs. Captain Augustus Brayton. Why has she been detained?" His straightforward way of speaking seemed at odds with his fussy uniform.

I admit Williams surprised me. As far as I knew, coachmen did not speak unless spoken to. Yet here he was, asking questions of the guard.

"A thief, that's what happened here. Or so she claims," Glebe said, tugging at the flaps of his own jacket. "He made off with her reticule. Strange, when there were all sorts of other fancy passengers. Yet he only picked on you, madam. Why?"

Williams stepped between the guard and me. "Mrs. Rochester, Mrs. Captain Brayton is expecting you. I trust this good man has made a report to the constabulary?"

"Not yet, I ain't."

"Then do so," said Williams. "Mrs. Rochester? Our carriage is this way."

Williams gave a neat half bow, the line of him interrupted by that stiff right leg that refused to bend. "Mrs. Captain will be happy to see you. Don't fret, ma'am. Mrs. Captain has all sorts of resources. She will help you get this sorted. See if she don't."

Ensconced in the Braytons' handsome carriage, I peered out the window to see London, as best I could through the rain. The number of people astounded me. My impression was of a moving sea of persons in all shapes, sizes, and colors! Soon, I was forced to bury my nose in my sleeve because the stink of this place was worse than a privy on a hot summer day. Moreover, there was a prevailing dank darkness to the sky. My gray dress had been quickly covered in a mixture of soot and grit that had entered through the window. This, added to the mud from my tussle with my attacker, rendered me quite unpresentable. I thought to close the curtain, but my curiosity got the better of me and I quickly went back to staring out the window. I felt certain there was much to recommend the place, but alas! Given the dirt, the smog, and the press of the crowd, I confess that I found London less than desirable! In fact, I was bitterly disappointed.

Unlike its redbrick neighbors, #24 Grosvenor Square wore a fresh coat of white paint. Rather than the usual black shutters, Mrs. Lucy Brayton had added a touch of yellow to the paint, turning her trim a dark evergreen. Bountiful pansies, their heads heavy with flowers, spilled over window boxes, making them as colorful as gypsy caravans. The scent of her spicy geraniums added a tingle to the air, although the droop of the leaves told me that the frosts of fall had already done damage.

As the carriage pulled up, the front door opened and a figure came rushing out.

"Jane! There you are, at last!"

As a footman helped me alight from her carriage, Mrs. Captain Brayton squealed with joy and threw her arms around me. "At last I have a sister!" she exclaimed. "And I want to hear all about the baby!"

To describe Lucy Brayton was to attempt to pin down a butterfly and examine it carefully as it flapped its wings. The woman stayed in constant motion, her curls bobbing, her lashes fluttering, her hands moving, and her overall posture one of preparation for flight. Taken along with the vivid colors of her wardrobe, the effect dazzled the viewer.

While she was quite handsome, I believe she was never beautiful. Somehow her features—while pleasant enough when viewed separately—were less than harmonious when assembled. However, a light of curiosity shone from her eyes, functioning as a beacon that drew you closer. Lucy's apparel paid homage to the highest art of the Parisian dressmakers, and yet she did not wear it stiffly and cautiously as a manne-quin might. Instead, she seemed wholly unaware of its delicacy and costliness. Indeed, after a small amount of time in her presence, I, too, forgot how fashionably she was dressed. That was nothing except butter on the bread. The true focus was not the artificial outer garments but the woman's sparkling character, which no amount of apparel could obfuscate.

I guessed her age at thirty and five years, or so.

Her embrace sent me moaning in pain.

"Oh dear, and I finally have a sister and I broke her already!" She stepped away from me, her face contorted with dismay. "Goodness! Just look at you! Your eye is the color of a bloom-ing pansy, and you have more dirt on you than my gardener moves each spring. Come along, Jane. I want to hear all about little Ned—and the story behind your disarray!"

Her use of my Christian name and her exuberant welcome confirmed my earlier suspicions that my hostess would not let our friendship develop as such relationships naturally did.

That is, slowly. No, based on our husbands' long-standing friendship, Lucy Brayton was apparently already confident that we would be good friends, too.

That had been a more fulsome welcome than I expected, though Edward had warned me not to be misled by Lucy's fashionable exterior and overt cheerfulness into thinking that she was lacking in intelligence.

"Lucy has more substance than many men I know. She travels with Augie, gets to know the natives, and generally explores the world on her own terms. In every way, she is remarkable. Such a shame that she and Augie have been unable to produce an heir," Edward had said as he kissed our Ned.

"Yes, well, hello—" I managed now.

The front door opened slightly and a small dog tumbled down the stairs and onto the street. At first, I thought him to be a white muff, sewn out of human hair, so silky was his coat. However, his high level of exuberance quickly altered my impression.

"Meet Rags," Lucy explained as she scooped him up. "He was a gift from Augie. Isn't he adorable? Everywhere that I go, he comes along to save me from getting overly lonely while Augie is serving the King in climes unfit for humankind."

She took my hand and helped me up the stairs. My lack of food and the nagging pain from my injuries rendered graceful movement nearly impossible, so I succumbed to Lucy's guidance. We stepped over the threshold and into a black-and-white marble foyer, where her staff stood in a line for introductions. I struggled to concentrate, but I did manage to note that Polly was Mrs. Brayton's personal maid, and Sadie was the kitchen and parlor maid. Higgins was the name of the butler.

"They are all at your disposal," Lucy said as she concluded her introductions. "Now we shall get you upstairs and see to your injuries."

Before I could protest, I found myself in an opulent guest

bedroom, decorated in shades of yellow and green, with extravagant gold brocade curtains, a four-poster bed, and a chair positioned in front of a roaring fire. One of the footmen brought up a bathtub. He returned with a housemaid, and both carried buckets of hot water. I was whisked behind a screen, where Polly helped me remove my garments. Lucy scooped out sea salts and lavender from a brilliant cut glass container.

"I believe more lavender is also in order," she said to the maid. Polly left us and came back with a tin of dried herb leaves. When added to the hot water, the fragrance of lavender relaxed me, even before I stepped into the tub.

As I soaked happily behind the screen, Lucy plied me with questions about Ned.

"He sounds like a perfect darling!" she declared.

When the water grew cold, Polly toweled me dry, bandaged my wounds, and helped me into a dressing robe.

"Polly will see to your frock," said Lucy as her lady's maid left the room. "She is the finest abigail in all of London. I've instructed her to unpack your portmanteau. Cook sent up a tray. I'll be mother." Lucy lifted a delicate teapot. "Weak or strong?"

"You don't believe in that old superstition, do you?" I helped myself to a slice of cold meat, a piece of bread, and a slice of cheese. My stomach warned me these would only partially slake my hunger, but dinner would not be served for four more hours.

"That two people drinking from the same teapot risk bad luck?" She smiled at me. "No. I am a contrarian. All that is conventional arouses my suspicions. That said, you have had a run of ill fortune. Care to tell me what happened? I do not imagine you left Edward's tender care in such a state of dishevelment!"

I sighed. "It is rather a long story."

"Do your injuries hurt much?"

"Yes," I admitted. "Especially around my eye, where the skin feels most tender."

"Polly?" Lucy called out. "Run and fetch my flask, won't you?"

Polly returned with a small silver flask. Lucy tipped some liquid into my tea. "Try that. It should help you feel better."

"What is it?" I sniffed it cautiously.

"Gin. I find refreshing beverages like it to be delightful. Alcohol does wonders for the disposition, and it will hasten the process of getting to know each other. You are lucky I am willing to share. Now drink up."

I followed her lead. The beverage scalded my throat. I sputtered.

"You will get used to it. I daresay you will even grow fond of it, given a chance."

After that initial shock, it went down as a treat. To my amazement, my injuries stopped throbbing. In fact, I welcomed another helping in my second cup of tea. The faint aftertaste of juniper intrigued me. "How did you come to develop a taste for this?"

My hostess laughed. "Augie introduced me to it. You see, in India our men drink this mixed with quinine. It helps mollify the effects of malaria."

"I see."

"Why not start your story at the beginning? Why did you quit Ferndean so abruptly?"

I told her about Adèle's letters and showed her the foul note that threatened the child's safety.

"I asked around about Maude Thurston," Lucy said after she had read the note and returned it to me. "She has survived a precipitous fall from the rarified levels of high society. Her husband used to belong to Boodle's, the same club at which Augie and my brother are members. But Mr. Walthrop Thurston gambled away his fortune, and then committed suicide. The wretch. He left his poor wife to face the bill collectors alone. Her employment by Lady Kingsley as the Alderton House superintendent is more than simply fortuitous; it is necessary for survival," Lucy said. "Now tell me all about your travel here. I want to know everything!"

I explained about the offer from Mr. Carter for a ride, concerns regarding Edward's vision, and how I overheard Mrs. Carter. "I could not hear everything, but I heard enough to believe that she rejected my company because she had heard scurrilous remarks about me from a woman named Blanche Ingram." The gin loosened my tongue.

Lucy nodded solemnly. "Yes, I, too, have heard what Blanche Ingram and her mother have said about you and about Edward. They are terrible gossips, I'm afraid. They have been telling everyone who will listen that Edward tried to marry you while he was still married to another. Of course, they never let an opportunity pass without pointing out that you were his ward's governess. The Ingrams have complained long and loud over what they term 'Squire Rochester's ill-bred behavior.' But do not let it worry you overmuch. I doubt that you'll run into them much while you are here."

"Not that I care!"

"Ah, but things might change, when Ned is older. You might well shun Society now, but later you will see the advantages it can offer your child. Take my word for it."

I did not respond. I had not considered my new responsibilities to my son's future. Instead I sipped my tea, trying to ease the cotton wool texture inside my mouth. We sat for a while without speaking. At long last, I gathered my courage and said, "What should I do, Mrs. Brayton? You are quite right; I need to look ahead."

"I absolutely must insist that you call me Lucy! What you must do is form alliances. To see and to be seen, my darling. If that sounds odious, do it for Ned's sake. And for Edward, because a squire never knows when he might need a favor from someone in London. You still haven't explained what happened to your eye."

I told her about my trip in the mail coach and the incident with the thief. I ended my recitation with, "I hate the thought of telling Edward I have lost the Rochester diamonds!"

"I can assure you, Jane, that Edward will not care one whit about the jewels. They meant nothing to him until you came into his life."

"I know that. However, he has changed since Ned's birth," I explained. "Before we became parents, Edward thought of his family's legacy as a painful situation that must be endured. After all, it was his father's desire to keep Thornfield unencumbered that got him tricked into his first marriage."

"I know, I know," said Lucy. "What a horrible injustice!"

"For years, Edward thought of family and felt only disgust. But since our son's birth, my husband thinks in terms of what he—and the Rochester family—can offer Ned. He keenly regrets that several portraits of Rochester ancestors burned in the fire. A portraitist has been commissioned to re-create one from a miniature. Even more surprisingly, Edward has communicated with a distant relative to see if he will loan us a painting of his mother to be copied."

"You are worried Edward will be angry not because you lost the diamonds but because he will miss the chance to pass his mother's jewelry to his son? I admit, that makes more sense to me. Every man hopes his family name will live on. For that very reason our system of primogeniture continues to exist. Any child is a blessing, but a son doubly so." Her voice wavered and she looked down at Rags, gathering him close and giving him a hug. His tail wagged merrily as he licked her face.

Lucy feigned absorption with a tangle in Rags's hair. But something in the slump of her shoulders told me she was thinking about her own situation.

I knew I should comfort her, but I could not. It went

against my natural feelings of restraint. As much as I liked her, I was not in the habit of pressing my affection on women I'd barely just met. I wanted friendship, but I was not sure how to pursue it.

"Edward will not so much be angry as disappointed. I hate being the instrument of his distress. It angers me that I did not fight harder."

"You must not say that." Lucy's voice turned forceful. Rags responded by hopping to one side and whining at her. "That is entirely wrong. Your assailant wielded a knife. You were lucky to escape with your life. Your courage is not at issue here. A victim should never be blamed for an attack! I am certain that Edward would wholeheartedly agree with me."

"Yes, I know. It is just that the jewels were entrusted to me such a short while ago, and already they are gone."

"These are early days yet. Do not give up so easily."

"Glebe, the mail coach guard, did not inspire my confidence. He made no attempt to run after the thief. He did not request a description. In fact, I am tempted to believe that he did not credit my story."

"Why do you think that?"

"Glebe pointed out that I was surrounded by other people who might have made better targets based on their mode of dress. And yet, the thief chose to attack me. Not someone who might have seemed more likely to carry valuables."

"I see." A frown creased her forehead. "You cried out for help. Others saw the thief running away. Clearly, you suffered in the attack. Besides, I know of several ladies who wear paste jewels today because their own fine gems were stolen by highwaymen!"

"Yes, but Glebe implied I'd brought the crime upon myself. He even hinted that maybe those were not *my* jewels that I had lost! That perhaps I was a lady's maid, carrying them for my mistress, and that perhaps I was in league with my attacker. Or maybe I had previously lost the jewels and concocted a story to protect myself."

"Hmm. I suppose I can see his line of reasoning."

"It upsets me, but I suppose I can, too. I do believe he plans to check up on me before following other lines of investigation."

"There are other methods of inquiry." Lucy stroked Rags's head.

"Such as?"

"You could hire a private inquiry agent to investigate. A person skilled in such matters."

"Such people exist? Do you know of one?" At Lucy's urging, I took the last slices of cheese and meat and ate them with much pleasure.

"Yes, in fact, I do. I know one quite well, actually. But before we pursue that course of action, I suggest we stop at the constabulary and make a full report."

"I should like to do that, but I have other more pressing matters to attend to first. I plan to visit Adèle early tomorrow morning."

"I would accompany you, but I cannot on such short notice. I have an eleven o'clock appointment with my mantua-maker that I cannot break. She is in such demand that if I tarry, I might find her sharing my newest designs with another client! After I see her, I have calls to return, so my early afternoon is similarly occupied. But I shall instruct Williams to take you to the school—and wherever you choose to go in my absence," she said. "I have another driver and carriage at my disposal."

As she spoke, my eyes grew heavy. The warmth of the fire, the light repast I had enjoyed, the hot bath—and the stress of travel and my robbery—all conspired to make me drowsy. I was still hungry, but sleep was of a more pressing need. "I believe I should like to lie down for a while before dinner."

"Of course." Lucy gathered Rags under her arm. "Sweet dreams, little sister."

But before I could allow myself the luxury of a nap, I quickly penned a letter to Edward:

Dear Husband,

I am arrived in London. I find myself more tired than I would have guessed.

Mrs. Lucy Brayton has welcomed me with affection, as you said she would. She is lovely and very gracious. I am afraid I was not much company. I could barely keep my eyes open over our tea. She graciously offered me the use of her carriage.

First thing tomorrow, I will visit Adèle.

Give our son a hundred kisses from his mother.

I already miss both of you terribly. I know you are coming soon, and I can scarcely wait to see you again!

Your loving wife,
Jane Eyre Rochester

P.S. There was an unfortunate incident at a coaching inn on the Great North Road. I am a bit bruised, but otherwise, I am fine. I shall write more later.

Chapter 6

I slept through dinner, vaguely aware that Polly had tried valiantly to rouse me. Thus refreshed, I awakened in the morning at seven, a habit derived from checking on my son. The sky hung black as a funeral crepe, and torrents of rain beat against the window glass. Polly heard me stirring and brought me my dress. Not a smidgeon of mud blemished the skirt. I thanked her profusely for her hard work. When she heard I planned to visit the school, she suggested my black silk worn with a tucker. However, it was one of my better gowns, and a quick glance outside told me the rain was not letting up.

"I shall simply wear my gray corded muslin again," I said to Polly, and asked her about breakfast.

"Cook don't make anything before ten because Mrs. Captain isn't up till then. Lady guests don't usually get up as early as you. How about a cup of tea, ma'am?" She went to ask Sadie to bring it up for me.

As I drank the reviving beverage, Polly assembled my clothing. I could tell by her lack of enthusiasm that she thought my choice ill-advised. Nevertheless, she helped me into my undergarments. I moaned a little with pain as she tightened my stays.

"Sorry, ma'am," she said.

After I was dressed, Polly brushed my hair, parted it, and, at my direction, pulled it neatly into two coils, one on each side of my head.

To finish my toilette, I added the tiny pearl pin from Maria Temple to the front of my dress. Compared to Lucy's finery of the night before, the brooch seemed whimsical, but it brought me such happy thoughts of my old teacher that I decided it must stay.

"Is Williams available? Please tell him to bring the carriage around front." With that—and more thanks—I dismissed the girl.

I had decided it was best to first see Adèle, assure myself that she was fine, and then return to the Braytons' home. The cook would have set out breakfast by the time I returned. Thus, I could eat at my leisure, pen a note to Edward, and perhaps visit Hatchards while Lucy was making her afternoon social calls.

But as the coach started rolling, I debated the wisdom of my plan. My stomach growled with hunger, recalling my missed dinner. The motion of the carriage produced a light-headed sensation.

Suddenly, we came to a stop. Peeking out the window, I realized we sat at the end of a lane, a goodly distance from any houses.

"Beggin' your pardon, Mrs. Rochester, but I dunno if I can get us closer to the school. There are several carriages blocking the way." Williams positioned himself half in and half out of the Braytons' landau door, his awkward straddle baptizing me with fresh torrents of rain.

"We have arrived?" The trip from the Braytons' to Alderton House was much shorter than I had expected.

"Yes, ma'am."

"That is the school up ahead? That large building on the right?"

"Yes, ma'am."

Braving the rain, I stuck my head out farther and surveyed our situation. "Can you not get me *any* closer, Williams?"

"I'll see what I can do, ma'am." The coachman doffed his cap—not the best idea since the rain ran over his head and shoulders—and took off to determine why the conveyances ahead of us were stopped. He returned shortly and said, "The jarvey up ahead warns me they ain't moving. We could turn around. Come back later."

I considered that perhaps I should return to the Braytons'. I could go back to bed and await breakfast, postpone my visit to Alderton House for a few hours, or even another day, and perhaps change into a dress more suitable for my status. Wasn't it Glebe who'd remarked that I didn't look like a lady who'd own diamonds?

But Adèle needs me.

With that thought uppermost in my mind, I made up my mind. I moved toward the door of the coach.

My right eye had swollen so alarmingly that sight was difficult. But I ignored my injuries and squinted out the window as the rain poured over the brim of my bonnet. Beyond the stalled carriages stood two figures in black, clearly involved in conversation, their heads invisible under a large black umbrella.

"That's a fine-looking Berlin," said Williams, staring at one of the carriages. He spoke more to himself than to me. "Fast and light, but hard to overturn."

"Is one conveyance markedly better than another?" My curiosity got the better of me.

Williams's jaw dropped. "Certainly, ma'am. Why, just look at it!"

What was it Edward had once told me? "In London, ostentatious style determines one's pecking order. The citizens of that town judge one another with the same sort of assessment a farmer generally bestows on livestock."

"I shall get out here," I declared, having made my decision.

"No, ma'am! Please, no, you cannot! Mrs. Brayton finds out, she will have my hide!"

I doubted that. Stuffed and mounted he wouldn't make much of a prize. Williams certainly would not enhance her fine marble entryway.

"I'll speak on your behalf. My mind's made up." I struggled to open the door, and Williams hurried to help me down. I swallowed a whimper as I stepped first on the lozenge-shaped carriage step and finally onto the uneven cobblestones.

The smells of London assailed me: damp wool, wet coal dust, moist peat smoke, running waste from chamber pots, and piles of fresh, steaming horse droppings. All this at a highly desirable address! I could only imagine the squalor of the rookeries in Holborn, those wretched quarters where I had been told that thieves, children, hogs, and dogs vied for food and shelter.

"Williams, those two men block the front door. How else might I enter?"

"See the wrought iron railing with the steps going down? That's called the area. But it's for the trade and servants. Wouldn't do for quality like you!"

Two years ago, I wouldn't have been welcome anywhere except through the servants' entrance. My wardrobe may not have changed, but every other aspect of my world had.

"Thank you, but it will have to do," I said, my tone brooking no argument.

Williams tipped his hat again and said, "Very well. I shall wait for you around the corner, ma'am!" With that, he hopped back up to his high perch.

I hurried against the wind as it buffeted me up and down, the way a kite gets tossed about on a fretful spring day. Picking my way through the puddles, I discovered a walkway. I gave a wide berth to the two men—who still stood on the front steps, talking in urgent tones and totally ignorant of my presence—and I continued until I could grasp the wrought iron fencing and follow it along. I was nearly at the bottom of the stairs when the two men ended their conversation.

One hopped into the Berlin and took off down the street. The other opened the front door of Alderton House and disappeared inside. He came right back outside, his hands gripping a long, low plank. On it was a bundle covered by a white sheet. A partner carried the other end of the burden, both struggling to keep their footing as they navigated into the wind.

Unexpectedly, the wind changed direction. The gust knocked the men sidewise—and pushed me against one of the house walls. I watched helplessly as the men struggled to regain their balance by juggling their load. A corner of the white fabric worked free from the stretcher.

The wet sheet rose up like a sleeping creature comes awake. The fabric swayed first this way, then that. Snapping and snarling in the wind.

I shivered at the sight of it, an inanimate object come to life to dance a demonic jig.

The new man shrieked and nearly dropped his end of the transport. The other man responded with guttural curses, first at his partner, then at the elusive fabric that jerked up and away from his grasp.

The cursing man reached high and snatched at the white sheet, finally dragging it. The pelting rain ought to have plastered it down, but the fabric refused to stay pinioned. It jumped free of his hand once more, and flew up to reveal what was in the bundle.

A body with skin as white as chalk.

Chapter 7

While the men loaded their burden into the hackney, I knocked on a heavy door. My repeated appeal brought no answer.

Desperate for shelter, I gave the door a push. When it refused to yield, I set my shoulder to it.

The door swung open with a loud groan. Hanging firmly on the handle, I spun about, making a tight half circle. Thus, I staggered inside, backside first.

"About time you arrived," said a voice behind me.

I completed another half turn and used my back to slam the door.

"Aye, and don't that just cap the globe?"

A woman stared boldly at me. She wore a cook's apron, and a trace of flour smudged her broad forehead. She squinted and stepped closer to examine me. "What a sight! Ain't only the rain that's been beating on ye! Someone has been giving ye a good what for!"

A low snicker drew my attention to a young girl chopping vegetables.

"That will be enough, Emma," said Cook.

Resting my back against the door, I caught my breath. The short walk in the elements—and the disturbing glimpse I'd had of a dead girl—had drained my reserves of energy. My compelling desire to see Adèle was all that fueled me.

"Wouldn't send me worst dog out in this weather, I wouldn't. Go on and get over by the fire."

Following her directives, I stepped nearer to the wide brick hearth, where yellow, orange, and red coals glowed brightly. There I proceeded to shake the rain from my garments. As I moved, my bonnet tilted. More water dripped down, splashing a wooden box lined with rags. One of these shifted, revealing a large, lugubrious black cat. He hunched his spine in a stretch before settling into a seated position, where he regarded me haughtily.

I stared back.

He didn't blink. His gaze suggested he felt quite my superior.

But then, *he* was dry, and I was not.

"Hope ye ain't superstitious. That there is Mephisto, and he is the very devil. Ain't got a spot of white nowhere. Mean, but a good mouser. Got a soft spot for the girls, he does. He'll scratch you and me till we bleed like we been stuck with knives"—Cook pulled up a sleeve to show me the proof—"but he don't never hurt the students. Never."

Mephisto twitched his nose at me, rolled over, and went back to sleep.

"Ah," was all I could manage. I unpeeled my wet shawl from my aching shoulders. With effort, I wrung it out on the floor. Water ran in rivers.

Cook kept up a rhythmic turning and slapping of dough against a flour-dusted tabletop. Small clouds of flour flew around and resettled. Emma chopped her vegetables in a stately cadence.

"Emma, put that down. Run tell Miss Miller that her

German teacher has finally arrived. All the way from Hamburg, she has come to us."

A correction formed in my mind as a wave of tiredness and hunger nearly bowled me over. One hand on a nearby counter steadied me, temporarily.

Emma took her time untying her apron, clearly using Cook's instructions as an excuse to examine me at length. "That is quite the black eye," the girl said.

"Aye, it is. Now run along." Cook left the dough and slid a long-handled wooden paddle under three fresh loaves in the oven. My stomach growled at the aroma of baking bread and caraway seeds.

I wasn't alone. Emma cast a rueful glance at the fresh-baked bread before aligning her knife with the pile of half-peeled turnips. "Aye."

"Mind, she might be too busy. What with what has happened and all. If she is, ask her what to do with this one." Cook spoke in an undertone, but I could still hear. "I cannot have her hanging around my kitchen, not with those beggar eyes. Well, one beggar eye. The other is all swelled shut."

I edged nearer to a shiny copper pot hanging from the ceiling. There I caught my reflection. The right side of my face resembled an angry purple pansy. My mouth was double its normal size. A bright red slash divided my lower lip in two.

I was glad I hadn't examined my injuries more carefully back at Lucy Brayton's house. They were horrible!

Suddenly, the purpose that kept me rigid, the force that had compelled me to keep going, vanished. My knees went weak and I wobbled a bit.

"Sit." Cook shoved a stool beneath me. From the cupboard she retrieved a white china teapot, festooned with forget-me-nots and finished with a gold trim. The piece took on an unexpected glow of delicacy in that dreary, heavy kitchen.

I sank down and rubbed my forehead. Closing my eyes, I surrendered to a parade of images: little Ned in his cot, the long carriage ride with Mr. Carter, the trip in the mail coach, the man who came from the shadows at the inn and—

"Here." Cook poured from the teapot, her chapped red hands thickly incongruous against the translucent white of the pot. She pressed a mug of lukewarm tea toward me. I took a tentative sip. I wished it had milk and sugar, but I was grateful nonetheless.

I closed my eyes to savor the brew. One more image impressed itself on my brain—a flapping sheet, the spectral silhouette I'd witnessed from the walkway.

I squeezed the thick mug, trying to transfer its warmth. I was cold and hungry and tired. When the senses are over-stimulated, the imagination naturally attempts mediation, doesn't it? I decided that my mind had taken my concern for Adèle, my guilt at not visiting, her fearful letter, and my own memories of Lowood and woven all these separate occurrences into a new and fantastical tale. Mixed together with the sight of a sheet flapping in the wind, I'd invented a dramatic intrigue. My mind had merely woven disparate visions together, hoping to create a narrative, even where none existed.

That couldn't have been a dead body that I had seen.

Taken in tandem with the threat to Adèle, it conjured up all sorts of wild imaginings.

Don't go there, Jane, I warned myself. *Keep to your plan. Surely Adèle is fine!*

Industry. I wanted motion and purpose to keep my emotions in check. I drained the mug. Before I could thank the cook, she took the cup from me and turned her back on me.

"Hamburg. That's a long way away, eh? Ye been running from someone. He done ye harm, eh?"

She had confused me with someone else. I opened my mouth to correct her, but before I could, she said, "No matter. Miss Miller will be happy to see ye. Especially after what happened this morning. She is going to need all the help she can get, I'll warrant."

"Miss Miller, the headmistress?" The name was familiar. However, there are nearly as many Millers in England as there are sheep on the hillsides.

"Who else would it be?" Cook laughed, a snort of derision that sent a cloud of flour flying. "Mrs. Thurston, the superintendent, would not be talking with the likes of ye. Nor would ye be passing the time of day with Lady Kingsley, the founder. If Mrs. Thurston did have a tick to spare for ye, wouldn't she give ye what for? Showing up like this. Three weeks late."

Clearly, she still took me for the errant teacher. By dressing in an improper manner for my station in life, I now realized how I invited misinterpretation. Breaches of etiquette did, indeed, send the wrong message, especially here in fashionable London.

I shivered. Digging deep into my skirt pocket, tunneling through the wet fabric, my hand bypassed the soggy note from Adèle, plus the offensive threat, and withdrew a limp handkerchief in time to cover my sneeze.

Cook looked up and set fists on her hips. Her watery blue eyes lingered on my bruises. "I had one of 'em once. Talked with his fists, he did. He was a good man, except when after he had himself too much whiskey."

I attempted to nod and was rewarded for my efforts by a stabbing pain in my temple. My fingers flew to my eye. They cautiously explored the swelling flesh. The bulge was big as an apple now. I believe that I whimpered.

"Well, ye're here and ye're safe. It's an ill wind that blows no good, I always say. Ye look smart enough, like ye spends all yer time reading. That'll make ye all skinny and pale. My daughter looked a bit like ye."

"Did she?" I perched on a stool. A pain shot through my ribs. I bit back a moan.

"Ye're hurt bad, ain't ye? I'll get ye a piece of meat to put on that eye. Just ready to turn it into a nice stew, but it won't hurt my cooking to wait, and it might do ye a world of good."

"Thank you kindly." What I really wanted was another hot cup of tea with milk and sugar, and perhaps a piece of that bread. My eye could not be helped, I feared, but my stamina was fading quickly.

"Ye speak English right nicely. Blimey. I bet learning German is awful hard."

With consideration to my mistaken identity, I quickly added, "*Danke.*"

"Aye. Don't hold much with foreigners."

"I was born in Thornton, Yorkshire." No need to tell her that my cousins and I taught ourselves German by reading great literature with a dictionary propped open on our knees. Thinking of Diana and her sister, Mary, I pulled my dripping shawl tighter around me.

"Good." My English pedigree thus established, Cook reached into a pot, withdrew a large hunk of uncooked meat, and transferred it carefully to my hands.

I raised the meat to my aching cheekbone. Perhaps the raw flesh could, indeed, provide relief. But I held little hope.

Emma reappeared and held the door open for another woman. When this second entrant raised her head, I gasped in surprise to see Nan Miller, a teacher from my days at Lowood. Relief rushed through me as I beheld a woman I once knew well.

"Jane Eyre! What on earth are you doing here? Your face!"

Nan Miller's careworn countenance had only grown more haggard over the years since I had left the school. When I first met her, she was an under-teacher with a ruddy complexion and a propensity to scuttle. About ten years my senior, Miss Miller was also an orphan who, like me, had been sent to Lowood and who aspired to a better way of life.

I juggled the meat with one hand and reached out to shake Miss Miller's outstretched fingers with the other.

"I will take that." Cook scowled and gestured toward the meat.

"*Danke*," I said.

"*Dan-kee*," Cook mimicked my earlier thanks.

"*Danke*," I repeated sternly, unwilling to let her atrocious accent go unchallenged.

"Emma, bring us tea. We'll take it in the parlor." Miss Miller jerked her head in the direction from where she had come, indicating she expected me to follow. "What a pleasant surprise, Miss Eyre. But I cannot visit for long. It is a very sad day. One of our students has died."

At that, I fainted.

Chapter 8

I fought to regain consciousness as the world came back into focus. A dull ache thrummed in the back of my head. My stomach rumbled with hunger.

"Miss Eyre? Please, wake up. I haven't time to play nurse-maid." A blocky hand waved a vial of strong scents under my nose. "Put the tray on the table, Emma. That will be all. Close the door on your way out."

We were seated in a highly decorated parlor, a veritable jungle of overbearing palms. Dark and gloomy portraits frowned down on us from all four walls. Vases, an obelisk, and a multitude of porcelain figurines competed for space on a white mantel. Reaching for opulence, the decor achieved clutter. The general stuffiness and the overabundance of items added to my mental confusion.

"Drink this. I added a touch of ratafia." Miss Miller guided a delicate rose-sprigged teacup to my lips so that I could take a fortifying swallow.

I gasped. The tea could not disguise the fact that the ratafia tasted like oak barrels, where I assumed the beverage had fermented.

I added more tea to my cup and asked, "What happened?"

"I am not sure. Emma summoned me to the kitchen. I thought to meet our long-lost German teacher. Imagine my surprise to find you in our kitchen, and in this battered state! Then you fainted dead away. From the looks of that fresh bruise and broken lip, it is clear that you have had a most trying experience."

"A highwayman robbed me."

"Oh dear! They roam the roads with impunity, do they not? You must have put up quite a struggle."

"I did," I said. I sought to direct our conversation into another channel. There was no reason to dwell on my past misfortunes. "Did you say that someone had died?"

"Yes." Miss Miller's voice was little above a whisper.

"Who?"

"Pardon?"

"I need to know. Who died?"

"Why, Miss Eyre! I hardly think it is any of your affair!"

"Which girl is dead? Is it Adèle?"

"Adèle? We have no student named Adèle."

"Adèle Varens. She is here. I know it! Tell me she is all right." My head began to swim with pain.

"Oh! You mean Adela Varens! You call her by her French name? You see, Mrs. Thurston issued strict instructions to only call the girl 'Adela' in order that she might become more British in her manner and—"

"Is she all right?" Her evasions proved so frustrating that I could have grabbed Miss Nan Miller by both shoulders and shaken her.

"Of course, Adela is fine."

I tried to organize my thoughts. Adèle was not dead. However, another girl was! What was happening here?

"How did that girl die?" I needed to know if this was

somehow connected with the threatening mail Adèle had received. Was my young friend in imminent danger?

Miss Miller sighed. "Selina Biltmore was found dead in her own bed this morning. An undisclosed illness, or some unknown weakness, appears to have felled her. Really, Jane, you are most provoking. As I said, I need to get to my responsibilities, especially given this sad occurrence. I shall see you to the door." Miss Miller attempted to stand.

I grabbed her arm and held her fast. "No," I said. "I cannot leave. Not yet." My hands flew to my temples where the pain stabbed through my skull like a pair of sharp daggers.

"I shall excuse you overstaying your welcome because it is clear to me that you are in pain. I can see it on your face. You carry no reticule. I assume that since you were robbed you are penniless and without shelter, like so many here in London. I would offer you a bed for the night, but unfortunately, I am not in a position to do so. I hate to send you away, but my presence is urgently required elsewhere." Miss Miller pulled away from me and tried to stand, her chilly speech bolstered by her stiffened posture. "Do come visit me again. I am sorry we lost touch with each other. Now that we are reacquainted—"

"Miss Miller! I must see Adèle. I have pledged to do so."

Miss Miller sat back down. "How do you know Adela?"

"Think back to our time together at Lowood. Do you recall that I advertised in the *Herald* for a position? And that I was offered a situation as a governess?"

Miss Miller pondered this. "Yes, I recall that."

"It was Adèle I was hired to teach, and as a consequence, the child grew very dear to me. I'm sure she's told you as much."

Miss Miller looked away and fingered her dress, meddling with its thin fabric. "No, I had not heard. Well then, you must have been one of several teachers she had! You see, Dowager Lady Ingram is a friend of our founder, Lady Kingsley. Through this connection, Mrs. Thurston heard that Mr.

Rochester had a governess who ran away from her post. Under circumstances most embarrassing and insalubrious."

A hot blush crept across my face. "What did Dowager Lady Ingram say?"

Seeing Miss Miller waver between telling me and holding her tongue, I added, "I might have heard a similar story."

"It is a wild tale of a wedding interrupted. See, there was a governess involved, a young lady with aspirations far above her station. Terribly unsuitable. Dowager Lady Ingram told Lady Kingsley how this tutor bewitched the lord of the manor. Had him quite crazed for wanting her. As a consequence, he proposed marriage and she accepted, causing the squire to spurn poor Blanche Ingram, who would have made him a brilliant match. Lady Ingram's daughter Blanche's heart was quite broken. But it was all for good, because that wicked man was already married! Can you imagine? When the upstart governess found out his true intent—bigamy!—she ran away, and the squire sent his ward off to school. That's how Adela came to lodge here. And there's more."

"Pray continue." Although I knew an honest version of this story by heart, I wanted to hear the gossip that Dowager Lady Ingram was spreading. I needed to know what tales were being told about me and Edward.

"Dowager Lady Ingram told Lady Kingsley that the wife was a madwoman, kept locked in the attic of Squire Rochester's country manor. Have you ever?" Miss Miller paused and took a sip of her tea. Her urgent business had been temporarily postponed in the excitement of sharing such scandal. "I guess the squire had a nurse who looked after the madwoman, but that old crone was given to drink. And one night the crazed wife slipped free of her drunken minder and set the old hall on fire! Squire Rochester was nearly killed as a consequence. Don't know but he's now an invalid. He hasn't been to see Adela since she came here."

"I see." It took me a minute to absorb this retelling of the events of my life, which, though twisted, contained elements of truth. "But the squire has married again since the fire—in which his first wife perished. Did Lady Ingram not say he had? Doesn't Mrs. Thurston know that Edward Rochester has taken a new bride?"

Miss Miller shrugged. "I don't know. Could be. Perhaps Mrs. Webster heard about his marriage. Mrs. Thurston came on nearly six months ago. She has had much to do, especially since our German teacher left."

"Has Adèle—Adela—made no mention of her guardian and his status?"

"Heavens, no. Maude Thurston cannot abide gossip."

It took all my self-control not to scoff at this. Clearly, the woman loved gossip! She had no compunctions about sharing unfounded, scurrilous remarks about Edward and me.

Miss Miller continued, "Mrs. Thurston expressly warned Adela not to talk about her guardian. She told Adela the man is a fiend and his name is not to be bandied about."

I gasped. Nothing prepared me for this. No blow to my body could hurt as much. How dare Maude Thurston subject Adèle to such restraints? How dare this woman judge my husband and label him so crudely! And what must Adèle think? She dearly loved her *bon ami*, Edward Rochester. The poor child. How confused she must feel!

It's of little matter, I consoled myself. *I am here now. I can set this right.*

My former colleague stood. "It has been good to see you. However, given the tragedy of this day, I really must cut our visit short. Perhaps you can come back and visit me and see Adela some other time."

"But I am here now, and I want to see the girl."

"That is noble of you, I am sure, but unnecessary. It is really quite impossible for you to visit with Adela today."

"Perhaps I have not made my position clear. I demand to see Adèle!"

"By what right, Jane?"

"I have every right. *I* am Mr. Rochester's wife!" I pulled off my glove and thrust forward my left hand.

Chapter 9

"I beg your pardon!" Miss Miller's mouth hung open. "I did not know! The governess? The one who ran away? It was you?"

"Yes. However, the tale that Dowager Lady Ingram told does not bear repeating. It is both cruelly slanted and spiteful."

"Again, please accept my apologies. My word, Miss Eyre, you are the wife of a squire? How fortunate for you!"

Nan Miller's frank admiration embarrassed me. It would take some time for me to sort through all the mischief that Lady Ingram had caused. In the meantime, I would need to set the situation right with Maude Thurston. More importantly, I needed to see to Adèle.

"Even if Mrs. Thurston did not know about our marriage, Adèle did. Mrs. Augustus Brayton is a family friend. She checked on Adèle regularly up until six months ago."

"Perhaps the girl did mention it. I can't say. Adela babbles in French so quickly that I find it hard to follow."

A fresh wave of guilt swept over me. That poor child! Until six months before I became her governess, she had lived on the Continent and had spoken naught but her native tongue. Edward brought her and her French-speaking nurse with him to England after her mother left. Although I had insisted we spend a portion of our days speaking in English, Adèle still preferred her native tongue, especially when she was tired or distressed.

"I never was very good with languages," Miss Miller said with a dismissive wave of her hand.

While most girls' schools offered Latin, Greek, and French—and occasionally German and Italian—as part of their usual curriculum, at Lowood, Miss Miller never rose above the position of under-teacher because her linguistic skills were so paltry.

"But surely the girl confided in someone," I insisted. "Was there no adult who could converse freely with Adèle?"

"Yes, of course. Our old German teacher, Fräulein Hertzog, and Adela got along famously. Fräulein could speak a bit of French. Not much, but some. She was the proctor for the Senior girls. You know, Adela is the youngest in her form. Most of the Seniors are thirteen and up."

"Why is she in the Senior form? She only turned ten this year."

"When Mrs. Thurston came, she moved Adela in with older girls, in consideration of the fact that the girl had been exposed to certain unsavory influences early in life." She paused and shook her head at me.

The fact that the child had been judged for the sins of her mother, who was an opera dancer and a courtesan, struck me as unnecessarily harsh. However, I did recall that shortly after meeting Adèle she had shown me a specimen of her accomplishments, which included a canzonet with a subject that was wildly inappropriate for such a young performer. Perhaps Mrs. Thurston was wise to separate Adèle from the younger children.

"There is one other question I have. Of late, Adèle's letters are different. The phrasing seems foreign to her."

Miss Miller laughed. "And much improved, no doubt? Yes, the truth is that the students are not the authors of their correspondence. Mrs. Thurston is. All the girls copy her letters from the blackboard."

"What?" I could not believe my ears.

"Really, it is quite an ingenious arrangement. Lady Kingsley, our founder, was furious when one girl complained to her parents about something or another and they responded by withdrawing her. Maude Thurston vowed it would never happen again. But parents do expect to hear from their children regularly. So Mrs. Thurston decided she would script out the messages."

My heart went out to Adèle, but I also experienced a feeling of relief—at least now I knew why her recent letters had been so strange!

"I feel horrible that Adèle has not seen us in so long," I said. "Do the other parents who send their daughters to Alderton House visit them often?"

"Most, I am sorry to say, do not. Her situation is not unusual. Sometimes parents stay away because their visits are disruptive. Each family is different. All of our parents choose Alderton House because they want a good education for their children. Many travel and have decided that a stable atmosphere is best, but others seem to want to be done with the rigors of parenting. To tell you the truth, many exhibit more affection for their little dogs!" She sighed. "Students often stay with us over the holidays and summers. The majority of parents visit the school infrequently if at all."

"Then how do they know that their girls are getting a good education?"

"A few ask for regular reports in the form of letters, which Mrs. Thurston provides sporadically. She feels it best not to bother the parents unless there is a problem. Involving parents only invites interference, as you can well imagine."

"Interference."

"Yes." This, a soft hiss of admission.

I could not contain myself any longer. I stood up. "Enough.

I'm afraid I shall have to 'interfere'—you must take me to Adèle at once."

"I am sorry, but that's not possible. She is sleeping."

"At this hour? She should be in class, should she not?" Adèle who never napped? Never showed any sign of diminished energy? My heart took an unwelcome tumble.

"After her friend's death, Adela grew distraught. When she refused to be comforted, the doctor examined her and suggested a tisane. Perhaps if you can come back later—"

"Either you can escort me or I shall find my own way."

Miss Miller put her hand on mine. "I might almost suppose you didn't trust me."

"It does not matter if I trust you," I explained. "I must see the girl. I *will* see her. I have promised my husband, and I must fulfill my promise." I would make it up to Adèle for being remiss, and I would start that process today, right here, right now.

"You are so . . . hard, Jane. So intractable! I remember you always asking too many questions. But I do not remember you being so insistent and challenging. What has changed you?"

Had I changed? Since my days at Lowood, certainly—and only for the better, I thought. "It is the responsibilities I now shoulder—some happily and some reluctantly. These are the burdens I intend to carry as my own from now until the day I draw my last breath. One of those includes seeing to the welfare of Adèle Varens."

Miss Miller rose from her seat and started toward the hallway. "You have convinced me. But we must be quick. Mrs. Thurston thinks I take time with you because you are our new German teacher. I don't believe we have the luxury of correcting her misunderstanding and introducing you properly at the moment. Not right now. She is understandably preoccupied by our tragedy. I believe she is making arrangements for us to go into mourning. Earlier she was writing a letter of condolence to the girl's parents."

Since I could do nothing for the dead child, I nodded my assent. I cared not a whit about Mrs. Thurston or what she thought of me. I cared only about seeing Adèle.

The parlor door opened into a spacious foyer. A fine silk rug covered a portion of the alternating black and white marble squares. A crystal chandelier dangled above us. Marble busts stared down from alcoves in the wall.

"To the right is Mrs. Thurston's office, and behind it is her own snug apartment," explained Miss Miller. Seeing the surprise on my face, she laughed quietly. "We could not imagine such a place as this, could we? I think back to our early days at Lowood, before it was rebuilt. How crowded the one schoolroom and dormitory were. The odor of burned porridge seeping through its every pore. There's none of that here."

She gestured toward an open room on our left, and I glimpsed two dining tables set with fine silver that sparkled in the light streaming through the windows. "A partition can divide this room in half," said Nan Miller, pointing to a set of folding doors. This space was approximately the same size as the whitewashed cottage in the good village of Morton where I taught twenty scholars during that sad interim when I was estranged from Edward.

Following Miss Miller upward along a broad staircase of polished mahogany, I glimpsed a first floor neatly sectioned into quarters. These were the classrooms. Through the closed doors, I heard the high piping voices of little girls chanting their lessons.

"At the back is a music room, complete with a cabinet piano. Each classroom has globes and reference books," she said with an abundance of pride in her voice.

We ascended another set of stairs. "Here we have our library. There is even a ten-volume set of *Encyclopaedia Britannica*. At night we gather here, so that the girls can practice their needle arts and read aloud. We have fifteen students—well, I suppose now fourteen students—in all. The dormitories for the five Infants, the five Juniors, and the five—four—Seniors are on this floor. The forms are divided into Infants, ages six to eight; Juniors, ages nine to twelve; and Seniors, ages thirteen and up."

At the top of the landing, we stepped inside a long room. A bed and small dresser sat apart, near the door, in an area cordoned off by a dressing screen. "The teacher usually sleeps here. Each dormitory has an adult in attendance. But because our new German teacher has not arrived, this bed is currently empty."

We stepped around the dressing screen and gazed upon five beds in two facing rows.

"Adèle!" I said. She lay on one side with her face turned away from us. Her copious hair with its abundant curls was easily recognizable as it spilled over the pillow. I hurried to her, expecting her to rise up and greet me sleepily.

How she had grown in the last two years! I could tell she was much taller. The clock of childhood sweeps along at a faster pace than that of adulthood. Although our parting seemed recent to me, for Adèle the separation had already lasted a large portion of her life.

I stepped around the bed and knelt beside her.

"Adèle?" I tucked a stray lock of her hair behind her ear so it did not dangle over her face. Poor child. Did she think we had forgotten her?

She made no response.

"Adèle!"

She didn't move.

Chapter 10

"What is wrong with her?" I demanded of Miss Miller. "Why will Adèle not rouse? Is she ill? What did the doctor say when he examined her? Is that why you wanted to keep me away? What aren't you telling me?" The last dregs of my control ebbed away. I was tired, I was angry, and I was frightened. Very, very frightened.

Miss Miller's bland face told me nothing.

"Answer me!"

"You must understand. She was hysterical. She sobbed. She pulled at her hair. She was making herself sick. The tisane had no effect. I put two drops of laudanum in a chocolate and offered it to her."

Chocolate? That would prove irresistible to my young friend. Sweets were among Adèle's greatest passions.

"See? She sleeps quietly." Miss Miller smiled. "She is at peace. The doctor suggested it, Jane. You were not here. Believe me, you cannot imagine how distressed she was. She worked herself into such a state that she started retching. We could not help her any other way."

I knew Adèle to be emotional, dramatic to excess, but the description of her behavior seemed beyond anything I'd ever seen from the girl. Yet if a surgeon had suggested dosing Adèle, perhaps that had been the wisest course. I had seen her when she was wayward, and I knew that because she had been spoiled and indulged when younger, she could prove to be quite vexing. Given the shock that must have occurred when a schoolmate died, I could well imagine the French girl's over-reaction. I stroked her cheek and kissed her forehead, noting the regular rise and fall of her chest. I took one of her hands, opened the fingers, and planted kisses on the palm. I murmured endearments to her in her native language. She sighed, smacked her lips, gripped my fingers in sleepy response, and snuggled deeper into the bed. Her partial response to my ministrations encouraged me. Yes, she was in a drugged state, but she was still with us, not entirely insensible. I watched her steady breathing and noted her healthy color and that she seemed thinner. Although I couldn't rouse her, she was not in danger.

Slowly, I rose to my feet. I bent over and kissed Adèle's cheek once more. In response, Adèle mumbled.

The sound of her voice did my heart good.

"You really do love her." Miss Miller's voice held wonder and appreciation.

"Of course I do. How could I not care for Adèle? She is a darling. Besides which she matters to Edward, and what matters to him is of paramount importance to me. But even if that were not true, I would still care for her."

I fingered the threatening slip of paper tucked deep in my pocket and considered my options. Was it wisest to remove Adèle at once, or would she prosper better at Alderton House? True, the surroundings here were opulent, and it was clear none of the girls lacked those basic comforts that are both necessary and pleasing to daily life. Clearly, the place was well-appointed for scholarship, and perhaps this dispassionate environment provided her with exactly the sort of cool clime she needed to quell those early disadvantages that rendered her overly emotional. I knew that Miss Miller had a good heart. She had treated me and my classmates with kindness. Yes, she was calloused, but the thick skin covered a tender core.

On the other hand, Adèle was unhappy at the least, and wanting from a lack of thoughtful adult interference at the most. Perhaps I should take Adèle with me, and once she awakened, I could interview the child and better evaluate what our best course of action might be.

"Is there someone who could carry her down the stairs? And run 'round the corner to hail my driver?"

"If you are planning to take her with you, I beg you to reconsider," said Miss Miller calmly. "Despite this morning's histrionics, Adela has adjusted to school life very well. When she came two years ago, she was unruly, but she has settled into a routine. She likes her schoolmates. Of course, she can leave if you wish, but I think you are making a mistake. Tomorrow she will want to discuss with her friends what happened. Who can understand it better than one of her peers?"

"And you are sure that she is not ill? That the girl who died did not harbor an infection? If so, I should remove Adèle immediately!"

"As I told you, there were no outward signs of anything amiss with Selina, the girl who died. We called the surgeon as quickly as we realized the girl was . . . cold. He saw no indications of illness," said Miss Miller.

I thought over her suggestion: She was right. Even if my presence was a comfort, if Adèle woke up here, she could mourn with the support of other girls. It would go a long way toward making her understand the value of friendship. And duty. Both were qualities that Edward wanted instilled in her.

Besides which, I was a guest in Lucy Brayton's home. While she had extended every courtesy to me, it would be impertinent and rude to return with an unexpected guest.

Miss Miller interrupted my thoughts. "I know it is a hard decision, but you don't want to undo all the good that has come to Adela over the past two years. She has been making friends and learning to use English rather than her mother tongue. If you take her now, she will likely regress. I suggest you let her stay. At least until tomorrow. Let her grieve with her friends before you take her home."

She paused. "Think on how you weathered the tragedies at Lowood."

A reasonable request. Schoolgirls often turned to one another in a crisis. My schoolmates at Lowood and I had relied on one another that cruel May when infection turned the seminary into a hospital. Such friendships could last a lifetime; I still stayed in contact with Julia Severn and the witty and original Mary Ann Wilson. I wanted that for Adèle. She would enjoy the society of others, as she was by nature a chatterbox who loved nothing more than an admiring audience.

"Then I shall leave Adèle here. At least for now."

"That is a wise decision."

I left a last kiss on Adèle's forehead and squeezed her hand, then moved with Miss Miller out of the dormitory. "When do you expect her to awaken?"

Miss Miller pulled the door closed behind us. "She will sleep for the remainder of the day and through the night."

"I must hear everything that concerns Adèle: how her studies are going, who instructs her, who her friends are, what progress she has made. Most importantly, you must grant me assurance that she is safe."

"I give you my word," she said, hurrying me along down the stairs. "It is true that we've suffered a tragedy, but the storm will pass. The girls will help one another to cope. Adela was overwrought. But nothing more. Since you know her, you're aware she tends to be dramatic."

My hand again touched the note in my pocket. I thought about sharing it. But that would betray Adèle's confidence—

and I might miss out on finding the truth. Perhaps another student wrote it to threaten her.

Schoolgirls suffered intense passions. They could fight one day and exchange kisses the next. I wanted to determine for myself whether Adèle's letter to us sprang from those variances in emotion—or whether she truly was being mistreated. Judging from my experience, Adèle might be unhappy, but I hoped her complaints were merely exaggerated.

I decided to keep both notes to myself for the time being. As long as Adèle was safe, they could wait.

Miss Miller turned and whispered, "We must hurry. Mrs. Thurston has a temper that heats up very quickly. Today will provide you an example if she sees me tarrying. It would be best for you to come back tomorrow. Do you have lodging for the night?"

I handed over one of Lucy Brayton's calling cards. It was damp but still impressive. Black embossed script letters spelled out my hostess's name and address.

Miss Miller rubbed her thumb over the thick ivory card. "Mrs. Augustus Brayton. She has been here to visit Adela several times. You are her guest? She is a member of high society." Miss Miller could not hide her surprise. Her eyes took in my dress, and I could tell that she still struggled to reconcile my plain appearance with the exalted station I now occupied.

"Yes, I am staying there. Mrs. Brayton and I planned to visit various shops," I said, by way of explanation for my simple mode of dress. "I believe she has an extensive agenda for us."

"Shops," she repeated, a tone of wonder in her voice.

The shift in my social status had clearly taken her aback. Since she remembered me as a waif, a persecuted and unwanted child, I suspected it was a particularly poignant and bittersweet change. I bit my tongue rather than tell her that even before I married, I had become independently wealthy. Miss Miller needed no more cause to feel envious.

"If Adèle awakens early, please seek me out."

"Tomorrow we can speak about Adela's progress," said Miss Miller, as we entered the entry hall.

"So good to see you again," I said politely, but I could feel the shift that had been made. We were no longer colleagues. I had progressed to a lofty station in life, a situation that Nan Miller would never achieve. My friend studied a potted palm spilling over an entire corner. It was not an especially interesting palm. Palms generally are not. Their placement hides deficiencies in decorating. They fill space but do not contribute much besides catching dust and hiding the odd mouse. In this case, they provided Miss Miller with a way to avoid my penetrating gaze.

"Yes. Likewise, it was a pleasure to see you, Mrs. Rochester," she replied, and I could tell the words "Mrs. Rochester" stuck a little in her craw.

Before I could depart, the *slap-slap-slap* of shoe leather announced a person coming down the hallway. A stout woman with a flat bulldog face stomped into our midst. Two piggy eyes peered out from a froth of ornate ruffles. She listed her squarish frame left then right as she walked, looking for all the world like a ship on choppy seas. While I make no claim to beauty myself, this was a person sadly lacking in any attractive traits. Her grizzled hair was escaping from its tight braid. Her nose was colored like a cherry and a vibrant pattern of veins ran up and over the bridge of it.

"There you are, Miss Miller! I have been looking for you. When you are finished playing ministering angel to our errant German teacher, come into my office." The woman sniffled.

"Yes, Mrs. Thurston," said Miss Miller with a slight bow. "May I introduce—"

"No, you may not." Mrs. Thurston shook a sausage-shaped finger at me. "Showing up late and in such disarray speaks very poorly of your future with us, young lady. You have already wasted too much of our time. Especially on a terrible day like today!"

"May I introduce—" Miss Miller tried again.

I extended a hand wearing a still-damp pair of gloves.

"No, you may not," snapped Mrs. Thurston again, ignoring my outstretched fingers. "Hold your tongue, Miss Miller. I don't have the time to coddle a teacher. Neither do you. This selfish chit has already tried my patience. Furthermore, her appearance is a disgrace. Someone certainly gave her a beating, and I warrant she deserved it. Perhaps it taught her a valuable lesson. Here at Alderton House, we have rules. The staff is not allowed followers. No gentlemen callers. Scandal is to be avoided at all costs."

I started to respond, but Miss Miller reached over and gripped my upper arm, hard. The pain surprised me so much that I yelped.

Mrs. Thurston either ignored my howl of pain or thought Miss Miller had done a good job of disciplining me. Again, the sausage wagged before my nose. "This disrespect is not to be repeated. I won't stand for it. Nor will we entertain any negotiations of salary. Am I making myself quite clear? Consider carefully if you can abide by my rules. I need your answer by this evening. After that, I shall look for a new teacher who can!"

Her unparalleled rudeness took my breath away. Mrs. Thurston took my silence for acceptance.

"See, Miss Miller? That's how you handle staff. I trust you've taken a lesson from this exchange. Present yourself in my office immediately." She concluded her remarks by wiping at her eyes and nose with a grubby handkerchief.

I intended to say I was not staff, and that she owed me an apology, but Mrs. Thurston had already turned away from us. I was still collecting my wits when she slammed a door in my face.

I wanted to march into Mrs. Thurston's office and set her straight, but in truth, I was too flummoxed to think clearly. "Is she always like this?"

"She is a bit more abrupt than usual today, but I beg you to remember our collective grieving for Selina." Miss Miller opened the front door. "I see it still rains. If you wait, I could send our Caje to fetch your carriage for you. He's rather more than an odd-jobs boy and a bit less than a footman."

"Thank you, but after that foul wind blew through"—I nodded toward Mrs. Thurston's office—"I believe fresh air will do me good. I will see you tomorrow. Early."

"Yes." Miss Miller nodded solemnly. Her mouth moved as if she wanted to say more, but she stayed silent.

We shook hands and I stepped out into a steady drizzle.

Chapter 11

Despite the rain, I relished my walk to the carriage and, my mind more at ease now that I had seen Adèle with my own eyes, I thoroughly enjoyed the ride back to Lucy Brayton's. The beauty of Hyde Park, with its graceful plantings and stately trees, provided a welcome relief after the oppressive and cluttered interior of the Alderton House School for Girls. As Williams drove, my mind turned over all I had seen and heard.

The demise of her schoolmate must have unsettled Adèle temporarily. Perhaps the doctor had been wise to suggest sleep as a natural remedy. It was well-known that laudanum could provide a useful antidote to jangled nerves. At Lowood, the teachers used cordials laced with laudanum for a variety of ailments from the infants' croup to the older girls' monthly discomfort.

Had Adèle not felt so alone, she might have weathered this crisis with more equanimity. But as it happened, she had every reason to be angry. And disappointed. Terribly, terribly disappointed. Twice in her short life, the adults charged with her well-being had deserted her.

How could any child thus abandoned learn to trust other people?

Perhaps she purposely exaggerated her misery when writing her note to us, and penned both notes as a way of punishing Edward and me—and getting our attention.

It was possible. Young girls are especially prone to fantastical thoughts. The concentrated boarding school atmosphere spurs the imagination to a fevered pitch. Added to this was Adèle's own nature. The girl possessed a fanciful mind, inherited no doubt from her mother. The child's personality could be as changeable as the weather, and just as given to extremes. She could be as bright as the noon sun on a June day or as dark as a moonless January night.

What Adèle needed was a secure foundation, a steady environment, an educational plan that encouraged self-discipline. Perhaps Alderton House had provided those things before, but this Mrs. Thurston struck me as the sort who jumped to conclusions and acted hastily. Witness her supposition that I was the new German teacher!

Although Miss Miller said Mrs. Thurston espoused a hatred of gossip, she had apparently been willing to repeat what Dowager Lady Ingram said—and did so with no compunction! This extremism and lack of logical thought exhibited the exact opposite traits of the role model that Edward had wished the school to provide. Furthermore, her subterfuge in demanding that the girls copy her letters was deceitful and self-serving. All this, taken together, proved to me that such a woman was constitutionally unfit to supervise any school. Edward would be disappointed when he heard my opinion of the place.

I arrived at Lucy Brayton's doorstep, feeling my spirits sag. Perhaps it was the recognition that I had reached the end of my journey. Or perhaps the tea I'd taken at the school had worn thin. But each step seemed to tax the last of my strength.

I handed over my soggy bonnet and shawl to Polly. "I assume Mrs. Brayton is still making her calls?"

"Yes, ma'am. She should be back shortly."

Glad to be alone, I struggled up two sets of stairs and into the guest bedroom, which was a veritable garden of yellow and green gaiety. As I fidgeted with my clothes, Polly knocked at the door and came to my aid. I wasn't accustomed to having help dressing, but as tired as I was, I had to admit I was glad to see the girl.

Polly was a bright young lass, probably all of thirteen. With a deft hand, she managed my buttons. Before stepping free of my skirt, I pulled the two notes from my pocket and tucked them into my chemise for safekeeping. As I stood there in my thin cotton, Polly loaded my wet things over her arm. She looked down at my skinned knees and shook her head.

"Sadie will bring a tray to you directly. I'll get you a poultice to put on your eye, and a sponge to clean up your knees. Might do with a bit of honey for your split lip, if Cook'll let me take a dab."

"Honey?"

"Helps with the healing. Keeps you from scarring. My mum always used to put a bit on my brothers when they scraped their elbows and such."

That would be good to remember, especially given all the physical diversions little boys found appealing. A quick prickle at the back of my eyes warned of impending tears at the thought of my little son, so very far away.

I changed into the dry chemise and sat on the side of the bed. Polly returned quickly and attended skillfully to my injuries. First she sponged the scabs off my legs and administered a balm. Then she offered me a poultice, heated to a perfect temperature and scented with soothing chamomile.

Holding the wet muslin to my face, I settled into the soft embrace of the bed and closed my eyes, only to be awakened far too quickly by a yapping in the hallway. I sighed and reconciled myself to the fact that Lucy Brayton was on her way, bearing down like a sudden squall sets upon boats in Newhaven Harbour.

"Polly? Is Mrs. Rochester here? Let me see her." After a

courtesy knock, the door flew open. The exotic scent of gardenias preceded my hostess into the room, and her little dog Rags followed at her heels.

I pried open my good eye. Lucy bent over me, her heart-shaped face glowing with the sort of interest that comes from a nimble mind. For an afternoon of social calls, she wore a high-waisted gown of yellow muslin, topped with a spencer in a darker shade of the same buttercup color.

"Are you any better? Let me see under that poultice." Lucy removed her gloves to touch my face. "I still think we need to call a surgeon to examine you. Your face is even puffier and your eye is nearly swollen shut. And you still went to the girls' school without me? Goodness. Such determination."

Rags jumped up against the bed to look at me and give a yip. He must have thought me a pitiful specimen.

"I might look worse than I did earlier, but I daresay I shall heal."

"I want to hear what you thought of the girls' school. Especially how dear Adèle is doing."

"I am afraid it is a rather long story."

She settled on the bed next to me and lifted Rags onto her lap. I shifted away. Lucy appeared not to notice how uncomfortable her informality made me. She simply continued her train of thought. "Tell me all. There must have been a powerful catalyst to spur you to such hasty action."

"Here is your tea and toast with cheese, Mrs. Rochester, madam." Sadie set the tray on a stand next to the bed. "Cook sent up scones for you, Mrs. Brayton."

After Polly helped me into my black silk dress, I took a piece of toast topped with melted cheese and ate it greedily.

"Get me my flask, please, Polly. Bring the tumblers, too," Lucy said to her maid. Then to me, "That bruise around your eye has ripened into a lovely shade of aubergine. I imagine the scrapes on your legs now cry out with misery. The gin will offer a bit of solace."

"Gin?" I couldn't have heard her right. It was one thing to have a sip of spirits in the evening, but this midday tippling—two days in a row—was unheard of for a proper lady!

When Sadie returned with the silver flask, scones, and glasses, Lucy poured our tea directly into the tumblers. To this she added a splash of Ladies Delight.

Lucy lifted her tumbler and admired the beverage in one hand while holding a scone with the other. "This certainly would have made my calls more interesting. For me, at least. Possibly for my hosts as well. Gads, but I hate returning calls. They are a crashing bore. Everyone talks of nothing, but they talk endlessly about nothing, compounding the tedium. I would have rather gone with you."

"My visit could not wait. I needed to assure myself of Adèle's well-being."

"Yes, of course. And how does she fare?"

"I don't know. At least, I have not heard a report from her own mouth."

"What?"

I explained about my visit, Selina Biltmore's death, and meeting my old colleague Nan Miller, and I finished by telling Lucy about Adèle's reaction to Selina's death and her subsequent dosing with laudanum.

"Miss Miller believes Adèle will not wake up until tomorrow morning," I concluded.

"Heavens!" Lucy threw up her hands. "What a day you've had! You say you saw them carrying out the poor girl's body? That's positively gruesome. But Adèle is in no danger? You are quite certain of that? We could bring her here. As I told you, my house is yours. That reminds me; I bought you a gift when I was in India."

From the depths of a dresser, she extracted a parcel wrapped loosely in silver paper. I opened it eagerly and lifted out a magnificent shawl. The material slid over my hands, a texture most amazing. I held up the length of fabric and reveled in the robin's egg blue shade, examining the wondrous silver stitching as it twinkled in the light.

"I have never seen the like!"

"Pashmina," said Lucy. "A variety of cashmere. The needle-work is silver thread. Edward described your lovely dark hair and your pale skin, so I thought it would look well on you."

"I shall cherish it for its beauty, but more so for the thought that you put into it." To my own surprise, I embraced her.

"Wear it in good health, dear Sister."

More and more, I found myself at ease with Lucy. Despite her fashionable exterior, she seemed entirely genuine. Of course, Edward had warned me not to judge Lucy by her gloss, and he had been rightly worried that at first I would be put off by her flounce and bounce.

"Your hospitality is most heartwarming," I said. "Miss Miller told me there is no evidence that the student died of infection. It would have been awkward to bundle Adèle up and carry her through the rain, and furthermore, I do think she might want to grieve with the school community as a whole. There is balm when like hearts share their pain."

A gentle smile warmed Lucy's face. "Yes. It is wonderful to have someone to share your trials with, isn't it? And your jubilation? I am so happy you are here, Jane. Edward told me of your numerous sterling points, and I daresay, even though his description was spirited, he understated your appeal."

A warming blush crept up my neck. Unaccustomed as I was to such a compliment, I desired to change the subject. "Now that I have seen the appointments at Alderton House, I must say that, frankly, the home is a bit overmuch for my tastes."

Lucy nodded. "When she had a sizable income, Lady Kingsley insisted on filling every inch of the place with trinkets and bric-a-brac. Over the years, however, she lost her fortune through her son, a hobbledehoy who preferred strong drink, cards, and women of low virtue to his education. By the time she reconciled her books, she was near ruined with no help in sight. Lord Kingsley had gone on to his reward a long time ago. Turning that extravagant house into a girls' school elicited a lot of whispers behind her back, but I've heard she's making a handsome living from that monstrosity. Certainly, it has kept Maude Thurston out of the poorhouse."

"What a detestable excuse for a human being she is!" The gin loosened my tongue and, I fear, destroyed any last vestiges of self-censorship.

"Yes, but remember what I told you: She has fallen from a high perch, Jane. When the lofty tumble, they either react with spite or humility. It seems, unfortunately, that she has chosen the former. Yet I do admire her for trying to pay her bills. Many would have crept off into the night and hoped the debtors went away."

"I am not certain it's the best fit for Adèle." I said this tentatively, mindful that Lucy had suggested the school to Edward.

"You are a far better judge of that than I, Jane. Believe me, it will not hurt my feelings one jot if you decide to remove her."

I appreciated her reassurance.

Before I could respond, Polly appeared in the door, looking flustered. "Sorry to bother you. There's a woman at the front door."

"Tell her I am unavailable," said Lucy. "She can leave her calling card."

But Polly didn't leave. She slipped into the room and closed the door behind her, giving us a semblance of privacy. Polly spoke in a low voice, so her words wouldn't carry. "I tried, ma'am, I did. I told her to go away. But she's upset something terrible. She says she has to see you, now. Says it can't wait."

"Blast." Lucy started to rise, but Polly shook her head.

"Sorry, Mrs. Brayton. It's not you she wants. The visitor came for Mrs. Rochester. It's a Miss Miller, and she says it's a matter of life and death."

Chapter 12

The water dripping off of Nan Miller formed a puddle in the middle of the Braytons' marble entrance hall. She must have run the entire distance from the girls' school, because she panted like a harrier after a foxhunt. More shocking, she wore no bonnet. No head covering of any kind. Hunks of wet hair worked their way loose from the bun at the back of her neck and dripped water over her coat and down her skirt.

"Is it Adèle? Is she all right?" I ran down the stairs, disregarding the stiffness in my bruised legs.

"She is fine, still asleep." With that Miss Miller commenced to shaking so violently I wondered if it was a prelude to a seizure.

Lucy must have thought the same. She turned to her butler and said, "Get me a blanket, Higgins. Do it quickly."

The chatter of Miss Miller's teeth was audible to everyone, with the marble tiles providing amplification. Although my old colleague was clearly in distress, her eyes darted this way and that as she took in the extravagant chandelier in Lucy's foyer, the richly textured wallpaper, and the velvet curtains.

Nor did Miss Miller's eyes miss Lucy's lovely yellow gown or my new shawl from India. I pulled the pashmina tighter around my shoulders.

Higgins brought a heavy wool blanket, and we wrapped it around Miss Miller's shoulders.

"Sadie, grab some towels to dry her hair. Tell Cook we need more tea. Hot with sugar."

"I came as fast as I could. You made me promise Adela was safe, and she is. But a Bow Street Runner came to the school. He asked so many questions. Questions about Selina and how she died!" Miss Miller grabbed my hands. "That man questioned me for nearly an hour! He asked about the school and our students! Mrs. Thurston was furious. With me and with him. As if I had any say in his visit! Any say at all! Yes, Selina died. It happens. I am sorrowful. But I am not to blame!"

I put an arm around my old friend's shoulder and asked my hostess, "What do you suppose has happened? Why would a man from Bow Street come around to ask questions?"

"I can think of one or two reasons, actually. None of them are pleasant," Lucy said to me in a whisper. To Miss Miller, Lucy spoke clearly and in soothing tones. "I am sure everything will be all right. Let's get you dry and cozy in front of a fire."

"Higgins, tell Williams to fetch my brother," said Lucy. "He's not to come back without him, do you understand? I don't care if he's at Boodle's. I don't care what state he's in. Bring him here, now!"

I thought it odd that Lucy was so disturbed about a Bow Street officer. The fact that one was asking questions seemed unremarkable to me. After all, they were little more than glorified night watchmen. Or were they? Lucy's heated response and her demand that Williams fetch her brother put a new spin on this top. Perhaps Nan Miller really did have reason to be worried!

"Come along now." Lucy took Miss Miller by the elbow.

"We shall go upstairs to the parlor. You can sit down in there. You poor thing. You have not eaten, have you? I believe we've met before—one time when I visited the school, perhaps?"

Lucy's voice stayed low and soothing, as all the while she guided my former colleague up the stairs. Miss Miller moved slowly and rested on us heavily, her blocky frame and plain face an odd contrast to Lucy's handsome visage and dazzling dress. Now that she had spent her anger at the constable's intrusion, Nan Miller's sobs dissolved into steady crying.

Lucy proved her good breeding and quality of character by showing Miss Miller the type of hospitality she might a baroness. I marveled at my hostess's charity and generous nature. Even as Miss Miller left puddles of water all over Lucy's carpet, my new "sister" neither flinched nor drew back.

"Here you go." Lucy settled Miss Miller into an armchair by the fire and began to blot her hair with a warm towel that Polly provided. "Let's get you dried off. Sadie, add more coal to the fire, please." Lucy rubbed the warmth back into Nan Miller's fingers. "Miss Miller, I think it would be wise for you to remove your boots."

A puddle was forming around Miss Miller's feet. Slowly she untied her brown lace-up shoes, revealing worn and raveled wool stockings. Polly removed them, emptied out the water on a fern in a terrarium, and set the footwear on the tiles in front of the fireplace.

Once we made Miss Miller more comfortable and poured her a cup of tea, Lucy whispered to me, "I suggest we wait for my brother. Bruce has experience with difficult matters, especially those involving criminal behavior. He even worked at the Bow Street station."

"Is your brother an inquiry agent?" This might explain why his presence was perceived to be invaluable.

"Yes. Bruce also studied at the Inner Temple to become a barrister, and he served the Crown in the Army. He is very conversant with problems such as Miss Miller seems to be describing."

Neither Lucy nor I asked our wet visitor any more questions. Instead, we worked toward restoring her sensibilities, which proved difficult. After her first cup of tea and a few bites of a scone, Miss Miller refused any sustenance and stared blindly into the red coals in the grate of the fireplace. Eventually, we plied her with more tea, a strong brew. I coaxed my friend into taking a couple of bites of the bread and cheese Lucy's cook had sent up.

A little less than half an hour passed. The room smelled of wet leather shoes and woolen stockings as the warmth of the fire began to dry Miss Miller's things. Lucy loaned her a linen handkerchief, and after thanking our hostess, Miss Miller vowed she would see that the scrap of fabric was returned to its owner, even as she examined the fine embroidery carefully.

"Hallo! Sister? You wanted me? I am here!" a voice called up from the foyer.

Lucy ran to the doorway and called down, "Bruce, we're in the parlor."

The house echoed with heavy footfalls. The parlor door burst open and there before us stood a man so nearly perfect, he hurt the eyes. His skin was burnished by time in the sun; his eyes were a lovely blue green. Golden strands threaded their way through his brown hair. Any artist's eye would have lingered on a specimen like Mr. Douglas due to the pleasing regularity of his features, but it was his coloring that truly set him apart. He lit up the room like Helios, the Greek god who daily rode his chariot across the sky to bring sunshine to us mortals.

All that saved Bruce Douglas from being as pretty as a woman was a feathery mustache and an oddly twisted nose, which I would later learn had been earned in a tavern fight. Or two. Or three.

In keeping with such, it was also obvious that he was in his cups. Horribly drunk. In fact, he grabbed hold of an armchair rather than fall over. The smell of liquor traveled with him as he wove his way into the parlor.

At first I thought his state quite shocking, but in reflection, Lucy had poured a generous amount of gin into our tea, hadn't she? Perhaps my life had been too sheltered. I decided to defer full judgment of Mr. Douglas until I knew more of him.

"Bruce! What am I going to do with you?" Lucy wrung her hands, but her eyes shone with delight.

"I'll be right as a line!" With two bounds, he crossed the room and scooped Lucy into his arms. He lifted her as easily as if she were a child and twirled her around. When they almost crashed into the fireplace, Lucy laughed. "Put me down! I repeat: Whatever am I to do with you?"

"Why, you must adore me, Sister. It is your job! That is what little brothers are made for!" Giving her a hearty kiss on the cheek, he set her on her feet.

Standing side by side, there was no question about their provenance. They were two peas from the same pod. But his coloring owed its vibrancy to hours in the out-of-doors, while hers showed the pale hues of a lady who never went without a hat.

"Miss Miller and Mrs. Rochester, may I present to you my brother, Bruce Douglas? Bruce, you remember Augie's friend, Edward Rochester? This is his young bride, Jane Eyre. I have taken her for my sister, which makes her kin to you, too, little brother."

"Shall I give you a twirl, too, Mrs. Rochester? I wouldn't want my new sister to feel left out."

"No, thank you." I managed to hide a smile.

"Well then, Bruce Douglas at your service, ladies." He executed a courtly bow to Miss Miller first and then to me. Like his sister, he clearly delighted in fashionable apparel, and his black cutaway coat perfectly conformed to his broad shoulders and narrow waist.

Miss Miller stared at Mr. Douglas, her mouth agape.

I understood. I fear I stared at Mr. Douglas myself, and for rather too long, because he reminded me of a work of art, so perfect was he. I admired him the way you stare at a fresh quince blossom, seeing the touch of the divine and wondering that the world could be so breathtaking. I believe he was accustomed to long looks, because he returned my frank gaze and stepped nearer. When he was close enough to touch me, he raised the tips of his fingers to my chin. "May I?" His glance drifted to my cheek.

I nodded. I know that I am plain and not usually inviting of a second glance, so I did not consider his approach an attempt at inappropriate intimacy. Instead, I understood it to be mere curiosity.

With exquisite gentleness he turned my face so that the candlelight shone on my disfigurement. "My, my. That's an admirable black eye you've got there, Mrs. Rochester."

"Yes, it is, rather."

"On the streets they would call that a mouse," he added.

"I wouldn't know. However, the term rather fits, doesn't it?"

Sadie reappeared bearing a tray and a huge smile. "I brought you that black tea from China, Mr. Douglas. Made it strong. Just the way you like it. Cook says she's sending up a plate of those shortbread biscuits you fancy and some lemon curd. And lots and lots of cream and sugar for you, too. Anything else you want, sir?"

"No, Sadie. But thank you so much. Extend my thanks to Cook, will you? You both take such good care of me."

She nodded and turned as red as a holly berry. Polly appeared on the parlor maid's heels. "Anything you need of me, Mrs. Brayton?" she asked, but her glance was at Bruce Douglas, who did not seem to notice.

"No, thank you." A smile teased the corners of Lucy's lips. "I'll ring if we need you, Polly."

"Yes, madam." She bowed and took her time leaving the room.

"Drink up, Bruce." Lucy poured him a cup of the dark brown brew. "We have need of your best thinking, I fear. Williams found you at Boodle's? Playing cards again?"

"Guilty as charged, Sister. I was actually winning when Williams came for me. Marcus Piper, the coroner, practically handed over his purse. I particularly enjoy playing with him because he often loses but also because he frequently provides me with the opportunity to acquire new business. On occasion, Piper recommends me to the families of victims because my services prove useful. But sometimes I simply sit and listen to the man talk about his work. Together we speculate about what might have happened. Like today. He had been called out this morning. Seems a doctor requested his presence at a school where a young girl was discovered dead in her bed."

Chapter 13

"Oh my!" Miss Miller gasped, a strangled cry that she quickly suppressed.

"Miss Miller is the head teacher at the Alderton House School for Girls," said Lucy. "It was one of her students who died."

"Of natural causes," Miss Miller interjected quickly. "We sent our footman to get the doctor immediately. But sadly, it proved to be too late for the student."

"Please accept my sympathies." Bruce Douglas inclined his head.

"Of course," said Miss Miller. She had dried her eyes and now, in the presence of a gentleman, sat a bit straighter and patted her damp hair self-consciously.

"As you'll recall, I recommended the Alderton House to Edward Rochester, for his ward, Adèle Varens," Lucy said to her brother. "That means I feel directly responsible for Adèle's well-being and safety. You remember Adèle, don't you, Bruce? I brought her home for the Christmas holidays."

"How could I forget that little French darling?"

"The very one! I think she stole your heart, Brother. I know she owns mine."

I swallowed hard and clung to this sentiment: I wasn't alone. Lucy also cared about Adèle. This camaraderie proved comforting. A willing ally bolsters one's courage; a formidable ally makes one bold.

Again, I debated the wisdom of bringing Adèle home with me. What did the Bow Street officer's visit to Alderton House signify? What exactly *was* a Bow Street Runner? Why had he asked so many questions? What if there was something seriously amiss at the school? Something much more sinister than a child dying of illness?

If I took Adèle home, her education would stop. At least for a while. I didn't see how I could care for Ned, assist Edward, and act as Adèle's tutor. She had never been a cooperative student. She required a good deal of time and energy or she wouldn't learn. More importantly, she needed guidance to become more refined and less prone to senseless dramatics. There were no appropriate schools near Ferndean. We could hire a governess, but our small family already occupied all the inhabitable rooms in the old hunting lodge. There was no place for a governess to enjoy even a modicum of privacy. I, more than anyone, knew how important it would be for a teacher to have a place of respite.

"How did Adèle cope with the tragedy this morning?" asked Mr. Douglas.

"Not well," said Miss Miller. "Very poorly, in fact. She became hysterical, and the doctor advised us to give her laudanum when she proved unable to calm down. Right now she is sleeping. I believe she'll stay asleep until tomorrow morning."

"What is the dead girl's name?" asked Mr. Douglas. "Marcus Piper was tight-lipped about her identity."

"Selina Biltmore. She has—had—been with us for three months."

"Bruce, a man from Bow Street came to the school earlier

this afternoon. He questioned Miss Miller at length. As you can imagine, it was very unsettling," Lucy said.

"Did he indeed? What was his name?" Mr. Douglas asked.

"Phineas Waverly," Miss Miller said, withdrawing his calling card from her pocket.

Mr. Douglas gave a low whistle through his teeth as he examined the writing on the card. "Miss Miller, I am afraid you have misconstrued his position."

"Indeed?" A bit of her confidence was returning, and Miss Miller's voice took on an air of imperiousness.

"Yes, Miss Miller. I happen to know Phineas Waverly rather well. He is not merely a man from Bow Street."

"But the address is there on the card!" she protested.

"He is from Bow Street, that is correct. But he is the senior Bow Street Runner, the most skilled investigator of the lot!"

"Who or what is Bow Street?" I finally asked.

"Bow Street is the home of a group of officers charged with policing the city. They do not approve of being called 'Runners,' but the populace has adopted that term. They answer to the magistrate."

"So they patrol the streets? Like the parish watchmen?"

"No, the Bow Street officers can go wherever they wish. They typically investigate crimes, serve writs, and make arrests—so it makes little sense for one to be assigned to the death of a schoolgirl. The top priority for the Runners has always been protecting our sovereign. I mean, someone must keep watch over His Majesty King George IV, especially now that the trial has gone on so long."

I nodded, remembering the conversation between Edward and Mr. Carter. "So why would one of those Bow Street men have questioned Miss Miller? Or visited the school at all?"

"I couldn't say, although when there are questions about whether a death was of natural causes, the assistant magistrate does order a plainclothes Bow Street Runner to investigate," offered Mr. Douglas. "If the Runner finds enough information to warrant action, the assistant magistrate will pass that along to the magistrate, who will ask the coroner to hold an inquest. But an inquest is very expensive, so the magistrate is loath to order one unless he determines there is good reason."

Miss Miller turned completely white. She swayed a bit in her seat, and I ran to my old colleague's side. "What is wrong?"

"Are you suggesting—are you saying the presence of Mr. Waverly indicates a problem?" Miss Miller barely managed to get the words out.

Lucy rummaged around in a sewing basket and pulled out an amber-colored bottle. Without ceremony, she poured a splash into Miss Miller's teacup. "Try this," she commanded.

Miss Miller sipped the drink, sputtered, and instantly her cheeks grew flushed. However, she did not meet my eye when she put down her cup. In fact, she avoided my glance and studied a pattern on the carpet. I stepped away from her and returned to my seat.

I wondered if Miss Miller knew more about Selina Biltmore's death than she let on. This realization sent fear coursing through me.

"Why don't you tell us everything that happened? Everything. From the beginning," suggested Mr. Douglas in a gentle tone.

"I cannot," said Miss Miller, biting her lip and pleating her skirt between her fingers.

Perhaps we stared at her too expectantly. Or perhaps all her fear and anguish had spilled out with the tears she had shed. I cannot say. But suddenly, Miss Miller shut us out. Although she sat with us, she no longer saw us, instead looking deep into the glowing coals of the fireplace.

"You are here now, and you need help. That much is obvious. You said you were questioned extensively. Bruce is an inquiry agent, a private investigator, and he has much

experience in such matters. He is offering you his assistance."
Lucy spoke in a firm tone.

"I can't! Don't you see? Mrs. Thurston would let me go!
She wouldn't give me references if she knew I had spoken with
any of you. Especially you, sir. I told her I was on an errand
fetching some things that the new German teacher needed
upon arriving in London."

"The new German teacher?" Lucy asked. "What on earth?"

I explained about that morning's confusion.

"Can you really speak German? As well as French?" Lucy
raised her eyebrows at me. "How impressive!"

"Yes. Although, of course, I read German far better than I
speak it." I did not mention I also knew a smattering of Hindostanee.

"Mrs. Thurston still thinks that Mrs. Rochester is our
missing teacher. I planned to explain everything, but Mr.
Waverly appeared at our door, and I did not get the chance.
Mrs. Thurston will be most unhappy with me when she
finds—if she finds—that I was less than truthful about my
visit here. What shall I do?" Miss Miller glanced around
wildly, as if there were answers to be found under the terrarium and antimacassars. "Oh! I was wrong to come here! It was
reckless of me. I will gather my things and go anon."

Before she could gather herself, I knelt beside her. "You
came for a purpose, Miss Miller. I doubt you ran all the way
in the rain merely to tell us you had been interviewed by
Phineas Waverly. There is more, is there not?"

She averted her eyes. "Not really."

I sensed she was holding herself in check, keeping the truth
from us. At least part of it. What was she hiding? Could I
trust her when she said Adèle was safe? Given the hysterical
tone of Adèle's letter, the threatening note that accompanied
it, and, most especially, Selina Biltmore's death, was I foolish
to let the child spend another night under that roof?

We all waited to hear what else Miss Miller might say. Our

silence pressured her, and she finally said, "When I told Mr. Waverly that we have been short one adult teacher since Fräulein Hertzog left us, he was adamant that we find another chaperone immediately."

"Why?" I asked.

Nan Miller looked around wildly. "I don't know why!"

"On the contrary, Miss Miller. I think you know exactly why," said Mr. Douglas. "Mr. Waverly fears for the safety of the students, does he not? Marcus Piper told me there are certain inconsistencies."

"Inconsistencies?" I repeated. "Please explain yourself, Mr. Douglas."

"In this case, there were . . . markings on the corpse that are inconsistent with a natural death," said Mr. Douglas. "As a gentleman, I am reluctant to share such distressing details with ladies."

"No, please, no." Miss Miller buried her head in her hands and started to cry.

"Bruce, what are you suggesting?" Lucy asked.

"Mr. Piper is confident that the girl was murdered. She did not slip away easily, either," Mr. Douglas said.

His words hit all of us hard. Lucy's quick intake of breath told me she was stunned. I managed to make it back to my seat, but the shock of that statement caused my senses to reel.

Mr. Douglas continued, "The girl was found dead in her bed, wasn't she, Miss Miller? Either someone gained entry to the school or a murderer roams the school community. It is highly unlikely a murderer came from without. Not impossible, but unlikely."

He let us absorb the import of his words, then added, "That is precisely why you came here, isn't it, Miss Miller? You believe a murderer roams the halls of Alderton House—and the idea frightens you."

"How dare you?" Miss Miller's head snapped up and her eyes sent him angry sparks of displeasure.

"Then why did you come here? Why did you seek out Mrs. Rochester? Why did you permit Mrs. Thurston to continue her misunderstanding about Mrs. Rochester's identity? You have a plan in mind, don't you?" Mr. Douglas asked.

Miss Miller hesitated, looking around the room wildly as if trying to find a solution, a resolution, or perhaps even an escape. "I am worried! How could I not be? There was no adult in the Senior dormitory last night when Selina died! None! The Senior girls have no one to watch over them until the new German teacher comes. Mr. Waverly was pointing this out—and suggesting the girls are at risk."

Miss Miller turned toward me. "You are the only one I trust, Mrs. Rochester. Mrs. Thurston thought that you were the German teacher. But I have no idea when Fräulein Schoeppenkoetter will arrive. Could you not perhaps take Fräulein's place—temporarily—and help me watch over the girls? We could do it together, you and I. Don't you see?"

And suddenly, I did.

Chapter 14

"What if Mrs. Thurston realizes I am Adèle's former governess?" I asked.

"That could work to our advantage. She had instructed me to find someone to fill the position temporarily. Certainly she doesn't want to serve as proctor for the Senior girls, because the stairs are too difficult for her to climb. I could tell her that you are between situations. That might work well, as she is aware that Adela's governess left under embarrassing circumstances," Miss Miller said.

"I'm not sure I understand why that is useful. Pray explain your reasoning to me," I said.

"If Mrs. Thurston believes she could get away with paying a teacher less than custom demands, the situation would benefit her." Miss Miller's cheeks turned crimson. "Lady Kingsley demands a strict accounting of all our expenses. This is a small economy, but one that should prove helpful."

"But Mrs. Rochester is no longer a governess. Her station has changed. She is married to a squire!" Lucy's gentle tone kept her remark from sounding like a reprimand.

"That is true," Miss Miller said. "But I am fairly certain that Mrs. Thurston does not know about the marriage. Poor health forced Mrs. Webster to retire rather suddenly. Paperwork piled up as a natural consequence. Maude Thurston has neither gone through nor distributed all the correspondence on her desk."

So that was why Adèle didn't congratulate us on Ned's birth! The girl never received our letter! It most likely sat in that pile of unopened mail on Mrs. Thurston's desk.

"You are asking Mrs. Rochester to put herself squarely in the path of danger," Mr. Douglas said, frowning at Miss Miller.

"I should think that Jane might be better served to remove Adèle at once and be done with Alderton House," said Lucy.

"I admit I did not consider the danger to Mrs. Rochester. Indeed, I was uncertain that there was a danger," Miss Miller said. "But Mr. Waverly pressed the point—and he is a compelling figure. So he forced me to wonder how to protect the girls. Of course, I knew Mrs. Rochester would share my worries for them. Especially given our history at Lowood."

She and I exchanged a wordless interlude. The memories of the dying girls came flooding back. No one spoke for them at the time. No one stepped forward to offer them protection or solace.

Miss Miller knew I could not refuse her. Not given our shared remembrances.

"Let me speak to my status: I care little about it. I am new to London, so I have no calls to make and no station to protect," I said honestly. "Since my husband will not be joining me for several days, I see no harm in this masquerade. As for the girls, I imagine that more than a few were sent to Alderton House because their parents have happily relinquished their responsibility. They are orphans in all but the technical term of the law. Beyond that, I am here to protect Adèle and to see if this school is right for her. This might present a useful manner for making observations."

"But Jane, it might not be safe! Miss Miller, could you hire another German teacher? Or rearrange the sleeping accommodations so all the girls have protectors?" Lucy spoke with great emotion.

"The layout of the school is such that each of the forms has a separate sleeping room. I watch over the Infants, Miss Parthena Jones is installed with the Juniors, and, thus, the Seniors alone are without supervision. There are too many students to move them all into one room.

"Since everyone is expecting a German teacher, this seemed like a good way to both secure the sleeping quarters and keep an eye on the different age groups," Miss Miller explained. "I also supposed that Mrs. Rochester's presence would go a long way toward comforting Adela."

"That might be the wisest course of action, putting a fox in the henhouse, so to speak, but it is a hasty response to the problem," said Mr. Douglas.

I wondered aloud, "Why doesn't Mrs. Thurston sleep in the room with the Senior girls?"

Miss Miller colored slightly. "She is such a sound sleeper that I think it would do no good. Also, I doubt that she could manage the stairs. She is rather stout."

This explanation strained the seams of credibility, but I let it pass.

"What questions did Waverly ask?" said Mr. Douglas, beginning to pace impatiently. "Pardon my interference, but before Mrs. Rochester puts herself in this situation, I would like to know what Waverly knows. That might shed more light on the dangers."

"Mr. Waverly wanted a recitation of the events of the morning," Miss Miller said.

"Review that for us quickly, if you would please."

"Staff rises at five thirty," said Miss Miller. "Emma, our maid of all work, rings the bell for the Senior girls at six. Ten minutes later, she knocks on their door. Since the previous

German teacher Fräulein Hertzog left us a month ago, we have had no adult in that dormitory. As a consequence, Mrs. Thurston devised a plan. Each Senior has a partner, who is responsible for seeing that her partner is dressed and ready for breakfast. The head girl oversees two partners."

"And the age of these girls?" Mr. Douglas asked.

"Adela is the youngest Senior at ten," Miss Miller said, and quickly explained how Mrs. Thurston thought she might be a bad influence on children her own age. Lucy shook her head in disgust, but Miss Miller continued with, "The rest are age thirteen and older. Many of the girls will stay with us until they make their debut at age sixteen. Selina was the eldest, just sixteen. The idea of partners has worked rather well."

"What happens if the partner proves incorrigible? A sluggard?" Lucy asked.

"Then they both are punished." Miss Miller spoke softly. The rest of us shook our heads in disgust. We could well imagine the difficulty for a child with a recalcitrant partner.

Could that have been a motive for murder? I wondered, but I discounted the idea. How could one schoolgirl kill another? The very thought sent a shiver up my spine.

"I admit that the problem lay chiefly with Selina," Miss Miller hurried to explain. "She is—was—difficult and did not take well to instruction. The girl was a beauty, had always been, and I believe her father especially was so captivated by her looks that he could not bring himself to discipline her."

"Would an intruder have had access to the Senior dormitory?" Mr. Douglas wondered. "That scenario—while unlikely—cannot be completely discounted."

"Yes." Miss Miller nodded. "It is possible an intruder climbed in through the window. There is a large horse chestnut tree with a branch that abuts the dormitory window."

"Did Waverly see any signs of forced entry?" Mr. Douglas asked.

"He did not, but he did recommend that, besides adding the chaperone, Mrs. Thurston ought to cut down the offending horse chestnut branch immediately."

"And her response?" asked Mr. Douglas.

I thought I knew what it would be. I could not imagine Mrs. Thurston accepting direction from anyone, even a Runner from Bow Street.

"She said she would take up the matter with Lady Kingsley. Such decisions about the grounds are beyond Mrs. Thurston's purview, to be honest."

Miss Miller colored and looked away. "I must also tell you that Selina liked to sneak out at night. I caught her at it once. I know Miss Jones did, too. Selina was like that. Challenging. Strong willed. Her parents live in Brighton. They are not well-to-do, so they sent her here while they saved up for her debut this spring. Selina was unhappy about the situation, as she expected finer lodgings and a grand staff and told us so at every opportunity. As a consequence, she liked to misbehave. We were quite unsuccessful in taming her."

"Let us get back to your review of the morning's schedule," said Mr. Douglas.

"The girls wash and dress to come downstairs. Prayers are at six thirty. Breakfast is served around seven. But at six twenty, Selina had not moved. Her partner railed at her, rewarding her with a few small shoves to the shoulder. The other girls ignored this. The morning seemed unexceptional, as Selina often refused to get up in a timely manner. Finally, Selina's partner grew angry. The two had gotten into a brief scuffle a few days ago. There was even some hair pulling. Despite the tussle they had, Selina had succeeded in making her partner late, and both girls were charged with memorizing extra Scripture verses. This morning, Selina's partner lost all patience. She decided to drag Selina out of bed. Of course, that is when she discovered Selina was dead."

I could only imagine the scene and how shocked the girls were. Especially the girl who grabbed Selina only to discover she was cold and stiff.

Mr. Douglas's face was thoughtful when he asked, "What is the name of Selina's partner?"

Miss Miller cut her eyes at me. "Adela. It was Adela Varens who found Selina dead."

Chapter 15

"No wonder she was hysterical!" I could scarcely contain myself. "How could you not tell me this earlier?"

"I planned to tell you when we met on the morrow. That way I could assure you that Adela was fine. After she'd had a good night's sleep and I'd had the chance to talk with her."

"This certainly explains *why* she was distraught!" I spat the words out.

"Mrs. Rochester, I beg you to remember that you were the same age when the nurse at Lowood carried you from the bed of your friend, Helen Burns. Helen's death did not frighten you overmuch. At least not that I observed."

"That is true enough, but Helen and I both knew she was dying—and I was taken from the bed before I realized she had died! More importantly, Adèle and I have different sensibilities. She is French and prone to emotions—"

"Whereas you are English through and through," said Miss Miller. "What upsets one child, another takes in stride. Yes, finding Selina dead did disturb Adela, at least initially, but I hoped to report to you that she had regained her self-control. She has been working hard to develop that quality over the past two years. I believe she has come a long way."

Mr. Douglas cleared his throat, bringing us back to the topic at hand. "What else did Mr. Waverly ask?"

"He wanted to know if Selina had made enemies."

"Had she?" asked Lucy eagerly, leaning forward in her chair.

"Enemies?" said Miss Miller. "I can't imagine so. But Selina was . . . provoking. She teased Caje, the young man who works at Alderton House. She flirted with him and mocked him. She bullied our previous German teacher, Fräulein Hertzog, until the young woman packed her bags and left in the night without a character reference. Truthfully, although she matriculated only three months ago, in that short time Selina managed to irk all the teachers, leaving her work undone, causing disruption in the classrooms, and generally being disagreeable."

"How did she act toward the other students?" I asked.

"Regretfully, I must admit she tormented them. I tried to correct her, but Mrs. Thurston would have none of it. Selina had become her pet."

"I do not understand," Lucy said. "You are saying that Mrs. Thurston ignored the girl's misbehavior? Astonishing. Particularly when you relate that she caused so much havoc."

Miss Miller nodded. "It is rather confusing. I cannot explain why Mrs. Thurston doted on the girl. In the beginning, Mrs. Thurston and Selina were frequently at odds and even once engaged in a shouting match. Soon after, I noticed Mrs. Thurston's attitude changed. She chose to ignore the child's failings."

"Given the tenor of our meeting today, she did not strike me as being exceptionally sensitive," I said.

"Our superintendent puts great store by controlling one's emotions. While her exterior is gruff, Mrs. Thurston can be very kind and compassionate. I know you did not see that side of her today, Mrs. Rochester, but believe me, it is there," Miss Miller said.

"That discrepancy, the change in Mrs. Thurston's behavior toward Selina Biltmore, is certainly a matter that needs to be explored. Meanwhile, let us summarize." Mr. Douglas steepled his fingertips. "Selina Biltmore was killed in her own bed sometime during the night. She was discovered to be dead when her partner, Adèle Varens, attempted to rouse her for breakfast."

Miss Miller nodded. "Adela's screams brought me running. I sent a girl to tell Caje to fetch the doctor. Miss Jones led the students to the dining room, where they stayed until after . . . after Selina's body was removed. That is about the time that Mrs. Rochester appeared for her visit."

"I saw men carrying the stretcher to the hearse. Of course, at the time I did not know it was a hearse, but now I understand the nature of the vehicle that had blocked our way when Williams and I arrived," I explained.

Mr. Douglas inclined his head and continued his summation: "There is a window leading into the dormitory of the Senior girls, and it is accessible by climbing a horse chestnut tree. There was, and is, no adult available to stand guard over the girls in the Senior dormitory."

"Waverly did say he would post a man on our street," Miss Miller said. "A Robin Redbreast."

"What is that?" I asked.

"One of the Bow Street horse patrols. Their red waistcoats announce their identity from a long way away," Lucy said.

"The horse patrol might prevent someone from breaking into the school," Mr. Douglas said, "but such a plan offers no help if there is already a murderer in your midst."

He paused and added, "There is another way the murder might have occurred. You say that Selina Biltmore often sneaked out, possibly to meet with someone, and the tree offered easy access. Is it possible she let someone in?"

"But the other girls would have overheard an intruder," I protested.

Mr. Douglas stroked his chin. "That raises the question: Why did none of the girls awaken when Selina Biltmore was struggling? Marcus Piper believes she fought her murderer."

"Yes, how could the girls have slept through such an event?" Lucy asked.

"They could have been dosed with laudanum!" I spoke so quickly that I surprised myself. "Adèle has been dosed. When I tried to wake her, she barely responded!"

"That could explain the other students' ignorance of the murder," said Mr. Douglas. "But it would also mean our villain was someone with access to the girls to dose them. Who could have done so?"

"There is yet another likely scenario. Perhaps the murderer had an accomplice inside the school," I said.

"Just so," he said. "Very good, Mrs. Rochester. I can see you are a natural at this! Who would have hated the girl so much?"

"I was sorry to tell Mr. Waverly that almost everyone in the school had reason to dislike Selina." Miss Miller sighed. "Since she came to Alderton, there have been many tearful scenes. Mrs. Thurston would not allow her to be disciplined, so Selina did whatever she wanted. I did not mind the disruption so much as I hated the way it hurt the other girls."

She sighed. "But despite all that, I cannot imagine anyone inside the school hurting Selina, much less taking her life."

"I can," I said. "And I have proof."

Chapter 16

I withdrew from my pocket the two pieces of paper that had precipitated my visit to London. "This one from Adèle came to us through the mail a few days ago. The smaller paper was tucked inside."

Lucy, of course, had seen both messages. She rose, left the room, came back with Rags, and, while holding him on her lap, silently stroked his hair with her fingers.

"Can either of you recognize the handwriting on this threat?" Mr. Douglas asked Miss Miller and me as he fingered the heavy piece of paper.

"No," I shook my head. "It could be Adèle's, if she took care to disguise her natural script. But I cannot say for sure."

"Neither can I," said Nan Miller. "Nor does it look familiar, though that is not surprising. Whoever wrote this took care to be unknown. What are these words that cross Adela's letter to you and Mr. Rochester? The same word written three times? Can you read it, Mrs. Rochester?"

"*Au secours*," I said. "French for 'help.' Of course, it could be that this threat has nothing to do with Selina Biltmore's death."

No one said anything. None of us believed the events to be discrete.

Mr. Douglas stood, legs akimbo, and stared down into the burning coals in the fireplace. "The only piece of information that Waverly does not possess, but that we have, is the threatening note written to Adèle Varens. We do not know if the threat was credible. We do not know the circumstances behind it. Or if it is connected in any way to Selina Biltmore's death. Therefore, I suggest we wait to share it. Right now, it casts a poor light on Miss Varens, as she found the dead girl and she might have felt threatened by someone."

I shook my head. "Adèle would never harm anyone. I swear to you, she wouldn't."

"Mrs. Rochester," said Miss Miller, "I beseech you. Come back with me to the school. Mrs. Thurston already believes you to be our missing German teacher. I shall explain to her that you have agreed to take on the position only for as long as Fräulein Schoeppenkoetter is delayed. To avoid confusion, I can call you by your maiden name, since she would never consent to having a married woman in the position."

"But Adèle knows that she and Edward have wed," Lucy said. "I told the girl myself, and I know she received a letter from the two of them."

"True, but Adela has been forbidden to talk about her guardian," Miss Miller said.

"What?" Lucy said. "Can you tender an explanation?"

"Dowager Lady Ingram told Lady Kingsley about Mr. Rochester's first wife. As a consequence, Lady Kingsley told Mrs. Thurston, who was so shocked about his conduct that she forbade Adela to speak of her guardian."

"How dare she!" Lucy's face contorted with anger. I am sure my visage was equally distressed.

Miss Miller deflected our dismay by shrugging and adding,

"Perhaps these attempts were misguided, but Maude Thurston was only trying to protect the girl from scandal."

I struggled not to show my disapproval as I turned to Lucy and her brother. "Mrs. Thurston also took it upon herself to mandate that Adèle be called 'Adela,' which she thinks is more properly English than the girl's given name."

"Perhaps her methods were injudicious. But her intent was for Adela to escape from her tawdry past," Miss Miller said with a hint of defensiveness.

"That is taking her responsibilities rather too far," said Mr. Douglas. "I do not suppose that working there as a teacher will give you much joy, Mrs. Rochester, but I do think your presence could be an incredible asset to the school, and more importantly to the girls. No one expects you to uncover the identity of Selina's killer on your own; only to help keep the girls safe and perhaps gather some information."

"Bruce, you are still asking Jane to put herself in harm's way. To thwart a killer!" said Lucy. "That's too much to expect. I think she should take Adèle and go home."

He smiled at her. "Doing so would safeguard Adèle, but what about the other girls? Let's say the killer wasn't only interested in Selina. Perhaps Adèle is not the only girl who received a threatening note. What if the killer is a fiend who preys on children? There's no adult to watch over the Seniors. Mrs. Thurston cannot insure their welfare, can she? And who would she find at this juncture who would risk her life for the students? I can only think of one person, and she is here in this room with us."

That had been my thought exactly. To hear him voice my concern so succinctly gave me additional confidence that I could make a difference. He turned to me and continued, "Mrs. Rochester, you do not know me well, nor I you. However, I can tell you in all candor that once or twice in a lifetime, fate presents a person with an opportunity to do tremendous good. To make a difference. But this opportunity always comes in tandem with personal risk. Sacrifice. Occasionally, embarrassment. I draw on my own experience when I say that if you turn away, you will always wonder. You will lie awake at night and feel remorse. You will always question your right to walk among decent people and hold your head high."

"You truly believe I can be of assistance?" I said.

"Provided that you keep a cool head. You will need to notice any and all discrepancies. From your vantage point as a teacher, you might thwart a murder and find clues to the murderer's identity. Without your presence in the Senior girls' dormitory, the killer might feel at liberty to strike again."

They all turned to me, waiting for my response. "I shall pack immediately."

"One more moment, please," said Mr. Douglas. "While I admire your courage, I refuse to send you willy-nilly into the path of danger. I suggest we meet together regularly so I can guide your investigation and keep apprised of your personal safety."

"How do you propose to do that?" asked Miss Miller.

"To meet regularly, and to speak freely, the meetings must be outside of the school," reasoned Lucy.

We all recognized the wisdom of that.

For a long time, nobody spoke. Only the ticking of the clock on the mantel reminded us that we must enact our plan quickly.

"I have it," said Miss Miller. "We lack a teacher who has any artistic skill with pencil and chalk. As I recall, you own a particular talent for sketching. I propose to tell Mrs. Thurston that you can teach drawing as well as German. That way, you will have an excuse to take your charges to Hyde Park, where Mr. Douglas and Mrs. Brayton can meet with you. The art class would run from two to three in the afternoon."

This ingenious plan met all our needs.

"But what do I do about references? Mrs. Thurston is rigid on the subject."

Lucy rose and went over to a writing desk. After pulling a sheet of thick ivory paper from a drawer and dipping her pen, she started writing. None of us spoke as she worked. After she blotted her message with sand, she read it aloud:

Dear Mrs. Thurston,

I present to you Miss Jane Eyre, an outstanding tutor whose reputation is impeccable. She is fluent in drawing, pianoforte, German, and French. I personally vouch for her integrity. In fact, I am so taken with this young woman that I propose to sponsor her. Enclosed is a bank draft for the equivalent of one year's salary.

Cordially,
Mrs. Captain Augustus Brayton

Chapter 17

"We need to get back," said Miss Miller. "I slipped out while the girls were taking their singing lessons with Signora Delgatto. Those will be over soon. Since she offers both individual and group lessons, the students are usually busy for several hours."

Lucy rang for Polly, and I rushed to my room to supervise her packing. While she bundled up my undergarments, a sleeping gown, and my black silk, I wrote a hurried note.

Dear Husband,

I have a few concerns about the environment at the girls' school. They bear more scrutiny, which I intend to apply immediately. Therefore, I must write this in haste.

Know that Adèle is safe, and I am well.

Lucy is everything you said her to be and more.

I send my love to you and our son. Tender my warm regards to Mrs. Fairfax.

Your adoring wife, who misses you—
Jane Eyre Rochester

"Polly? Please make sure this goes to the post," I said, handing her my letter. A pang of sadness ripped through me. How I missed my son and husband! And what could I do about the missing Rochester gems? But this was not the time for self-pity. This was a time for action.

With the abigail's help, I changed back into my gray dress. The hem drooped in the back from the weight of the water it had collected. Although Polly had cleaned it, the gown was not totally dry. I sighed knowing it would be wet again in minutes. The damp fabric clung to my skin, but that could not be helped. Reluctantly, I folded my new pashmina. It was far too fine for me to wear in my charade as a poor teacher. I stared down at my portmanteau and questioned it as well. Would a simple governess own such a fine trunk? "Polly? Could you find me a muslin bag? I need something less elaborate to hold my clothes."

She nodded, left, and returned quickly with a worn pillowcase.

"That will do nicely," I said.

Polly's nimble fingers held open my boots as I wiggled my toes into place. The scuff marks reminded me of the skirmish at the coaching inn. My ribs ached from my struggle with the thief, and one touch to my eye assured me the episode had not been a dream. I had barely escaped unharmed. How could I protect a small clutch of young girls? Girls who had no experience with rough-and-tumble living? Young women who might be harboring a killer in their midst? I sank down onto my bed, pretended to adjust my stockings, and took a few moments to collect my thoughts. Was it possible that one of the students was a killer? Or had a teacher ended Selina Biltmore's young life?

Edward, my darling husband, had never seemed so far away. I imagined he would worry about my safety if he knew of my plans. He would point out my elfin size and modest demeanor as inadequate resources for besting a murderer. He might even scold me for exposing myself to possible injury.

But he wasn't here. And he often remarked that my outward appearance was at odds with my formidable spirit. This could work to my advantage. The killer might underestimate me, and therefore, I might discover the identity of Selina Biltmore's murderer before he—or she!—recognized my true purpose.

Not only was our beloved Adèle in danger; a murderer roamed the halls of the school. A frisson of fear crawled up my spine. Might another girl fall victim? I hoped not.

Polly handed me the pillowcase packed with my things. I thanked the girl as she started to tidy up the clothing we had rejected.

Miss Miller's voice drifted up from the parlor. Adèle and the other girls were in her care, but Miss Miller seemed as pliable as a willow branch—not at all the sort of personage who might thwart a killer!

Why, she had been frightened of Mrs. Thurston while considering the consequences of her visit this afternoon! Was it possible that she worried more about her responsibility to Mrs. Thurston than about the safety of her charges? I knew Miss Miller to be a dependable and kind person, a generally fair teacher, though one who had been overworked and weather-beaten even in those days, and seemed even more so now, since our first meeting more than ten years ago. But she had never been authoritative, and I could not imagine her having the presence of mind to protect the students at Alderton House. If confronted by a superior or by a personage with more status, I was positive that Miss Miller would give way.

She needed my help, and as I reviewed what I knew about Alderton House, I wondered: How could the two of us watch over all the girls? Were there other teachers who also could be called upon to safeguard the students?

I caught a glimpse of my reflection in the dressing table mirror, as Polly continued her efforts. My plain and youthful visage belied the harsh conditions I had endured as a child.

My simple hairstyle—parted in the middle, pulled back, and braided—contrasted with the complexity of my thoughts, the tangled strands of my emotions. My posture was unbowed, and so was my spirit, but to the outside world I looked as meek and mild as a spring lamb.

My face was still swollen, my eye was black, and my lip was split. I touched these tender nodules and marveled at the damage that had been done to my person. Yet when confronted by a thief armed with a knife, I had fought back! I had not given way!

What an unlikely savior I would prove to be for these girls!

Yes, I was small and unassuming, but I was also determined.

I would have to do.

Lucy rapped sharply on my door and stepped inside. "Have you finished, Polly? I wish to speak to Mrs. Rochester in private, please."

Polly gave a half curtsy as she left and closed the door behind her.

"You do not know my brother," said Lucy, "so I must tell you this one thing to ease your mind: He is a powerful ally. Bruce is cunning and brave, and when it comes to the safety of those in his care, he can be positively ruthless. Be advised, you can count on him."

I nodded. "I see that in his manner."

"I sense your determination. However, I beg you—do not put yourself or Adèle at risk. Your bravery is evident in your bruises and scrapes. You fought so hard for a handful of jewels! I can only guess how you would defend a child. But if you sense danger, do not try to soldier on alone. Instead, call for help. I am suggesting a prearranged signal. We know there is a horse chestnut tree near the Senior dormitory. You could tie a handkerchief to the branch nearest the window, couldn't you?"

I nodded at my friend. "That should work well."

"One of Bruce's men will be watching for it. He has a group of like-minded former military men who work for him on a regular basis. They served together in India, so they are tested and true. You will never be without resources."

I stared at her. Lucy was more thoughtful and more versed in the art of subterfuge than I ever would have expected.

As if reading my mind, she smiled. "At a later date, we can discuss how I came to be so conversant with such matters. But this is hardly the time. May I suggest that you do not share this information with Miss Miller?"

I quickly grasped the reason. Clearly Lucy and her brother also felt a pinprick of doubt regarding Miss Miller's loyalties.

"I shall keep the existence of a watchman our secret. The prearranged signal will go no further than the two of us."

Impulsively, my new friend—for such she was proving herself to be—embraced me, a gesture I accepted with pleasure. "What courage you have! We'd best get you on your way. Williams will drive you and Miss Miller to the school and let you out two streets away, as to avoid suspicions about your arrival by carriage. My brother and I will be in the park tomorrow afternoon and every afternoon thereafter. We shall wait for you on a bench. You can expect at least one of us to be there daily."

She stepped back and stared into my eyes. Hers had changed, deepening from that springlike shade of bluebells to the midnight blue associated with the fathomless depths of the sea.

"You can count on me for anything. Anything at all," she insisted again. "When I said I wished to be your sister, I offered you my home, my hearth, and my heart. After glimpsing your character, I am proud to be your sister. You are not alone in this venture. I stand in the shadows, but I am here. I am ready to assist you in any way possible."

This embrace was quicker, but the emotion that welled up inside us made us grasp each other much more tightly. A signal, perhaps, that we both feared those rocky shoals and storm-tossed seas ahead.

As we parted from our hug, she gave my hands one more quick squeeze of affection. The pressure from my wedding band reminded me of the part that I would be playing. Lucy must have read my mind because her fingers lingered against those of my left hand.

"Your ring." A sadness filled her eyes as she turned my hand over before clasping it with both of hers.

I stared down at my wedding ring. I had expected to never remove it, to wear it with my shroud to the grave, but here I was, less than a year and a half later, tugging at it. Reluctantly, I worked the simple gold ring down the length of my finger. My skin fought the ring's slow progress. The removal tore my heart in two. When, at last, it slipped over my fingertip, I grasped and squeezed the band tightly, hoping to burn the shape into the flesh of my palm.

Lucy plucked the ring from my hand. "It's not the ring or the ceremony that binds you and Edward. It's your heart. I see it in your face, in your eyes as they light up when you say his name. Do not despair. Gold is a soft metal, easy to dent or ding or melt. But a woman's heart is a substance immutable even to the most skilled alchemist. Have no fear, Sister. With or without this ring, you are still his, and Edward is still yours."

With that, my friend left to instruct her cook to pack up a bit of cheese and bread for Miss Miller and me, in case she and I had missed our supper. Higgins was getting Miss Miller's coat when Mr. Douglas intercepted me in the hallway. He motioned me into the library.

"I must be quick. I sense that you are that rare person who finds strength in adversity. Good. I have served with such men in India, and I tell you they are the strength of any organization. Since you lack neither the will nor the intellect, I shall endeavor to give you self-preservation skills that should serve you well if you are confronted with a deadly adversary. Pay strict attention, please. The first is simple: Never underestimate your opponent. Trust no one. Stay alert. Do not allow yourself the luxury of an unguarded moment."

"*Maim samajh guyi,*" I said.

"You speak Hindostanee!"

"Only a little. Thank you for your good advice. I shall follow it carefully."

His eyes widened in wonder. "You are welcome. Entirely welcome."

Chapter 18

Once in the carriage, Miss Miller shrank so far back into the shadows that I could only discern the outline of her fingers pressed against her mouth. The *clop-clop-clop* of horse hooves drummed us away from the Brayton home. Over the course of the day, my muscles had stiffened, and each bump and bounce along the cobblestones sent lightning bolts of pain through my body. After one particularly rough jolt, I gasped in pain.

"Does it hurt much?" asked Miss Miller.

"I shall be fine."

"I hope we both shall be."

Another carriage passed by, its coach lights illuminating our cabin and highlighting an anxiety in Miss Miller's eyes.

"I rarely ride in coaches." She ran her hands over the horse-hair seat covers. "My, my."

My heart softened toward her. "You have done right to tell us about your fears, and therefore, you have done your duty to Alderton House."

"And what of you? Surely taking Adela home would have been a simpler solution. Your husband would applaud your good sense, and you could rest easily at night with his ward under your roof again. It's not too late, Mrs. Rochester. The driver could wait outside Alderton House. You could take Adela and leave."

The thick landscape of the park presented an impenetrable fortress. Tree leaves moved against a sky of gray, a ceiling that pressed heavily upon us. I moved restlessly, feeling closed in and panicky. My thumb rubbed the spot where my wedding band had been. Miss Miller was right: It would be easier to take Adèle and go home. No one would blame me. Besides, I had a husband and son to consider. My life was not mine alone anymore. Their own lives and well-being depended upon my safe return. My scheme threatened those sacred obligations.

But as Bruce Douglas had pointed out, how could I live with myself if I did nothing to aid the girls at Alderton House?

I straightened my shoulders. "My course of action is set. Perhaps we should turn our efforts toward making me a credible German teacher, even if my hire is temporary."

"You do possess the necessary language skills, don't you?"

I sighed. Why were we going over old ground? Was she that fearful that our plot would be discovered?

I bit back my impatience and said, "I have studied German. I can read and write in that language. As for conversation, I have mastered enough to teach other beginners. Before we met, my husband traveled through Europe, spending time in all the capitals. He has a good ear for languages. He corrected my pronunciation of simple words."

"'My husband traveled through Europe.'" Miss Miller echoed what I had said in a tone of wonder. "How different your world is these days! Well, you should feel at home at Alderton House. At Lowood, we were trained to serve others. At Alderton, we train girls to be served by others. There is merit to both ways of life. In truth, the more I learn about the expectations visited upon these children of privilege, the sadder it makes me. They have less freedom than one might suppose. Mrs. Webster, our former superintendent, once compared a hothouse orchid to a common thistle. Both may be delicate and luminous in their beauty. But one can only survive under the constant, tender care of a gardener, while the other can scratch out an existence in the most meager of soils."

Miss Miller fingered her skirt thoughtfully and said, "Mrs. Webster would then ask us, 'Which flower is to be envied?'"

"I have no doubt. I know I am the thistle, and glad to be so." I sat deep into the well-worn carriage seat. The day had tired me, and my eyelids begged to close. The end of day had the opposite effect on Miss Miller. The darkening gloom and the rhythmic swaying of our carriage rendered her garrulous.

"I concur. The plant is useful, sturdy, and distinctive."

Suddenly her voice sounded just like our old superintendent, a woman we had both known and admired, Maria Temple. Miss Temple had challenged us to use our minds, finding rote repetition and mimicry offensive. "A split-tongue rook can be trained to repeat words," said she back then, "even if they be nonsensical. But God has granted you the gift of reasoning. Use His gifts wisely!"

I wondered: If Miss Temple were here, would she applaud our scheme?

I fervently hoped so.

The carriage lurched to a stop. A storm of emotions assailed me. Could I follow through with this charade? Would my masquerade fool Mrs. Thurston and, possibly, a killer? If I learned that someone had murdered Selina Biltmore, what might I do with that knowledge?

Williams rapped on the carriage door, and before he could send water cascading over me for the second time in one day, I quickly rose to exit. He gravely handed me my pillowcase full of clothing. Miss Miller and I made our way to the curb, waving him on.

My colleague and I stood side by side, watching the light

of Williams's receding coach lamps glint and skip along in the running rainwater. Neither of us spoke. The task ahead loomed large before us, a steep hill, a Sisyphean ordeal far too arduous for two tired women. Silently, we turned and started to trudge toward Alderton House.

"I assume he is much older than you?"

She did not need to specify whom she was speaking of. "Edward is twenty years my senior."

"Then he is old enough to be your father! Although that is not unusual, is it?"

"I scarcely gave the matter any thought. Edward is my ideal match; the two decades between us mean nothing to him or me."

"We can use the age difference to your advantage. I suggest you emphasize your innocence," Miss Miller said. "If Mrs. Thurston questions you about the rumors she heard, tell her of your lack of experience with the opposite sex. Proclaim how little you knew about Squire Rochester and his designs on you."

"Is that truly necessary? The circumstances were extraordinary." A catch in my chest squeezed hard, and I found it difficult to speak. This was the first time that I fully realized how at Alderton House, I would need to adopt a far different relationship to the man I loved! Why, Nan Miller did not even know that I was a mother! During my first visit, she and I had focused on Adèle's welfare. On this second visit, we had concentrated on the safekeeping of the Alderton House students. Suddenly I realized how little I had told my old friend all about my new life. I gasped slightly, and she reached out to steady me, thinking I had stumbled upon a rock.

"Are you all right?" she asked.

"Fine. Just momentarily overcome with homesickness," I said. Seeing her expression and recalling the scandalous gossip she'd heard, I gave Miss Miller the brief—correct—details of my past three years, concluding with the news of my baby.

She stopped. The rain punished us, but Miss Miller stood there, soaking it up. "You have a child? Of your own?"

"Yes," I said, and a smile came to my face. "He is six months old, and his name is Edward Rivers Rochester. We call him Ned, and he is beautiful."

"A happy ending," said Miss Miller.

"Yes."

We walked a bit without conversation. I asked, "What of yourself? What has happened in the years since we last met?"

"After you were successful with your advertisement, I placed a similar note in the paper. A school in Liverpool required a headmistress. I served there for a year and a half."

We both wiped water from our faces, as the rain showed no signs of slowing and the droplets hit hard with venom. "And then?" I encouraged her.

A hesitation, a catch in her voice, warned me that she was fighting a strong emotion. "Circumstances changed. I came to London, and then Miss Gryce—do you remember her from Lowood?—mentioned in a letter that Lady Kingsley needed a headmistress."

I sensed there was more, but a fresh gust of wind sent a shiver down my spine. My injuries cried out in protest. I gritted my teeth and struggled to keep pace with Miss Miller, whose legs were longer than mine and presumably not stiff with pain.

"What sort of woman was Mrs. Webster?" I asked at last.

"In temperament, she was Mrs. Thurston's opposite. Quiet. Unassuming. We had hoped she would not retire for years to come. Unfortunately, her health took a turn for the worse. You would have liked her. We all did. I miss her. Which brings me to the situation ahead. Mrs. Thurston must hold you blameless in regards to the machinations of Edward Rochester. You must appear to be without guile or she will reject you out of hand immediately." To this bald indictment, Miss Miller added a harsh gesture, a chopping sweep of the fingers that signaled she would brook no discussion.

Swallowing hard, I nodded. "I was but an innocent."

This much was true, but our story did not end there, thank God!

"You must warn Adela not to talk about your abortive wedding," said Miss Miller. "If she does, we are lost."

"But we did, indeed, marry!"

"Yes, and you know that Mrs. Thurston would not hire a married woman. No superintendent would."

The enormity of my duplicity was beginning to weigh on me. "Leave Adèle to me," I said. "Are any of the others fluent in French?"

"*Un peu*," said Miss Miller. "Mrs. Thurston purports to speak French. Indeed, she styles herself as our French teacher. But I can assure you that she is far, far from fluent. If you and Adela need to converse, you are correct, it would be well for you to talk in her native tongue."

So I had surmised. Knowing we could converse freely without fear of being understood could prove useful.

We came closer to Alderton House. Its neighboring mansions hunkered over us, dwarfing and crowding us as we traveled by foot. Two-story colonnades fronting stucco villas surrounded us on every side. Back in the safety of Lucy Brayton's parlor, courage guided my decision. Here on the wet sidewalks of London, a creeping fear nibbled at my bravado. What had I done? Why had I agreed to this foolhardy venture?

I gritted my teeth. My temples ached. Despite the rain soaking my clothing, I stopped walking and tried to massage the tight muscles. But my ministrations did not help. They only made matters worse.

"Jane? Have you changed your mind?" Miss Miller's voice prodded me.

"No," I said firmly. "Just a pain in my heart. That is all."

It was truer than she would ever know.

Chapter 19

"I'll show you where to hang your things. We can check on Adela while we are up there in the dormitory. There's no need for you to carry that pillowcase and your wet shawl and bonnet along to see Mrs. Thurston. But we need to hurry. It will soon be time for dinner."

I followed Miss Miller as she trudged through the house.

While she was clearly enamored of her surroundings at Alderton House, the opulence of the decor meant little to me. After all, Lucy Brayton's home dazzled with the latest in fashionable furnishings, and Thornfield Hall had boasted ancient treasures that signaled the long-standing and exalted rank of the Rochester family.

Yes, unlike Miss Miller, I was accustomed to finery—and I knew to look beyond its gloss and peer deeply at the raw material within.

I could not help but compare this grandiose place to the girls' school in Morton, where my cousin St. John Rivers had offered me a post as mistress. There, in a humble cottage, I had taught twenty scholars, coarsely clad little peasants for

whom education was the only means of progress. Those moun-
tain surroundings were simple but wholesome, and my pupils,
while raw and ignorant, proved teachable. That scene took me
back to Lowood, and its wholly uncongenial surroundings,
where for eight years my routine varied little, even though I
moved up the ladder from student to teacher.

For all my wanderings, one constant remained: I enjoyed
teaching. Planting germs of thought in an eager mind gave
me a sense of purpose. Even if my students peered ahead into
an uncertain future, they would take with them on their lifetime journey a rich inner world of ideas and a nodding
acquaintance with good literature. While few choices for occu-
pation beckoned them, at least they could cipher well enough
to avoid being cheated. They could imagine other worlds,
other times, and other lives. As long as they could read, any
book that presented itself might offer an escape from the
drudgery that would circumscribe the rest of their lives.

Miss Miller narrated our tour. "As I understand it, all the
best homes in London have similar floor plans. Beneath us, as
you've seen, are the kitchen, scullery, pantry, and a servants'
dining room, plus a small sleeping room for Cook. Caje, our
young man, sleeps on the floor in the kitchen in front of the
hearth. He is rather a recent hire. When Mrs. Webster was here,
we had a butler and two maids, but Mrs. Thurston likes her
economies. On the ground level here, as I showed you this
morning, Mrs. Thurston's apartment occupies the right side as
you face the building, and her office is the first room to the
right of the front door."

I followed Miss Miller from front to back of the house so we
could take the servants' stairs up to the dormitories. The same
partitions in the dining room again presented themselves on
the left, turning the long room into two smaller ones. As we
ascended and passed the first floor landing, the sweet sound of
young voices drifted from the music room as they sang a hymn.

From the back of the house facing the front, we had the

Infant dormitory on the left, and then the Junior dormitory at the front of the building on the left. At the right front was the library with its globe and encyclopedia. "This is where the girls practice their needle arts and we say prayers at night," Miss Miller said.

At the back of the building was the Senior dormitory. We paused by the door as Miss Miller indicated the stairs going up yet one more time.

"Emma, our maid of all work, sleeps in the garret above you."

"There is but one maid?" I was astonished. This was a large house, and the full complement of students would mean a demanding work load. By contrast, Lucy Brayton—who lived alone—employed a butler, driver, lady's maid, cook, and parlor maid.

"Yes. There is much work to do, but we manage. Caje acts like a footman, carrying water and coals. We also have a laundress who fetches our dirty linen, cleans it, presses it, and brings it back on Mondays."

Because Miss Miller was talking to me, and I was intent on learning my way around, it wasn't until we were nearly inside that we heard the voices in the Senior dormitory. We stopped outside the door and listened.

"Blood on the pillow linen. I'll be taking this with me," said a man.

What was this? I wondered. Then, with a start, I realized Adèle was in that same room! Was she safe? Heedless of repercussions, I rushed inside.

There I encountered Mrs. Thurston's angry presence, and that of a middling tall man with narrow shoulders who was smoking a pipe. I hurried past him with my head down and knelt beside Adèle, noting that the laudanum still held her in thrall. Taking her hand, I soothed her brow.

"You?" Mrs. Thurston's face reddened at the sight of me. "What is the meaning of this?"

"It's only the new German teacher. Remember? You met her earlier and asked me to go to help her acquire some necessities upon her arrival," said Miss Miller as she rushed in behind me, although her voice nearly cracked with the strain. "Pardon us, Mrs. Thurston, but she"—and here she gestured in my direction—"once served as Adela's own governess. Naturally, she's happy to see the child again."

Ignoring me further for the moment, Mrs. Thurston turned to the man and said, "See here, Mr. Waverly. What is the meaning of this? You have no right—"

"Madam, I answer to the Bow Street magistrate, Sir Robert Blake, and only to him." So this was the officer Miss Miller had met, the one whom Mr. Douglas had seemed in awe of. Truly, Waverly's presence commanded respect. He smoked a cherry pipe and had a battered-looking face.

"You . . . you impertinent . . ." Mrs. Thurston's florid face puckered in inchoate anger as she pointed a finger at Waverly's chest. Added to the fact that she was struggling to breathe—a situation I assumed was in response to the exertion of climbing the stairs—the woman seemed almost ready to explode, or expire, or both.

"That's true, ma'am. I am that. One of my worst faults; but it serves me well now and again. If I could trouble you to move back so that I may examine the area around the bed." Waverly executed a courtly half bow, holding a black baton under one arm. As he bent, light glinted off a gold coin embedded in one end of the truncheon.

"This is unconscionable!" Mrs. Thurston's hands churned the air. "Ridiculous. I demand that you leave at once! I plan to complain to your superior personally. In fact, we'll see what Lady Kingsley has to say about this intrusion," she sputtered.

"Sir Blake will contact Lady Kingsley himself if he hasn't already done so. You can count on it," Waverly assured her.

"So shall I, sir! So shall I! Take it to the Bank of England!" Mrs. Thurston stomped out of the room. Her footsteps echoed down the hallway and finally, she huffed and puffed her way down the stairs.

"Miss Miller?" he asked as he turned toward my friend. "Can you identify the owner of this trinket?" With that he held up a length of sky blue grosgrain hair ribbon.

"Adela Varens." Miss Miller spoke without hesitation.

I rocked back on my heels, hanging on to Adèle's bed with one hand, thankful to be near the floor.

"She's the girl who found the body, right?" Waverly continued.

"Yes, sir. You see, Adela and Selina were partners."

"Partners? Explain that to me."

She talked about the system of joint responsibility.

"But Selina was also responsible for Adela, right?"

Miss Miller nodded. "Unfortunately, Selina often had problems getting out of bed in the morning."

"Was that a source of friction for the girls?" he asked.

"On occasion." Miss Miller sounded meek, regretful.

I shook my head. Although I would never have suggested that she lie, I wished with all my heart that her answer would have been different.

"Adela is that child there? The one who was administered laudanum? The one with the teacher hovering over her?" He cocked his head toward my sleeping charge.

"Yes, sir."

"Why are you lingering there?" he asked me.

"I'm checking on her," I said before adding, "sir."

"I shall want to talk with her when she wakes up."

"Of course," Miss Miller said.

"You have come in from outside? Recently. And it is raining. Why? What sent you wandering on an evening like this?"

"I was fetching some necessities needed by Miss Eyre, our new German teacher." Miss Miller gestured toward me. "She is a former colleague of mine, newly arrived in London. We are fortunate that she was available on short notice."

I gained my feet and stood straight as a chair back, but I kept my eyes downcast, hoping to both appear modest and discourage his curiosity.

"You requested that we find an adult to act as chaperone in this dormitory, and we have. I went to run an errand. That's all." Miss Miller's voice faded, and if her explanation sounded a bit fulsome, well, Waverly seemed not to notice.

I bobbed my head in greeting.

"Who beat you?" his gruff tone demanded.

"A thief at a coaching inn. I was robbed." I did not return his gaze.

"Did you report your misadventure to anyone? Wasn't there a guard traveling with the coach?"

"A man named Glebe took the report, sir."

"Glebe? That cork-brained fool. All right. I'll see what he's done about your loss."

He turned toward Miss Miller. "Miss Eyre looks scarcely older than your students. Both of you better dry off. You'll catch your deaths!"

With that observation and quick dismissal, he moved to the doorway of the Senior dormitory. Miss Miller scurried along after him. I stayed where I was. As the officer and my old friend crossed the threshold, she glanced quickly back at me with a look both apologetic and embarrassed. "Miss Eyre? You can hang your things on the coat stand. I shall wait for you outside the door. The first bed in the row on the left will be yours, the one set apart with the modesty screen nearby."

I thanked her and did as she bid, moving quickly but quietly. I overheard Mr. Waverly ask Miss Miller, "Is it possible that the hair ribbon was a gift? Or a loan to the dead girl?"

"I doubt it, sir. Adela was exceedingly fond of that particular ribbon. She was looking for it the day before . . . before Selina died."

With a last kiss for Adèle's brow, I hurried to join Waverly and Miss Miller. The three of us walked downstairs together, where he bid us good night. She closed the door behind him and leaned her forehead against the wood panels. "At last, he's gone! Now we must deal with Mrs. Thurston."

The superintendent reluctantly responded after Miss Miller knocked on the door of her office for the second time. "There better be a good reason for disturbing me—" She stopped abruptly when she saw me.

With hesitation, Maude Thurston stepped aside. Her face was still florid from her struggle with the stairs. Miss Miller and I entered her office. A large desk squatted in the middle of the room, crowding us into the edges of available space. Every cubby overflowed with papers. A mountainous heap on the desk surface wobbled and threatened to topple over. Papers lined two wicker baskets and covered the cushion of the only available chair. The magnitude of the mess shocked me.

"What are you gawking at? Why are you here?" The superintendent directed her tirade toward me.

"Excuse me, Mrs. Thurston, but I believe you may want to read this correspondence. It is urgent. I would have given it to you sooner, but it's none of Mr. Waverly's business." Miss Miller's trembling hand offered the letter from Lucy Brayton.

"I'll have that man's job. See if I don't." She fixed a glare at me. "I suppose now that you've arrived you'll need a place to sleep. There's an extra bed in the Senior dormitory. Miller? Tell Cook we have one more for supper. On second thought, she can take my place."

I blinked in surprise, so taken aback by her gruff kindness that I could not muster a response.

Mrs. Thurston snatched up a magnifying glass and perused the return address on the message from Lucy. After reading it, she made a shooing motion toward me with her free hand.

"You wait in the entrance hall. This is none of your concern."

I fought the urge to say, "Oh, but it is." Instead, I managed a half curtsy, left her office, and walked loudly to a spot in the hallway. When I heard the door slam, I stepped toe-heel, toe-heel back to Mrs. Thurston's room. Pressing my ear against the smooth wooden panels of her door, I could catch a word or two: "Idiotic inspector . . . How dare he? . . . an accident . . . ruin us . . ."

At that point, her diatribe ceased. Miss Miller must have reminded her about the note from Lucy. A long pause ensued.

"This would be temporary? Only until Fräulein Schoeppenkoetter reaches us?" I heard Mrs. Thurston ask.

An urgent appeal came from Miss Miller, but I could not make out the particulars. I caught the words "German" and "chaperone" and "for now."

"Bring me Jane Eyre!" said the superintendent.

Chapter 20

"You are dripping water on my carpet," Mrs. Thurston muttered. So was Miss Miller, for that matter.

Standing there in my wet clothes, I rued my appearance. As a rule, I prided myself on my respectable, nearly Quaker-like neatness, and this misadventure had cost me the chance to keep my appearance tidy. Now, here I stood, looking and feeling unkempt, which left me sorely at a disadvantage.

"You lied to me today! You allowed me to think you were Fräulein Schoeppenkoetter." Mrs. Thurston pointed a finger in my face and shook it angrily. Her hot, fetid breath assaulted my face.

I considered reminding her how she had not given me the chance to introduce myself. Instead, I held my tongue and allowed her to continue her harangue. She lectured me about proper conduct. Teachers in her employ were expected not to chew tobacco or use snuff, not to give themselves airs or ape their betters, not to act overly familiar with the parents or students, and not to question her.

Though I chafed at her tone, the rules were the same in

every other educational institution in the land. But rather than point out the redundancy of her recitation, I said nothing.

"While under my roof, you are not to have followers. Is that clear? So whoever it was who beat you, well, he is not welcome at Alderton House."

I wholeheartedly concurred with that! But I bit back a smile because I couldn't conjure up the spectacle of her turning away my "follower," Edward Fairfax Rochester. Indeed, I hoped I would be done with this assignment before my husband arrived in London.

Mrs. Thurston continued, locking bleary eyes on my person. "You will, of course, join us for prayers in the evenings and on Sundays. Once you prove suitable—and if Fräulein Schoeppenkoetter does not come—I may grant you a half day off every third week, but that is at my discretion. We do not mollycoddle our students. So you were that French girl's governess? Then I have a low opinion of your skills as an educator, Miss Eyre."

An uncomfortable heat started at my neck and crawled up to my cheeks. I longed to rebut Mrs. Thurston's remarks! I wanted to set her straight, to explain that Adèle had made admirable progress under my care, but I had not been her teacher for the past two years—Alderton House was responsible for her recent education. However, I knew that if I quarreled with the old woman, all advantage was lost.

It came to me: Could it be that Maude Thurston had written the threatening note to Adèle?

I swallowed hard and decided I would find out.

"As for her guardian, Mr. Rochester, I have heard all about your misadventure with him. That is what comes of setting your cap so far above your station! Throwing yourself at a country squire. Have you no sense of decorum?" She drew herself up. I found my attention riveted to a stray chin hair that switched back and forth like the tail of a playful dog. This image—ridiculous in the extreme—helped me cool my rising temper.

"Are you listening to me, Miss Eyre? I trust you are not applying to teach here so that you can be close to Mr. Rochester's ward. Do you see this position as a way to wiggle your way back into his good graces?"

"No," I said honestly. I told myself the woman would be quiet soon. I reminded myself she would eat enough crow to vanquish all the ravens at the Tower of London. But containing my ire became increasing difficult as she continued.

"Oh ho! I see by your face that you do harbor feelings for him! While London is a town of sophisticated tastes, illicit behavior is still frowned upon."

Why is it, I wondered, that boorish people persist in repetition? Do they assume that you cannot hear them? Or is it the nature of a boor to repeat the same tiresome phrases over and over?

"You wish gainful employment? And you have hoodwinked a sponsor into recommending you? You hope to be welcomed back into the fold of decency? We shall see, we shall see! Get me my Bible, Miss Miller."

Turning back to me, Mrs. Thurston held her thumb and forefinger an inch apart. "You came this close to becoming a bigamist!"

No insult to my person could have knocked me harder. I blinked back strong emotion, and Maude Thurston frowned as she noted my response.

Miss Miller rummaged through an overloaded étagère. Obnoxious gewgaws, statues of dubious provenance, and other awkward tokens crowded the shelves. After a quick search, she pulled out a dingy leather-bound Bible. The forceful smell of must and mold mingled with the scent of strong spirits.

"On this Holy Book, you must swear to put aside all your feelings for Mr. Edward Rochester, Adela Varens's guardian. Come! Place your hand on it!" Mrs. Thurston grabbed the book from Miss Miller's hands and thrust it toward me.

My old friend's pleading look told me all I needed to know.

She was asking me to forswear my husband, even at risk to my soul. If I backed down now, Miss Miller's part in this misadventure would go hard on her.

"Really, Mrs. Thurston. Is this necessary?" I said peevishly. "I am here, I can teach German—and Mrs. Brayton vouches for my character. Are you suggesting her recommendation is without merit?"

I had her. Mrs. Thurston paused. Confident that the threat of Lucy Brayton struck the old woman a sound blow, I continued, "Is her approval not reason enough to accept me? Or should I return to her home and take her check with me?"

"Place your hand on my Bible!" Maude Thurston repeated.

Miss Miller's lips formed one word: *Please.* I could imagine her fear. The Holy Book was inches from my fingertips, yet I could not move toward it.

How could I swear to put aside my love for Edward? Even in our darkest hours, when I had concluded that my only salvation came in putting distance between us, even as I'd run blindly away from the only person I had ever loved, I had never been able to say that I did not care for him. Regardless of the humiliation I had once suffered—I could not sever my feelings for him. No, from the instant I'd first seen him thundering over the hill on his black steed Mesrour, he held my heart in his hands.

This beastly woman demanded that I swear on the Holy Bible that he who meant everything to me meant nothing!

I hesitated. Miss Miller bowed her head and clutched her hands together against her breast. Her lips moved in a prayer.

As did mine.

"Repeat after me," Mrs. Thurston said. "I, Jane Eyre, do solemnly swear on my true faith as a Christian—"

Eeeekkkkk!

A scream interrupted her.

Chapter 21

Since I was closest to the door, I flew out of Mrs. Thurston's office and raced up the stairs, following the noise. I worried that it was coming from the Senior dormitory, so I climbed faster and faster, thinking of Adèle.

Miss Miller followed me into the hallway, but Mrs. Thurston did not. One quick backward glance affirmed that the superintendent was planning to remain in her rooms. I didn't spare a second look.

As I mastered the stairs with increasing difficulty, I reminded myself that my young charge had been fine when I left her mere minutes ago. Sleeping soundly, totally insensate to her surroundings, but fine.

The scream dwindled to whimpers.

When I reached the second floor landing, I spotted the open dormitory door. The setting sun had darkened the room somewhat, but my eyes quickly adjusted to the gloom.

I discovered a figure sprawled on the floor. "Are you hurt?" I called out.

"No," sobbed a childlike voice.

"Adèle?" I said to the lumpy covers, a quiet mound signifying her still-drugged form. I leaned close enough to hear her snore lightly. Her skin felt warm to my touch, but not overly so.

I turned to the child on the floor. Ragged sobs came from her throat. A sliver of light revealed a tangle of auburn hair, a body curled tightly into a protective ball like a threatened hedgehog.

"Are you all right?" I asked, touching her shaking shoulders with a gentle hand.

"Sc-scared. Gh-ghost! I want Miss Miller!" The name came as a wail of misery.

"I am her friend. Where are your classmates?"

"Lining up for dinner," she said without once looking at me. "Are you a ghost?"

"No. I assure you that I am quite real. Here." I located both of the child's hands, which she had pressed to her face. Slowly, I peeled her fingers away. Her hands clutched mine in mortal terror, and still she refused to open her eyes.

"Come now. It's all right. Look at me."

"Miss Eyre, where are you?" Miss Miller called up the stairs.

"In the Senior dormitory." I raised my voice, hoping it would carry my message to her.

Cautiously, the girl on the floor opened her eyes.

"Eeek!" she cried again. "What is wrong with your face?"

I had forgotten my bruises. I choked back a laugh. All the students would be curious about my injuries. That was the nature of the young, to approach the world with unrestrained wonder, unfettered by the faux sophistication that society encouraged adults to affect. Only as we grew older did we learn to practice the art of dissembling about our natural, healthy interest or shutting down that miraculous facility of a wondering mind.

"I've been hurt. That's all. Tell me what has happened. Miss

Miller is on her way." I could hear my friend's heavy footsteps leading the way on the stairs, followed by the tromping of a group of other, lighter feet.

Miss Miller's voice mixed with others, and I realized she was diverting the students, who had responded to their friend's scream by swarming the stairway. They sounded like a bunch of magpies chattering, trying to make sense of a confusing situation.

But of course they were upset. They had every reason to be. One of their classmates had been discovered dead—and their imaginations had run wild.

Reaching into my pocket, I located a handkerchief and mopped the wet cheeks of my crying companion.

"Come along. There's a draft along the floorboards." After I helped her to her feet, I coaxed the girl to sit on an empty bed. Even in the fading sunlight, I could see that she had a curious delicacy, suggesting she would grow up to be a beauty. Tears dripped from long lashes set in an oval face and balanced by tiny rosebud lips.

"Wh-who are you?" she asked of me.

Miss Miller finally made her way through the clutch of hysterical students crowding outside the dormitory door. "Rose, this is our new German and drawing teacher. Meet Miss Eyre."

But the girl refused to calm down, almost throwing herself at Miss Miller. "Don't let Selina hurt me! She's haunting us!"

"She's dead, child," Miss Miller said sternly.

"No! She . . . she's here!" Rose pointed at the coatrack, draped with my wet things. The imaginative mind of a frightened girl had given them substance and a human shape.

"I see naught but a coatrack and sodden outer garments," Miss Miller said. "Rose? Cast a good look yonder. Do not let your mind play tricks on you. See? There is no ghost, merely wet clothing belonging to Miss Eyre."

To help support this claim I went quickly to the coatrack

and held out my shawl and bonnet for Rose to inspect. Afterward, I replaced everything on the pegs.

Rose peeled herself away from Miss Miller and peered, first through squinted eyes and finally through wide-open lashes, at the bonnet and shawl. I lifted each of them again, moving more slowly.

"I thought . . . I thought . . . she had come back for us," said Rose. "I only came up to find my wrap because I was cold, and then I saw . . . I saw that . . . and I . . . I guess I was silly."

"No," Miss Miller said, "you were not silly. You had a fright, that's all. We're all upset. Let's splash water on your face and tidy you up."

Below us a clock bell chimed six times. Miss Miller nodded. "Good. Time for dinner. Come along, Rose. Let's show Miss Eyre to the dining room."

"Give me a minute to check on Adèle," I said. After again noting the even rise and fall of her chest, I readjusted the sleeping child's covers and planted a gentle kiss on her cheeks. She sighed in her sleep but made no effort to awaken.

As Rose, Miss Miller, and I started down the stairs, I paused to extend my hand to the girl. "I assume your name is Rose?"

She took my hand and shook it solemnly. "Rose Amanda Taylor. How do you do, Miss Eyre?" As children often do, she had moved from panic to self-possession in the twitch of a cat's whisker.

The other girls had already preceded us down the stairs. They waited for us in front of the dining room. I could tell from the expressions on their faces that Rose's screams had left them terrified.

And they had a right to be.

Chapter 22

Our arrival in the dining room caused scant attention. I presumed that the girls were either accustomed to having guests or so exhausted by the emotions of the day that my insignificant presence caused little commotion.

The students took their seats and waited quietly with their hands in their laps. To a one, their eyes were red and puffy from crying.

The table settings represented the finest of their ilk. Eggshell porcelain teacups, white with blushing red roses and trimmed in gold. I must admit, the splendor surprised me. The delicately translucent teacups and gleaming silver brought home the differences between my new situation and my past. At Lowood, we'd supped from tin cups and plates as battered and tarnished as our dreams—there was nothing delicate about our lives. If one was not hardy and tough, one did not survive.

Quickly, I corrected my thinking. What had I expected? I had been a charity case. These girls were privileged members of the upper class. As if thinking the same thing, Miss Miller leaned into me. "Mrs. Thurston believes, as did Mrs. Webster, that the girls should be familiar with the dining habits of their class. Not only do I concur, but I have certainly come to appreciate it. It adds a dollop of civility even on the worst of days."

Miss Miller stood, clapped her hands together, and announced, "Ladies, may I present to you our new instructor, Miss Jane Eyre. Miss Eyre is a former student of mine. Please line up to shake her hand and tell her hello."

The Senior girls led the queue, each introducing herself to me.

Rufina Garland-Simmons, an untidy child of about fifteen whose hair was coming out of its braids, shook my hand with surprising strength. "Welcome."

Nettie Inslip managed a tiny bob and a quiet, "Hello, miss." I judged her to be a little younger than Rufina, but not much.

Rose Amanda Taylor curtsied low to me, her delicate hands spreading her skirt gracefully. "It is a pleasure to see you again, Miss Eyre. I do hope you've been well since we last met," Rose said gravely.

I replied that I had, indeed, been well, as I struggled to keep a smile of amusement to myself at such formality when we had met just five minutes earlier.

While Rose's face retained the plump cheeks of a young girl, her features were more adult. I would guess her to be around fourteen. That meant that all of the Seniors were at least four years older than Adèle.

One by one, the other students filed past me. A moppet from the Infants' group twirled a curl on one finger, took my hand with the other fingers, and stared boldly at my black eye. "Does it hurt you much, miss? Your eye?"

"Caroline! One does not make personal comments about the appearance of one's elders," admonished Miss Miller.

All eyes turned on me. I knew the import of this moment.

The girls were waiting to see my response. Would I be harsh? Churlish? Or kind? My decision would set my course here, as the students watched me carefully, hoping for clues to my demeanor.

I leaned close to the girl. "Yes, my eye hurts terribly. I advise you to avoid getting hurt like this, if you can help it."

This set all the girls to giggling, and the strained atmosphere eased immediately. Rose cupped a hand over her mouth and said to her sister Seniors, "She was ever so nice to me when I was scared. Really she was. And I saw her lean over and kiss Adela, but Adela didn't notice, of course, being so sleepy and all."

After the youngest students marched back to their seats, Miss Miller led us in prayers. After the last "amen," she reached for a small crystal bell to signal that the serving should begin. Emma staggered in under a tray heavily laden with loaves of bread and three soup tureens. She set the offerings down on a tablecloth of snowy white damask. A young man—Caje, I presumed—came along behind her, carrying a tray with two platters, one heaped with sliced venison and the other, I could smell, with baked fish.

I noted that for all his youth, and I judged him to be about eighteen, he wore an expression of weariness. Although he was wearing a jacket, no one could have missed the fact that he was lean and muscular, clearly accustomed to hard work.

After the servers made a second trip to bring another set of trays and assorted dishes containing peas, salad, and beetroots, Miss Miller said, "You may eat."

She turned to me and said, sotto voce, "I know that some suppose children do not need much food, but Mrs. Thurston believes in feeding the girls well. That way they present good figures for their debuts. Can you imagine how this would have delighted us at Lowood? Even at the best of times, the food there was still meager."

Emma stood at the doorway and gave the table one final

glance, checking to make sure she'd forgotten nothing. Her attention moved quickly, efficiently, but I deemed I caught a hint of her naked longing. I turned my own gaze away, feeling embarrassed for both of us. I knew how Emma felt. Being an outsider nettled, and worse yet, there was nothing anyone could do. You were born into your status; you most likely would also die there.

Miss Miller and I sat next to each other. An older woman, as thin and spindly as a winter-stripped sapling, took a seat to my right. An oversized black shawl drooped carelessly from her shoulders, and her grizzled hair escaped from a crocheted snood.

"Allow me to introduce myself," she said to me in formal, heavily accented English. "I am Signora Ambrosia Delgatto, the Italian tutor and singing mistress."

With this she touched one hand to her chest, closed her eyes, and executed a charming half bow from the waist.

"*Piacere di conoscerla, signora.*" I returned her bow similarly, but wondered: If Signora Delgatto was here, why weren't there enough adults to chaperone the girls?

She broke into a large smile. "Ah! You speak my native tongue." If she was curious about my bruised face, Signora Delgatto hid it well.

"Alas, only a few words," I said. "I have an affinity for languages. My name is Jane Eyre—" I caught myself before "Rochester" could slip out.

"Miss Eyre is our new German and drawing instructor," Miss Miller hastened to add.

"A pleasure to meet you, Miss Eyre. I am Parthena Jones," said a tall woman to Signora Delgatto's right, as she extended a cool hand to me. She was probably the same age as I, with an open face and wide-set eyes under finely arched brows, but her nose was a bit too wide and her mouth a touch too small for her to be pretty. Her robust stature and proud profile reminded me of the Amazon women in ancient mythology.

She towered above me, as I was much closer in scale to the Junior students, while Parthena Jones could have easily been mistaken for a man. "I am the Juniors' proctor, and I also teach math, Latin, and needle arts," she said.

"For the record, I teach English literature, grammar, and composition. And history. That has always been my passion." With that Miss Miller buttered a large slice of bread. "And of course, as I told you, Mrs. Thurston teaches French. Deportment as well."

Signora Delgatto helped herself to the butter, too. "Oof!" she exclaimed in a voice heavy with irritation. "I could not get the girls to pay attention to their lessons today. I stayed late this evening to help them. I shall have to ask Caje to help me home. My eyes are no longer good in the dark. I have very poor vision for one of my species!"

I smiled to myself, since *del gatto* was Italian for "of the cat."

"Signora lives in Clerkenwell with her brother, who needs her assistance," Miss Miller explained.

"Some call Clerkenwell 'Little Italy,'" said Parthena Jones to me.

"Ah, he has the bad heart. I have the bad leg. We are a pair!" Signora Delgatto said. "But together we manage."

"I am certain you are happy to be shed of us today, signora. This has been a sad day, Miss Eyre, what with the loss of one of our students," Miss Jones said.

"So I have heard," I said. "Please allow me to tender my condolences."

Signora Delgatto finished her meal hurriedly. "I must go now. My brother will be wondering where I am. Oh! What a day I have to share with him! One of my own students—dead!"

As she stood, she leaned close to me and whispered, "*Lei è morta e ne sono contenta.*"

Surely my translation was wrong. Could the old woman really have said, "She is dead and I am happy"?

While Signora Delgatto struggled out the door and I considered her surprising parting words, Miss Jones turned to me.

"So you are the unlucky individual who arrived soaking wet in the kitchen just this morning, are you not? I heard Emma remark on your injuries," she said.

"Yes, a thief accosted me at a coaching inn."

"Oh dear! What a dangerous place this world is for an unmarried woman. What a shame. For a woman, being unmarried—without a male protector—and safe are mutually exclusive. Our inferior status forces all of us into a role as chattel."

I found this curious. I did not think of Edward as my protector. He was my spouse, my helpmate, and my equal. We were both charged with protecting our son . . . and Adèle. A sudden wave of homesickness engulfed me. Surrounded by other women's children, I missed my own Ned. So physical was this longing that my breath caught in my throat.

"Are you all right, Miss Eyre?" asked Miss Jones. "For a moment, your face showed extraordinary sadness. What might I do to help? I want to be your friend as well as your new colleague."

How peculiar. Twice in as many days, women I'd barely met professed to desire my friendship.

Miss Jones rephrased her offer. "Forgive me if I am being forward, but I do hope to get to know you. There are so few of us, and having the society of other teachers makes this post much more desirable than the solitary position of being a governess, don't you agree?"

"I do." A governess could not mingle with the staff, nor was she generally accepted as an equal by her mistress and master. Save in one instance . . . mine.

Miss Jones stared at me.

"Yes, I understand what you are saying. Being a governess can be very lonely."

Miss Miller sent a sidewise glance at me, then quickly studied her serviette.

"Where were you in service last?" Miss Jones asked.

"North of here, in Yorkshire," I said, and to channel the conversation in another direction, I stifled a yawn. "Pardon me! It has been a rather long day."

"Yes, Miss Eyre, it has been a trying and troubling day for all of us," Miss Miller said. Her eyes caught mine and her tone sent another message: *And you must not let down your guard. Not yet! A killer may walk among us!*

Chapter 23

Recognizing I would have to rehearse even my most casual and mundane speech with care added to my overwhelming sense of exhaustion. Every part of my body ached, and the bruising around my eye pulsed with sharp arrows of pain.

After dinner, Miss Jones, Miss Miller, and I conversed about desultory topics as the students quietly occupied themselves with their assignments and reading. The women shared with me a general overview of the school's routine, along with a sense of what rules and expectations there were for the students. Discipline, I learned, was left largely to the individual teacher's judgment.

"What happened to Fräulein Schoeppenkoetter?" Miss Jones asked Miss Miller. "There's nothing seriously wrong, is there?"

"Fräulein has been unavoidably detained. Mrs. Thurston did not share specifics with me. When Miss Eyre happened by to renew our friendship, I conceived the idea that she could step in for a short while."

Miss Jones started to speak again, but one of the girls came to ask her a question about geography. I had the sense I was fortunate that the interruption occurred.

Needle art projects consumed the final hour before bedtime. Emma served tea and biscuits in the library, where a small coal fire had been set in the hearth. At long last, my clothing started to dry out.

I struggled to keep my eyes open, telling myself that I must take heed of the surroundings and note the different personalities so I could report to Mr. Douglas. Perhaps he could tease out information that would be useful. So far, I could see nothing that might help us conclude the identity of a killer.

Some girls stitched steadily; others fussed about with their floss and needles. Rufina grumbled that she hated needle arts, Nettie seemed particularly cross about her own work, and Rose mainly sat with her project in her lap and stared off into space.

Miss Jones pursed her lips. "The girls are all out of sorts. You cannot imagine how distraught the students were about Selina Biltmore's death. How many children were in the family that you served? You said your post was in Yorkshire?"

"Just one and yes."

"Was the family good to you? Why did you leave?"

"Circumstances changed."

Miss Miller intervened, obviously tiring of Miss Jones's attempts to pry into my past. "Miss Eyre served as Adela's governess."

"Indeed! So you must have met her guardian!" Miss Jones threw her hands up in horror. "How lucky you were to have escaped with your virtue intact! That man must be a monster! Hiding a wife while wooing a governess!"

My teacup rattled as I set it down.

"Please forgive Miss Jones for speaking out of turn. She knows that Mrs. Thurston takes a strict stand against gossip." Miss Miller glared at Miss Jones, who met her stare and returned a benign expression. "Tonight we seem to have forgotten our manners. Perhaps it is because the events of this morning were so distressing."

Little Caroline approached Miss Miller for help unraveling a knot. While my old teacher's attention was diverted, Miss Jones whispered to me, "You have heard about Selina Biltmore, haven't you? Adela found her lying there, dead, this morning. She was already cold to the touch! Can you imagine?"

"Miss Jones! Please!" Miss Miller sent Caroline on her way as her own voice sharpened with irritation. "Let us not dwell on it. Of course Miss Eyre knows about the tragedy. Please do not pander to nervousness by remarking on the circumstances surrounding the girl's death."

"One can hardly call it pandering! I simply seek to warn Miss Eyre that her students might suffer from nightmares. Adela sobbed and sobbed until we dosed her. That's her French blood, I daresay. They are an excitable people. Prone to dramatics and reckless behavior. They take little heed of the impact on others. The women especially. She must have been quite the trial to you when you were attempting to teach her."

"On occasion," I agreed. "Her French blood and years in that country cannot help but evidence themselves. However, she is a good child at heart. Most adults would suffer agitation, too, when confronted by a dead body. Surely you don't blame Adèle for responding as she did? She is, after all, just a child."

"I was only remarking on what happened and her response to it so that you will be informed." Miss Jones shrugged in a manner that betrayed petulance.

"Of course," I said, to smooth over this hiccup.

She continued in a more conciliatory tone, "I, myself, have burst into tears several times today. The news of Selina's death was shocking for all of us. Horribly so. I think it best to warn you that tonight of all nights, your charges might awaken you

with bad dreams. I daresay this would be a good night to give
them all a drop or two of laudanum. It might help them get
through the long evening without interruption, poor dears.
Remind me, Miss Miller, to tell Cook to buy more when she
does her shopping."

"Ma'am? May I begin the readings?" Rufina curtsied to
Miss Miller, all the while sucking on a bloody index finger.
When she withdrew it from her mouth, I could see that the
skin had been broken by several needle pricks.

The three Seniors—Rufina, Rose, and Nettie—took turns
reading Bible passages out loud. Rufina spoke haltingly, stumbling over difficult words. Rose read with a clear voice and
dramatic flair, while poor Nettie's recitation was marked with
incessant interruptions as Parthena Jones corrected the child's
lazy tongue. The rest of the girls hid behind their stitching to
muffle their giggles, while Nettie suffered no end of embarrassment. The child's face grew redder and redder with each
stumbling pronouncement.

When Nettie finished, Miss Miller turned to me with a
frown. "I am not a martinet, but her father has sent strict
instructions that we teach his little girl to talk like a proper
Englishwoman and cure her of this silly lisp. His words, not
mine. I think she's adorable."

At long last, the Bible passages came to an end, for which
I sent up a silent prayer of thanksgiving.

The girls began to pack up their needlework, and Miss
Jones turned again to me. "Where did you learn German?"

"My cousins are scholars. They taught me."

But she was not finished. "Are your cousins here in
London?"

"Actually, I am the guest of Mrs. Captain Augustus Brayton." The words slipped out before I could weigh and measure
them. The expression of surprise on Miss Jones's face told me
she found this fascinating.

"My! That's lofty company for a governess, isn't it? She used to visit the school quite frequently, but then her interest ceased."

"Her husband is serving the Crown in India, and he took ill. She, naturally, went to his aid, but has now returned."

"Oh! That explains her recent absence. I was wondering why she lost interest in us. My! I can't imagine visiting with a society lady like Mrs. Brayton at her home. Much less having her as a hostess! How did you meet her?"

"Through my former employer, Adèle's guardian."

"Have you known her long?" Miss Jones was nothing if not insistent.

This was exactly the sort of conversation I hoped to avoid, since any mention of Lucy might lead to explaining our real relationship, the bond that came from our husbands being best friends. No, such a discussion might lead me to slip and announce my true status—I was too exhausted to think clearly. Yet here I was in the thick of it with no way out. I set my teacup down rather too clumsily and the clatter caused Miss Miller to face me. I sent her my unspoken cry for help— and she responded by saying, "I suggest we escort the students up to bed early, since it might take a while for them to get to sleep. Ladies, put your work away. Let's have a hymn before bed. What might you suggest, Miss Jones?"

"The girls practiced a nice one with Signora Delgatto just this morning. Come along now. Stand in your places." She rose and directed them into three neat rows, where the girls waited for their cue. Miss Jones raised her hands then dropped them to signal the start of a well-loved hymn with a verse that included the words "make us thy sorrow feel, till through our pity and our shame love answers love's appeal."

I could not know it then, but it proved oddly prescient.

Chapter 24

After singing, the students lined up with their proctors at the head of the queue. Rufina, the head Senior, led the way to the dormitory. Her face wore an expression of tense resignation. The dragging of the Seniors' feet, the abject silence, and the general aura told me they were all terrified.

Once in the Senior dormitory, I checked on Adèle while the three other young ladies untied their pinafores, hung them up, and washed their faces. I was tucking the blanket up under Adèle's chin when Miss Miller knocked on the door.

"This is our schedule, and a roster of our students. Here is the German primer we use. There's a notebook, a sketch-book, and several pencils in the muslin bag. The classrooms have slates and chalk for each student." She pressed the pile upon me and asked, "Have you considered where and how to begin?"

"My first task will be to assess where the girls are in their learning."

"Good idea. Fräulein Hertzog wasn't with us long. Perhaps

three months? So I imagine the girls have retained little, if any, real skills."

She leaned close and whispered, "Remember, I am across the hall from you if you need me. The walls do not muffle noises as much as one might like."

Setting the book and bag on top of my dresser, I returned to my charges. All had undressed and were climbing into bed. I stepped behind the modesty panel and removed my dress, shivering as I did. After pulling my night rail over my head, I slipped my arms into my white lawn wrapper. Tying the belt caused me to stop and look down. This would never do. Both my night rail and wrapper were trimmed with deep ruffles of lace, an embellishment totally out of keeping with the post of a humble governess.

It is only lace, and nothing more, I thought as I ripped the frothy trim from the garments.

I turned the lace over and over in my hand. Feeling the pattern of holes and stitching, I recognized this torn fabric as a metaphor for my life—I had ripped myself from my husband and son, from the life I loved, a world rich and fine. Now I pretended to be something less than what I was.

I tucked the trim into a pocket of my wrapper. Perhaps no one would have noticed the extravagant embellishment, but I couldn't take any chances.

No, I had made my choice. I was committed to this course of action. I sighed and prepared myself. I surmised that the girls would watch my every move, the way a frightened dog watches his master for proof that all is well.

My instincts were correct. When I stepped out from behind the screen, three sets of eyes stared at me. Their expressions ranged from curious to cautious. Adèle snored lightly and rolled over.

"That was her bed," ventured Rufina, pointing to the empty cot beside mine, with covers twisted 'round and 'round like a stork's nest. The pillow appeared to be missing, but a glance told me it rested awkwardly between the wall and the floor, as if it had fallen there.

"Caje is supposed to come get her mattress at some point," said Rose. "If she was sick, he's to burn it. He's the houseboy and he's awful strong."

"He isn't the houseboy," corrected Rufina. "He's the footman. Sort of. Only he doesn't wear a uniform. And he isn't that strong. That bed does not weigh much." To prove her boast, she walked over and hefted the head of the cot, lifting it easily.

"Wonder if we can have our things back," said Nettie in her babyish lisp. "Miss Eyre, do you suppose we can have them?"

"What do you mean?" I pulled pins from my hair and shook it out.

"Selina took all my sweeties and put them in the top drawer of her dresser. I was just thinking, she will not be eating them, so do you suppose I could have them back?"

"May I have my sash? It is my prettiest one, and it is all satin, and my papa gave it to me," said Rose.

Rufina scratched at a scab. "I should like my kite. I worked a long time on the tail. It's rather a good flier."

"Why does—did—Selina have these items? You say they belong to you?"

"Yes, ma'am," Rufina said. "They are in her dresser. Top drawer. She showed them to us from time to time."

"Why does—did—she have possession of them?"

The girls exchanged looks. No one spoke. I sat on the bed, resisting the urge to lie down. Once I moved to a prone position, my eyes might snap shut and I'd be fast asleep.

"Because she took them," Nettie said finally. "She told us we had to share with her. She said we were like her sisters, and sisters are obliged to share, and then she took them."

"But if she said you were to share, then you must have her possessions as well." I folded down my sheet and spread the wool blanket over my bed.

"No, miss. I don't have anything of hers." Rufina shook her head emphatically.

"Nor do I," added Nettie.

"Me, neither, and Adela told all of us that Selina took her hair ribbon," said Rose as she slipped into her bed and pulled the covers up into a neat horizon under her arms.

"She got so angry." Rufina sighed and wiped a spot of blood off her elbow with the hem of her gown. Her covers were already halfway off the bed.

"Who got angry?" I fought to concentrate, but the lure of sleep tugged at me.

"Adela did. She and Selina started pulling each other's hair." Rose added a dismissive roll of her eyes.

Oh dear. I was reminded that their quarrel had gotten so heated as to become violent. Did Waverly know that? If so, he might suspect Adèle. Perhaps that was why he wanted to talk with her.

As I struggled with this disturbing line of thought, the girls again gave each other sideways looks. As if reaching a consensus, Nettie said, "Miss Eyre, are there really ghosts?"

Before I could answer, Rose said, "We're worried that Selina will come haunt us." Her lower lip trembled.

"Don't be silly!" Rufina guffawed. "There is no such thing as a ghost! What gooses you two are!"

"Geese," I corrected her. "The plural of goose is geese. Come here, girls." I patted my mattress, and with no more urging, they tumbled onto my bed.

Another adult might dismiss their fears out of hand, but I knew better. When I was but ten, I saw a beam of light, complete with dancing motes where no ray should have entered. This came with sound I was confident portended a visitation from my dead uncle. To this day, I remembered the experience of raw terror, a sensation too vivid to allow me to make jest of my young charges or their similar concern.

"Although Christ our Savior rose again, I have heard naught

of other people rising from the grave. The creed tells us this will happen when Christ comes again to judge the quick and the dead. Until that time, I am sure we are safe." I paused and added, "From Selina's return."

They huddled together, clinging one to another as if shipwreck victims. Their bleak expressions told me they found my explanation hard to credit.

"Selina would come back. I know she would. It would be just like her to come and scare us," Rose said.

Nettie's eyes widened. "Mrs. Thurston says Selina died in her sleep, and I know that it happens to bad girls all the time. But I do not want to die! I am so sorry for all I have done! I am a sinner and I am afraid!" With that, she burst into noisy sobs.

I took her into my arms and patted her back. "There, there. It's all right," I half whispered to her.

The other girls stared at me in surprise. Was it possible that Mrs. Thurston forbade affection between teachers and their pupils?

Rufina guessed my concern. "Mrs. Webster was awful kind to us, but Mrs. Thurston, well, she don't think the teachers should spoil us overmuch."

"I see," I said. And I did. Some superintendents believed such attention would ruin children, but the lessons of my childhood remained perfectly clear in my mind. A bit of kindness went a long way with me then, as it did now. I couldn't see how comforting a frightened child could be wrong.

As Nettie dried her tears, the others girls snuggled closer to me. This past spring, a wild dog gave birth to puppies in our shed. Her babies writhed and wriggled their way, following the comma of her body, until they believed themselves to be safe. So, too, did the girls attach themselves to me.

"There, there," I whispered, gathering them in my arms. "No ghost can bother you. Neither can any human while I am here. And if you hear anything, come wake me. Now, time to say your prayers. After you do, I shall tuck all of you in."

Making the rounds of the beds, I plumped pillows for the girls, tucked them in, and gave each a quick peck on her forehead. Rose reached up to grab my collar. Her small fingers gripped me. "Miss Eyre?" She pulled me close. "You will not let Selina hurt me, will you? She was awful mean to me, just awful."

"No, lamb. I will not let her hurt you. Close your eyes. I'll be here if you need me."

"Do you promise? Promise she will not hurt me." Her moist, hot breath warmed my face.

"I promise," I said, and I crossed my heart, wondering if I could, indeed, protect these girls. My intentions were good; I could shout for help and warn off an intruder.

But would that be enough?

Worry is no substitute for action, so I made yet another circuit of the beds, tucking in covers for young women now nearly asleep, before concluding my journey by checking on Adèle. I wandered back to my bed but stopped along the way, where the moonlight streamed through the window, illuminating the empty bed that had been Selina's.

Who was she?

Why had she died?

The branch of the horse chestnut rubbed against the side of the house, making a scratching sound. Cupping my hands around my face, I stared until I could see the outstretched limb. What a fine step stool it made! Broad, rough, and horizontal. Climbing out on it would be easy.

I rested my elbows on the sill, wondering if Mr. Douglas's watcher lurked in the bushes below.

Who was out there in the shadows?

A killer?

This same lunar light beamed down on Ferndean. I knew from experience that it bathed my husband's stern features as it slipped past the window dressings. I would often awake to study my husband as he slept. How far away Edward seemed—and yet, strangely, how close to me, as each beat of my heart matched his in a lovers' duet.

"Sleep tight, my darlings," I whispered, touching my fingertips to my lips and sending a kiss to my husband and Ned. Then I climbed into my cot, which proved uncomfortable, especially after the luxurious, cloudlike mattress at Lucy Brayton's home. It seemed there was a lump in this bed. I tried to get comfortable, and mainly I failed. Once, I was nearly asleep, but startled awake to the sound of footsteps outside the dormitory door. Before I could rouse, they went away, leaving me to study the softly snoring forms of my charges. Each snuffle and sigh prickled my senses into high alert. Would an intruder dare visit us? If so, could I scare him or her away? I wouldn't sleep through an attack . . . would I?

Gradually, a heaviness weighed down my limbs pleasantly. At last I slept.

Chapter 25

Sometime later, Adèle rooted around in her covers, making enough noise to awaken me.

"Adèle?" I slipped from my bed to hers. "It is I, Jane Eyre."

"Oh, mademoiselle! *Mon Dieu*, I am so happy! So, so happy! How I have missed you." She peppered me with kisses and hugged me with all her might. Lucy had been quite correct in saying that Adèle had lost weight, I noticed as the child bumped against my bruises. Despite my best efforts to stay silent, the pressure on my black eye proved too much and I moaned with pain as Adèle's head bumped mine.

"You are hurt? Oh, your face."

"Just a fall at the coaching inn. Nothing more," I said. "Now shhhh. The others are sleeping."

"Others? Ah, I am not at home? Not back at Thornfield? This is but a dream?" Her voice trembled.

"We are both at Alderton House. I am here to watch over you." I slipped my hand into hers and gave hers a squeeze. "I have taken a position as your German teacher."

"And our proctor? You will be our proctor?"

"Yes. I shall be sleeping in this dormitory each night."

She propped herself on one elbow. "So that was not a dream, either, was it? Selina is dead, is she not?"

Before I could stop her, Adèle tumbled out of her bed, hit the floor hard, bounced to her feet, and ran to the empty bed, whimpering, "Selina!" as she threw herself against the pallet.

"Stop, you must stop!" I grabbed at Adèle. I did not want the others to awaken. Not until I could coach Adèle in her new role.

Rose sat up in her bed and looked around with unseeing eyes, then settled back to sleep. Nettie whimpered, and Rufina mumbled.

"She is dead," Adèle sobbed.

"Shhh! Adèle, you must be quiet. You will wake the other girls. Yes, Selina is dead and there's nothing to be done but to keep her in your prayers."

Adèle turned to me, wide-eyed and wild. "She was cold, mademoiselle! So cold! I tried to wake her. I tried and tried, but she wouldn't get up, and her skin was—"

"Do not think about it. Do not!"

Adèle commenced to crying in earnest. "Mama went away, too. To the Holy Virgin. I remember when they came and told me she was gone—never to return. I cried and cried."

I said nothing. Adèle's mother Céline Varens was not dead. She had run away to Italy, leaving her child with her landlord and his wife, who had told Adèle her mother had died, rather than betray her unnatural act. Though not the girl's father, Edward had taken charge of Adèle and thought it better not to correct her rather than admit to the loving daughter that her own mother had abandoned her.

Adèle continued to wail. "Now I shall never see Selina or Mama again! And it is all because I am wicked. A wicked, wicked child. That is what Miss Jones says about me. And Mrs. Thurston says I have an imp inside me!"

"You are not wicked." I pulled Adèle closer to me. She

wrapped her thin little arms around me and buried her face in my neck, sobbing for all she was worth. Rocking her back and forth, I did my best to calm her.

"I know you well. It is not in your nature to harbor ill will toward anyone. Selina is dead; that is so. But you are not the cause. Trust me."

"What about Mr. Rochester? My *bon ami*? Why has he not visited me? Is it because you two are married? He must hate me, because he sent me here and he has not written me in ages! Neither have you!"

"When did you last hear from us?"

"Years ago!"

"Years ago? Think carefully, Adèle," I cautioned her. I knew her predilection for exaggeration.

"Before Easter last."

I nodded. That was only about six months ago, not nearly "years ago." The timing would coincide with Mrs. Webster's departure and Mrs. Thurston's arrival.

The full import of my situation struck me: I could not now tell her about our son. Not yet. She would be too happy about our new life, her new "sibling"—and she would want to tell her friends, tell everyone. That would ruin my plans. If I left things as they stood, I could continue this charade. But I would have to ask her not to talk about my marriage to her *bon ami*.

The necessary duplicity saddened me immensely. I hated keeping the truth from Adèle.

But what choice did I have?

"I am here now, dear child. You know I care for you, don't you? Else why would I be here?"

"Y-yes," she admitted.

I believe I can be forgiven if a few of my tears mingled with hers. My longing for Edward leapt up inside me, as powerful and as electric as a sudden summer storm. The thought of my baby, Ned, caused my arms to throb with the ache of longing. My throat tightened with emotion.

I rocked my old student in my arms, amazed at how her shoulder blades protruded through her night dress. "Sh, sh, sh," I repeated as she refused to let go of me. Exhaustion swept over me, and finally, I decided to carry her to my bed.

"Hush now." I tucked her in and crawled on top of the covers, beside her. Her arms wound tightly around me the way a sweet pea vine grips a lattice. There we lay, two weary travelers clinging to each other. What was I doing here? Why didn't I take Adèle and run? What had happened to Selina was not our concern, was it? I had nothing to offer the other children. Nothing.

We could hold on until tomorrow. At the dawn, we would dress and gather our things. I would march downstairs and announce my true identity to Mrs. Thurston. Despite her apologies, which I expected would be copious, we would turn our backs on Alderton House. With Adèle's hand in mine, we would skip down the street to Lucy Brayton's house. I would put this godforsaken school behind us, safeguarding what was dear to me.

With that plan of action firmly in mind, I dozed off. As did Adèle.

Chapter 26

❦

I awakened well before dawn. A voice soothed a whining child in the next room over. Miss Miller must have been roused by one of her charges in the Infant dormitory.

My arm tingled as I pulled it out from under Adèle. Despite the movement, she didn't wake up. That was fine; she still had time to sleep. I climbed out of bed and hurried behind the modesty screen to dress. Remembering how God told Jeremiah to gird his loins before meeting his enemies, I spent extra time neatening my hair and pinched a bit of color into my cheeks. The swelling in my eye provided its own rainbow hues, but that could not be helped. As the sun began to chase away the dark, a mockingbird sang outside our window, his song so glorious that my spirits lifted despite how little sleep I'd gotten the night before.

I folded my nightclothes, putting these articles and the rest of my things back into the empty pillow casing, to make it easy to leave. Although I moved quietly, my industry awakened Adèle from her slumber. Rubbing sleep from her eyes, she blinked twice and stared at me, squinting.

"*Mademoiselle! C'est vraiment vous?*" She bounced upright in the bed and nearly shouted with joy, her childlike voice speaking in rapid French.

I knelt by her side and hugged her tightly. She smelled of warmth, sleep, and the faintly sour odor of childish sweat. "Shh, darling child. Don't wake the others. Not yet!" I said in her native language.

"You did come! You did!" She burrowed her head against me. "I thought it was a dream!"

I brushed aside her tousled locks so that I could look her in the eyes. "Listen to me. This is important. Very important."

"La," she said. "You are here. That is what is important. I must tell my friends. Girls—"

"Shh! Not yet. We must talk first. You must answer me as honestly as you can."

Who had threatened her? I needed to know before I confronted Maude Thurston with the note. Did the threat to Adèle play a part in Selina's death? Were both girls targeted by a killer? If I could discover this before we took our leave of Alderton House, I could pass the information on to Mr. Douglas. I would have secured justice for Adèle and done the other girls a service.

"Mr. Rochester and I received your letter. You had written *au secours* on it. Why did you ask for help? What prompted your request?"

"I wanted him to come for me! I am so unhappy here! Mrs. Webster was kind, but Mrs. Thurston does not like me! She makes me write Bible verses because I twirl and dance and sing like my mama did."

"I see. And the other teachers? Are they kind to you?" I needed to get at the threatening note, but the roundabout way often worked best with Adèle. Besides, I couldn't risk her being frightened. That might cause her to expose me and, therefore, to endanger all her friends. I would start with a general summary of the atmosphere.

"They are all awful! Miss Miller is a rainy cloud. All the time, sad and dreary, but she is not mean," Adèle said. "Signora Delgatto stamps her foot when I don't pay attention. She smacked my fingers with a ruler. But one time only. Fräulein Hertzog is gone; she was not here for long, but I miss her because she could speak French as fast as I do."

"When did Fräulein Hertzog leave?" I wondered if it was possible that, for some reason unknown, she had written the threat to Adèle.

"A month ago. And Miss Jones smiles all the time, even when she is angry. That makes her very dangerous, I believe."

"How about the servants?"

"Cook is ever so nice. She knows I miss croissants, and she sometimes buys them for me when she goes to market. She says that even though I am a Frenchie, I am a luv. Emma does not talk much to any of us."

I imagined not. From what I had seen, the maid of all work toiled unceasingly. In fact, I wondered if the girl got more than four hours of sleep a night. Although such servants were common in private households, only a cheapskate like Mrs. Thurston would expect one small girl to clean, polish, mend, and serve an entire school population.

"And Caje? Is that not the name of the young man who works here? How does he act toward you?"

"He does not like to talk."

"And the other students?"

"I like most of the Juniors. With the Seniors, well, Selina, she told everyone what to do. She decided if the Seniors would be mean. Or nice. They were all scared of her. I do not care. Not much."

"How are they mean?" I asked, wondering what a ten-year-old girl considered cruel.

"They tease and they pinch and they tell tales."

"All of them? All of the time?"

She considered this. "No. *Comme ci comme ça.* It might be

different now. Sometimes Rufina is bossy. Sometimes Nettie is a big crybaby. Rose pushes me out of the way. She wants everyone to look at her, all the time."

"How did Selina act toward you?"

"Bah, she was the worst. Always calling me names. Always teasing me and pulling my hair." She stopped a minute and thought. I did not interrupt. "Now they might be nicer. Truly they might."

"Was she unkind to only you?"

"No. To all of us. To everyone. All of us girls. And to Emma. And to Caje. She teased and she hit us and she stole—" Adèle's voice became louder as she warmed to her subject.

"Shhh," I warned my little friend. Rufina sat up on one elbow, rubbed her eyes, looked around without really focusing, and lay back down, pulling her covers over her head.

"But Mrs. Thurston liked Selina best. So she could do anything she wanted. Anything!" With that, Adèle realized, "But she is gone, is she not? She is dead!"

I took her hands in mine. "Yes. She is dead. Let us pray that her soul rests in peace."

"But it doesn't! I know it won't! She will come back to haunt us! She will sneak around and grab us when we sleep! That's what she will do! I know it!"

Adèle started to sob.

Chapter 27

"Did anyone threaten you?" I finally asked. "Anyone at all?"

"Yes, yes, all the time."

"In writing?"

She tore her hands away from mine and jumped out of bed. At her dresser, she opened a drawer, rummaged around, and withdrew two pieces of paper, both of similar weight and type as the threatening note in my pocket. One message said, "You and your French people should perish from the earth! Death to all of them! *Toi aussi!*"

The other bore this message: "You should be sent to the guillotine! *Ta tête* will roll in a puddle of blood!"

I gasped out loud. "Did you show these to anyone?"

"Only to Mrs. Thurston. She said I was trying to make trouble. But I wasn't!"

I would not stand for this. Someone would pay, and pay dearly. But who? While Miss Miller had said no one here spoke French well, these scraps of phrases were elementary, neither extensive nor complicated. Anyone, even the children, could have written them.

Fräulein Hertzog might even have penned them before she left.

"You must . . ." I stopped and thought better of what I planned to say. I started again. "You and I are going to play a game, Adèle. When you have something important to say, speak to me only in French at all times. *Français seulement, d'accord?* Also, do not go anywhere alone. Stay with the other girls in a group. Like a flock of birds. Always. Can you do that?"

Her face tilted to one side and she regarded me with intense curiosity. "Mademoiselle, that is a very odd game!"

"Yes, I know. I ask because it is essential. Can you trust me?"

I intended for us to leave after breakfast. Lucy would not be up until after ten. That would give me several hours to see what I might learn about Selina's death—and perhaps to collect enough information to confront Mrs. Thurston. I intended to speak my mind at last. Although I planned to remove Adèle, I would not leave without letting the superintendent know I found her methods reprehensible—and I would insist she punish the author of the threatening notes to Adèle.

A bell rang, signaling time for all to rise.

"Go tidy up your bed," I instructed her. "Remember? French only."

"*Mais certainement,*" she said, and she threw her arms around me and gave me a kiss.

I turned my attention to gathering the teaching materials Miss Miller had brought me the night before, as I aimed to return them to her.

The girls slowly pulled themselves out of the cocoons they'd made of their covers. They stood around their beds, yawning and stretching. Reluctantly, they dunked their hands in the cold basins of water. Finally, when it could be avoided no longer, they splashed their faces with the water.

Nettie turned her back to me; the straps of her night rail

slipped down over her thin shoulders and exposed a portion of her spine.

To my horror, four dark red stripes marred her flesh. The scabs were long and thin, crisscrossing one another, with bruised skin on either side. They had healed, but they were angry.

She'd been struck with a cane.

My hand flew to my mouth, as I choked back my inclination to cry out loud.

Who had beaten Nettie? And why? How could such a timid creature have aroused such anger? Did Mrs. Thurston condone corporal punishment?

I should have to find out. This could not be ignored.

"Adèle?" I asked her in French to come over near me, then I queried her gently. Had anyone ever hit her? Did she know if the school allowed caning?

"*Mais non*," she said, giving me a look of pure bewilderment.

I sent her back to finish making her bed.

Who had administered the caning? Of course, Mrs. Thurston was at the helm. But was she culpable? The question niggled.

I had never seen value in corporal punishment. However, many of my colleagues relied upon such strong inducements. They quoted the Biblical axiom that sparing the rod would spoil the child. Since teachers served in *loco parentis*, that is, in the place of parents, our mandate included delivering both punishment and praise.

But the marks on Nettie were beyond the scope of light corrections. Weeping canals that cut so deeply into the flesh could only be the result of an unrestrained application of force.

When I thought of the fury that must have accompanied such a whipping, my stomach turned. What manner of "crime" could be deserving of such punishment? Had Nettie forgotten an assignment? Or neglected to pay heed during a lesson? Or chattered when she should have been silent?

Paltry misdemeanors, indeed.

As I reined in my emotions, the girls went about their morning rituals. Rufina grumbled at Rose. "You splashed water on my coverlet."

"Did not." Rose turned to face her accuser.

The bell rang again, causing the girls to put a bit of snap into their steps. They helped one another tie their pinafores. They stood for one another's inspection. In quick order, they queued to go downstairs.

I fell in step behind the girls, my mind turning all this new information over and over. The urge to let Mrs. Thurston know she'd offended the wife of Mr. Edward Rochester, Esquire, was keen, but a new sense of purpose had snuffed out that fire and replaced it with a frosty resolve. What would such a revelation gain me? A few morsels of satisfaction?

It would not help these girls at all!

The desire to humiliate that awful harpy faded next to the need to expose the truth.

No, wait, I scolded myself. *Think this through carefully.*

My best option would be to circumvent Maude Thurston entirely. I could gather my proof and present my findings to Lady Kingsley. That would put me in a position to demand Maude Thurston's dismissal!

But what if she was the killer? If it was Maude Thurston who killed Selina Biltmore, a dismissal might give her a credible reason to flee London. If she disappeared into the countryside, she might never be forced to pay for her crimes. I slowed my steps as I pondered this new insight. I could not expose these other wrongdoings until I also could prove the identity of the murderer.

Before I approached Lady Kingsley, I needed to find out who wrote the threats, who caned Nettie, and who murdered

Selina Biltmore. I owed this to the girls. My plan to leave with Adèle dissolved as an unaccustomed ferocity grew within me. I would protect these girls. I had to!

As if she knew what I was thinking, Adèle rewarded me with a quick hug as we paused at the first-floor landing. Nettie followed suit. Rose reached for my hand, squeezed it, and mumbled, "I'm awfully glad you're here, miss."

Rufina mumbled, "Me, too."

Rose stared up at me, her eyes full of trust. "Will you stay, miss? You won't leave like Fräulein did? She ran off in the middle of the night!"

"I shall stay as long as I am needed."

I meant every word.

There was more wrongdoing afoot than the threat that had initiated my visit. Something evil had begun. Its hunger was not satisfied by one girl's death. Someone had struck a child's tender flesh. Taking full advantage of Mrs. Thurston's blind eye, a malevolent force had wormed its way into the very marrow of this school.

Was this a manifestation of the superintendent's own character? Or something more sinister and alien? I had to seek out its origins so I could weed it from this fertile soil.

Each step brought me closer to Mrs. Thurston and a decision.

Should I or should I not reveal my true identity?

Chapter 28

Prayers began promptly at six thirty in the dining room as a prelude to breakfast. I followed the girls, but once I crossed the threshold, Miss Parthena Jones motioned to me to join the teachers at the head of the table. I took a seat between Miss Jones and Miss Miller. Mrs. Thurston sat to Nan Miller's right.

Toast soldiers stood at attention in silver toast racks. The yeasty fragrance of the fresh bread caused my mouth to water and my belly to rumble with hunger. Generous pots of jam, cheese, and butter also decorated the white tablecloth.

Chairs scraped as girls took their assigned places. We opened the Book of Common Prayer. Mrs. Thurston mumbled her way through Psalm 119, as well as the first and the second lesson.

When Mrs. Thurston finished, all of us waited expectantly to hear what the woman would say.

"We shall all observe strictest mourning for our departed friend, Selina Biltmore," she said. "Her remains will be returned here to Alderton House. Tonight during your quiet time, the dressmaker will measure each student for her white clothing, as is appropriate when a child passes. Teachers, I've instructed the dressmaker to measure each of you for white dresses in a suitable fabric. You will also be expected to purchase mourning shoes. As I speak, Emma covers the mirrors and windows. During this time, I expect all of you to act with proper seriousness and decorum."

Mrs. Thurston started to sit, glancing around as she did. Miss Miller jerked her chin in my direction and mouthed, "Introduction?" With that, the superintendent froze halfway to her seat, and added, "Miss Eyre joins us to teach German and sketching."

No words of welcome accompanied this pronouncement, nor was I asked to stand and greet the group. Perhaps Maude Thurston believed that Miss Miller had introduced me the night before. Or perhaps her rudeness knew no bounds. I thought it the latter.

The aroma of breakfast grew more tantalizing with every second. How different this was from Lowood, where the scent of bad food caused our stomachs to turn even as they rumbled with hunger! Although Miss Miller had warned me that life at Alderton House would be different, in no way did her comments prepare me for the continuing surprise of bounteous spreads of food.

Struggling with the weight of a heavy tray, Emma first brought in teapots of steaming tea and pitchers of milk, cool with foam on top. The girls took turns pouring tea for their schoolmates, and at last serving themselves. The students' manners rivaled those of the gentry, holding the cups just so, pinkie fingers extended. Stirring the tea without splashing or making noise. Passing the sugar and cream to one another. When necessary, lifting snow-white damask serviettes from their laps and dabbing at their mouths.

Miss Miller's plate overflowed with delicacies, and great portions disappeared faster than I could imagine. I sipped my tea and watched my old colleague out of the corner of my eye. She chewed contentedly, staring silently at her plate.

So this was how the wealthy schoolgirls lived. Coddled and cosseted.

A superintendent might budget the needs of her pantry in a lavish manner, while actually serving nearly inedible food. I expected similar economies from Mrs. Thurston. Her acceptance of Lucy's "sponsorship" and the meager salary she offered me proved the woman's avarice.

But Mrs. Thurston was shrewder than I'd credited. By delivering well-fed girls to their families, Mrs. Thurston prepared her students for the marriage market, where well-rounded figures were a badge of desirability. From the looks of it, she settled on a strategy: "Feed the girls and please the parents."

"Manners, Elspeth," warned Miss Jones, as a girl from Miss Miller's Infants' group reached across the table for a pitcher of milk.

The child withdrew her hand abruptly and apologized. Other students flinched with obvious distress. Miss Jones smiled at the girls. "Remember, Miss Eyre has just joined us. We all want to make the right impression."

What is the right impression? Especially since I saw your schoolmate dead and cold on a stretcher?

That led me to wonder, was Miss Jones as aware of the danger as Miss Miller and I? I needed to ask. But what if we shouldn't trust Miss Jones? What if *she* was the murderer?

My mind traversed broad circles, following each idea around and around. In short order, I found myself suspecting everyone I had met at Alderton House except the elderly Signora Delgatto.

Was there any benefit to my staying? What if it had truly been a random act? If so, it might be impossible to trace the killer's actions.

This will never do! You must seek out information and have a reason for your thinking, I admonished myself.

I set down the bread I was eating and massaged my temples. Despite my various scenarios, I could not shake a deep conviction that Selina had been the target all along.

If what I'd learned about the girl was correct, there was no shortage of possible killers!

Chapter 29

More morning prayers and singing followed breakfast. The sound of Rose's pure soprano brought me back to the melancholy of the day. The sweet intonations of her voice dipped and soared and created a sacred space, a reminder that heaven awaited all of us.

As we left the dining room to start our school day, the girls elbowed one another, vying for the chance to take my hand. Adèle pouted when Rufina usurped her accustomed place.

"She is my mademoiselle. Mine." Adèle gave Rufina a rough push with her shoulder. Rufina, sturdy as the crossbeam in a roof, absorbed the blow and carried on, never loosening her grip on me.

I paused and whispered in French, "Adèle, I shall always be 'your mademoiselle.' However, right now you have to share me." This reassurance brought on a dismissive Gallic shrug and a stomp of her foot.

"I am so glad you have come, miss," said Nettie.

Unable to compete with Rufina and Adèle for my hand,

Nettie contented herself with wrapping her fingers around the trailing end of my shawl. Rose held herself apart and walked a bit ahead of us, but an occasional glance over her shoulder proved she, too, wished to stay close.

I found these gestures touching, and the girls' affection fortified my intention to see that they were safe. Together the children and I climbed the stairs to the classrooms.

I bid the Seniors good-bye as they went to their first class. Since I had decided to stay, I needed to prepare for the German lessons, so I carried the primer and a notebook under my arm as I searched for a quiet room.

The music room was unoccupied. There the pianoforte took pride of place, guarded by a gaggle of black music stands. Sinking into a comfortable wing back chair, I began flipping through the German text. The door opened and in walked Signora Delgatto with a group of Juniors ready to take their piano lessons.

"Stay. Please stay. My students are very talented." The morning light cruelly highlighted the woman's age-ravaged face, and she smelled strongly of unwashed hair. Walking was very hard for her, and she limped her way across the music room slowly, awkwardly. It was impossible to imagine her breaking into the school, climbing two flights of stairs, and subduing a student.

"I would enjoy remaining to listen. However, I must prepare to teach my classes. Another time, perhaps?" With that I carried my German primer up to the Senior dormitory.

I sat on my cot and tried to concentrate, but Emma showed up to empty the washbasins and slop jars. Her small frame was at odds with the heavy job, but her approach to her work spoke of efficiency. I paused to watch her, thinking of how few options were open to young women, especially those of a less fortunate station.

"Sorry to bother you, miss," she said, noting my attention

but misreading my thoughts. "If I don't get this done now, Mrs. Thurston will not be happy. I have got hers, the Infants', and the Juniors' yet to clean. Also I am supposed to strip Selina's bed and take everything down to the laundry."

"Yes, of course." I bent my head to the German text. But only for a moment. I realized that Emma probably observed more interactions than any other denizen of the school. "Emma, what was Selina Biltmore like?"

The serving girl froze midway through yanking the sheet from the bed next to me. As she tugged it, a puff of white dust flew up, swirled around, and finally settled lightly on the wooden planks of the floor, like a fresh falling of snow.

Bath powder. Selina liked her luxuries.

Except that most powders featured floral fragrances, and this had none, at least none that I could detect.

"Emma?" I prodded the maid. With her back still to me, her posture went rigid as a red deer in the forest. Twisting toward me, her eyes wore an anxious look. "Miss?"

"I wondered what you thought of her. Selina Biltmore."

"It ain't my place to say." She turned away, knelt down, and wiped the powder from the floor around Selina's bed.

"But you must have formed an impression. Did she get along with the other girls?"

Emma paused with a rag in one hand. The white powder had mixed with water from the bucket to form a pastelike slurry. Slowly, Emma dunked the rag in the bucket, then wrung it out, hard. "I couldn't rightly say."

"I heard she took their belongings."

Emma scratched her head, scanned the room, and picked up her bucket. "I might have heard something like that, too."

"Was she kind to them? To you?"

She had missed mopping up a bit of the powder, but that did not matter. Not really.

This provoked a stronger response. Emma's eyes narrowed

and her mouth flattened into a thin, straight line. "I can't say as how she was."

"Would you call her cruel? I ask only because I sense she was not well liked, and I wonder why. The girls were frightened last night. They seemed to fear that Selina would come back to haunt them."

Emma's face moved through a variety of emotions. I held my breath.

"The others were scared of her. I guess it don't change just because you're dead, does it? I mean, she weren't any better than she should have been. Because she had this wonderful hair, and she were a little older, see, she knew how to get her way. With the littler girls especially."

I nodded. "I grew up in a charitable institution. I saw how certain girls bullied their classmates. Perhaps Selina did the same."

"Be careful what you say, miss." Emma lowered her voice and glanced at the partly open door. "Selina was Mrs. Thurston's special pet. You don't want to get on Mrs. Thurston's bad side. Now, if you don't mind, I best be about my business." With that she started dumping, rinsing, and wiping in a fit of furious activity.

Emma was warning me, trying to help me—and the oddity of the situation did not escape me. Here I was, the wife of a squire, being cautioned by a serving girl about getting on the bad side of a lowly superintendent. Instead of worrying about pleasing Mrs. Thurston, I could be at home, in Ferndean, the mistress of my own hearth.

That small amount of powder left on the floor bothered me. It struck me as just one more bit of unfinished business. Grabbing a damp towel from near my washbasin, I marched over and started to mop up the thin film of white dust. My curiosity—a faculty that can be both blessing and curse—got the better of me. Wetting a fingertip, I touched it to the powder. Cautiously, I brought it closer to my nose. Try as I might,

I could still detect no fragrance, and the consistency of it was not slick the way bath powder usually is.

How odd!

Nothing about this place or its occupants conformed to any logical premise. I fought an impulse to toss down the book of German, grab Adèle by the hand, and march out of this wretched warehouse for abandoned children. Worse of all, I had abandoned my own son in order to help a group of girls who were strangers to me.

I should leave.

I should.

Bruce Douglas's words ran through my head. How would I hold my head high if I turned away from these children? Especially now that they eagerly put such trust in me? What if one of them had been my own flesh and blood? Would I choose differently then?

Emma pulled another chamber pot from under a bed, her thin arms bowed under the weight of the porcelain jug and its contents. Her dress hung on her thin frame. Her shoulder blades protruded through the fabric of her apron.

"How old are you, Emma?" I asked.

Continuing her steady efforts, she sighed and said, "I'll be sixteen at the end of the year, ma'am."

Fifteen. Barely any older than most of the Senior girls.

If the killer targeted young women, this poor child was at risk, too.

I had to stay. At least for a while. The ache of homesickness was fleeting, but the blotch on my soul would remain forever if I turned my back on this situation.

I wondered if my son had noticed his mama was gone. I wondered how Mrs. Fairfax was getting along. Of late, she'd wound down, moved more slowly, like a tired clock with little energy left in its spring. And Edward? How was my husband doing? Had he taken Mr. Carter's advice and rested? Was his eye improving? Did he miss me as much as I did him?

With any luck, I would return home in a day or two. Surely it would not take long for the police to find Selina's murderer. How difficult could it be?

Think, Jane! This is but a problem to solve. Put your mind to it. How can you help discover who killed Selina? Why was she killed? If the murder was not random, there must have been a reason, an inciting incident. Perhaps if you found that event, it would point to the culprit.

First I would need to learn more about Selina.

How? Interviewing each person increased the risk of my exposure. Even Emma seemed cautious when I asked her questions.

There had to be a better way.

I could assign the Seniors an essay to test their German skills. The subject would be their friend Selina. They would write down their thoughts so I could see their skill level—and share their notes with Mr. Douglas.

With a plan in place, my thoughts circled back to Edward. Mrs. Thurston expressly forbade me to correspond with him, but her authority meant nothing to me. I would write him and give the letter to Lucy to mail. Even though he was joining me soon, and realizing that the letter might not arrive before he left Ferndean, I knew he could enjoy it later—and writing it would go a long way toward helping me sort through my thoughts. With that intention, I put pen to paper, but the distraction of Emma's industry caused my mind to stray.

In desperation, I pulled the modesty screen around me. The resulting privacy pleased me even though the lump in my bed still confounded all my attempts at comfort. My makeshift "walls" allowed me to block out my environment. At length, Emma's footfalls told me she had quitted the room. However, the screen provided me a sense of separation from my surroundings. With my mind freed of these restrictions, I wrote:

Dearest Husband,

I hope this finds you well. I trust that you are taking care to rest for the sake of your vision.

I miss you more than words can express. At night, I reach for you and when I discover—alas!—I am alone, I think my heart will burst with pain. I miss our conversations, our daily rituals, and of course, I miss your affection. It is comforting to think that you will be here in London soon.

When I came to visit Adèle, I was surprised to see that Nan Miller, a teacher from Lowood, now serves here as head teacher. One would think that should alleviate our fears, but I admit the situation perplexes me. The new superintendent, Mrs. Thurston, is not the sort of woman who sets the proper tone for a school. Because we met under trying circumstances, I struggle to be fair to her. However, so far she has failed to impress me.

Complications abound. The choice of replacement for Mrs. Webster is but one problem. The other problem—and I hesitate to tell you lest you be unduly alarmed—involves the death of a schoolgirl.

Right now Adèle is not at risk. If the situation changes, rest assured that I shall take the necessary actions to secure her safety and well-being.

Please let Ned know that his mother misses him terribly.

All my love—
Your Jane

P.S. Tell Mrs. Fairfax she was right. Next time I shall take heed of her suggestions regarding the importance of fashionable clothing when one is in London. Perhaps Lucy and I shall go shopping while I am here.

I folded the paper and tucked it inside my bodice. The note succeeded in making me feel closer to Edward, but it also brought a pang of guilt. Was I really that confident that Adèle was safe?

And then the concern that I had pushed to the back of my mind demanded my attention: What on earth was I going to do about the missing Rochester diamonds?

Chapter 30

The bell rang and I descended the stairs to start my duties as a teacher. One by one, the Juniors filed past me, heads up and shoulders rolled back, their erect posture guaranteed by the backboards they wore. My five students took their spots on the benches in the lecture room. I asked them to introduce themselves while I took note of their names.

Elizabeth Morrow was the Junior head girl, her intelligent eyes at odds with her squirrel-like inflated cheeks. Mary Tolliver squirmed in her seat, unable to keep her spindly frame still as she twirled a curl of yellow hair around and around her finger. Winifred Dalton-James seemed a jolly sort, whose bright smile rarely wavered. Victoria Falmouth wore a sad frown under a sprinkling of freckles. Patience Chesterfield sat like two stone blocks, set one over the other, solid and thick, broken up only by a tumbling mane of dark hair.

The German primers sat on the bookcase near the front desk. I asked Elizabeth to pass them out, then I instructed the girls to get their slates ready.

The last girl in the row, Patience, stared at me with empty hands and a bovine placidity.

"Are we missing one?" I asked as the predictable cloud of chalk dust settled. The wet stone–like scent of the girls' blackboards filled the air as they steadied them on their laps.

Elizabeth said, "Ma'am? I bet Selina put her book in her dresser."

"But she wasn't in your form. So how do you know this?"

"Everyone knows what Selina was like, miss!" said Mary. "Selina hated Fräulein Hertzog and hated German, too. She was always hiding books from the teachers. Because we all use the same books, we were always one short. But it is all right, Miss Eyre. Patience can have mine. Winnie and I can share."

Mary handed hers to Patience, scooted closer to Winnie, and took ahold of one side of the textbook's cover.

"If Selina hid the German textbook, where might it be?" I asked.

"She usually kept textbooks in her dresser under her things. It's probably still there, next to that bottle of perfume she liked and that bath powder. The one that smelled like camellias. Fräulein Hertzog would send her out of class to get her book. Selina would take her time and visit the kitchen or wander about."

"She liked to steal biscuits from the larder. But she wasn't the only one who did. Cook got awful angry but could not stop her," Patience chimed in, speaking so slowly I wanted to nap between words.

The other student, Victoria, remained silent and stared straight ahead during this cataloging of Selina's misbehavior.

When I gave the children a sentence to translate, and the *skritch-skritch-skritch* of chalk on the boards accompanied the students' efforts, Victoria continued to sit quietly. Catching my eyes on her, she said, "I can't write. It's my hand, you see," and she held up her right arm and pushed up her sleeve to display a white wrapping.

"What happened to you?" I asked.

Sly glances flew from one student to another. One snickered.

"I got hurt."

"Yes, but how?"

"I got bitten." She paused and held up two fingers on her left hand. "Twice."

"Bitten? By that cat in the kitchen?"

"No, Miss Eyre. Old Mephisto stays with Cook. He bites and scratches everyone but her and us girls. I got bit by a person."

"You say a person? Goodness. Who was it?"

Victoria dropped her head to examine the tucks on her pinafore before mumbling something.

"Pardon?" I asked. "What did you say?"

Her bench mate Patience sent Victoria an expression of sympathy. Behind her tablet she grabbed Victoria's uninjured hand and squeezed. It was only for a second, but the flesh-to-flesh contact seemed to bolster Victoria's spirits.

"Selina did it to her, miss," said Patience, slowly.

Victoria's lower lip trembled. "Selina got mad and bit me. And then she bit me again. For good measure."

"Oh my!" In my years of teaching, I'd never heard of children older than infants biting one another. "I'm sure Mrs. Thurston had something to say about that!"

Elizabeth rested a fist on her hip and harrumphed, sounding more like a parent than an eleven-year-old girl. "Nothing happened to her! Nothing ever did! Selina never got punished! She was Mrs. Thurston's favorite!"

The head girl rolled her eyes and screwed her mouth into a moue of disgust. Now the cork was out of the bottle, and Elizabeth had plenty to say. "Mrs. Thurston thought Selina made the sun come up in the morning and the moon glow at night, she did. Selina was her favorite for sure. She could get away with anything. Because she had a special friend."

"Selina had a special friend?" I repeated. Finally, a piece of information worth sharing with Mr. Douglas.

"Right," Mary said, arching her eyebrows. "Prinny."

I wondered who Prinny was, and I planned to ask Mr. Douglas and Lucy if they knew.

"Is that so?" I tried to recover my authority, but I must admit, this new revelation caused my head to spin. Was there no one in this school who'd stood up to Selina?

"Mrs. Thurston said *I* was to blame," sniveled Victoria. "She said that if Selina bit me, I must have deserved it awful bad, and I should be ashamed of myself. But I did not deserve it. I swear to you, miss! I only asked Selina real polite-like not to take all the strawberry jam. I said please, too. And she said, 'Why? Because you are hungry? I am hungry, too. I will show you.' Then she bared her teeth, grabbed my arm, and bit me hard. When I cried, she said, 'I will give you something to cry about,' and she bit me again."

"Oh." That was the best I could muster.

Why had Mrs. Thurston allowed the girl to behave in such an outrageous manner? Favoritism occurs naturally in every environs, but most particularly when adults mix with children. In my experience, children who purposefully curry favor receive it. But by all accounts Selina flouted basic niceties.

"I believe we have talked enough about Selina, God rest her soul. Let's get to work." I changed from English to German and gave the girls a few simple commands.

In short order, I concluded that my predecessor had been either negligent or incompetent. Or possibly both. Not a one of the students could respond to any of my requests. Nor could they conjugate a verb. When I asked them to translate a simple sentence from English into German, they failed miserably.

"Let us begin at the beginning," I said, offering them a simple *guten Tag*.

Relieved of the need to conjure up skills they clearly lacked, the girls responded by working hard. The rest of our time moved along at a satisfying pace. At the twelve o'clock chime, I followed my students to the dining room for our luncheon. Nan Miller's chair sat empty. Mrs. Thurston thundered her way through a prayer of thanksgiving for the food. As she did, I thought I caught a whiff of alcohol.

Surely not. Your imagination runs away with you, I told myself.

Cold meat slices and cheeses sat on the sideboards. Fresh bread with brown crust sent a yeasty warm fragrance into the air. I took the end portion of the loaf, plus a slice of cheese and a bit of apple, and resumed my seat just as Miss Miller hurried into the room. Her eyes were puffy and red, and her manner agitated. From half a table away, I heard the rattle of the teapot against her cup as she poured for herself.

Mrs. Thurston leaned toward my friend and whispered a question.

Miss Miller shrank back. She shook her head emphatically and guided a shaky spoonful of sugar to her tea. Mrs. Thurston still did not relent. The words were lost to me, but the import wasn't. The superintendent wore the same expression as a terrier when it clenches a rat between its teeth. My friend looked the part of the rodent.

I wondered anew—if Selina had been her favorite, where were Mrs. Thurston's outward signs of grief?

Miss Jones leaned toward me and whispered, "Mr. Waverly came. Again. He questioned Mrs. Thurston once more and asked to see the place Selina's body was found. Again. I heard him puttering around overhead while I taught."

That must have happened while I held my first German class.

"He questioned Mrs. Thurston?"

"Yes, but I think that he primarily came to interview Miss Miller again. Took her right out of class. They were in Mrs. Thurston's office for an hour. It must have been terrifying for her."

"Did they question anyone else?"

Miss Jones raised an eyebrow. "No. I know he intends to talk to Adela, but he had to leave abruptly. I don't know why. He asked me a few questions, of course. But I had nothing new to tell him. I suffer terribly from sick headaches. The night Selina died, I'd taken my medication and fallen asleep quickly. The door to the Junior dormitory stayed shut all night. The children know to wake me if they need me, or to go get one of the other proctors, but none did. So I am of no interest to them. However, Miss Miller is."

"Oh?"

"This is not the first time one of her schoolchildren has died."

"But that was typhus!" My mind flooded with wretched images of my schoolmates dying. I added hastily, "Many of the students took ill with the contagion at Lowood. It is true that the poor living conditions led to more deaths than one might normally expect, but it was still a natural phenomenon. Surely the police cannot blame Miss Miller for that."

"Typhus, you say? At the charitable institution? What a ghastly situation. But no, that was not the rationale for his inquiry. I refer to the *other* incident."

Other incident? I choked on a bite of my bread. After coughing repeatedly, I finally dislodged the piece. What was Miss Jones talking about? I must have misunderstood. She could not be suggesting that Miss Miller had been involved in yet another student's death. Could she?

More importantly, what didn't I know about Nan Miller's past that I needed to know?

As so often happens, the girls sensed a conversation that was not fit for their ears. Nettie, Rose, Rufina, and Adèle all turned their attention to us. I lifted my teacup with both hands to control the tremor, and after a fortifying sip, I changed the subject and addressed the listeners directly. "Girls, I am planning for us to take our sketching class out of doors, where we can study birdlife. How does that sound?"

"Hurrah!" cheered Rufina. "Can we go to Hyde Park?"

"That is exactly what I had in mind. You will have to help me with the Juniors, however. Can you do that?"

"I have a little brother at home," lisped Nettie. "When Mama lets me, I help with him. The Juniors will not be any trouble, miss."

The girls wriggled with enthusiasm.

"How lucky you are to have a reason to take the girls outside. I so enjoy doing plein air watercolors, but since my duties here keep me indoors, I rarely get the chance." Miss Jones pouted.

"Mademoiselle and I loved to watch the birds at Thornfield. The antics of crows in the farmers' fields amused us greatly. John—he's our manservant—he kept a rookery in one of the towers. Such noisy birds. And so smart!" Adèle babbled happily to her friends.

"My, but you have a lot of patience with her. Was she as flighty then as she is in the classroom?" Miss Parthena cast a glance at Adèle.

"On occasion," I said, as a spike of loyalty to my student caused a burn in my cheeks.

"That is the French for you. A nation of pompous fools lacking self-control. Oh, they prance about, shouting for brotherhood and equality, but since they fall on their knees to worship the Pope—who is nothing more than a doddering old man wearing a red gown—one finds it hard to believe they understand God's basic command to love Him first. Much less following His secondary edict that we should love one another. And all this talk about equality? So a cat can not only look at a queen, it can aspire to be one? What nonsense. We are born into a class and cannot rise above it. And beyond the limitations society imposes on us because of our low birth, women like us are forced to bear the burden of men's shameful impulses. If we are not gifted with beauty or youthful charms, then we have nothing to barter."

"Yes, well . . ." I could not formulate a proper response. Miss Jones's opinions were as oversized as the rest of her.

Fortunately, the remainder of the conversation did not require my participation. She prattled on regardless of my attention, while I let my mind wander back to the strange events at the school, until one of Miss Jones's comments nearly knocked me off my chair.

She lowered her voice a half an octave, presumably out of deference to the presence of the girls. "I count myself fortunate to be a teacher at a school rather than a governess. So often, a governess is naught but a plaything for the master of the house or his sons. They use and discard young women like they were pieces of blotting paper. Quite disgusting."

How I longed to set Parthena Jones straight!

Chapter 31

That afternoon, we set off for the park, the nine students—five Junior and four Senior girls—and I. When I spotted Lucy Brayton, her brother Bruce Douglas, and the merry little Rags sitting on the bench at Hyde Park, I waved in greeting. Rags jumped to his feet and barked happily, his tiny body shivering with joy as he displayed a fashionable set of apparel that outshone mine. His navy blue patent leather collar particularly proved adorable, and the students flocked around him.

Lucy had met Adèle and the other girls once before, when she'd invited the classmates to her house for tea when Adèle first came to London. But it had been a while, so the students were a little shy around her at first.

Lucy formally introduced her brother. Mr. Douglas endeared the girls by offering his hand and bidding each of them a solemn, "How do you do?" Rose stared at him with unabashed admiration. When it came her turn to say, "Hello," she presented Mr. Douglas with a winsome smile and sank into a deep curtsy.

Give her a few years, and she will be a society darling, I decided.

Too quickly, the meeting became a contest, a jousting match. Half the girls were clearly in awe of Lucy and her fine clothes. The compliments flew thick and heavy.

The other half of the girls doted on Rags, who responded with cheerful snuffles and licks.

All the girls cast covert glances at Mr. Douglas, painfully conscious of him and shy all at once. This signified their awakening womanhood, when the presence of a man caused contradictory emotions.

Lucy gave the girls her complete attention, and very quickly, the younger children felt at ease, admiring her parasol and stroking the silk flounces on her dress. Victoria wiggled herself into a spot right next to Lucy. Rose sniffed the air. "What is that lovely smell? Gardenias? My mama likes them, too. I like lilacs more."

"Do you?" Lucy asked. "We shall have to wait until next spring for them. That seems very far away, doesn't it?"

Nettie buried her face in Rags's coat. Rose managed a spot next to Mr. Douglas's knee.

Chatting with first one girl and then the other, Lucy glowed with affection. She clearly adored children—how unfair that she had none to call her own. I resolved then and there to name Lucy godmother to my son. If Providence hadn't provided her a child to love, I would. For I could see that she was a woman full of love, a woman who would have made an excellent, doting mother. Imagining her as a part of my son's life gave me a sudden sense of satisfaction.

"Girls, attention, please." I clapped my hands to bring them nigh and begin our drawing lesson. Holding up a sketch pad, I introduced various pencil strokes: thick, thin, hard pressure, soft, and shading. Next I pointed out a robin hopping along the ground, and in preparation for drawing the bird, I asked what sorts of shapes comprised his silhouette.

"That one's round as a globe," said Victoria. "Looks like he could roll downhill without any trouble."

Rufina snorted. "Sort of like our Mrs. Thurston."

This brought a fit of giggles.

I instructed them to sketch a robin and to include the bird's surroundings. Once given their assignment, nine heads bowed over the sketchbooks and started to work in earnest. Moving from student to student, I offered suggestions and corrections.

So engrossed was I in my teaching that I startled when Bruce Douglas set a hand on my shoulder and leaned in to say, "Ladies, may I interrupt? I need to speak with your instructor."

"How do things fare with the girls?" Lucy raised her eyebrows at me once I was seated next to her on the bench.

"They are so thankful for my presence that I feel at sixes and sevens for carrying through with this charade. Worse luck, I have learned little of value. Here is a list of all the instructors' names, which I gleaned from a schedule that Miss Miller gave me."

"I shall get men to investigate these women as soon as possible. Perhaps we can turn over a stone and find a missed grain of information that will be helpful." Mr. Douglas pocketed the list.

"Beyond that, what I have seen and heard only serves to confuse me! Most importantly, Selina was sneaking out. She had a beau, or so one of the girls told me. They called him her 'special friend.'"

"That bears further scrutiny." Mr. Douglas stroked his chin. "Did she supply a name?"

"Nothing proper. Only a nickname."

"That wouldn't do us much good. Try to find out, please."

"I will. It appears that Selina was Mrs. Thurston's favorite, yet the girl was cruel to everyone. It makes no sense."

"I am sorry, but I fear I must add to your confusion," Mr. Douglas said. "As I told you before, Marcus Piper, the medical examiner, and I have known each other for years, and he often consults with me when he is puzzled by what he finds. However, for the first time in our long friendship, he has refused to talk to me."

"You mean he refused to discuss Selina Biltmore's death," Lucy said.

"No, Sister." Mr. Douglas shook his head. "He refused to talk to me at all. I arrived at his office, his assistant announced me, and Piper ran out the back door. Fortunately, by slipping a few coins to his second-in-command, I have still been able to advance our cause. I now know how the girl was killed."

"I was present when Mr. Waverly examined the fabric and noticed a blood smear on the pillow slip," I said. "I assume that was used as a weapon?"

"Yes. They found a feather inside the girl's mouth. She also had a small broken bone here." He touched his throat.

"What does that signify?" I said.

"Pressure was applied to her face. The killer must have been someone strong enough to subdue the girl. The injuries to Selina Biltmore's body came as a result of her struggle to survive. The murderer might sport a bruise or a scratch from the encounter."

I had been sitting forward, watching the girls as they drew their cheery robins. Now the import of Mr. Douglas's words struck me hard, and I sank back onto the park bench. My sketch pad was open, and I began to draw the same assignment that I had given the girls. The motion of the pencil against paper worked to help me stay calm.

"Have you learned anything else?" Lucy asked me. "Observed anything that might be a fingerpost pointing toward a suspected killer? Although it is intriguing that Selina was sneaking out, do we still believe she was murdered by someone inside the school?"

I thought about that. "I find it hard to believe that someone entered the building off the street, came upstairs to the dormitory, and left without arousing anyone."

"I concur," Mr. Douglas said. "It would be one thing to dose a group of schoolgirls, but quite another to also dose the servants."

"Mr. Waverly visited again today—the third time in two days!—and spent more than an hour interviewing Miss Miller. He also spoke to Mrs. Thurston, but that was a short session."

Mr. Douglas shook his head. "Waverly is paying too much attention to your friend Miss Miller. If she was the killer, why would she have involved you? Your presence only complicates the situation."

I decided not to share Miss Jones's accusation that Nan Miller had been involved at one time in the death of another student. Until I spoke to Miss Miller directly and confirmed this gossip, there was no reason to cast aspersions.

I added a second robin to the first in my drawing.

"And there is another question that nags at me," Mr. Douglas said. "This does not fit the profile of those cases to which Waverly is usually assigned."

"What do you mean?" his sister asked.

"Until I know why a senior Bow Street Runner is investigating the death of a schoolgirl, there is a huge gap in our knowledge. This ignorance makes it nearly impossible to figure out the identity of the killer," Mr. Douglas said. "What else have you seen or heard?"

"Not much. Nothing that seems important. I have tried to pay close attention to every detail, but I have no idea what I should be looking for!" With that, I gripped my pencil rather too hard in frustration and broke off a portion of the lead.

Mr. Douglas leaned forward, clasping one gloved hand in the other and resting his elbows on his knees. "Are you familiar with the concept of ratiocination? It suggests that we look for discrepancies in word and behavior. Lies and coincidences. Most importantly, watch for an aberration or abnormality that might point to the criminal. Finally, think about who wanted this girl dead and why. Also consider the timing. Why was it important that she be murdered now?"

"You are asking me to solve a puzzle with most of the pieces missing."

Mr. Douglas smiled. "Welcome to the world of detective work. Rarely does one even know what that missing piece might be. Or how we shall turn it up. So, we watch, we ask questions, we look for discrepancies, and we try to piece together a tapestry from bits of fabric and thread."

"You cannot share anything useful, dear Brother? No tricks you have mastered?" Lucy gave him a light tap on the shoulder.

"Only this—in most crimes, we see three variables, three conditions that must be satisfied. Opportunity. Motivation. And method. Think on those and you'll quickly understand why they matter."

"Is it possible that the killer suffocated the wrong girl? How close is Adèle's bed to Selina's?" asked Lucy. "I have never ventured up to the dormitories."

"The beds are right beside each other. So yes, perhaps the killer got the wrong girl. Perhaps Adèle was the intended victim all along. In fact, I might have proof of such." I reached into my pockets and withdrew the new set of threats that my little friend had given me. I also handed over the original note, so that we could compare the handwriting.

"This looks like a match to me," Mr. Douglas said. "But I am hardly an expert."

"All these threats make me wonder if I should simply take Adèle and leave. But I worry about the other girls!"

"These messages are outrageous," Lucy said after reading them.

Mr. Douglas frowned and stared off at the girls. "I wonder if Adèle is the only one who was threatened. Perhaps you can find out."

As we talked, my fingers moved restlessly along with my emotions, and the two birds were fleshed out by my efforts. Mr. Douglas glanced over at my work.

"Mrs. Rochester, you are most talented. I wonder, have you any ability when it comes to capturing the image of a person? If so, could you sketch your assailant from the coaching inn? I have not forgotten about your stolen jewelry. If I take Glebe a sketch, perhaps it will spur action. The lost items have been added to the list of stolen property that the Bow Street Runners keep on hand."

I thanked him and assured him I'd make a drawing of my assailant that night and bring it along tomorrow. I was glad he'd brought up the subject of my loss. The jewels were secondary to the problem at the school, but I was pleased that he remembered my plight.

I then shared what I had learned about Selina from my students. "She was not well liked. It seems that she could be quite cruel, and would set out specifically to cause the younger girls distress—indeed, took pleasure in it. In fact, she took from them objects that they loved." I explained about the drawer full of purloined possessions. "In each case, Selina seemed to know exactly what each child treasured, whatever small trinket made that particular girl feel loved."

I mentioned that Victoria sported bites on her wrist, and Lucy whispered, "Oh my stars. What a despicable child you are describing!"

"Universally disliked? That does make pinning down a killer rather difficult." Mr. Douglas sighed. He then smiled indulgently as Rose got up to shake a blade of grass off her skirt. Despite the fact that all the girls wore the same uniforms, Rose managed to look as if her pinafore had been sewn by a designer in Paris. Her hair glinted with a shine and softness the others lacked. There was a radiance about her, a natural loveliness. I wondered what her life would be like. Would that beauty be an asset or a curse?

"Selina seems to have displayed a callous disregard for others. When I asked Emma, the maid of all work, what Selina was like, the poor girl turned pale and shook with fear."

In front of us, Rufina coaxed Nettie and Adèle and most of the Junior girls into a game of blindman's bluff using Nettie's handkerchief as a blindfold. I should have demanded that they sit down and finish their lesson. But I enjoyed watching them cavort, and it was a pleasant distraction from our dark discussion. Fresh air has a healthy effect on the young and old alike. The sweet scent of oak leaves perfumed the air, as did the rich, dark fragrance of decaying grass blades.

Perhaps by letting the girls run and play now, they would sleep more soundly tonight, free of fears that Selina would return to haunt them.

Mr. Douglas said, "In summary, we have the death of an unlikable girl who made a lot of enemies. We have the best of the Bow Street Runners on the case. Someone has advised the medical examiner to keep the details to himself. We know that a pillow was used as a weapon. We do not know if the killer attacked the right person—or whether the killer might strike again. Someone has been issuing threats, to Adèle at least."

"There is more." I told them about the marks on Nettie's back and about Adèle's ignorance of the beating. "Of course, the scars have long since healed, and the caning might have nothing to do with Selina's death."

"But it might," said Lucy. "It surely might."

I suddenly realized the time. "Girls, tell Mrs. Brayton and Mr. Douglas good-bye. We need to get back to school."

The initial shyness returned to all except Adèle. She threw her arms around first Lucy and then Mr. Douglas. In babbling French she praised them, told them she adored them, and prayed she would see them again soon.

A spot of worry niggled at me. How would I explain it when we saw them here again tomorrow?

As if reading my mind, Lucy came to the rescue. "Mr. Douglas and I shall be here every afternoon this week. Rags needs his outdoor exercise. So we shall hope to see you again on the morrow."

"Nicely done." I leaned close and embraced her, pressing my letter to Edward into her hands.

"Ah, improvisation. It's a critical skill, isn't it? Too bad they don't teach it at girls' schools." She smiled at me, then turned to Adèle. "*Au revoir, ma petite.*"

"Trust your instincts," Mr. Douglas said to me in Hindostanee. "My man awaits your signal for help."

"I understand."

With Rags yapping and racing to keep up, Lucy and her brother headed for home. The girls and I started back toward Alderton House, but we hadn't gone far when some instinct encouraged me to stop and turn around. Lucy and Mr. Douglas were poised on a grassy hummock, watching my charges and me as we ambled back toward Alderton House. My "sister" waved to me, a subtle gesture that spoke volumes. Even from this distance, I could read the affection in her eyes.

A thrill coursed through me. Whatever happened in this adventure, I was not alone. I had a true friend, one with considerable resources—including a worldly, wise brother.

I took Nettie and Adèle by the hands. "Come along, girls," I said.

I had a murderer to catch.

Chapter 32

We walked through the front door and nearly bumped into Mrs. Thurston, her squat form an ugly gargoyle in the midst of the elegant entry.

"Miss Eyre? Where have you been? What were you doing with my students?" she snapped.

"Practicing our plein air drawing work, which is—"

"Varens." The superintendent interrupted me by snapping her fingers at Adèle. "Come with me. Mr. Waverly is here, and he has a few questions for you."

Adèle shrank behind me, her fingers gripping mine so hard that she hurt me.

"Is something wrong, Mrs. Thurston?" I asked, as I turned and put my arm around Adèle's shoulder in a protective manner.

"Wrong? A girl is dead! Under my roof. And Varens found the body! The Bow Street Runner is here to investigate. That is what is wrong—so hand Varens over!"

Terrorized by the woman's ugly countenance and shrill voice, Adèle began babbling in French. I interrupted her and responded in her native tongue, reminding her to keep speaking French, and to speak no English to anyone until I told her to do so. The other girls caught wind of Mrs. Thurston's predatory behavior. They clustered together and moved away, almost as one creature, trying to slink off.

I gave them instructions. "Ladies? Hang your cloaks up. Wait for me in the first classroom upstairs. Finish working on your sketches. Help one another, if necessary. Rufina? Take charge, please."

Mrs. Thurston might be the titular head of this institution, but her overwrought actions showed her to be a weak leader. I did not mind that I had superseded her. In fact, a frisson of pleasure rippled through me. The girls responded immediately to my request, moving with alacrity and purpose.

My triumph proved short-lived, as Mrs. Thurston called after us. "Varens? Speak English!"

I bent over and whispered in Adèle's ear in French. "Do not. Absolutely do not. If you love me, Adèle, you will do as I say."

"*Oui, m-mademoiselle*," the child stuttered.

"You have frightened her beyond all sensibility." I stared coldly at Mrs. Thurston. "She's terrified and unable to access this second language. If Mr. Waverly insists on meeting with her regardless, I am able to translate."

"So, you insist on putting yourself in the midst of this? You simply must meddle? She speaks too quickly for me to follow, so be off with you. Take the girl into my office," Mrs. Thurston said. "Go. Get out of my sight."

Adèle held on to me so tightly that I stumbled over her feet. "I am frightened," she managed. "Does he plan to send me to the guillotine? That's where all the French peasants belong. Am I a peasant?"

"Of course not, *ma petite*." I hugged her slender shoulders.

I tapped on the office door and Mr. Waverly bid us enter. He cocked an eyebrow at my appearance. "The new teacher, right? Your eye is looking better. Leave me with the girl." His voice was gruff. After adjusting his glasses upward so that they perched on his forehead, he tucked his fingers inside his vest pockets and rocked back on his heels. This unusual posture gave him a bit of a swagger.

I was not intimidated by him. "Sir? She is French. Her English is inadequate. Mrs. Thurston suggested that I volunteer to translate for you." I lowered my eyes and stared obsequiously at the carpeting as I told this small fib. I also held my breath.

"Translate? She does not speak the King's good tongue?"

"No, sir. Not well."

With that, Adèle started chattering like a squirrel in French. She told me she was frightened, she said she wanted to go home, she asked why his nose was so crooked, and finally I said, *"Ferme la bouche, ma chère."*

She did as she was told and closed her mouth. However, her blathering had done the trick. Waverly leaned back against the fireplace and stared hard at both of us. "All right then. Sit down. Both of you."

I "translated" this command.

"Miss Varens, is it true that you and Selina quarreled the day before she died?" he asked.

Adèle told me in French, "She took my ribbon. The one that *mon bon ami* gave me when he sent me away. She would not give it back. I asked and asked and asked for it. I was so angry"—and here she stomped her foot—"so I told her she was mean and cruel and that I hated her."

I translated. "Adèle resents the fact you question her relationship with Miss Biltmore. They were dear friends. Yes, Miss Biltmore borrowed Adèle's ribbon, but that is all. The girls often share personal items."

Mr. Waverly stroked his chin and considered all this. Taking his glasses off to polish them, he said, "Indeed. Is it true that Miss Biltmore refused to wake up in the mornings? And that Miss Varens was responsible for getting Miss Biltmore out of bed?"

I translated his questions.

"That lazy, no-good cow," Adèle said. "Selina would sneak out at night. She climbed down the tree. God only knows who she was meeting. Then she would be too tired to wake up. We would both be late but only I would be punished. It made me so angry."

"Miss Biltmore was also responsible for getting Adèle out of bed. Adèle hates getting up in the morning."

"Indeed?" He tilted his head and adjusted his spectacles. "Could you ask Miss Varens if she smothered Miss Biltmore with a pillow?"

My mouth dropped open. He could not suspect Adèle! But she understood him.

Adèle stomped her foot so hard that all the whatnots on the étagère jumped and did a St. Vitus dance. She began to say things in French that I could not and would not translate. All of them, I am sure, were learned at her mother's knee. None of them suitable for polite company.

No matter how emotional she was, she could never hurt another living soul. She would cry for hours when we happened upon a dead baby rabbit in the forest or a baby bird that had fallen from its nest. Surely anyone could see how honest and guileless she was.

"*Non! Non!*" Adèle shouted. As she wound down, she said she would have liked to strangle Selina many times. Yes, she would. But she would never actually *do* such a thing. If she did, that would be committing a mortal sin, and therefore, she would never go to heaven. So, of course, she didn't kill that stupid cow. How could he accuse her so unjustly? With the suddenness of a summer storm, she burst into torrents of tears.

"But you wanted to kill her. Are you sure you did not do it?" Speaking perfect French, Mr. Waverly asked this directly of Adèle.

Before I could intervene, Adèle said, *"Mais non!* I am not a bad girl. I would never do that." Adèle faced him, stomped her foot, and spoke in a manner that brooked no questions. *"Jamais.* Never. Do you understand me?"

"Parfaitement," said Waverly. "Perfectly."

"You!" I pointed a finger at him. "You speak French!"

"And you, miss, you are a sneak and a liar!" he retorted.

"How dare you? Of course I would protect this child from you. Is this how the much vaunted Bow Street Runners work? They throw their weight around and frighten little girls? How proud you must be of your position!"

He burst out laughing. "I say, for a tiny house wren, you attack like a trained falcon. Run along, Miss Varens. I need to talk to your 'interpreter.'"

My body stiffened with anger. I leaned over, hugged Adèle, smelled the sunlight on her hair, and kissed her. "Go to the classroom with your friends, darling. You are fine. You did just fine."

She cast Mr. Waverly an imperious look over her shoulder. "Humph," she grunted, and she stomped out of the room.

"I bet she ruins a lot of shoe leather." Waverly watched her go. "All that stomping breaks down the soles."

When I turned to see if he was serious, he shrugged. "My father was a cobbler. Sit down, Miss Eyre. We need to talk."

I stepped backward and bumped into a chair overloaded with papers. I scooped them aside unceremoniously and sat down.

"I say, I was quite taken in." He packed his briarwood pipe full of tobacco and propped his feet up on Mrs. Thurston's tea table. "I have to admit, I thought you a regular green girl, but you gulled me. You do realize I have a serious job to do, do you not? Your interference won't make it easier. Nor will I find the killer faster if you manipulate my witnesses. Until then, you and she both are in danger."

My anger drained away. Chagrin replaced it. Seeing the

situation from his point of view discouraged me. "I owe you an apology, sir. I only meant to protect her."

He nodded. "So I heard. I understand your desire to be protective. However, you may have protected her but put the other girls at risk."

"You do believe her, do you not? Adèle is the tenderest of souls. She is incredibly gentle and loving."

"She also possesses a formidable temper. Miss Varens had many reasons to want to see Miss Biltmore dead. At least, that is what I have been told, and what I need to explore."

He suspects her! Truly he does! My heart fluttered uncomfortably in my chest. Involuntarily, I squeezed my fist to my mouth. Edward had faith in me. I could not fail him or Adèle. "She has a schoolgirl's temper. Not to mention her volatile French blood. A sudden response. A quick flare-up. It is over as fast as it arrives. I have never seen her unleash it on other people. She may stomp and pout, but she will not raise a fist in anger. Furthermore, she feels genuine regret when she speaks out of turn or hurts someone's feelings, so tender-hearted is that child." I ended my discourse with an appeal. "Does that sound like a killer to you?"

"Not at all. But your meddling might have cost me the killer."

The stem of the pipe pointed at me accusingly. The lump of tobacco showed red against the blackened bowl.

"What do you mean?"

"If you had not have interfered, it was possible that Miss Varens might have told me something useful. Something that would lead me to the killer. Now I have nothing. From her at least."

It is possible to wallow in guilt and yet to still feel virtuous. Protecting Adèle was my priority. Solving a murder was his. We both wanted to safeguard the girls in this school. Our goal was the same; our methodology differed. Mr. Douglas had said Waverly was the best of the Runners, their most experienced man. Whereas I was an amateur, he knew what he was doing.

"Surely you have something? An inkling of whom to suspect?" I couldn't believe he didn't, and I knew him to be a trickster.

He lit his pipe and took a deep draw on the stem, closing his eyes and shaking his head. "I have nothing. No forced entry. No motive. No particular suspect. Just a method. And a dead girl. Perhaps also an entire school community at risk."

"You do not suspect the girls, do you?"

He opened one eye and surveyed me thoughtfully. "I suspect everyone. That is the nature of my job. I accuse no one. I keep an open mind and observe. I consider the evidence and try to concoct a likely story from it. I ask questions and listen carefully. Once in a great while, a discrepancy points me in a certain direction. When the killer lets down his guard, I redouble my efforts. God willing, I am successful."

"What did you hope to learn from Adèle?"

He closed his eyes again and steepled his fingers over his chest. Leaning back in the chair, he appeared to be a man in repose. However, I imagined that I could see the gears in his mind shifting, testing the speed, and shifting again. The whole time, he chewed on the stem of his pipe, causing it to travel from one side of his mouth to the other.

"That is my business and not yours."

I sighed and waited to be dismissed. He let the silence between us stretch on and on before he spoke.

"I need to know what manner of girl Miss Biltmore was. I need to know what sort of passions she inflamed. My aim was to eliminate Adela Varens as a suspect. You see, Miss Varens had cause, opportunity, and means. But finding her hair ribbon under the pillow struck me as a bit too neat. If Miss Varens had wanted her ribbon so badly, bad enough to kill for it, why would she then leave it behind? You see my dilemma? All the stars align to make me suspect your little friend.

However, as she just illustrated so aptly, she wanted that ribbon. It held meaning for her. So I repeat, why kill Miss Biltmore and forget to take the ribbon?"

I nodded slowly. "The scenario is flawed as it stands. I can come to only one conclusion: The murderer wanted Adèle to look guilty."

"And in doing so made a mistake." A sparse curl of smoke rose from the bowl of the pipe. It smelled of cherries.

"Yes."

"The murderer knew about the girl and the ribbon."

"Yes."

"So the murderer is someone in the school community."

"Most likely."

He opened his eyes. "You are quite intelligent for a woman. Your command of the facts and the inferences one can make is most impressive. Too bad many of the constables I work with are not as bright. I was not entirely honest with you earlier. I do have my suspicions." Leaning forward to stare at me, his eyes were gray, devoid of liveliness, full of remorse and sadness. They brought to mind the color of a tombstone after the rain soaks it. "Tell me. How well do you know Nan Miller, Miss Eyre? Or should I call you Mrs. Rochester?"

Chapter 33

I sputtered for a moment, then managed, "How did you know my married name?"

Mr. Waverly puffed on his pipe. "It is my job to know with whom I am dealing. I wouldn't be effective if I didn't have a keen memory for faces, names, and descriptions. Every day, I read the incoming reports, as well as the *Hue and Cry and Police Gazette*. You mentioned that you gave your report to Glebe regarding your robbery, and I recalled a guard's report mentioning a woman named Mrs. Rochester. He noted that she had received a black eye in a scuffle with a thief at a coaching inn. The chances of there having been two such incidents involving two women with the same sort of injury, within the same week, seemed unlikely. For future reference, ma'am, most ladies simply hand over their purse. Few dare to fight their attacker. So I inferred that you were Mrs. Rochester from your injury—and one other event. The name 'Jane Eyre' was written in pencil and appeared last on Mrs. Thurston's list of teachers. Hence, I could deduce that you are a new addition, which would be in concert with your being a traveler who was robbed."

His logic was impeccable, and I enjoyed hearing him explain how one deduced fact led to another. The method of thinking was simple and elegant at the same time.

A slow puff of smoke preceded his next question. "What inspired you to take a mail coach here? They cost more than a regular coach, and they offer fewer comforts. I suspect something inspired you to come to London in a hurry. Am I right?"

"Adèle is my husband Mr. Rochester's ward. When her most recent letter arrived, it became clear that she is deeply unhappy here."

"Why did your husband not check on the girl himself?"

"His surgeon advised him not to travel."

"So he sent you? A mere slip of a girl?"

"Mrs. Brayton had encouraged me to visit. My husband plans to join me."

"I see. I am acquainted with her brother, Mr. Douglas. Quite the military hero. And tell me again how you knew Miss Miller?"

I told Mr. Waverly about Lowood, and how Miss Miller started as my superior and eventually became my colleague.

"After I left Lowood, we wrote each other once or twice, and I regret to say, we fell out of touch. Our meeting here was by chance. When I arrived to find the school in uproar over Selina Biltmore's death, I had thought to withdraw Adèle immediately, but Miss Miller convinced me I could do more good here. She said that you had strongly urged them to add a chaperone in the Senior dormitory, so she invited me to substitute for their missing German teacher, and as you know, the opportunity suited me. It is for just a short time. I thought it would give me a chance to observe the inner workings of this school, and to ascertain whether it was a good fit for Adèle. The ruse would only work if I claimed my maiden name."

"So Mrs. Thurston does not know you are married?"

"The situation is complicated. Mrs. Thurston made a rash assumption about who I was. I had originally intended to tell her my real identity, but she did not give us the chance." I paused. "Surely you have noticed that she adheres firmly to her opinions without listening carefully to what others say? And without gathering facts?"

He laughed. "Well put."

"I decided to use her rash behavior to my benefit. Besides, the position is vacant only temporarily. You yourself convinced Miss Miller that the Seniors needed a chaperone and that the post should be filled quickly. Given our history, Miss Miller knew she could trust me."

He said nothing, and that caused me a bit of unease.

"I am here only for a few days. Mrs. Thurston does not need to know I am a married woman. You and I would both agree the girls are safer with me being here." I was acutely conscious that my rationale sounded a bit like a plea.

Mr. Waverly sat there, seeming totally disinterested, his posture relaxed and his face slack, as if he were ready to drift off. My impulse was to continue pleading with him, begging him to let me stay. How odd it seemed: Only hours earlier I was determined to leave Alderton House. Now I was just as determined to stay the course.

Suddenly the man snapped to attention. "I have made my decision."

Rather than woolgathering, he had been considering all his options.

"I shall keep your confidence, Mrs. Rochester, for one reason only. It suits my purpose. I agree that you do a good turn by staying here."

"Thank you." I paused. "Sir."

I hoped that I had convinced him. But I worried that I had actually made the situation worse. Panic seized me; my mouth went dry. I spotted a carafe and glass on one end of Mrs. Thurston's desk, so I stepped nearer and poured myself a drink.

Unfortunately, the liquid was pure spirits.

I coughed and choked and coughed some more. I thought I'd never catch my breath.

Mr. Waverly watched me with amusement. "Bit strong for you, eh?"

My embarrassing interlude gave me the chance to think about his focus on Miss Miller. What *did* I know of her? The gaping hole in my knowledge of Nan Miller's recent past did not escape me. What had Miss Jones meant when she said that another student had died under Miss Miller's care? What had happened?

I hoped to tread safely around the circumference of my ignorance, but the deep crevasse worried me. Once I fell in, I might not be able to climb back out.

"I am not in the habit of drinking strong spirits," I managed with difficulty.

"I see." He slapped his knees and laughed again. "I say, you are a pip! Indulge me. Have you any suspicions of Miss Miller? Or any of the other instructors?"

"No, sir." I sat there, intent on allowing my hands to lie loosely in my lap rather than wringing them, which would be a sure display of my nervousness. "Each one seems capable. I have seen no untoward behavior. The only surly person in the bunch is Mrs. Thurston, and I rather doubt that she would ruin the reputation of her school by committing murder. Besides, from all that I have heard, Selina Biltmore was a particular favorite of hers."

"Hmmm. You have not heard of any disappointments that Mrs. Thurston might have had with the dead girl?"

"None, sir." I had no idea what he was on about.

"Invitations rescinded? Agreements made and broken? Any quarrels between them?"

My confusion must have shown on my face. "Are you suggesting that they had an argument, and that it led to—"

"No, madam. I'm not suggesting anything at all. Nothing at all. I'm merely—"

But his commentary was cut short. From outside the room came the sound of fists beating on the front door.

Chapter 34

Emma answered the relentless pounding on the front door, but her timid welcome was cut short as a howl of anger reverberated through the building.

"Where is Mrs. Thurston? Get her! Bring her to me!"

"Sir, calm yourself!" came Mrs. Thurston's plea from farther down the hall.

"You fool! You stupid, careless fool! How could you let this happen? You . . . you imbecile!" the man bellowed.

"Mr. and Mrs. Biltmore, please accept my—" But before Mrs. Thurston could tender her sympathy, a woman's keening interrupted.

"They won't let me see her!" the woman sobbed. "I want to hold her—but they turned us away."

My gut twisted into a knot as Selina's parents poured out their misery. What if I lost my Ned? My dear, sweet son? I fought to hold tight to my senses, but my body tasted the bitter herb of grief. A teeth-rattling chill swept through me.

Waverly shook his head and sighed. A deep frown creased

his forehead as his whole face closed down. Behind his spectacles, his eyes grew narrow and flinty.

"You are excused, Mrs. Rochester. Or Miss Eyre. As you prefer. We are done here. For now."

I slipped out of the superintendent's office and ran up the stairs, stopping briefly at the first landing, trying not to call attention to myself. Waverly had come out of Mrs. Thurston's office to introduce himself to the Biltmores.

"Mr. and Mrs. Biltmore, may I tender my deepest condolences? I am here at your service," he said before bowing deeply. "I am sorry to bother you, but we have much to discuss."

"This has ruined everything! He will be furious!" yelled Mr. Biltmore. "And you, you are complicit as well. Bringing her here was your idea."

This last salvo was directed at his wife, who continued to cry only harder.

"Really, sir," Mrs. Thurston said.

"Do you have any idea what has happened here? Tell her, Waverly!"

"This matter demands privacy," said Waverly. "Come. We can talk behind closed doors."

Waverly escorted Mr. and Mrs. Biltmore into Mrs. Thurston's office. The superintendent brought up the rear, sniveling loudly into a soiled handkerchief.

"Where is Caje? Where is he?" Mr. Biltmore asked. "I shall tear him apart with my bare hands! He was supposed to watch after her!"

Then the door closed with a bang.

The exchange struck me as exceedingly odd, but this was not the time to stop and ponder it.

"*Laboro, laboras, laborat.*" Miss Jones droned her way through the forms of the Latin verb.

The students' heads cocked with attentiveness as they tried

to make sense of the shouts from the ground floor. But they turned as one when they heard my footsteps, and their faces cheered at the sight of me, although they wore a sense of confusion like a heavy blanket tossed over their small frames.

Miss Jones continued her recitation in a voice as steady and measured as a clock hand. Evidently she had powers of concentration that exceeded mine, because she continued on about Latin verb formations as if nothing amiss or unusual had happened in the hallway one story below.

But she must have heard the commotion! Or the upset it caused!

A wet trail of tears streaked Nettie's face. Rufina was digging at a spot on her knee. Rose twirled a strand of hair as fast as the spinning of a dragonfly's wings. And Adèle's pale skin took on the unwholesome pallor of chalk.

"Come with me, Seniors." I gestured toward the secondary classroom. "Thank you, Miss Jones, for attending to my young ladies while I was detained."

"But of course." She nodded.

My students seemed rooted to the spot and stood there looking dazed and confused. Instead of chastising them, I reached out and took Adèle by the hand. In return, she took Nettie's hand, who took Rose's, who in turn grabbed Rufina by the fingers. Thus our human chain moved to the far end of the second classroom. They waited as I slid the divider in place and latched the partition closed. "Sit down, girls. Let us chat for a moment." Any notion we could get to work right away was absurd. Instead, I chose to address the commotion they had heard.

"Come, sit close to me," I said, directing my charges to bunch up while I took a spot in the middle. "I am here. Do not be frightened."

"That man who was yelling," Rose said, "he must be Selina's papa."

"And her mama is here, too. I remember the day they

brought her. She came in a big black coach pulled by twin bays." Rufina sighed. "The horses were lovely. I wanted to pat them."

"It is natural for her parents to grieve, girls. They have lost a child they love."

Nettie's lower lip quivered. "Lucky Selina."

"Pardon?" Nettie didn't seem the kind of child who would either employ or understand sarcasm.

"Her papa loves her. He is awful broken up about her being gone. I wish my papa cared as much for me. He does not want me around. Mama does not, either. Not since my little brother came. They only care for him because he's got hair."

I believe she meant that her parents were pleased because the boy was an "heir," but this was definitely the wrong time to discuss homophones.

I pulled Nettie close to me. "It might seem that way, but I am sure they love you very much. And you have a Father in heaven who loves you. All of you. Remember that, won't you? Now, would you show me your drawings, please?"

Their work ranged from accomplished (Rufina) to disastrous (Adèle). After a quick glance at the sketches, I said, "I want each of you to write a paragraph for me in German. The topic is Selina. I find it helpful, sometimes, to put my thoughts and feelings on paper. I think you will, too. Please get started."

The girls bent over their projects, letting the noise of pencils rubbing against paper fill the quiet spaces between us. As they worked, I roughed out a sketch of my assailant at the coaching inn. Thus our faculties were occupied until the commotion of voices and footsteps told us the Biltmores and Mr. Waverly were leaving.

My students barely registered the departure. They kept at their work until the bell rang for dinner. The girls fell into line behind Rufina, who led us downstairs.

What did Mr. Biltmore mean when he said, "This has ruined everything"? And when he singled out Caje? I vowed to press Miss Miller for answers about this and about the marks on Nettie's back.

However, when we arrived in the dining room, Nan Miller's chair again sat empty, as did Mrs. Thurston's. Miss Jones led us in saying our prayers over the food.

After our meal, the girls worked on their needle arts. Once they seemed occupied, I took a seat very close to Miss Jones and whispered, "May I speak to you in private?"

We moved to a corner of the room. "Is harsh punishment allowed here?"

She almost laughed. "Good heavens! Only if you think copying Bible verses is harsh. Why do you ask? Does one of the students vex you?"

"No. This morning when they were dressing I noticed scars on one of the girls' backs. I have no experience to judge these things, but they looked to me like caning marks."

"Indeed!" Her eyebrows shot straight up. "Then she must have been disciplined at home, because neither Mrs. Webster nor Mrs. Thurston would ever allow such a thing here. I believe the worst punishment ever meted out has been sending Adèle to bed without her supper."

I nodded, wondering if that were truly the case. Miss Jones leaned over and said, "One of the girls showed me the assignment you gave them, sketching the robin. I long to improve my artistic abilities. Would you critique some of my work?"

"With pleasure," I said. For the rest of the session, we viewed her portfolio. She had a good eye for color, but her technique needed refinement. I made a few suggestions, which she seemed to take to heart.

I admit, however, that it was difficult to focus. My eyes strayed to the door, expecting to see Miss Miller return at any moment. I rehearsed the suspicions I harbored, recalling that she had not elaborated on her life during that time when we lost contact.

"Circumstances changed," she had said. A neat sidestep.

Was there a portion of her history that bore relevance to the situation at hand?

Was my old friend a murderer?

ROSE'S ESSAY

Selina was my friend. She told me secrets. She said we were both beautiful, but that I was not nearly as lovely as she, and everyone took notice of her. She took my sash because she liked it and it looked well on one of her new dresses. She did not like school or teachers. She said this is a waste of time and youth. I will miss her, but I do not want her to come back and visit because she's dead.

NETTIE'S ESSAY

Our friend Selina is dead. I pray that God takes her to heaven. I will pray for her tonight. She liked sweets. I wish I had shared my sweets with her. She said she was special and {this was smeared} loved her. He would send carriages for her.

RUFINA'S ESSAY

Selina was mean especially to the little ones. Once she pushed Rose's face into the water basin. I did not like Selina. She said no one would ever fall in love with me because I am ugly. That made me cry. I don't care if she is our next Queen, I hated her.

ADÈLE'S ESSAY

I won't miss Selina. She was stupid like a cow. Now she will rot.

Chapter 35

Mrs. Thurston escorted a careworn spindle of a woman into our midst. "This is Mrs. Grover. She's here to measure for the mourning clothes." The shabby twig of a guest silently measured up each of us, first with a pair of red, swollen, and crusty eyes.

As head girl, Rufina took the lead, standing on a footstool and submitting herself to Mrs. Grover's quick ministrations with a tape measure, waiting patiently as the fast-moving woman stopped to scribble notes on a dirty scrap of paper. Children no older than these students would sit up all night sewing the mourning clothes by candlelight. The garments would be ready for wearing tomorrow.

This industry gave me pause. The many reversals of fortune in my own life led me to question what determined our fates. What unseen hand decreed that one child would stitch all night in a rookery and pay tuppence to sleep in a bed with a half dozen others, only to be turned out on the street in the morning, while the girls of Alderton House yawned and stretched, splashed in basins of clear water, and broke their fast with a table full of food? Where was the justice? Why the vast inequity? What loving God so neglected the majority of his children to spoil and pander to the rest?

The door flew open and Mrs. Thurston again waddled her way to the center of the room, pushing aside poor Mrs. Grover and causing the seamstress to lose a mouthful of pins.

"Attention!"

Miss Miller shuffled along in Mrs. Thurston's wake, but my old friend did not look at me. She kept her eyes on the floor.

"Selina Biltmore's earthly remains will come back to Alderton House," said the superintendent. "Since the family is from Brighton, this will allow friends in London to pay their respects before Selina makes her final journey home. She will be displayed in the front parlor. None of you have any reason to gawk, and I shall give strict instructions to the midwife in attendance that anyone lingering there will be reported to me."

Seeing the confusion on my face, Miss Jones leaned over and whispered, "The midwife safeguards the body, to keep it from being snatched by resurrectionists. Not a problem outside the city, is it?"

No, it certainly wasn't. The superintendent concluded that "there will be no reason for any of you to use the front parlor except to pay your condolences."

When Mrs. Thurston speared the Amazonian teacher with an angry look, admonishing Miss Jones for whispering to me, my colleague spoke up. "I was only telling Miss Eyre that I would be happy to make a funerary brooch from Selina's hair. Rather time-consuming, but a lovely remembrance. I made one last year when my brother died."

"Do so," said Mrs. Thurston. With that, she turned on her heel and left us.

"Please accept my condolences regarding your brother. That must have been horrid." I could only draw on my deep feelings for my Rivers cousins, though I had to assume those between siblings were many times stronger.

Miss Jones dabbed her eyes. "I come from a family of scholars. My brother Adonis was a historian, who traveled to France to do research. Sadly, he fell in love with a disreputable woman and was killed by one of her jealous lovers. We had hoped to open our own village school. Ministering to poor children was our dream, you see."

That explained her harsh words about the French people. "Words prove inadequate; however, again, I am sorry for your loss. He sounds like he was a wonderful person."

"The brightest mind I have ever known. A gentle soul who never stood up for himself or struck back. We often argued over whether a Christian should always turn the other cheek or whether 'an eye for an eye' was the more valid philosophy. He was the most forgiving and accepting of any person I've ever known."

I understood the conundrum. "What did you decide?"

Her smile stopped short of her eyes. "I firmly believe we have a duty to strike back at those who harm us and their minions. Elsewise they escape to do evil again and again. The least among us lacks a champion, unless each of us takes a stand against wrongdoing."

The evening dragged on, and a minor squabble broke out among two of the Junior girls. The prospect of Selina's body "coming home" preyed on all our minds, making concentration difficult.

Trying to redirect my own thoughts, I returned to my sketch of the thief who had stolen my reticule. His eyes captured the bulk of my efforts, as I made them large and protruding. As the image grew under my pencil, I shook off a strange sensation that I knew this person.

Of course he looks familiar; he robbed you, said a voice in my head. But even so, a certain bulging of the eyes prickled at my memory. Did I know someone with similar features? As I finished the sketch to my satisfaction, I reminded myself that my entire life had been turned topsy-turvy. Perhaps I was seeing resemblances where none existed.

Miss Miller did not appear until midway through the reading hour. Her boots were raised on patens covered in mud, and a border of wet fabric dragged down her hem. Her bonnet sat askew on her head, as hair worked its way loose from her bun and her cheeks glowed pink with exertion.

"Where have you been? We must talk," I whispered to her as she slipped into a chair next to mine. She bit into two pieces of bread with a thick slice of Stilton between them.

"Yes," she managed around the food. "But not now." Despite the mouthful of food, she engaged Mrs. Grover in conversation about the cost of the mourning clothes.

A glance at the mantel clock told me I needed to prioritize my questions. I culled Miss Miller from the group of students who were knitting hand towels.

"Does Mrs. Thurston administer canings?"

"Pardon?" Miss Miller's surprise turned to shock. "Heavens, no. A rap on the wrist or knuckles, perhaps, but that is all."

"Nellie has marks on her back. Stripes cut into her flesh."

Her ruddy face turned scarlet. "Surely you are mistaken. I tell you, Miss Eyre, you tread on dangerous ground. Such an accusation is inflammatory!"

"I have seen the stripes with my own eyes!"

"I daresay you were overtired. Your eyes played a trick on you."

Cutting our conversation short, Miss Miller led the girls in prayers and reading of psalms, taking care to position herself so that we could not talk privately. Inwardly, I fumed, but her evasion only served to strengthen my resolve. Given the closed environs of the school, she could not avoid me for long.

That evening, I took my time changing behind the modesty screen. Despite the news that Selina would be returning to Alderton House, the girls seemed to welcome sleep with

more ease than they had the night before. I attributed this to
the wholesome influence of fresh air and physical exertion.
Perhaps in sleep they would find their heart's ease and leave
behind the cares and worries that tied them to this place.

Perhaps Selina would leave them alone.

Unlike the girls, however, my own sleep was not restful. It
took a long time for me to fall asleep. The lump running
crosswise the length of my bed bothered me. Last night it was
a petty disturbance, but tonight its shape jabbed me relent-
lessly. Yet there was naught I could do with the nuisance that
wouldn't disturb the girls. I knew from experience that they
slept lightly. Remembering the tread of footsteps outside my
door last night, I had an idea. The girls had mentioned that
Selina kept bath powder in her dresser. Lighting a candle and
finding the powder quickly, I crept out of my bed, moved
silently to the landing, and there I dusted a bit of it on the
floor. The scent of camellias rose up to greet me.

If someone really was walking about at night, there should
be footprints in the morning.

Thus relieved that I had at least done something to help
catch our killer, I settled onto my uncomfortable bed. My
mind reviewed the events of the day—the images Mr. Douglas
had described regarding Selina's injuries; the sounds of her
mother crying and her father's angry accusations; the injuries
among the children—Nettie's wounds, Victoria's bite marks;
Mr. Waverly's feigned ignorance of French. After tossing and
turning, I eventually fell into a fitful sleep.

Jane!

I sat up in my bed. Moonlit squares brightened the wooden
floor of the dormitory. Shadows moved silently. I tried to parse
the darkness. Then out of the shadows, a form coalesced,
though at first it seemed little more than a disturbance in the
air, a blurring of certain outlines.

"Who or what are you?" I demanded.

It is I, your friend Helen. In slow stages, she revealed herself to me, as she once was. I was certain now that I was dreaming! But what a pleasant dream it was, to see my old friend again, that winsome girl with long, dark curls. She smiled gently, familiarly, and my fears subsided. The soft scent of violets perfumed the air. They were Helen's favorite flowers. She had often pressed them between the pages of her prayer book. *Do not be afraid,* the dream image said. *Listen carefully. There is pain here and great suffering. Explore each person's Hades. Expect no safety. Be on your guard. As Virgil said, "A snake lurks in the grass."*

"Helen, I am frightened. The girls! How can I protect them? They are vulnerable, and there is but one of me."

You will find a way. I know you will. God bless you, my darling friend. I watch you from afar and send you my everlasting love.

Her form turned porous, the edges indistinct, and she dissolved before my eyes. And as she disappeared, I sank back into a dark and dreamless sleep.

Sometime later, I awoke with a start. My mind immediately returned to the image of my dear old childhood friend Helen Burns, who had succumbed to consumption when we were students together at Lowood. Perhaps these surroundings brought back vivid memories. Perhaps the soft snuffles and sighs of sleeping children took me back to that brief time when Helen walked this earth.

Tossing off the covers, I put my feet in my slippers. Once again, my muscles had grown stiff and moving caused me pain. Nevertheless, I went from bed to bed, checking on my charges. They slept with innocence, without concern for modesty or appearance, the way young animals do. At night we drop all those pretenses foisted upon us by civilization. We become who we really are.

One bed sat empty.

"Who were you?" I mused. "And why did you die?"

No answer came, so I checked on Adèle. Her pulse beat steadily and her breathing was regular. For a long while, I sat in my bed and kept watch. In the twilight between sleep and wakefulness, I imagined the touch of my husband's searching hand and the pleasant weight of my baby in my arms. I was at Ferndean, and I was happy.

Once during the night I startled awake, thinking that I heard footsteps. Outside the window, rain began, steady and heavy drops splashing hard against the glass. Then came voices, low and urgent outside the dormitory door. At last, however, I could not keep my eyes open any longer, and sleep reclaimed me.

Chapter 36

I dressed in the dark, well before Emma's knock, lit a candle, and took a look at the landing. I found there two sets of footprints in the powder, in two different sizes. One set was large and wide, and led up to the garret where Emma slept, but did not come back down. Somehow during the course of the day, I would have to see the maid's feet for comparison. The images seemed exceedingly large for a girl so small.

The second set of prints indicated feet that were long and narrow, and that set led downstairs. Using a towel, I carefully wiped the powder away.

There was nothing to do at this hour but to mull this information over.

Since it was so early, I hoped to write another letter to Edward, outlining my task and my thoughts. Such an endeavor might help me to organize my thinking and better prepare myself for the day. But words would not come easily, and I set down my pen feeling frustrated by the jumble within me . . .

Mr. Waverly's questions about Nan Miller had proven particularly nettlesome. Although I had assured him that she could not be culpable, discrepancies niggled at me. These would need to be resolved. A list might help. Reluctantly, I

wrote down the names of all the Senior girls. Plus those of all
the instructors and the household staff.

I tapped the end of the pen against my chin. What was it
that Mr. Biltmore had said? "He will be furious."

Of whom was he speaking?

Another item claimed my curiosity. In her essay about
Selina, Nettie mentioned someone sending a carriage for the
girl. Who was that?

I added "Person Unknown" to my list of suspects and then
paused. I scratched off one name: Adèle. I knew that she could
not and would not have hurt Selina. Mr. Waverly seemed to
agree. But all the Senior girls had opportunity. So any one of
them could have killed their classmate. While this seemed
unlikely at best and outrageous at worst, I took to my heart
Mr. Waverly's motto, "I suspect everyone; I accuse no one."

My list went as follows:

1. Rufina. Selina took her kite.
2. Rose. Selina stole her sash.
3. Nellie. Selina took her sweeties.

    *(At this point I was tempted to put a line through all the girls'
    names. If any one of them killed Selina, surely the others would
    know. Besides, how could they have subdued her? Furthermore,
    it would have been easier to take back the stolen articles than to
    kill a classmate!)*

4. Cook. No motive I could discern, but admittedly I
   needed to know more about her.
5. Caje. Same as with Cook. But what had Mr. Biltmore
   meant when he called him out by name?
6. Emma. Selina had been cruel to her. But how cruel?
   And Emma was slight, albeit very strong.
7. The German teacher, Fräulein Hertzog. Why had she
   left so suddenly? Had it been because of Selina?
8. Parthena Jones. Something about the woman struck
   me as off. I could not say why, but it resonated through

me the way a false note sounds when played on the pianoforte. Perhaps it was only her grief over her brother's death, unresolved and fresh.

9. Signora Delgatto. She admitted that she was happy Selina was dead. Why? But I struck through her name. The woman was too feeble to climb the stairs.

10. Nan Miller. As much as I hated to add her, her actions of late had been very odd. What had transpired at her previous post? Why did Miss Jones say a child had died while under her care? Why was she not more forthcoming about her past?

11. Mrs. Thurston. Was it possible that some action had turned the superintendent against her favorite?

12. Person Unknown. The person who sent the carriage for Selina.

A rap on the door cut my work short. I hastily folded my list and slipped it into my pocket. "Good morning, Emma," I said as the maid bustled in.

"Good day, miss. The mourning clothes are here. I'm to set out each girl's things. In these boxes are the mourning shoes. Here's yours."

She withdrew from the pile a white dress made of cheap fabric. Pinned to it was a scrap of paper with my name.

As Emma distributed the mourning wear by setting it on each girl's dresser, I tried to get a glimpse of her feet, but the task proved impossible without betraying my motives.

The morning bell sounded, and the girls began their slow struggle to rouse themselves. One by one they shed their nightclothes. When Rose's chemise bunched up as she pulled it over her head, I choked back a gasp. Rust-colored stripes crisscrossed her shoulder blades and ran down her back, angry and egregious looking. These were far worse than the similar marks on Nettie's back.

Either Miss Miller had lied to me about the use of caning

as punishment, or she was unaware of this outrage. Was it possible that Fräulein Hertzog, the previous German teacher and Senior proctor, had doled out the lashes? And wouldn't the recipient have cried out? How could it be that the other teachers knew nothing about the inflictions?

I wanted to say something to Rose but decided against it. An overreaction might make it impossible for me to get at the truth. The girls were slowly coming to trust me. When the time was right, I could ask my questions—and be assured that they would be answered honestly.

The girls stood in a line, faces solemn, looking like bleached-out birds on a tree limb. The cheap white dresses fit them poorly, and the slippers were all a bit loose on their feet, but the point was driven home: We were officially in mourning for the death of a young unmarried girl.

After our morning prayers, Mrs. Thurston announced that Selina's body would arrive during the first class session.

"Once all is prepared, you will queue up and file by to pay your respects. Ladies, I remind you that this is a solemn occasion. None of you are to linger in the parlor or to gape at the important visitors who will, no doubt, be arriving to pay their respects. I expect you to wear your mourning shoes inside the school and to keep your voices low as befits a place of sorrow. The mirrors have all been draped. I had better not see any of you trying to glimpse your reflections in spoons and such, as this is a time to reflect on your immortal souls, not on earthly vanities. Dust to dust and ashes to ashes, none can escape death."

With that cheerful start to the day, Mrs. Thurston sank back into her chair as gracefully as a milk bottle toppling over.

Miss Jones encouraged the girls to "eat up" and attacked her food with her fork as though she were digging a ditch.

At nine o'clock the sound of boots clomping through the foyer alerted us to bearers carrying Selina's coffin. A few minutes later, Mrs. Thurston stepped into the classroom and bade us to queue up, with Rufina taking her spot at the front, since she was the Senior head girl. The child swayed on her feet, a greenish pallor replacing her usual healthy skin color. "Sit down." I shoved a chair under her. "Put your head between your knees."

"It's the lilies, ma'am," she managed. "Reminds me of when I lost my mum."

Pots of hothouse flowers spilled out from the parlor and lined the hallway. The worth of the floral tributes must have been immense. The quantity and quality of the offerings proved that all of London Society marked this farewell to the Biltmores' daughter—at least, in absentia. The smell of the blossoms approached a treacly crescendo that overwhelmed the senses, coating the nose and mouth. Every breath was a fight for survival, which, coupled with the cloying smell of decay, provoked my own stomach to roil. I instructed the girls to use their handkerchiefs to breathe through, and as expected, Rufina's was missing, so I loaned her mine. She took to her feet unsteadily, so I linked arms with her. Thus acting as a pair, we set off, leading the others through the viewing area at a stately pace.

When we reached the shoulder of the coffin, Rufina and I stopped to "say good-bye." We both pivoted slightly so as to be facing Selina Biltmore's mortal remains.

What a shock!

Selina Biltmore had been no child—she was a full-grown woman!

Miss Miller had said Selina was just sixteen, but one glance affirmed that she had been quite mature for her age. Although death had distorted her facial features, it was clear that Selina Biltmore had been blessed with a noble profile. As for her figure, the contours of her shroud revealed that she tended toward corpulence. I lingered, trying to get a better sense of this young woman, but Rufina's hand flew to her mouth and she made a retching noise. Fearful that she was going to be ill, I hurried us along.

No wonder she'd been so successful at bullying the others. Selina had been an adult in a world full of children.

* * *

After I prepared for the day's lessons, I revisited my list of possible murder suspects and decided to start at the bottom of the building and work my way up.

"Lo and behold! Our scholar! Bet ye've coming sniffing around for somethin' to eat, right?" A puff of flour blew up around Cook, enveloping her in a powdery white aura.

"Please, ma'am." I settled on the kitchen stool. It was as good a pretext for my presence as any.

She slid a scone onto a plate, generously slathered it with clotted cream, and slopped a dollop of jam on the side. From the stove, she grabbed a kettle and poured water in her china teapot. The gold trim on the lid and graceful forget-me-nots painted on the body suggested a grand provenance—although the two large chips marred its beauty. The triangle knocked from the spout made pouring tea a challenge, but the chip from the pointed handle on the top of the lid was more of a cosmetic failing than a functional one.

"Your teapot is lovely."

"Aye, it was a gift from my daughter. The toffs at the manor where she worked planned to toss it into the bin. Larissa asked for it. They took a half crown from her pay. They who was going to get shod of it! On account of a chip in the spout! My darling daughter knew how much I likes my tea," she said in a gruff voice as she poured me a cup. "It's all I've got left of her. That and a lock of her hair. Such a dear girl. I use that teapot every day and it makes me feel closer to my baby. Can't visit her grave, you see. It's too far. Feels like she's far away, too."

"Maybe," I said. "But I would guess she's close to you, nearer than you think."

"I hope so." Wiping the back of her hand across her eyes, Cook smeared more flour on her prominent forehead and bustled away from me.

"I am sorry for your loss."

"Thank ye. Ain't just my loss. The world lost an angel."

"That's a shame," I said with sincerity. "I regret that I'll never have the chance to meet her. No one thinks that way about Selina, do they?"

Cook's laugh was more of a short bark of derision than a nod to real humor. "That one? She's probably busy dancing with the demons!"

A neat segue, and I seized upon it. "Mr. Waverly has been questioning people regarding Selina's death. Hard to believe, but they say the girl may have been murdered."

Cook bustled around the kitchen, keeping her back to me. Finally, she said, "And what if she was? Whoever did it would have rid the world of one of Satan's own. They ought to be thanking whoe'er done it, and that's a fact."

"You didn't like Selina?"

"Weren't nobody liked that one." Slapping a large glob of dough onto the counter, Cook turned it over twice. "There was a mean streak in her, miss. I suspect her parents hoped Mrs. Thurston could cure her of it, discipline it out of her, but that's rot, ain't it? You cannot turn a cat into a dog, or a dog into a rat, and you cannot make a body something they ain't. Besides, Maude Thurston ain't nobody's fool. She closes her door at night and lets the girls fend for themselves, don't she?"

Cook worked the dough. She did not turn to face me, but her words rang loud and clear. "A bad seed. Fruit of a diseased tree. That girl caused a world of hurt and heartache in her short life—and she would have done more mischief if she could! Her father thought the sun rose and set on his precious child. She could do no wrong in his eyes. Well, he was a blind man."

With that, she gave the dough a ringing slap.

"The world's a better place without that she-demon." Cook punched the dough so hard that it tore. "I'm telling you the God's honest truth."

Chapter 37

Miss Miller continued to evade me. I tried to catch her in the hallways, but she proved more elusive than the dream ghost of Helen Burns. Once she stuck her head in my classroom and borrowed Rufina to mind the Infants for "a while." By the time I was on my feet and within whispering distance, she had turned tail and vanished. At the luncheon table, she sat stiffly and played with her food. All the while, she took elaborate pains to avoid my glance.

The girls changed from their mourning slippers into boots so we could go to Hyde Park. On our way out, we bumped into Miss Jones, coming from the parlor and carrying in her hands a fulsome hank of long chestnut hair. Selina's hair.

"For the mourning jewelry," said the tall teacher. "I have a braiding frame made from a man's top hat, and a new pattern for a finished brooch that resembles a bow. It should look quite lovely, I think."

She winced and touched her fingers to her temple.

"Sick headaches," she said. "They attack me regularly and keep me up all night. I believe I shall be forced to take a bit of medicine and lie down. Would you ask Signora Delgatto to take over my class when you return from your plein air class? I fear I will be sound asleep. Probably right through dinner. It is an inescapable side effect of the drops."

"Yes, of course. I shall do so when we return. Meanwhile, allow me to help you upstairs. Rufina? Lead the girls outside, please."

I bore the teacher's weight as best I could while Miss Jones and I climbed the stairs. Because she towered above me, her limbs put a heavy burden on mine. After she took to her bed, she directed me to look in her top drawer. There I found a dark brown glass bottle labeled LAUDANUM. There was also an eye-dropper and a small jar of honey. As per her instructions, I added the tincture and a spoonful of honey to a glass of water. While she drank, I arranged her pillows and helped her remove her mourning slippers, noting the length of her feet—they certainly could have been the same size as the footprints leading down the stairs because hers were long and slender. As I tucked her slippers next to her boots, my fingers brushed against the leather. Soaking wet. She must have worn her boots outside!

My mind raced. Sometime in the night, Parthena might have left the building—and since the footsteps only went down the stairs and not up, she must not have returned until after I mopped up the powder.

"Please, could you see to the dead girl's hair?"

At her direction, I started to wrap a hank of it in a clean linen square.

"There are two large pieces of hair there, am I correct?" she asked.

"I see but one."

"Ah, then I dropped the other. I hate to ask but . . ."

"I shall go downstairs and retrieve it." I retraced our steps to the landing, down the stairs, and through the hallway, but I did not see the missing locks of hair. There was only one other place to look. Opening the door quietly, I let myself into the parlor.

The snoring of the old midwife shook the ornaments on the shelves of the whatnot cabinet she leaned against. Each shudder included a snort at its end for punctuation. The slack-jawed look of the woman told me I need not worry about being seen. She was sound asleep, and from the stink of her, too drunk to care about my presence.

I walked around the coffin but did not find any hair on the floor. There was only one other place where the hank of hair could have fallen. I steeled my nerves for the examination I planned to conduct. Disregarding the unpleasant sensation of cold flesh, I gently tugged at the muslin wrapped around the dead girl's head to keep her jaw in place. When the fabric was removed, it disclosed two bare spots, one on each temple. The denuded areas were huge! The hair had been completely shorn! Miss Jones had cut the hanks, and in the process robbed the corpse of its natural adornments. This shocked me. Although I knew little about the making of such a keepsake as a piece of funerary jewelry, logic suggested that any hair taken could be cut from the back of the scalp, thereby doing the least to disturb the appearance of the dead. Of course, one could argue that the theft would have gone unnoticed, except for my poking about. But even so. There seemed to be something wantonly cruel about this harvest.

With my eyes, I traced the length of Selina's body. Again, her size astonished me. She probably weighed nearly as much as Edward. Although death had started its inexorable task of destruction, it was clear that the girl's skin was smooth as porcelain, the shape of her countenance a perfect oval, her hair lush and dark as it fell in loose curls, and her mouth perfectly contoured.

The midwife sighed in her sleep. One lonesome eyetooth stuck out from the roof of her mouth, and a thin rivulet of drool hung from her loose lower lip. I needed to find the missing hair in a hurry and go.

I stooped down to look under the coffin, and finally I found the curls coiled in a shadow over by a large floral offering.

I tiptoed out of the parlor and took my prize back up to the Junior dormitory. Miss Jones opened one sleepy eye to watch as I tucked the second hank of hair next to its twin.

"Your kindness overwhelms me," she said. A grimace of pain overtook her, but she managed to add, "Thank you, my friend. I will not forget this."

She could barely keep herself awake when she bid me good-bye.

I climbed back down the stairs, thinking about what I had seen, and the rapidity with which Miss Jones had fallen asleep.

Was it possible that Miss Jones had dosed Selina? She had access to the Senior dormitory. She could easily have put a few drops of her laudanum in Selina's evening tea. But what would have been her motivation?

Walking briskly through the foyer, I went down the front steps and a few yards along the sidewalk to where the girls were gathered around a dog, a small terrier, held on a leash by its owner, an elderly woman. Rufina succeeded in making the pup dance for a bit of bread. The girls turned to me expectantly.

"Oh bother!" I said as I reached into my pocket and discovered only one glove. "Rufina, pray continue to watch the others."

Back inside Alderton House, I crossed the marble tiles of the entryway once more, being as silent as possible. My movements were quiet, as the dead seem to demand of us a certain reverence. Perhaps we feel compelled to rehearse the silence of the grave. I made no sound as I slipped into the parlor.

Signora Delgatto stood with her back to me, leaning slightly over the polished walnut coffin. I froze there in the doorway, so as not to startle the elderly woman, who cleared her throat, hawked, and spat. Her spittle landed on Selina Biltmore's face with a splat.

"You no-good spawn of the devil." Signora Delgatto spoke directly to the corpse.

I gasped. The music teacher turned to stare at me, her eyes twin pools of milky brown, the clouds within them obscuring any sense of the woman's soul.

"Have you come to spy on me?"

"No, signora. I lost my glove. Is it on the floor? I cannot afford to replace it." Such a simple lie, one that came easily to my lips.

"You will tell Mrs. Thurston what you saw?"

"No."

"Why not?"

"Why would I?"

"Let me tell you about this, this *demon*." She pointed at the body. "You have heard of Fräulein Hertzog? The teacher you replace? She was a long-suffering sojourner. A woman who had endured much, and who recognized the same in me. Such a friendship! So much in common! So rare to find another soul with whom you have such a connection. Fräulein Hertzog loved singing, but God in His glory denied her a voice. But oh, how she loved music. So one day when we were walking at the market, she bought a canary. She named him Figaro. What a singer he was! So glorious! He brought my friend much joy."

In her exuberance, the old woman threw open her arms and nearly lost her balance. Slipping my hand under her elbow, I walked her to a chair and eased her down onto the seat.

"Do you know what Selina did? That evil girl twisted the bird's neck and fed it to the cat! She did it only to hurt Fräulein Hertzog, who loved her little pet."

"Why?" I asked. "Why would she do that?"

"It was an act of revenge. Pure and simple. Fräulein caught Selina slipping out of the building. Two times. Fräulein told Mrs. Thurston—and there was a quarrel."

"Between Mrs. Thurston and Selina? Or between Selina and Fräulein Hertzog?"

"Mrs. Thurston and Selina. They screamed at each other. Mrs. Thurston decided to punish the girl."

"Did she?"

"Mrs. Thurston told Fräulein to make Selina copy verses from the Bible. But the girl refused. Back and forth they went." Signora Delgatto raised a dingy handkerchief to her eyes and wiped away tears. "Then came a man in a handsome carriage to visit Mrs. Thurston. They spoke in private, and everything changed. Poof!" The woman snapped her fingers. "Like that, Selina became the favorite of Mrs. Thurston. I could not understand why. No one could."

"And your friend? Fräulein Hertzog?"

"She was told to leave Selina alone. Of course, the girl understood she had this new power—and everything was worse. She could do whatever she pleased! Selina teased Fräulein about the dead bird. Putting the feathers on Fräulein's pillow! And in her food! My poor friend went mad with grief. And what did Mrs. Thurston do to help? Nothing. Nothing at all!"

"So Fräulein left?"

"Home to Germany."

"I am sorry." My words sounded inadequate, but I was struggling to find an explanation for this odd turn of events. Who, I wondered, was the man who visited Mrs. Thurston— and what did he say that changed the balance of power?

Signora Delgatto grabbed my arm, her nails digging into my skin. "Listen to me. Leave this place. Leave it now. These children, they care nothing for us. Do you know what this girl did to her own governess? She pushed that woman down a well! Broke her arm! Left her there for two days while she cried for help."

"Oh my," I said. "How awful."

"That is not all. Then Selina found a snake and dropped it on the governess just to hear her scream! Finally, someone heard the teacher and she was rescued. But a few days later, the poor girl went mad and hanged herself from a rafter in the carriage house."

Pulling me down to her level, the signora locked her eyes on mine. "Find another way to survive, but do not surrender your life to the children of other people! Especially children like this! They have so much and they give us nothing in return! Nothing! They do not treat us like humans. They treat us worse than the dumb animals!"

We both heard the noise of horses stopping outside. I disentangled myself from Signora Delgatto's grip and ran to the front window to see a carriage on the street.

"Hurry! Someone is coming! We must go," I said to the Italian woman, taking her by the arm and heading her toward the door. "Ah! There it is! I spy my glove. Under the coffin."

Leaving her in the doorframe, I ran to grab my missing glove. As she waited for me, Signora Delgatto's narrow shoulders slumped, tenting the fabric of her mourning dress. "You do not listen. You do not understand."

"On the contrary, I have listened and understood you. And I share your sorrow. But Selina Biltmore will answer to a greater judge, Signora Delgatto. This I believe. Now please, we must go."

Leaning heavily on me, she limped into the hall. There I bid her good-bye and hurried outside, where I glimpsed the Biltmores as they were climbing out of a carriage. Fortunately, they did not see me. I hurried down the street to where the girls were still being amused by the little dog.

"All right now, ladies. Tell the dog good-bye," I said as I herded my charges farther from Alderton House.

Away from the morbid atmosphere of the school, the girls giggled among themselves. After a while, Rufina added a hop to her step and skipped toward the park. In short order, the others joined in. Their gaiety did my heart good, so I chose not to admonish them to act like ladies.

I walked at a brisk pace to keep up with the students. Perhaps Miss Jones had a perfectly good reason for clipping so much of Selina's hair. I knew nothing of funerary jewelry. Was it possible that Miss Jones needed locks of a certain length or thickness? Was that why she robbed Selina of her beauty? Or had Miss Jones intended to deal the corpse one last indignity? Was she as bent on revenge as Signora Delgatto was?

As puzzling as these questions were, Lucy and Mr. Douglas would help me think through them. There was so much that I was eager to share! What with the footprints on the landing and all the new knowledge I had about Selina. Especially the visit from the mysterious man who had interceded on Selina's behalf, and how his visit marked a change in the girl's privileges.

Taken individually, these bits of information probably meant nothing, but in the aggregate they might form a pattern. The question was, could we see it?

Chapter 38

Lucy and Mr. Douglas sat on the same bench, waiting for our arrival. I could tell as we approached them that Lucy fairly hummed with excitement. Today she wore a dress of maroon, trimmed with black. The girls swarmed around first her and then Mr. Douglas and Rags to say hello. They lingered to stroke the soft muslin fabric of her dress. "Thank goodness you are here," Lucy whispered in my ear as she embraced me. "I have important news."

"So have I," I said. "Let me start the girls on their lesson."

Taking the girls a few yards away, I lectured my students about the different shapes of birds' beaks, and how those beaks are suited to the industry of the species. In the school's library, I had found a copy of my old favorite Bewick's *History of British Birds*, and this I showed as a reference. The girls were assigned the task of drawing and writing an essay, comparing and contrasting four or more types of birds. With my students thus involved in their work, I would be able to speak freely with my friends, taking care to act as if we were having the most casual of chats, although we were actually discussing a matter of life and death.

"Do you feel safe, Jane? I need to know. If at any time you feel endangered, don't hesitate to send for us. Bruce is staying at my house for the interim. Higgins and Williams might not look like much, but they both served Augie in Bombay. They are tested and true."

Once she was assured of my well-being, Lucy took a deep breath and said, "I have been asking questions about the Biltmores while out making my morning calls. What I have learned puts everything that has happened into a new framework—and it might well color whatever you have discovered since we talked last."

"Pray continue. You have my complete attention."

"As you know, the Biltmores are from Brighton. In fact, Mr. Biltmore sold our King the farmland on which he built his Marine Pavilion."

Even in secluded Ferndean, we had heard how our current King, back when he was Prince of Wales, decided to turn a simple farmhouse on the southern coast into a pavilion, a fabulous showplace for his collection of Chinese wallpaper, furnishings, and pieces of art. By 1815, the villa seemed overcrowded, so the Prince hired John Nash to transform it into a palace. While His Majesty's trips to Brighton began as a way to improve his health, the seaside resort quickly became known for encouraging His Royal Highness to indulge in habits destructive to his well-being: gluttony, drunkenness, and carousing.

"Seems that the Biltmores eagerly pursued an invitation to one of King George IV's many parties. It was there that His Majesty took notice of Selina." Lucy paused.

I buried my face in my hands. Oh, to have such a man on our throne! But before I could regain my composure, another thought came. "Lucy, you can't mean . . . that Selina and our sovereign—"

"No," Mr. Douglas said solemnly. "She was not his paramour. But I have heard a rumor that her mother was."

"Then that means it is possible Selina was . . . his daughter?" I gasped as I realized the full import of this.

By all accounts, when he was younger, the Prince of Wales was intelligent, charming, and socially precocious. But he also had a disastrous weakness: He fell head over heels in love often and indiscriminately, frequently pursuing women who spurned him. In fact, the more they rebuked him, the harder he chased them, until he went so far as to marry one woman, Maria Fitzherbert, in a wholly illegal ceremony performed by a curate sprung from debtors' prison just for the event. Of course, his father, George III, turned a blind eye, and the powers that be protested that his marriage was but a sham. After all, our nation depended upon the heir to the throne to do his duty as a sovereign to produce his own royal heir—and for that to happen, the Prince would have to participate in a legitimate marriage to a royal princess. Caroline of Brunswick became his wife, and soon after, his enemy. When George III descended into madness, the Prince of Wales, his son George Augustus Frederick, was named Regent. Then George III died and the Regent became King George IV. Now our new sovereign and his estranged wife, Caroline, were locked in a battle playing itself out on the grand stage of the British Parliament as he accused her of committing adultery.

"Selina could have been one of his many illegitimate children," Lucy corrected me.

We three sat there silently, each lost in thought, until Rags whimpered for affection.

"But one of the girls told me that Selina had a special friend, whose name was Prinny," I said.

Lucy covered her mouth and smothered a guffaw. "That's the nickname that Mrs. Fitzherbert's adopted daughter gave the King."

"That explains a lot," I said. "Especially why Selina's 'friendship' was an open secret."

"Yes," Mr. Douglas agreed. "Also why Marcus Piper was reluctant to talk to me and why Mr. Waverly is involved."

"No wonder Mrs. Thurston stood aside and let the girl have her way. In the beginning, the superintendent must not have known about her parentage. Then Fräulein Hertzog caught the girl sneaking and tried to exact a punishment. In retribution, Selina killed the woman's pet canary and teased the woman by scattering its feathers around."

"What a monstrous thing to do!" Lucy said.

"Oh, there's more. I learned today that Selina pushed her own governess down a well and dropped a snake on the woman. She seems to have been a truly horrid girl." I paused. "But back to Selina's status at the school. It seems that Mrs. Thurston rescinded the punishment for sneaking out after a man came to visit the superintendent. I surmise the man must have been a representative from the King," I said. "But I don't understand why Selina was enrolled at Alderton House at all. Wouldn't the King have given her suitable lodging and an allowance?"

"Gads, no," Mr. Douglas said. "He is more likely to pay her to go away than to foot the bills to keep her!"

"But to house one of the King's children at a school?" I persisted.

"Let me suggest a reason, based on what I've heard," Lucy said. "The Biltmores are heavily in debt. A house in London is always expensive. More so during the Season. And staffing a suitable dwelling only adds to the cost. However, the cost for Selina to attend school here was, in comparison, a pittance. And this prime location kept their daughter easily accessible to His Majesty."

"What did her parents hope to gain?"

"I imagine they hoped the King would find favor with her, and perhaps give her an allowance or a place at court." Lucy frowned thoughtfully. "Any of those choices would have improved the Biltmores' fortunes."

A faint smile played on Mr. Douglas's lips. "Remember that we said Mr. Biltmore was a gambler? I believe he was gambling that his daughter could win the prize. Not a crown, not a place in line to the throne, but a settlement. It has happened before."

"That is the saddest part of this scheme." Lucy shook her

head. "Prinny has never acknowledged any of his illegitimate offspring. He barely paid attention to his legitimate daughter, Princess Charlotte. And then she passed on."

Yes, I had heard all about that. Princess Charlotte had died in childbirth. The poor girl had already miscarried twice before that third, fatal, attempt. My mouth filled with a bitter taste. "If that is how our royal family treats their children, I want no part of them! If a child is born on the wrong side of the blanket, it certainly is not the fault of the child!"

"You must understand what is at stake here." Mr. Douglas sighed. "It is His Majesty's duty to provide a legitimate heir. That secures an orderly transfer of power. With the death of his only daughter, and his animosity toward his wife, he has failed—and he is keenly aware of it. One reason he would like to be rid of Queen Caroline of Brunswick is so that he might remarry and fulfill his responsibilities. Perhaps if that happens, he might be more willing to acknowledge his illegitimate offspring."

My disgust for our King must have been fully apparent.

"Jane, our sovereign was forced by his father to marry a woman wholly unsuitable to be his wife. He had no choice in the matter. In fact, he was forced to give up the one woman he truly loved. Does that not sound familiar to you?" Lucy put a gentle hand on mine.

In response, I gave hers a light squeeze. "Yes, I guess that it does," I said, recalling my own Edward's first marriage.

"I imagine that the Biltmores hoped Selina would be given a settlement that would make a fine dowry," Lucy said quietly. "Perhaps they thought that our King might make a match for her."

"Prinny has been known to be extraordinarily generous on occasion," Mr. Douglas said. "And whether he acknowledged Selina or not, it's true he adores children."

"But she is—was—no child," I said, jumping in to clear up that misunderstanding by explaining how I'd seen the body of a mature and rather robust young woman.

"No wonder she could bully her friends," Mr. Douglas said. "Now that we've had our soupçon of scandal, what else do you have for us, Mrs. Rochester?"

I told them about the Biltmores' visit. "Selina's father said that Caje was supposed to keep an eye on his daughter. It sounds as if they had some sort of an arrangement."

My students passed the copy of Bewick's around as they talked among themselves. I could see the girls marveling, as I once had, over the vignettes describing a desolate coast far away. In that place, one could be miserably cold, but free of all painful human contact. The bleak settings both captivated and appalled me, as they predicted a sad future for those of us who were plain, obscure, and alone.

But I never dreamed that an attractive young woman who had a loving family might also face an uncertain future.

"After spending the past two nights in the dormitory setting, I am more and more confident that all of our students were dosed with laudanum. That is the only way that everyone would have slept through Selina's struggle." I explained about seeing the effects of the drug on Adèle and more recently on Parthena. "Unfortunately, it is common enough that almost anyone would have access to it."

Rufina ran over to show me her work. I praised it and sent her back to her schoolmates so that I could share another discovery. "There is yet another girl who has marks on her back. Rose has also been struck with a cane."

"Who would mar such beauty as your little Rose?" Bruce Douglas immediately looked toward the girl as she sat with her schoolmates on the grass. "That is simply unconscionable."

Lucy's jaw dropped and she turned on her brother. "So it's permissible to hit unattractive girls, but God forbid one might mar a beauty?"

I agreed with Lucy, and I was disappointed by her brother's comments. It is painful enough to be overlooked because one lacks regularity of features, but more painful yet to be reminded that one is thought to be of lesser value because she has not been blessed with beauty. On the other hand, Selina's death was a powerful reminder that even the most lustrous of us must finally meet decay.

Mr. Douglas grasped his chest as if he'd been stabbed in the heart and coughed loudly. "Sister Lucy, you wound me to the core. I am only human, and as a man, a lower form of such!" He continued in a quieter voice, "I talked to my source at the medical examiner's office. Selina Biltmore's back was also scarred."

"Miss Miller claims the punishment could not have taken place. Miss Jones agrees. Adèle knows naught of it." I pulled a face.

"But it must have," argued Lucy. "Otherwise why would such marks be found on more than one of the girls?"

"There are three questions: Who administered the thrashings? Why didn't anyone hear anything? Would such beatings have been a reason for murder?" I asked.

"Another avenue to explore," Mr. Douglas said with a sigh.

I recounted for Lucy and her brother my meeting with Mr. Waverly, his interview with Adèle, and his hidden mastery of French. Mr. Douglas couldn't keep a grin from his face, for which he apologized. "I am sorry, Mrs. Rochester, but I do admire Waverly. He never ceases to surprise me."

"Speaking of surprises." I handed Mr. Douglas the sketch I'd made. "It is a rather good likeness."

"This could be a powerful asset in finding the thief." He carefully folded his pocket handkerchief around the sketch. "Perhaps one of my informants will recognize him."

"I sincerely hope so." For the most part, I pushed that unhappy problem from my mind. The return to teaching and the intrigues of Alderton House aided me immensely in this, but not entirely. I dreaded talking with Edward about the loss of his family heirlooms. Now a slight glimmer of hope lifted my spirits.

Chapter 39

❦

When Lucy hugged me good-bye, she slipped me a packet. "Letters from Ferndean," she whispered. I shook Mr. Douglas's hand and headed toward Alderton House with my charges.

I walked with the Juniors while Rufina, Adèle, Nettie, and Rose chased one another toward an Oriental plane tree that might have been one of the originals planted in the park nearly two hundred years ago. Under the last vestiges of its lacy leaf cover, the Seniors circled 'round and 'round until they felt dizzy. All was laughter and shouting until Nettie slipped and fell. She landed hard, twisting her foot under her. I raced to her side.

"I'm not hurt, miss. Not much," said the lisping girl as I offered her my hand to pull her up. But once on her feet, the color drained from her face and she turned an ashen white. "Ow!" She flinched. "It pains me something fierce."

Rufina rushed to her classmate's side. "Nettie, put your arm over my shoulder. Adela? Get on her other side."

Rose offered Nettie a quick kiss on the cheek, but no physical assistance.

For a while, Adèle, Rufina, and Nettie struggled across the

grassy lawn of Hyde Park, but soon Rufina shook off the French girl's assistance. "I know you are trying to help, but I think Nettie can hop along better with just one of us, and I am fine, honest I am. She does not weigh much. Not really."

Rufina and Nettie managed without my interference. The two girls were roughly the same height, but Rufina's endurance astonished me. Rufina was sturdy, but the strength she showed amazed me, as did her leadership, because under Rufina's command the situation was quickly in hand.

Yesterday I doubted that any of the girls could have smothered Selina. I didn't believe they had reason—and I doubted they had the strength. And I wondered that they would pull together as a team.

Now I knew differently, and the scars from the canings suggested a new reason for animosity.

A rather more disturbing thought: What if the girls had worked in tandem? What if two or more of them had pressed the pillow to Selina's face? What if Selina had been the one responsible for canings—and they decided to put a stop to the torture? Especially since no adult was there to supervise them?

What exactly were my students capable of?

I didn't have the luxury of pondering this overmuch. We arrived back at Alderton House just as Mr. Waverly was leaving. "Ah, Miss Eyre." He emphasized my last name to send me a message: I know your secret.

"Mr. Waverly." I nodded. "Run along, girls. I shall be there shortly. Rufina? Tend to Nettie, please."

"How goes the investigation?" I waited until the front door had shut behind the girls.

He wasted no time on niceties. "Were you aware that another girl died at a school where Miss Miller was in charge?"

"They called it typhus, but the real killer was starvation," I said, remembering our deprivations at Lowood.

"Indeed? Well, I have also learned that she slips out at night."

This confounded me. Yes, I'd noted that she'd been missing for large portions of the day yesterday, but . . . could the long and narrow set of footprints have been Miss Miller's, not Miss Jones's?

"What do you intend to do?" I struggled to keep my voice calm.

"You shall see soon," he said cryptically, removing his pipe and blowing out a stream of smoke. "I have one other person in the school yet to interview. That young footman. Confound him. He manages to scurry out each time I arrive. Someone must be assisting him in giving me the slip. But I shall catch up to him!" With that, he turned on his heel and left.

Purposefully holding myself erect, I made it inside the doorway before collapsing against the frame. What did his questions about Nan Miller mean?

After climbing to the first floor, I saw the Junior girls racing down the stairs from their dormitory after depositing their bonnets and exchanging their boots for mourning shoes. "Ladies," I warned them sternly, "this is still a house of mourning."

In the main classroom, Rufina situated Nettie with her foot propped up on a leather ottoman. Rose took her injured friend's bonnet and cloak and went to borrow a rag from Cook. When she returned with the length of cotton fabric, I wrapped Nettie's ankle as tightly as was comfortable.

With our injured party taken care of, I asked Adèle to collect the girls' essays comparing bird beaks. While she picked up the papers, I wrote German vocabulary words on the blackboard and instructed the girls to use these words in simple sentences. Instead of correcting the girls' assignments, however, I opened my letters and read:

Dear Jane,

I trust this missive will find you in good health. Mr. Rochester and little Ned are fine, as am I. It will please you to know that the master has followed Mr. Carter's instructions to the letter. He has stayed recumbent more than I can ever recall, and I've known him all of his life, and he has been diligent about applying hot compresses to his eyes on a regular basis. It causes him no end of aggravation, but he has committed to improving his status. Meanwhile, he meets with workmen and hears their proposals for rebuilding Thornfield. I do believe the project has acted as a tonic on his psyche.

Ned's appetite is good. Yesterday he smiled at me when I held him. I believe he will have your hair color and Mr. Rochester's nose. It will be a fine combination; Ned is bound to grow up to be a handsome lad.

Enclosed you will find a letter from Mr. Rochester. Although I am more than happy to serve as his secretary, John and I came up with a plan. By scoring a sheet of paper with a stylus, we created raised guidelines, much like the lines printed on paper for students who are learning their letters. John nailed together a half frame, consisting of two pieces of molding set at right angles. A clasp completed his invention.

We presented this to the Master, who was quite pleased with our efforts. By securing the paper within the two-sided "frame" and using his sense of touch to follow the raised lines, Mr. Rochester is able to write to you without assistance, although I do suspect you'll find his writing a touch wobbly.

I send you warmest regards.

Your humble servant,
Alice Fairfax

I smiled and tucked that letter back in my pocket. A lump formed in my throat as I read about Ned and Edward. How thoughtful of Mrs. Fairfax to work with John to create a contraption to help Edward write! My heart filled with warmth toward the old lady. How lucky we were to have Alice Fairfax in our lives! Oh, how I missed my family back at Ferndean!

On the second sheet I found a wobbly script, occasionally overlapping itself, but on the whole easy enough to decipher.

Darling Jane,

Oh, but I miss you, my dearest wife. Letting you go was torture to me! I feel like God reached down and ripped out my heart. I listen for your footsteps. I wait for your touch. I awaken in the night and feel such emptiness as I have never known.

I curse this blasted eye and my infirmities! A man should not be at the mercy of his deficiencies, as I am at mine. I pray we shall never be separated again, my darling Jane, for I tell you, I can scarcely breathe for the pain of missing you.

At least, I take solace in knowing that soon we will be together again!

I will come to London as quickly as I can, my sweetheart. I miss you so much!

Your loving husband,
Edward

I wiped the tears from my eyes with my linen handkerchief. Why was I here when he was there? What possible use could I be to these girls? For a long while, I turned the letter over and over in my fingers. It was a spider's silk thread that bound me to my real life—and I worried that at any moment that thread might snap and I would find myself all alone.

Chapter 40

At dinner, Miss Miller was missing. Mrs. Thurston rapped on her water glass with the blade of her knife and looked out over the girls. "You comported yourselves well this morning. Please keep up the good work. There will be important visitors coming in and out, no doubt. I expect you to carry on as usual. Also, Miss Miller has been confined to her quarters. Teachers? Please see to her students. Remember, I tolerate no gossip. None! Have I made myself clear? Very well. Carry on." She raced through a prayer and punctuated the word "amen" with a hearty slam of her fist so that all the serving utensils jumped and clattered. Milk slopped over in one of the pitchers and spilled onto the tablecloth, lending a pungent fragrance to the setting.

As she sank back into her seat, I caught a whiff of gin. A quick glance her way told the tale. She had been drinking!

I gripped the edges of my chair seat to steady myself. *Carry on.* Yes, that was exactly what I must do.

Miss Jones's expression was largely unreadable; the laudanum seemed to have dulled her responses. The students exchanged quizzical looks, as they did not immediately grasp the import of Mrs. Thurston's comments. But Rufina understood and blurted, "Miss Miller must be in trouble! It's that man who keeps questioning her, isn't it? What is he? A constable?"

"That's enough, Rufina," I said.

"Yes, miss." But tears welled up and one dripped down her face.

Rose stared into her soup, Nettie sniveled a bit, and Adèle seemed largely unconcerned. The Juniors whispered to one another. Without their proctor, the Infants seemed lost. For the most part, however, they were unsure of what all the uproar meant. But after much whispering, little Caroline said, "They're going to put her in jail, aren't they?" and burst into sobs. One by one, the others joined her until even the Seniors were wiping their eyes. We adults were islands of solemnity, surrounded by crying children.

Mrs. Thurston continued eating as if nothing untoward was happening. She mopped up her plate with a slice of bread.

I offered what comfort I could by talking with the students. Miss Jones seemed strangely unmoved. The crying did not stop. Finally, Mrs. Thurston slammed down her food, shoved her chair back in disgust, and stalked off to her office, presumably to drown her problems in strong spirits.

The excellent baked hens that Cook had prepared went largely unappreciated; even the aroma of sage and parsley could not entice. I found I had little appetite.

"I feel quite torn, I do," Miss Jones said with a long sigh. "Miss Miller brought me on, and I held her in high esteem. However, if the Bow Street Runner believes she's guilty, that is rather a sure sign, isn't it? I mean, what with the dosing of the children and all."

"What dosing?" I toyed with a piece of chicken.

Miss Jones shrugged. "She is the one who doses the children. As headmistress, that is Miss Miller's responsibility.

Whether they have croup or fever, she administers the medicines. Since none of the Seniors awakened, Mr. Waverly must assume that Selina was dosed with laudanum before bedtime. Probably all the girls were."

I sat there stupefied. Miss Jones spoke in such a casual manner, but she had come to the same conclusion that I had. Was there more that she knew? I decided to encourage her to talk freely. Who knew what she might share?

"I find this . . . astonishing. Do you really think Miss Miller would kill one of the students? And why? What would have been her reasoning?"

"Who knows? She is an enigma to me. What with her sudden disappearances and her history."

This bothered me. Should I tell Miss Jones that I suspected *she* was sneaking out as well? Perhaps the roundabout path was best. "I have heard noises on the landing at night."

"I have, too," said Miss Jones. "In fact, I frequently wake and investigate, but to no avail. I understand how you feel. This whole situation distresses me, too. I have had trouble sleeping, and I can tell by the circles under your eyes that you worry also. I think we are much alike that way. As a gesture of friendship, I made a small gift for you."

Reaching into her pocket, Miss Jones withdrew a palm-sized rectangle wrapped in brown paper and tied with twine. "Please understand, I am just a beginner, but I hope to improve. Perhaps even with your help?"

I opened the gift to reveal a tiny watercolor sketch of a robin.

"This is so unexpected. I scarce know what to say beyond giving you my thanks." I openly marveled at the fine detail. Her proportions were slightly askew, but the effort showed talent. "Your sense of color is extraordinary."

"I did it while the girls were working on their math problems. I do hope you like it."

"I am delighted."

A skirmish ensued at the other end of the table. Victoria burst into sobs, pushed her plate to one side, and rested her face on the table to cry in earnest. I went to her. "Try not to fret. Come on now, be a good girl. Chin up." I patted her on the back.

"I do hope they can calm down," I said as I returned to my seat. "I wish Mrs. Thurston had been more comforting. Perhaps if she had spoken with more . . . caution or compassion. See how upset the students are! They are too young to have these worries."

"I suppose." Miss Jones cast a quick look over at the girls but mainly kept her attention on the bread she was buttering. "But remember, Miss Eyre, these are children of privilege. They will never know deprivation or hunger or thirst. This will bother them for a short time, and they will forget it ever happened. Neither Miss Miller nor you nor I mean anything to them. Yes, right now they feel shock. But the upset will fade. If not, perhaps it will even do them good. It might prove edifying." She shrugged and took a bite of her food. With a full mouth, she added, "It might just teach them a good lesson."

"Yes, but these are children. They are frightened!"

"Perhaps. But they have no reason to be."

"Their teacher is being questioned, their schoolmate was killed, and you have no sympathy for them? Or even for the dead child?"

"She was no child, just a nasty piece of baggage who teased her classmates and the teachers unmercifully. Because of her relationship with our debauched sovereign, she was accorded special privileges." Miss Jones studied me. "Yes, I guessed you would find out about her royal connections. Not much of a secret, was it? Obviously, the King grew tired of her. I am certain he found the girl as disruptive as all of us did. One could safely assume he had her dispatched with, rather than put up with her or pay her off. As for the rest of the students,

I have limited sympathy for them, which is more than they
have for me. Or for you. They will hire and fire women like
us when they are grown. They will pay us less than they would
spend on a nice frock. They will dismiss us on a whim. They
will accuse us of kindling their husband's affection. They will
grow furious when their children run to us for comfort. Meanwhile, we will care for their children, mop up their little ones'
tears, bind their wounds, and when they are grown, we shall
be tossed out into the cold. Unlike Emma or Caje, our working
lives are short, our services needed but for a brief window of
time. Nor are we valued for what we do, because we do not
enhance the lives of our employers.

"On the contrary, we irk them. They look upon us as necessary evils. We encourage their children to think"—and
here she tapped on her temple—"to learn, to grow beyond
their own narrow, well-prescribed lives. In short, we threaten
them."

"Sad to say, you are right." Back at Thornfield, when I was
still Adèle's governess, Mr. Rochester had entertained a gathering of the local gentry, including Blanche Ingram; her sister,
Mary; and their mother, the Dowager Lady Ingram. Blanche
had said that she and her sister had had at least a dozen governesses, half of them detestable and the rest ridiculous. Her
mother joined in to say she had suffered a martyrdom from
the incompetency of "our class." When another guest pointed
out that because of my proximity, I could hear this ugly commentary, Blanche and her siblings discussed the various methods by which they had tortured, belittled, and persecuted their
tutors. All of which they seemed to think droll behavior that
they looked back on fondly, though to me it revealed them as
hard-hearted and spoiled creatures, cruel to the extreme and
self-aggrandizing as well.

Of course, the cruelty that the Ingrams had displayed was
minor compared to pushing a governess down a well and drop-
ping a snake on her! My cousins Mary and Diana Rivers had

served briefly as governesses, and both of them had been exceedingly pleased to surrender their posts when I shared my inheritance with them. Once supplied with income, they chose to cast off the yoke of servitude that had been forced upon them by poverty.

"Our world is larger than theirs," continued Miss Jones, "and so we cause the parents grave discomfort. They repay us by spurning us. We are what they shun, and also what they aspire to be: educated. Thus, we are relegated to the margins of their society. We are the outcasts, the pariahs—women who do not trade solely on our looks, but who aspire to a higher calling, because we possess cultivated minds."

In this way, the union between Edward and me was unique. Although he admired my appearance, plain though I might seem to the world at large, he praised my intellect for having captured his heart. It was my spirit—my will and energy, virtue and purity—that he'd wanted to possess. These attributes taken together were what he said drew him to me and knit our heartstrings.

"The mothers who employ women like us are empty-headed dolls, prized only because they are petite, pretty, and precious, whether that means they bring a coffer of money to the marriage or confer some status. It does not matter. Such is the way of the world. They do what they are born and bred to do without thinking."

She finished with, "I feel no sympathy for the mothers—and only a little for their daughters. This is just a new generation of silly, addlepated women. We can pour all the education into these vessels that we want, but they are flawed. Thanks to their social status, they care little about what they learn. It is as if these particular vessels suffer from a large crack that lets the knowledge flow right out onto the table."

With that she folded her serviette and looked at me curiously. "You think me cold and unfeeling, I am sure. That is not the case. I accept my lot in life and enjoy my students during that brief overlap of their lives and mine. Who knows what the future may bring?"

"Yes, I think it well to dwell in the moment."

"There is nothing we can do about our status, Miss Eyre. We shall always stand with one foot on the bottom rung of life while hanging on for dear life with the other!"

Hunger had finally gotten the best of the girls. Most of them now turned to the task of eating. Seeing that we were being ignored, I took the opportunity to ask Miss Jones one more question. "What do *you* think happened to Selina? Whom do you suspect?"

"I have every confidence it was Caje."

"Why?" Her accusation surprised me. Especially in light of Mr. Biltmore's ugly suggestion that Caje should have watched over his daughter more carefully. Perhaps I needed to pay more attention to the young man, and certainly to consider him with more suspicion.

"Selina flirted with him shamelessly. I wouldn't doubt he grew weary of her cruel games. Since he sleeps on a pallet on the kitchen floor, he could easily climb the back stairs and gain access to the Senior dormitory."

This was something I hadn't considered. The young man was so quiet, so unobtrusive that I had largely discounted his presence.

But not anymore.

Chapter 41

The rest of the evening seemed to drag on and on. The girls were particularly subdued during our reading hour. When Selina died, they had felt both relief and fear, but the potential loss of Miss Miller shook the foundations of their world. She, more than Mrs. Thurston, was their safe harbor. Miss Miller had remained when Mrs. Webster left, and her stabilizing impact had helped the girls make the adjustment to Mrs. Thurston. Now, they were bewildered. They wandered around the room aimlessly, unable to concentrate on the tasks at hand.

This evening, I was the first to leave the sitting room, and as I did, I caught a glimpse of Nan Miller's skirt as she slid behind the door and into the Infants' sleeping area. Her hem was damp, and a single green leaf hung from it.

I was puzzled. I knew that Cook had been told to lock the door to the area, so no one could enter the building from there. As we left the dinner table, I had personally observed Emma turning the key to lock the front door as she did each night before returning the key to Mrs. Thurston. Miss Miller was supposed to be confined in the dormitory. So where had she been?

I decided to ask her myself. "Rufina? You are in charge. I shall be back quickly. I have an errand to run." With that, I crept down the hall. The mourning slippers rendered my steps soundless. I opened the door to the Infant dormitory quietly, and I stood to one side watching Miss Miller without her noticing.

She seemed withdrawn but calm as she instructed the Infants to get dressed for bed. She spoke in soothing tones, but the girls practically shrank away from her. At long last, she glanced my way and mouthed, "Anon."

Back in the dormitory, it was clear that my Seniors were also were confused and upset, so I gathered them around me on my mattress, where I told them a short story about a plain princess. As expected, all the girls thought the story to be about them—except for Rose. I doubted that she had ever felt unattractive, though she did find the story entertaining. "To be ugly would be horrid! Just horrid! I should rather die!"

Rose should show more compassion, but . . . why should she? She would never be less than lovely.

Rufina rolled her eyes at her chum, and I hid a smile. I delighted in the girl's sense of self and her strength of character. She proved herself to be resilient, reliable, and intelligent. However, it was her physical strength that led me to wonder if she could have smothered Selina. Perhaps Rufina had grown tired of watching the older girl bully her classmates? The more I learned about their dead schoolmate's cruelties, the harder it was to muster up revulsion toward her killer.

"Off to bed," I instructed, and when every girl was under her covers, I tucked each one in and planted a kiss on her forehead. The gesture came naturally, for I regarded each of them with affection. It was true, though, that I lingered a bit with Adèle, murmuring promises to her in French. The moments with her were to my benefit, as much as to hers, as I promised myself that soon I would be home and able to shower my son with similar affection.

After soft snoring and regular sighs settled over the dormitory, I closed the window by the horse chestnut tree and locked it. Leaving the door open, I crossed the hall and slipped into the Infants' room, where Miss Miller sat on a chair pulled up to a window, her arms crossed under her chin, as she stared out at the city. I touched her shoulder lightly and she turned.

"Miss Eyre, I knew you would come. Time to say good-bye, dear friend."

"Miss Miller! Are you saying you are guilty of this crime? I cannot imagine it."

In the pale moonlight, she wore what was almost but not quite a smile. But more importantly, tears stood in her eyes, which held no hope.

"I *am* guilty."

"What? You killed Selina Biltmore? I cannot believe that! Why then would you insist that I come safeguard the Senior girls? It does not make sense."

One of the Infants whimpered.

"Hush." Miss Miller rose and patted the child's back. I waited for her to come back and sit down. I perched on the edge of her mattress so I had a clear view of the Senior dormitory and its open door.

"Of course I did not kill Selina. However, I am guilty all the same. I told you that circumstances changed, remember? And those changes were why I quit teaching at the village school and came to London? That much is true. You had served in a similar capacity, or so you said. But you left and married your Mr. Rochester. My story did not have a happy ending."

"Tell it to me," I said. "You owe me that much. I came here at your behest."

She sighed. "Like you, I taught in a small school, in Liverpool. And like you, I fell in love. The object of my affection was the Anglican minister Francis Gilbert. Somehow I let myself believe that he returned my affection, and so when a large group of Irish immigrants flooded our town, I took my concerns to him. I worried, you see, because the children were clearly hungry."

Pausing, she pinched the bridge of her nose. After a moment, she picked up her tale. "Reverend Gilbert wouldn't hear of giving the Irish immigrants Anglican charity. In fact, he refused to allow me to distribute baskets of food to them, although the ladies of the church regularly made these up for just that purpose. I wanted to curry his favor, so I did as he ordered. You see? I closed my eyes to their suffering. I told myself that their own kind would help them. Once in a while I would leave a bit of my own leftover bread on the school steps so the children could eat a little something if they came to class early. But I never suspected that they took my meager offerings home to share. Or that they fed the youngest ones first. My imagination did not encompass the extent of their suffering. I lied to myself! But they were so hungry.

"One day after school, I discovered two of the Irish girls eating dirt and grass. Another time I found them eating a piece of paper that had been discarded, the wrapping of other students' lunches. I spoke about all this to Reverend Gilbert, but he was adamant. If I chose to feed their bodies, I would condemn their souls to hellfire, he said. And I bowed to his wishes, because I thought that he would see my obedient nature and know what a good wife I would make!"

I fought the urge to condemn her but I wanted to cry out: "You know better!" This story paralleled the sort of religious claptrap that we had heard so often in our youth. How could she not have seen through it?

"Then one day I came to school early, as was my habit," she said haltingly, "and found a hollow-eyed child slumped against the front door. Little Mary O'Brien was stone-cold dead. Mary loved school, but the two-mile walk that day had proved too much for her tired heart. Of course, I was not responsible. Not in the eyes of the law. But in the eyes of God? Ah, that is different."

She turned to me and grasped both my hands in hers, which were as cold as if she had handled snow. "That is why I came and got you. I could not stand by this time. I knew I did not have the courage or the wit to safeguard these girls, but after your visit on Monday morning, I got to thinking . . . Jane Eyre does!"

I said nothing, lest I say too much. I always allowed Miss Miller a good heart, and now I questioned my assessment. She, who knew better and who had already seen suffering in the guise of religious conscience, had stood idly by while a child starved.

And then . . . I recalled what Mr. Carter had told me. About the hunger of the people farming Edward's lands. Was I really without sin? Did I have the right to cast the first stone?

No. I was equally guilty. And so was Edward. We would have to rectify the situation—and soon.

I withdrew my hands from hers, and kept them knotted under the skirt of my wrapper so as not to give away my distress.

"Shortly afterward, I came here. And I discovered that thousands of Irish have also come to London because the potato crop has failed. You see, they rely too heavily on it. There was a blight in the last century and their problems continue. Their families are so large, and there's no other work besides that in the field. So they come here, hoping to find jobs in the city."

London was a stylish lady who beckoned you to come closer, and when seen from a distance, she looked remarkable. Only on closer inspection did you notice her diseased sores, her filth, and her soiled apparel.

"The abundance of food here fairly shocked me, so I slip out when I can and take food to the poor. As much as I can, as often as I can."

"But Emma locks the front door. Cook has a room next to the door of the area. How do you manage?"

A faint smile played at her lips. "Cook is a good woman.

She likes her spirits, as does Mrs. Thurston. She left her keys out one day, and I took them to be duplicated. But I am confident she knows, and is, I believe, in sympathy with me. Certainly she never remarks on the food I slip into my pockets, and she often leaves out bread and cheese wrapped in paper.

"You must understand," she pleaded, taking my hand in hers and leaning close to me. "I need to do penance! I must save my soul! You see, I was a fool to think a man like Reverend Gilbert could ever love a woman like me. If I hadn't been so addled, if I had been more honest with myself, I would have followed my conscience. Instead, I listened to my desires—and I wanted him to love me. I wanted . . . a home and . . . a family."

With that, she started sobbing.

Her story could well have been mine. I understood the power of love, and how, coupled with the desire to be admired as a woman, it could lead a person astray.

"Do you think God will forgive me?" she said. "I am not worthy!"

She sounded most earnest, but I could not find it in myself to give her absolution. Not when I thought about that poor dead child! "You must seek His forgiveness, not mine."

"I cannot believe in a God who wants little children to go hungry, can you?" She grabbed my hand, capturing it again between both of hers.

"No. Of course not."

"Tell me, Miss Eyre. Do you hate me?"

"No." It wasn't hate. It was confusion, and disappointment. This place seemed to bring out the worst in all of its inhabitants. I could not wait to quit it!

But first, I would finish what I'd set out to do: find a killer. "I do not hate you, and I do not believe you hurt Selina Biltmore. There was no reason for you to injure that girl, or was there?"

"No. I did not like her, but she did not bother me. I rather think that somehow I was beneath her notice. Probably because I am unattractive. She had a magpie nature that drew her to persons who were bright and shiny or interesting. The rest of us she ignored."

"I have observed more caning marks. Do you know of this? Who might have administered such beatings?"

"Two girls?"

"Three, actually. I have it on good authority that Selina also bore the marks of a caning."

"Mr. Douglas? He has his resources."

"Yes."

"I . . . I don't know what to say. Except that I am appalled."

She said nothing, turning her face back to the deep darkness of the night.

"Tell me about Fräulein Hertzog. Could the Fräulein have caned the girls?"

Miss Miller thought about this. "I suppose it is possible. But unlikely. I sometimes heard whimpers from that dormitory. That would be on my head, too, wouldn't it? I have always been one who looked away rather than face what disturbs me. And that is why the prayer reads, 'Forgive us, Lord, for what we have done and what we have left undone.'"

I had no patience for Miss Miller and her recitation of the Anglican prayer of confession. Not tonight. More important matters concerned me. "I know about the circumstances under which she left. Is it possible that she stayed nearby? That she exacted revenge on Selina? Could Fräulein Hertzog have climbed in through the window to avenge her loss?"

"It is possible, but not likely. She was devastated over the death of her bird, yes, but she planned to return to Germany. Stuttgart, I believe. Wait!" Miss Miller rummaged through her dresser and returned with a piece of paper. "These are her details. Perhaps Mr. Douglas can locate her."

I took the paper and stood to leave. "Good night, Miss Miller."

"Miss Eyre, again I ask—do you hate me?" She sighed. "I was foolish, I know, to ever imagine that such a man could love me!"

The shadows obscured the eyes of a woman who had been kind to me when I was a child. But her voice trembled with her sorrow, and this unfulfilled longing radiated from her person.

I understood her hunger for love. I had tried to reject my feelings for Mr. Rochester, admitting honestly that I had little to recommend me. There were my irregular looks. My lack of social or political connections. And certainly, at that time, I had no fortune to offer.

But despite my shortcomings, I still felt my passions deeply. I still loved. Indeed, I could not stop, no matter how hard I tried!

What a boon it was to my soul when Edward Rochester said, "I think you good, gifted, lovely; a fervent, a solemn passion is conceived in my heart." When he claimed that he had found in me all that he had wanted and needed.

So, yes, I understood what it was like to want to be loved.

But I didn't understand how she could let a child starve. Nor could I imagine loving a man who thought God would be pleased to see suffering foisted on the least among us.

She spoke softly. "There is nothing more you can do here. Take Adela and go home. Go now before she is in more danger."

"What about the others? And the real killer?"

"I . . . I do not know what else to do for them. Let Mr. Waverly puzzle it out. I beg you. Please go, and take my love with you. You have been a true friend. If you stay, you might be tainted through our association. That would be more than I could bear. Go, just go."

And I did.

Chapter 42

I hoped to sleep, but thoughts of Miss Miller and her confession paced around and around in my head. There were three ways to enter the school: the area, the front door, and the Senior dormitory window by way of the horse chestnut tree. Given the apparent proclivity of Mrs. Thurston and Cook to like strong spirits, all three of the exits were accessible. In theory.

We had discarded the idea that the killer came from outside the school community. Perhaps we needed to revisit it. Was it possible that the murderer came from outside but had an accomplice here in the building? The accomplice could have dosed the girls and let the killer in. If there was an accomplice, who would it be? Why would anyone here have come to the aid of a murderer?

Mulling all this around, I finally fell asleep only to awaken with a start. There was a noise in the stairway. I strained to hear voices. Rising slowly from my bed, I slipped my arms into my wrapper and tied the sash.

Two people whispered on the other side of the door. I paused to listen. These were no ghostly apparitions.

After a few steadying breaths, I threw open the door.

Caje and Emma jumped apart, severing a loving embrace. In one outstretched hand, Emma held a lit candle, only a stub, and flickering, but casting enough light to illuminate their fearful faces.

"Miss, please. Don't tell on us. I beg you!" Caje said.

"Mrs. Thurston will sack me for sure, miss." Emma shivered, but she raised her chin defiantly. Over the shoulders of her thin night rail, she wore a tired quilt, a small rectangle sewn together from faded and patched materials.

Caje stood defiantly before me, fully dressed, except for shoes. He wore only much-darned socks on his feet. He stepped between Emma and me in a most protective manner. It was obvious that his had been the large footprints I'd seen in the powder I'd spread on the landing.

"I shall decide how to handle this later. After we talk. That is, if you are both honest with me."

I decided to press my advantage. Perhaps they could help me figure out who killed Selina, if I could conjure up the right questions to ask. "Let's go to your room, Emma. No need to wake everyone up."

We climbed the dark stairs to a small room with a sloped ceiling and a narrow bed under a dormer that leaked cold air.

"I'll tell you whatever you wish, miss. And it is my fault, it is. See, I love Emma. I do with all my heart. I'm saving up so we can marry," Caje said, standing with his head bowed because of the low ceiling.

"And I love him, with all my heart." The maid took her place beside him and slipped her arm through his.

I sat on the edge of her bed and studied them.

They exchanged longing looks, their eyes saying more than their lips ever could.

"But if Mrs. Thurston sacks us now, we cannot afford to

marry," Emma said. "Just a few more months, miss. That is all we're asking."

I sighed. I knew exactly how she felt, the hope, the love, and the strain of waiting.

Caje mistook my sigh for condemnation. "I never touched Emma. I mean, not in that way. I have been a gentleman—and she is a good girl. Good, through and through, miss. Ain't our fault we fell in love."

"In eight weeks, I'll be sixteen. Caje will get a job on the docks. A man promised him one. That's all we need, a few months. Then we can go to Gretna Green and get married, proper, over in Scotland."

The desperation saddened me. Why should it be dangerous for them to fall in love? I waved away their concerns with my hand. "I am not here to question you about that. In fact, I wish you both the best. But I do have questions about Selina. Caje, I heard Mr. Biltmore say you were to look after her. What did he mean?"

Caje stared down at his feet, his calloused hands clenching and unclenching at his side.

"Go on," said Emma, urging him forward. "You can trust her. He don't like to talk much, miss."

Haltingly, he said, "I worked for Mr. Biltmore back in Brighton. He got me this position. Told me to watch after his daughter because she were special. Paid me extra for it."

"Did Mrs. Thurston know what you were supposed to do?"

"No, not at first. She hired me because I said I'd work cheap."

"The Biltmores tricked Mrs. Thurston, they did," Emma said. "It was only later that she learned what was what—and oh, but she was fit to be tied, miss. Then the King sent that man around to talk to her, and she, well, she softened right up. Imagine! That girl being part of the royal family! No wonder Selina acted like she did."

"But my mum still works for the Biltmores, and I did not

want to make them angry with me, because of Ma," Caje said. "So I kept my mouth shut and my eyes closed."

"Did you tell Mr. Waverly this?"

His eyes darted frantically toward Emma and back to me. "No. He were supposed to talk to me, but so far I've managed to dodge him."

"I told Caje, I said, 'There is nothing they can do to you!' On account of, he was just doing what he was ordered to do, you see? He was working for Mr. Biltmore and the King both, after a manner." Emma tightened her protective clasp on Caje's arm.

"So Selina was visiting the King? And only him?"

He and Emma exchanged pained expressions. She nudged him and pulled up an empty crate for him to sit on. "Tell her."

"As far as I know," Caje said, taking the seat. "See, in the beginning, I don't think he believed she was his kin. It took some convincing, I guess. When she first came here, I had to help her get a carriage, and then make sure the front door was unlocked so she could get back in. Then, one day, a man I knew from Brighton came 'round. He gave me a pack of letters for her. From her mother. I think she must have shown them to the King, because soon after that, the King started sending his own carriage for her. I could tell because of the colors, you see. Yellow with maroon blinds. After that, she could come and go as she pleased." Caje scrubbed at his eyes with his fist and yawned loudly. Poor lad, he must have been bone-tired. Emma, too.

I patted the bed beside me, and she tentatively took a seat. Their regular duties required them both to be up before dawn and stay awake after the house was asleep. Meeting in the middle of the night clearly had taken a toll on both of them.

"No," Caje continued. "She weren't no angel. But it weren't all her fault. Her brothers. They were a bad lot. They taught her tricks. See, she learned from them how to get her way with people."

"What sort of tricks?"

"Mean ones. She switched out the sugar and the salt, and poor Cook nearly lost her job because the meat was ruined and the tea was spoiled, too. When the girls weren't paying attention, she'd blotch their work. Because Selina hated it here," Emma said.

"She thought she should be living in a fine house with lots of servants and be her own mistress." Caje's tone grew more urgent. "Her father thought she could do no wrong. Not in his eyes, leastwise. When she was born, she was a late baby— or so my ma said. Everyone adored her. Especially after all those brothers. Then she got awful sick and nearly died. After that, Mr. Biltmore spoiled her something fierce. Because he came so close to losing her. But her brothers were rough with her, and she always wanted to keep up with them. I think that's how she became so mean, being teased by them."

"But the King wouldn't have hurt her, would he?" I was thinking out loud.

"Can't see why or how. He must have liked her if he kept sending his carriage, right?"

I nodded. "Could a killer have climbed that tree and gotten into the dormitory?"

Emma shook her head. "We had rain all night before Selina died. I didn't see no water to mop up on the floor by the bed when I went in to clean. If a killer climbed in, wouldn't he have left a puddle?"

Emma was right: The rain had been heavy. Any intruder from the outside would have left water on the floor, given the heavy rains. There was no way a person could sneak in and out of Alderton House without getting wet. Or without leaving a trail along the way.

So I was back to imagining that the killer had to be someone within these walls. Someone with access to laudanum. Someone strong.

I said good night to the young couple and returned to my

uncomfortable bed. Lying there, trying to get comfortable, and staring up at the ceiling, I went over and over what I knew, what I had learned.

Far too early, the sunlight peeped around the curtains and lighted the heavy bunting from behind. The girls awakened slowly and splashed water on their faces.

Emma came in and avoided looking at me.

"Good morning," I told her. The lilt in my voice signaled that I harbored no ill will toward her.

She lifted shy eyes to me. "You won't tell, will you, miss?"

"No."

Venturing a little smile, she handed me an impressive leather portmanteau.

"Mrs. Thurston wants you to gather Selina's things from her dresser and put them in her valise."

I tried to sit up. Instead I could only groan because my back hurt so much from trying to sleep on my uncomfortable mattress. Although I did not reckon on many more nights here, this could not continue. "Emma? Could you help me? I want to switch out this pallet for that one, the one on Selina's bed."

She helped me lift the old mattress off my cot and lean it against the wall. I turned and looked down to see a cane resting on the mattress ropes.

"That's your problem, miss." Emma nodded toward the object that had caused most of my misery at night. A cane. Two feet long. Three-eighths of an inch in diameter. I picked it up, set it aside, and gestured to Emma that we could return the mattress to its original position.

"Thank you so much," I said to her. Then I asked in a whisper, "Do you have any idea how that got here?"

"No," she said, her gaze steady and honest. With that, she left the room.

The girls had turned to watch our housekeeping efforts, and now they stared at the rod.

"Is this the one that was used on you? Nettie? Rose?" I plucked it from the floor and displayed it in my hands. "On your backs? Were all of you struck with this cane?"

None of them spoke. All examined their feet and the floor with great interest.

"*Je ne sais pas.*" Adèle shrugged. "I have never seen that before."

"Ladies? I asked you a question. Is this the instrument responsible for the marks on your backs?" When no one met my eyes, I said, "Rufina? You are the head girl. Tell me. Was this used to punish you and your friends?"

"Yes, miss."

"Did Fräulein Hertzog strike you, Nettie? Or you, Rose?"

The two girls exchanged guilty glances at each other, but neither spoke. Nettie bothered a ruffle on her pinafore, a habit she employed as a prelude to evasion. "It is a secret," she said in a low tone.

"Girls, this is not a secret you should keep. Either you tell me what happened here or we shall all go down and talk to Mrs. Thurston about this." I did not intend to do any such thing, but leverage was sorely lacking, and any minute Emma might reappear and ask why we weren't on our way to breakfast. I knew that my best chance to get the girls to talk was right now.

Still, no one spoke.

"Rufina? I am counting on you. Talk to me. I do not intend to punish any of you or share your secret, if I can keep it quiet in good conscience. Rufina, did you strike your mates?"

"Oh no, miss! I would never! Not ever! It was Selina! See, she let us join her club, but only after she punished us with the stick." Rufina twisted a corner of her pinafore into a tight, angry knot.

"Getting hit was how you joined." Nettie lifted her chin. "But Fräulein Hertzog caught us and she took the cane away."

"But Fräulein Hertzog didn't tell Mrs. Thurston?" I found this confusing.

"No, Miss Eyre. It was right after Mrs. Thurston told her to leave Selina alone. So, see, she couldn't do much, except make it disappear. That's why she put it under her mattress."

"Did Selina's father beat her?"

"No, it was her brothers who showed her how they got the cane at school," said Rufina with wide eyes. "That's how they joined their clubs! And we wanted to be in a club, too."

"But none of you cried out?"

"Selina tied stockings together—clean ones—and we put them in our mouth to bite down on. See? Her brothers showed her how. Like when the headmaster would strike them. They bite on something. Hard."

A sick feeling coursed through me and I had to sit down. Edward had told me of such behavior—and its ugly consequences. As young men in boarding school, he and Augie had been hit many times. "Some scars heal," he had said. "Others never do."

"Selina never punished me." Adèle pouted. "I would hate to be hit."

"That's because Selina decided you were too young to belong to our club," Rufina said loftily, but with an air of exaggerated patience.

"But Adela, men like women who submit to them. My mother says so." Rose gave a knowing nod of her head. "My mother explained that we must do as our husbands command, no matter how disgusting. Each of us has a responsibility to do her duty as an Englishwoman."

"And Selina must have known what she was on about because the King fancied her mother." Nettie offered this as incontrovertible truth. "So there you have it."

I shuddered. This was both unexpected and revolting.

Confounded by these revelations, and amazed by the mixture of confusion, bad information, and general twaddle shared under the guise of wisdom, I said, "We shan't speak more of this right now. Rufina, take the others down to breakfast. I shall join all of you later."

They didn't move. The girls watched me expectantly.

"Do not worry about the cane. I shall keep your secret. We can talk more about your ideas on marriage and men later. For right now, you must trust me: Selina was wrong. Run along to breakfast, girls."

With sidewise glances they signaled each other that the worst was over. A collective sigh escaped from my students. One by one, they walked past me and the dreaded instrument of "duty." When Nettie closed the door behind her, I sank down onto the frame of my bed and rubbed my temples with my fingertips. My bones ached, I was tired, my heart hurt, and I could not think clearly.

Best to keep busy. I stood up, took a deep breath, and opened Selina's dresser. Since I had been ordered to pack the girl's belongings, no one could fault me for inspecting her things. I also planned to take the opportunity to return to the other girls those items that had *not* belonged to Selina.

What a strange and malicious girl she had been!

When I opened the drawer, I found quite a collection of trophies from her misdeeds: the missing German text, several silver forks bearing a royal crest, two lengths of ribbon, a loose stack of papers, a broken nob of china with gold trim and a touch of blue, a paper box with chocolate biscuits inside, and a handful of yellow feathers, which must have come from poor Fräulein's beloved bird. Under all this was a small packet of letters, tied with a royal blue ribbon. One quick glance told me that they were from His Majesty.

With shaking hands, I read the first one, skipping quickly over the endearments and moving straight to the heart of the message.

I quickly realized there was no reason to keep these. Glancing through the other letters, the sentiments were all the same.

One by one I fed them into the flames. But the last one caught my attention:

My Darling Pansy,

I miss you more than I can say. My love for you threatens to burst my heart! Never have I met such a woman as you! What a treasure you are. Hearing that you are with child worries me. Will your husband treat you well? I hope so, because as you might guess it is beyond my power to intercede on your behalf at the present time. Not when my own situation is so distressful!

As you might have heard, I am estranged from that loathsome creature who pretends to be my wife. God knows that our marriage is naught but a sham. Had I not been wholly desperate with my debtors pressing on me from every side, I would never have consented to a public spectacle. But my father was quite out of his mind, as you know, so I had no choice but to proceed and bow to his wishes, for the good of the empire, by agreeing to an alliance that would help me preserve my ascension to the throne—even if it cost me my immortal soul. Such a humble servant I am to our nation! But as I told you before, and as you well know, I had already honestly sworn before God and in the presence of a priest to love and honor another woman. A woman I met in my younger days before my father met his end, a death that could not cede the throne to me soon enough.

Together she and I have had a daughter, a darling girl, who is the joy of my life. Although circumstances have forced that lady and me to live apart, she and she alone is my true wife. So as you can see, as much as I care for you, I am already bound to another. If that were not true, I would certainly spend every resource at my disposal to elevate you to the status you deserve, and to provide for (and this was scratched out and written next to it in a tight hand) *you.*

On the last page, he had dropped down to the center, scribbled a few last lines, and signed his name.

> *Pity the poor head that wears the crown! No one can imagine what dangers and pressures assail me on every side. The dreams I have of my time on the battlefield! The terror I relive! Sometimes I fear that I am every bit as mad as my father!*

> *George*

I hesitated. This letter was different. It laid a solid foundation. I held it over the flame. An edge curled with heat—and then footsteps echoed in the hall.

I tucked that last letter deep into my pocket. I could burn it later.

Chapter 43

"I packed up Selina Biltmore's belongings," I said as I set the portmanteau on the floor of Mrs. Thurston's office. I went there immediately after checking out the footsteps on the stairs. It turned out to be a Junior girl, Patience, who'd come to fetch the history lesson she'd left in her dresser.

Without glancing up from her desk, the superintendent said, "Good. Tell Caje to fetch it and take it in by the coffin. They're coming to take her down to Brighton for the funeral later. Odd. I'd have thought there would be visitors to pay their respects, but none came." Raising a teacup to her lips, she slurped a mouthful, then paused, dog-eared the page she was reading, and finally acknowledged my presence. "That reminds me. After classes today, your services will no longer be required and you will need to find other lodgings."

My heart plummeted—and she watched for my reaction. As much as I wanted all this to be over, I was sure that Waverly hadn't found the killer. Nan Miller might be guilty of sins of omission, but she hadn't murdered Selina Biltmore. Solving this crime from outside of the school community would be much, much more complicated, if not impossible. Especially now that I'd begun to hatch a plan to expose the killer.

The stack of loose papers that I'd found in Selina's dresser was filled with nasty observations she had made concerning her schoolmates. As I'd looked them over, a plot began to form. After all, it was Adèle's letter that brought me here—why shouldn't another set of communications send me packing? As I folded Selina's expensive undergarments, I wondered, what if she had written a diary? She clearly knew how to pick at other people's sore spots. Did I really need to find such a journal? Couldn't I prevaricate? Wouldn't it be enough to let the school population think that a diary existed and that I had it in my possession?

"Fräulein Schoeppenkoetter sent a courier with a message. Her coach arrives at the Bull and Mouth at eight this evening." The old woman spoke in a gentle voice. "Have you anywhere to go?"

"Yes," I said without moving.

She went back to her reading but watched me out of the corner of her eye.

Looking up, she added, "Of course, Mrs. Brayton would give you a reference."

"Yes."

"Is there anything else, Miss Eyre?"

"No."

I took my leave of Mrs. Thurston, and as I closed her door behind me, I heard her sigh. Miss Miller had been right: The superintendent was not all bad.

Hurrying down the hallway, my mind raced along with my steps. My time would be cut short! I had to see Lucy and Mr. Douglas right away. They could carry out the important second step of my plan—securing the blessing of Mr. Waverly. I needed a viable excuse for visiting them. But what? What could I say?

I would have to climb out the Senior dormitory window. And do it quickly while my girls were at breakfast and then at their first class. There was no help for it. If anyone knew of my exit, this entire scheme would wither on the vine. I'd also have to avoid the Robin Redbreast as he made his rounds.

I had never climbed a tree. Looking out over the branch of the horse chestnut tree, the task daunted me. But I was undeterred. I could do it. At least gravity would "assist" me, since my immediate task was to climb down and not up. After sliding up the window sash, I leaned my torso half in and half out.

Do not look down, I warned myself. But of course, I did, and my! The ground was at least thirty feet away! How small and thin the grass looked!

You can do this, Jane. Take it one step at a time.

Stretching forward as far as I could go, I grabbed for the closest branch. My fingers grasped a small protrusion, only enough to use as a grip. I pulled myself out onto the limb and rested there on my stomach, sprawled across the largish branch and hanging onto a smaller one slightly over my head. With effort, I turned so that my boots rested against the trunk. That left me staring into the dormitory with my feet wedged uncomfortably in the crux of the tree. Below me was a tangle of branches. My foot searched blindly for the limb I knew was beneath me, but my skirt inhibited my movement. Where was it?

I could see another branch below me that might serve as a step downward. Turning myself toward the trunk, I reached my right hand to grab a thin offshoot before stepping down with one foot, and then the other.

My heart raced from both exertion and fear. Where to next? If I could transverse my path to the other side of the tree, I would be less visible. Unfortunately, in my thin white mourning dress, my form was easily distinguished from the gray tree trunk.

Feeling my way along with one foot, I touched another branch to my right. Testing it, there seemed to be no problem of it bearing up under me. To reposition myself, I would be forced to grab a limb above my head and swing myself over.

Which I did. For a tantalizing beat of my heart, my feet dangled in the air without support, and my palms cried out to let go, but I held on. Huffing and puffing, I rested on this new perch. Below me two branches formed a V.

Feeling rather pleased with my abilities, I quickly dropped down into the new landing spot. From there it was another easy step, a branch to my right that dipped closer still to the ground.

But that new spot could only be gained by a leap forward. Could I do it?

I had to. I closed my eyes and pushed off.

Only to be yanked back midflight.

My skirt had caught in the branches above me and hauled me backward!

My left hand slipped and lost its purchase on the new branch. To my horror, I hung there, swaying back and forth, my skirt over my head. Unable to see. Fully aware that my undergarments were exposed.

Slowly my fingers on the right hand lost all feeling. Added to this came the slow *rrrrrrr-rrrrr-rrrr* of ripping fabric. The waistband of my skirt pressed hard against my ribs, cutting off my air. I couldn't see. I couldn't breathe. I couldn't hold on much longer. I wiggled and wiggled, rocking myself left and right, hoping the fabric would finally give way.

Rrrrrr-rrrr. How much longer would the cheap fabric take to rip? And when it finished, would I be free? How would I explain lying on the ground in my chemise? I redoubled my efforts to grip the tree, but my fingers burned. I reached up with my other hand, but the fabric occluded my vision.

I was growing light-headed. And my fingers cramped with pain.

A voice called up to me: "Just let go!"

I did.

I fell.

Chapter 44

And Edward caught me.

I tumbled into his arms. He wrapped them around me, and I responded by planting kisses all over his face. "Darling husband! How I have missed you!"

John, Edward's manservant, hooted with laughter. "That was a near thing, miss! I positioned master just right!"

"Jane, I did not know you to be so athletic!" Edward twined his fingers in my hair and kissed me. "That is a promise kiss. More will have to wait. Williams holds the carriage for us, and Lucy is most impatient to see you."

"But my skirt!" I pointed to the shredded fabric caught in the tree. He followed the direction of my finger with his eyes. Was it my imagination or did the one eye seem clearer?

"Confound that silly frock. I suppose we can't depart and leave your skirt flapping like a pirate's flag, can we? Dash it all." Setting me on my feet gently, he caressed my face and wrapped his cloak around me. "John, will you tear that down? My poor dear wounded sparrow. I can tell your eye is still swollen."

He ran a gentle fingertip around the bruise. "Does it hurt much? When I catch the thief who hit you, he will wish he was never born."

John tugged at my disheveled frock until the fabric tore free. I shivered in my chemise and Edward's wrap. With fabric in hand, we headed toward the street where Williams sat in the driver's seat. "Hurry!"

Once the carriage door closed and John had joined the driver in the dickey box, I showed my husband all the affection he'd been lacking. In turn, he stroked me and petted me until warmth ran up and down my body. "When did you get here? How did you know I needed you right this minute?"

"John and I set out several days after you left, but that blasted carriage kept sticking in the mud on the way to Millcote. Then I realized: John could lead my mount, and we could ride faster on horseback. What a fool I was not to think of it sooner! I arrived this morning at Lucy's house. Lucy told me what you are doing at the school and why."

"Are you angry?" We had not been married long. Although I knew Edward, and understood him, I had long ago realized that we might occasionally disagree. This could be one of those times.

"Of course not. I know why you went along with such a dangerous ploy. I would have expected nothing less of you than to step forward to help these girls. I promised our hostess she could come with me to see you, but again—"

"You couldn't wait."

"No, I couldn't. I missed you too much. When Williams pulled up with the carriage, he spied you out on a limb, as it were."

"Just in time." I ran my hands over the rough fabric of his suit and tucked my hands in his pockets. I pressed my face to his throat and breathed in the scent of him, tobacco, whiskey, and masculinity. I kissed him and wrapped his arms around me. "Thank you for understanding me so well. How is our son?"

"He is splendid. Big and fat and jolly. I do believe he is trying to coo like a turtledove. Mrs. Fairfax is delighted to have him all to herself for these few days."

"And how are you?"

"Besides missing you with every fiber of my being, I am well. In fact, my sight has improved tremendously. Mrs. Fairfax has been quite the ogre, forcing me to submit to warm compresses almost hourly. I have spent most of the time since you left reclining. Although I can't see as well as I did before the fire, I am surprised at what I can discern. Even without John's help, I could see the shape of you dangling from that tree like a woman's eardrop."

He lifted my chin and kissed me softly on the lips. "I shall always be here for you, my darling. Always. You need never fear. You are never alone. Never again."

The privacy we enjoyed inside the carriage ended too soon. At Lucy's house, we greeted our hostess and Mr. Douglas, then adjourned to the parlor. I set out my plan. "Lucy, can you keep these on your person? I shall need them soon, but it is best that I do not carry them."

I handed her the threatening notes, including the one that had started everything in motion.

"Mr. Douglas, can you convince Mr. Waverly to help us?" This was vital to my scheme.

"I am sure I can," Mr. Douglas said. "The Bow Street Runner has little to lose and everything to gain."

"Lucy? Can you dispatch Higgins or Williams to waylay Fräulein Schoeppenkoetter? I am not sure how you can identify her, but I know she arrives at the Bull and Mouth at eight o'clock this evening."

"One of my men can go there and hold up a placard with her name on it. It is done all the time," she said.

Next I explained my plan, going step-by-step. I concluded with this warning: "My scheme cannot be postponed. We cannot detain Fräulein Schoeppenkoetter for long. They have not yet charged Miss Miller with a crime. Mr. Waverly is gathering all his information and the magistrate will issue the summons. Once that happens, we shall be too late to help Nan Miller—and the real killer will go free."

"I understand what you are doing, but I do not like it, Jane," Edward said. "Before, you were simply an observer, and you posed no threat to the killer. This bold plan sets you up as a target! Let Mr. Waverly bring charges. That is his job. You have done yours—and this is far too dangerous!"

"I believe I have a way to protect Mrs. Rochester," Mr. Douglas said. He rolled back his sleeves to display a small dagger and its sheath strapped to his forearm. "Take this kirpan. Straps at the elbow and near the wrist keep the apparatus steady. The Sikhs believe the kirpan can only be used in self-defense or to protect those who cannot protect themselves. In their teachings, one should never stand idly by and let another come to harm. Mind you, the blade is incredibly sharp. It has saved my life more than once. I suggest you never let it out of your sight. No one needs to know you carry this."

I nodded, grimly. Suddenly I realized the enormity of the task ahead.

"You should wear it to bed tonight. Especially then, given your plan! If you can practice reaching up your sleeve and withdrawing the blade, so much the better. In addition, I can climb the tree and position myself right outside that window you've spoken of. If Mrs. Rochester raises the sash, entrance will be no problem. I'll never be more than a few feet away."

Edward nodded. "That sounds much better."

I touched the small handle and withdrew the instrument from its sheath. I marveled at the size of it—the blade could not have been more than three inches long. I handed the weapon to Edward so that he could examine it more closely.

"By Jove, that's a dandy."

"It has served me well," Mr. Douglas said. "Saved my life several times. I hope you don't mind that I gave it to your wife. Like you, I value her courage but am also concerned for her safety. Beg your pardon if my actions give you offense."

"Caring for my wife will never be offensive to me. I thank both of you for extending your help to her and to Adèle." Edward returned the kirpan to me. I replaced it and pulled my sleeve down over the ensemble.

"However, Jane, you do not have to do this," Edward said, drawing me close. "We could take Adèle and go home. I understand that you are concerned for the other girls, but really, my dear, that's not your responsibility."

"I am armed. I am prepared. You will all be outside and able to respond to my cries. There is no other way to flush out the killer."

"Let me impress this upon you: Your opponent is a murderer— and you are issuing a direct challenge to this killer," warned Mr. Douglas. "Once a person breaks that sacred pact with society and takes one life, crossing the line a second time is much easier. If you are threatened or if you sense danger, I urge you to action. Do not fall victim to the rules that society impresses on your gender. Never let societal whims cloud your own good judgment. You have a duty to protect yourself and to protect others."

"I understand."

My life, and perhaps the lives of others as well, was in my hands.

I must have presented an incongruous sight, armed with the knife and wearing Edward's cloak around my waist while Polly mended my skirt. I did not dare return to Alderton House wearing another dress. That would produce unwanted questions and might lead someone to suspect that I had left the premises.

"Lucy, won't Augie enjoy hearing all about this when he comes home?" Edward remarked, with somewhat forced gaiety. "He will think us all quite daring or quite daft. I am not sure which. Is Jane's skirt ready? I believe we need to get her back into the school."

Lucy watched Polly refasten my freshly mended skirt as I stood in the middle of the guest bedroom floor. "I wish I could go on calls today. Honestly I do. For the first time I can remember, it would be entertaining. Think of all the gossip and slander I could contribute. Instead I must content myself with helping you catch a murderer. Ho hum."

Once I was fully dressed, Lucy and I returned to the parlor, where the men had been talking in low tones. "Any ideas on how to spirit me back into Alderton House? If anyone suspects I have been away, my plan will be worthless."

Reclining in the wing back chair, and crossing his legs, Edward grinned at Mr. Douglas. "You are not the only schemer among us. We also need to get Adèle out, to make sure that she is safe. Here is what Mr. Douglas and I have in mind . . ."

I hunched down in the space between the seat and the wall of the carriage. Edward leaned over. "Are you quite miserable? Luckily, we haven't much farther to go."

I couldn't help laughing at the ridiculousness of our desperate machinations, and my location on the floor of the carriage. The possibility of being discovered and tossed from Alderton House so close to the end of my mission was both appealing and appalling. Had it not been for the girls inside, I would have happily walked away.

The carriage rolled to a halt. Before stepping out into the street, my husband tugged his navy blue waistcoat down into place, smoothed his jacket, and gave me a half grin. "Ready, Jane?"

"Yes!" It came out in a half whisper.

"Off we go!"

"I'm here, sir," John said, joining Edward on the cobblestones.

I was happy that Edward didn't catch John's expression of chagrin. The old servant wasn't accustomed to subterfuge, and he valued decorum far too much to approve of Edward's plan. But he loved the boy he'd helped to raise, and so he was willing to play along, even if he did so glumly.

Williams pretended to close the door after Edward and his manservant, but in truth left it ajar, so I could follow their progress. My husband used his cane and John's shoulder as his guide up the front steps of Alderton House. Once there, he banged on the door with the head of his walking stick. When no one came immediately, he banged again, harder. Finally, Caje opened up and Edward bellowed, "By God, where is she? What have you done with my Adèle? Where is your superintendent? Tell that woman I expect her here now! Immediately! Move it! By Jove, I shall beat sense into you and everyone else in this ridiculous excuse for a school!"

"You heard him!" John pushed the door so hard it bounced against the interior wall. "Do not just stand there! Go fetch Adèle Varens! Bring her here, right now!"

Both men stood in the doorway shouting as loudly as possible. From inside came the shrill sound of Adèle screaming, "*Mon bon ami! Mon Dieu! Il est ici! Je suis libre!*"

I smiled to myself. In a life full of surprises, some things could be counted on.

Adèle appeared tout de suite.

Edward spoke to her in rapid French, telling her not to say another word. Especially not about me. "*Entre*," he said and pointed to the carriage. In her native tongue, he told her to stay there no matter what and not to talk to anyone because they were off to Mrs. Brayton's house in just a tick.

"Jane?" Adèle paused to ask.

"*Tout va bien. Ferme la bouche*," he said.

On Adèle's heels trotted Mrs. Thurston, calling after the girl, "Come back here!" and then turning on Edward with, "You, sir! What is the meaning of this?"

Williams wrapped his reins around the rein guides, hopped down, and ran around to the carriage door on the opposite side of the school. Opening it, he helped me out. Mr. Douglas jumped off the back, where he'd played the part of a rather too tall coachman. Together he ran with me to the side of the house by the horse chestnut tree. By now, Edward and John were inside Alderton House, causing a commotion that capitalized on Adèle's excitement at being "rescued" by her *bon ami*.

"Remember, leave the window open for me. I'll climb up to that limb tonight and stay just outside the dormitory in case you need help."

"Will do," I said.

"Good luck. Up you go." Mr. Douglas boosted me up to a low limb, keeping watch while I climbed one branch after another until my waist was even with the windowsill of the Senior dormitory. Pushing off from that last branch, I inelegantly shoved myself back into the window I'd earlier exited. I hit the floor with my hands and walked on my palms into the dormitory until my legs were inside. Then I rolled onto my backside.

I was still on the floor catching my breath when Emma burst through the door. "Miss! There's a terrible commotion downstairs, and Mrs. Thurston wants you to come right away."

"Pardon? I dropped a button under the bed. Can it wait until I find it?"

"I'll help you." Emma started toward me.

"Here it is." With great exaggeration, I pretended to pocket my "lost" button. "My goodness! Who is making all that noise?"

Despite my "pleas" that she be allowed to stay, Adèle rode off with her guardian within minutes. Edward did his utmost to look upon me with disdain, while I played my part of mewling former governess as best I could. As he walked past me, he gave me a solemn wink. It was torture not to hop into the carriage with them. Hearing the front door slam behind them caused my heart to pound wildly.

This has to work. It has to!

I moved through the remainder of the morning's lessons as if nothing out of the ordinary was happening. The Seniors missed Adèle, so I suggested that they write letters to her in German.

We were heading down the stairs to eat our lunch when a street urchin in ragged clothes and a cap that covered most of his face appeared at the front step. I overheard him barter a letter for a shilling. Emma called Mrs. Thurston to make the exchange. The superintendent gave the boy a ha'penny and he went running as fast as his legs could carry him on his make-shift shoes of newspaper tied on with string.

"Miss Eyre?" Mrs. Thurston called to me from the foyer. The upheaval had taken its toll on Mrs. Thurston. Social nice-ties fell by the wayside.

"Yes, madam?" I gave her a half bow. "I am packed and ready to depart, directly after classes finish."

"There has been a change of plans." She waved the letter at me. "You can stay a little longer."

"Yes, ma'am." I bobbed to Mrs. Thurston. "Thank you, ma'am."

"Good heavens, what is on your dress?"

I looked down at the dirt I had gathered while climbing the tree.

"Change immediately into something presentable," said Mrs. Thurston.

"I will do so."

We were in the midst of eating luncheon when Mr. Waverly rapped at the front door, demanding to see Mrs. Thurston. After a hurried conference in her office, she entered the dining room. All of the girls were already there, as were Miss Jones and myself. Miss Miller remained sequestered in the Infant dormitory. Mr. Waverly, however, also called in Caje, Emma, and Cook. The staff members took places at the back of the room.

"Go get Miss Miller," Mr. Waverly instructed a constable, "and escort her to the carriage waiting outside."

Mr. Waverly took the floor. "I am sorry to tell you that we believe that Miss Miller is Selina Biltmore's killer. Therefore, we are now taking her into our custody. If any of you have evidence pointing to Miss Miller's guilt, it is your duty as a loyal subject of the Crown to bring those facts forward. Do not share them with each other. I repeat: Do not share any information you have. I shall return on the morrow, at breakfast. You can give whatever information you have directly to me. That is all."

Mr. Waverly left, and our meal concluded shortly after. Back in the classroom, a subdued mood settled over the group. The girls were oddly quiet. Rose's brow puckered and she said, "Will they hang Miss Miller?"

"Let's keep her in our prayers." This was an evasion, but one that satisfied all of our needs.

The afternoon lessons dragged along. A soft rain started, gathering effort as it went on, until thunder burst like a drumroll demanding we snap to attention. "I believe we shall work indoors today," I said.

Once again, loud knocking at the front door disturbed our studies. This time it was the undertaker removing Selina's body. His assistants also carried all the floral tributes out into the waiting hearse. Twice now she had left this building in the rain. This time, I knew she would not be returning.

This sorrowful event further dampened my students' spirits. I lectured on birds of prey. Even my thrilling description of how a barn owl can find a field mouse failed to elicit a flicker of interest. Each child turned her fears inward rather than express her worries. Nettie chewed on her fingernails, and Rose twisted a strand of hair around and around her finger. Rufina dug at a bump on her knee. The Juniors mainly sat huddled together, hunched over, and bleak as an outcropping of small stone protrusions.

Another spate of banging interrupted our session, but this noise came from directly overhead. Leaving Rufina in charge, I slipped out to ask Emma what was happening. "Mrs. Thurston asked Caje to nail the windows shut."

"What!" My plan depended on Mr. Douglas being able to enter the dormitory from the horse chestnut branch.

"Since Miss Miller won't be here in the Infant dormitory, this way no one can crawl in or out."

This would prove an impediment, but there was no help for it. I would have to carry on regardless.

By dinner, the girls had recovered somewhat. Their bright chatter did me good. Children seem incapable of dampening down their natural buoyancy for long periods. By the time we repaired to the sitting room, a modicum of normalcy had returned. Without Miss Miller, Mrs. Thurston was compelled to join us during the sewing hour, as I had hoped she would.

"She plans to sleep with the Infants," Miss Jones whispered in my ear. "I guess that Mr. Waverly told her in private that under no circumstances were the girls to be left without chaperones again. He was most adamant on that point!"

The superintendent's presence had a distinctly dreary effect, though she largely ignored the girls. The novel she had been reading must have been captivating, because she stuck her nose in the book and never spoke to the rest of us. After a while, the book fell from her grip, and she slumped over in the big brown tapestry wing back chair, snoring loudly. When Emma brought the tea and bread, Miss Jones tapped Mrs. Thurston on the shoulder. The rotund woman awakened in time to heap her plate high with savories.

I had carefully chosen a spot in the middle of the room, on an ottoman, where I was the centerpiece of the group. As the girls poured tea, I leafed through the handful of papers that

I'd found in Selina's dresser. They were nothing but poorly done homework assignments and her unkind thoughts about her classmates; however, for my purposes they worked nicely. I waited until Emma brought a second tray of cheese and then gasped loudly.

"Oh my!"

"What is it?" Mrs. Jones set down her teacup.

"This is a diary that Selina must have started."

That elicited a snort of laughter from Mrs. Thurston. "Selina? A diary? I heartily doubt it. Our Selina wasn't much interested in introspection."

"Nevertheless, I found these papers in her dresser earlier. I meant to throw them out but decided I should look through them first." I made a show of glancing over the papers before clutching them to my breast dramatically. "They are dated shortly before her death. What time is Mr. Waverly arriving tomorrow? He will certainly want to read these. I believe there is information here that points to a motive for her murder."

Mrs. Thurston snapped her fingers at me. "Give me those."

"I cannot. You heard the inspector." I folded the papers and tucked them into my pocket. "He specifically told us to keep any information to ourselves, didn't he, girls?"

Little faces nodded, looking from me to Mrs. Thurston and back again.

"How could I face him and tell him I was disobedient? For tonight, this will keep. I shall hold them close to me. I plan to sleep with them under my pillow."

"Confound you! I say, hand them over!" The superintendent thrust out her chubby hand.

"No. Considering all that has happened, I plan to adhere to instructions. To do otherwise would reflect very poorly on all of us!"

That capped it for her. Mrs. Thurston heaved herself from her chair and stormed out of the room, stomping along and muttering darkly. Miss Jones sighed. "I am going down to the kitchen to ask Cook to make hot chocolate. It might settle our nerves."

"Yes," I agreed. "On such a dreary night, I'm sure that would be most appreciated by all."

A few minutes later, Miss Jones reappeared with a tray, and the girls perked up considerably as the rich scent of chocolate filled the room. As she had predicted, the treat improved everyone's mood.

Afterward, we went to the dormitories. Mrs. Thurston's voice drifted through the wall as she fussed at the Infant girls about some small matter.

I pushed the curtains aside and checked. Yes, the sill had been securely nailed shut. There was no remedy except to move forward. While behind my modesty screen, I fingered the kirpan. The sleeves of my night rail would not cover it. The wrapper caught on it. Frustrated, I took the dagger from its sheath. When I stepped out from behind the screen, I quickly tucked it under my pillow.

Although the rain had quit, clouds covered the moon. I'd never known a darker night. My pulse raced. Would my audacious plan work? The stillness absorbed all light and gave nothing back.

"Miss? Are you going to tuck us in?" Rose called to me from across the room.

"Of course I shall. That is the best part of my job," I told her as I picked up my candle and headed her way. Although I yearned for my own son, I would also miss these girls. I pulled up the covers and gave each child a kiss on the cheek. Rose surprised me by reaching up and hugging me—hard. "You are the nicest teacher we have ever had." Her words were slightly slurred.

Rufina tried to speak and also tripped over her own tongue.

There was only one explanation: The hot chocolate had been dosed with laudanum.

In short order, the girls fell fast asleep. I moved from bed to bed to be sure they were tucked in. Rhythmical snores and sighs came from all my young friends. With any luck, tonight I would flush out the killer—and none of the children would be the wiser. They would sleep through any commotion. In the morning, we could assure them that the school was safe again.

At long last, I climbed into my bed and stared at the ceiling while I waited for a signal—Bruce Douglas's tap on the windowpane. That noise would tell me that he was up in the tree and in place. I planned to pantomime that the sash could not be opened.

Perhaps I could use the kirpan to somehow pry the nails loose. I climbed out of bed, lit the candle, and tried, but it did not work. The struggle seemed to tire me, and I was increasingly clumsy. After a few halfhearted attempts, I staggered back to bed.

My last waking thought: I've been drugged!

Fighting the call to slumber, I fell fast asleep.

Chapter 45

The first part of my plan had been simple: I would set up a scenario that suggested that I had incriminating papers. Thus, the killer would need to come to me to get them.

The second was more complex: Once the killer tried to wrestle the papers from me, we would seize him or her.

Mr. Douglas would be right outside my window, where he could hear any scuffle and immediately come to my aid. One of his men would be positioned under the tree, and he would sound the alarm to bring the others running.

Edward would be waiting with John in Lucy's carriage, parked two houses down, so as to be less conspicuous. Williams would be sitting in the driver's seat, armed and ready to spring to action. Waverly had been instructed to have the roaming constable shorten his rounds, keeping Alderton House within his sight at all times.

I had planned to feign sleep, but the drugged cocoa was too powerful to resist.

I dreamed of Ferndean. Ned was on my lap, cooing up at me, squinting in the sun. Mrs. Fairfax bustled around and poured me more tea. Adèle danced and twirled until dizziness overtook her. Edward stood beside me with his hand on my shoulder. We sunbathed in the gentle spring light, enjoying the nodding daffodils and cheerful red tulips. I picked a purple violet and showed it to Ned, who laughed out loud.

Then I glanced down and spotted a snake.

My face was pressed down into the pillow.

I struggled. A weight on my back pinned me to the pallet.

I couldn't breathe. I twisted and turned. Fighting the pressure on the back of my head, I attempted to rotate my face. But the weight on me proved too much.

The kirpan!

My hands had been beside my head when the intruder pressed on me. Now I wiggled my fingers under my pillow. My lungs cried out for oxygen! The pain was nearly unbearable! Then an image of Ned came into my mind and I bucked like a wild horse.

Had my scheme worked so well that the murderer decided I was a threat? Why wasn't it enough to simply steal the incriminating papers?

The unexpected motion knocked my assailant off-balance. I lifted my head long enough to gasp. The gulp of air clarified my thinking. My right hand burrowed under the pillow, but the person leaning on my shoulders held me captive. I bucked again, but this time my assailant was prepared for my upheaval. The pressure never eased off.

I grasped the knife by the handle, but I could not work my hand free.

My lips were forced against my teeth. My assailant gave a mighty downward shove. A gush of warmth told me my lip had split. The blood ran toward my nose, wetting the pillow cover. The wet fabric molded to my nose.

I was drowning in my own blood!

In a panic, I raised my hips and managed to flip onto my back. The pillow fell to the floor. With my one free hand, I reached up and grabbed a handful of hair. I yanked hard.

I heard a woman sob as she put the pillow over my face again. "No, stop. I don't want to hurt you!" she whispered near my ear as she pressed down. "Sleep! Go back to sleep!"

Was it possible that she really meant me no harm?

The world faded. Stars circled the edges of my vision. Darkness closed in on me.

I yanked the hank of hair again and used the strength in my legs to roll my body to one side. In order to stay with me, my attacker needed to shift her weight. We were close to toppling off the side of the bed. With one mighty tug, I struggled to withdraw the hand with the kirpan—and succeeded! My hand was free!

I raised it overhead and plunged it into my attacker.

She screamed in pain and rolled off of me, falling hard onto the floor, still grasping the pillow. I jumped to my feet and stood over her, with a dripping knife blade in my hand.

Whirling on me, she grabbed me around my ankles and pulled them out from under me. I hit the floor with a crash.

Edward! Help me! I thought.

Everything went black.

Chapter 46

❦

"Jane? Darling girl, come back to me," Edward called from far away.

"Try the smelling salts," Lucy said.

An odor assaulted me, causing me to gasp and choke.

"That is it, my sweetheart. Come on. Breathe!" Edward commanded me. "For God's sake, Jane! Come back to us!"

Sputtering and fighting, despite the pain in my chest, I sucked in fresh air.

"I do not doubt that her ribs are broken," Mr. Douglas said.

He might have been right. Each breath hurt, a pain so intense that I never wanted to breathe again. I wanted only to rest, to slip away. To leave the agony behind me and go back to that twilight of nothingness.

With enormous effort, I took one agonizing breath and then another. A strange voice said, "Good job. Keep it up, Mrs. Rochester."

I struggled to open my eyes. Edward held me in his arms the way a mother cradles an infant. His face looked down on me as we half sat and half reclined on a settee in the parlor.

His brows knit in concern. "I thought I had lost you!" He kissed my forehead.

"Sir, I believe she might breathe better if I bind her ribs. The wrapping stabilizes the bones." A serious-looking young man pushed his wire-rimmed spectacles up on his nose. The black bag in his hand led me to think he was a surgeon.

"Wha . . . what?" That was the best I could muster.

"You are safe, Jane." Edward squeezed my hand.

"Mrs. Rochester, a surgeon is attending to Miss Jones in one of the classrooms. A constable is with them." Mr. Waverly leaned over me.

"We burst in on her as she was trying to smother you," Edward said.

"It was a near thing." Mr. Douglas turned his cap over and over in his hand. "I tapped on the window, but you didn't respond." Lucy, dressed as a street urchin, stood at his side. She had a frightened expression on her face, which was mostly covered by an oversized newsboy's cap. This costume had served her well when she delivered the message to Mrs. Thurston that Fräulein Schoeppenkoetter had again been delayed.

"Mrs. Thurston had Caje nail it shut," I explained. "And the cocoa I drank was dosed. I should have expected that. It only had a little laudanum, but enough to keep the girls sound asleep. They are unaware of the scuffle, aren't they?"

"Yes," Lucy said. "I checked. They are sleeping, as is Mrs. Thurston. Emma and Caje are awake. They are making tea in the kitchen. Cook is also asleep. Caje explained she takes a nip at night and might be hard to rouse."

"I couldn't keep my eyes open," I said. "Where is Miss Jones? How is she? Did I cut her badly?"

"No," Mr. Waverly said. "You merely managed to nick her, but it was enough to make her cry out. Mr. Douglas heard her. He yelled to his man, who alerted the rest of us. We were stymied by the front door until Mr. Douglas volunteered to pick the lock."

"My skills are rusty." Mr. Douglas broke into a roguish grin. "So is the lock! Took me longer than I had hoped. Meanwhile, with the help of his man, John, your husband broke down the door in the area. Somehow he managed to race upstairs and straight to your bedside. Thank God you called out to him!"

Of course, I hadn't done any such thing. At least, not out loud. But my heart had called to Edward.

And he had heard me.

"There is only one problem," I said to the assembled group. "Miss Jones didn't kill Selina. And she never intended to kill me."

"But I pulled her off of you," Edward said. "John came on my heels and helped me wrestle her to the floor. She is a large woman. A strong one, too. Your lip still bleeds."

"She was simply trying to snatch Selina's papers from under my pillow—and because she is such a large woman, she was suffocating me."

"But she had your pillow in her hand—" Edward interrupted.

"Yes, but I believe she panicked. I do not believe her original intention was to do me harm. After all, she dosed the hot chocolate. She had every reason to think I would be insensate. Her goal was to stop me from sharing Selina's journal—a journal that doesn't exist."

"So she murdered Selina Biltmore, is that right?" Mr. Waverly asked.

"No."

"I am confused," admitted Lucy, removing her cap and running a hand through her hair.

"Someone else murdered Selina. But my plan flushed out Miss Jones because she was worried about the journal, which I invented to enact this scheme. You see, Miss Jones was slipping out at night. She was meeting someone, and Selina found out."

"How do you know all this?" Edward asked.

"I sprinkled powder on the landing and saw her footprints. Later, I examined her shoes and they were wet. That was why Miss Jones had to get a look at the faux journal. She worried that Selina noted her disappearances—and Miss Jones feared she would be sacked without references if Mrs. Thurston found out. On the other hand, Miss Jones *is* responsible for writing the threatening notes."

"What threatening notes?" Mr. Waverly said. "No one has mentioned this to me."

Lucy reached in her pocket and handed over the notes I'd given her earlier for safekeeping. Edward explained to Mr. Waverly about the threat that had fallen out of Adèle's letter to us.

"I withheld the threats from you, but my reasoning was sound," I said to the Bow Street Runner. "With the first one, I worried that it might have been written by Adèle in a bid for our attention. Because of various circumstances, we hadn't visited her in some time—and our letters did not get through, either. Adèle was angry at being ignored, and rightly so. Writing such a note would have been an easy way to punish us. If I gave it to you, it would only make her look bad. You were already suspicious of her."

"But now you say Adèle did not write it? She did not pen a threat to herself expressly to force you to visit?" It was Waverly's turn to be confused.

"No, sir, she didn't. Miss Jones did."

"But why?" Edward said. "Adèle was no threat to Miss Jones. Whatever could have aroused the woman's ire?"

"I believe Miss Jones was determined to make Adèle suffer for the sins of her mother." Mr. Douglas stepped forward. "You see, Mrs. Rochester gave me the names of all the staff members right after she arrived. I instructed my associates to go and see what they could learn. This afternoon one told me that only last year, Parthena Jones's older brother, Adonis, traveled to France, with the goal of improving his ability to speak their language. However, once he was there, he became enchanted with an opera dancer."

"Céline Varens?" Edward asked, speaking of Adèle's mother. "When last I heard she was in Italy."

"No, not Madame Varens, but a young woman who often appeared in the same venues with Adèle's mother. It seems that this opera dancer already had a lover—and that man suffered a fit of jealousy and stabbed Adonis to death. The murder caused quite a scandal in Paris."

"But why would Miss Jones want to threaten Adèle?" Lucy asked.

"Miss Jones believed in retribution. She wanted to make Adèle suffer. When you left for India, Miss Jones realized the girl had no champion, and thus she stepped up her campaign."

"Oh no," Lucy shook her head. "What a shame!"

"Do let me help Mrs. Rochester," the surgeon said, urging my friends to step back. "She is obviously in pain."

"Please do," I said. "Afterward we must go confront Selina's murderer."

I allowed the doctor to perform his services, and once he was finished binding my ribs, I continued. "I suggest that Mr. Waverly and I go together. I believe that she will come along with little fuss." The wrapping around my ribs eased the sharp stab that accompanied each breath. If I could make it down the stairs, I was certain I could convince Selina Biltmore's murderer to give up.

"But will you be safe?" Edward asked.

"I am certain of it. She has no reason to hurt me. None. In fact, I doubt this person would ever kill again. The circumstances were extraordinary."

"I will go with you and stand guard," Mr. Douglas offered.

"Mrs. Rochester, you say there is nothing to fear," Mr. Waverly said. "I beg to differ. This was a cold-blooded act, not an impulsive decision. How can you brim over with sympathy for a murderess? A woman who suffocated a child sleeping innocently in her bed."

I shook my finger at him. "Sir, Selina was no child. Nor was she an innocent. Come, I shall show you your dastardly murderer. When you hear her story, you will change your mind about the crime, I promise you."

Mr. Waverly led the way, while Mr. Douglas helped me down the stairs. Through all the commotion, the girls remained asleep, as did Mrs. Thurston. Caje stepped forward to meet us when we entered the kitchen, his face bleak with understanding. "There's only one reason you'd come down here. To get her."

Emma stood behind him, hanging on his sleeve, her eyes brimming over with tears. "She's a good woman, miss. Really she is."

"I know," I said.

The cat Mephisto's bed was empty. That further confirmed what I'd suspected. What I knew. I knocked on the door and waited. A voice called, "Is that you, Miss Eyre? I was expecting ye. I was only pretending to sleep earlier. Let yourself in. It ain't locked."

"I've brought Mr. Waverly with me."

"I'm decent." Cook sat facing us, her back against the wall. Mephisto nestled in the well of her lap and she stroked him rhythmically. Opening his coolly indifferent yellow eyes, he stared at me, before closing them again. On a wooden box, pressed into use as a table, sat a lit candle stub. Its flame danced and dipped, sending ghostly shadows across the ceiling and wall.

With one work-roughened hand, Cook held closed a faded and torn blue wrapper. Her hair was neatly twisted into a bun. She'd been crying. A tired and threadbare patchwork quilt stretched tightly across one end of the pallet, perhaps once colorful, but now the shades were pale versions of themselves. Beside her rested an open Bible. A ladder-back chair with a leather sling for a seat completed the furnishings. Cook's entire wardrobe hung on four hooks along a wall.

"You the Bow Street Runner? Aye, I thought as much. Take a seat, sir. Miss Eyre? You can sit on me bed, if you wish."

Moving gingerly, I did so.

"I knew you was coming. Just a matter of time. Ye're a smart one. Like my own darlin' Larissa, ye are. Mind if I stay here while we chat? Me feet ache somethin' terrible at the end of a day. Of course, that'll soon be over, eh?"

"Mr. Waverly needs to know what happened." My voice shook only a little.

With a sigh, she said, "I reckoned as much."

"Cook, your given name is Belinda Connelly?" Mr. Waverly said, looking over the list of staff members that Mrs. Thurston had given him. "You need to come with me. There'll be a hearing before the magistrate."

"And a trial, and then you'll hang me by the neck, right? I ain't going to lie to you. I killed that evil girl. Dosed her and the others to put them to sleep. Made me way up the back stairs. Pressed that pillow over her. But she fought me. She was a big one, and I guess she didn't get enough to make her sleep."

I nodded. The first day that I arrived, Cook had attributed the scratches on her arms to Mephisto. But later, the girls told me that he never scratched her. Ever. There was only one reason she would have lied about the marks.

"I held that pillow down until she was good and gone." Cook sounded weary. "Couldn't leave her to live all high and mighty like a princess, now could I?"

"Right." Waverly stood. "So we'd best be going."

"So's you can take me to Tyburn, put me in the cart, and let me dance from the short drop?"

"You would have let Miss Miller hang for your sins?" I tried to sound fierce, but the pain in my ribs made speaking difficult.

"No, it would never have come to that."

"But it almost did!" I put a little more force behind my words.

"I was only waiting until the Biltmores came to see that girl in her coffin. I had to know they suffered . . . like I did. They deserved it!"

Mephisto had begun to purr, a sound rich and throaty and totally at odds with our purpose.

Mr. Waverly stared at Cook coldly. "Justice is for the judge and jury to decide at the Old Bailey."

"I done the world a service, I did. Ye should be thanking me." She smiled at Mr. Waverly, offering a grin half mischievous and half ugly. "As for punishing me, I plan to die in me own bed!" With that, she relaxed her grip and a brown bottle rolled from her hand onto the coverlet, coming to rest at her side.

The label on the bottle: LAUDANUM. I handed it to Mr. Waverly, who read it and cursed under his breath. Tucking the bottle in his pocket, he stepped forward and grabbed Cook roughly under her arm. "Come on with you!"

"Sir, I ain't got long! Won't ye at least hear my tale? Miss Eyre, they said Larissa fell down the well. She didn't. See, I asked Selina. Confronted her one day. She was a great one for sneaking down here and stealing biscuits from the pantry," said Cook, ignoring the fact that Mr. Waverly held her arm.

Mr. Waverly's eyes moved from the woman to me and back to her again. In her faded blue shift and her slumping frame, she didn't present a threat. He let go of her arm but remained standing nearby.

"I told you about my Larissa, didn't I, miss? I ain't got a picture of her, but she were a lot like you. A great one for learning, that girl. Had a lot of gumption. She weren't afraid of much. No, sir. Just anything that slithered. So's after Selina and her brothers threw her down that dry well, they tossed in a snake. Just for sport."

Cook wiped her eyes. Her pupils were nearly the size of pinpricks. She shivered. I pulled the quilt up and helped her arrange it over her shoulders. "Larissa's arm broke in the fall. She lay there two days, screaming at first. Terrified, she was, of that snake and no way out. Imagine what when dark came. She cried and whimpered all the time. That's how the gardener found her. She were only moaning. Couldn't talk none."

Cook reached into a pocket of the wrapper and showed us a long, auburn curl. "See? She had the prettiest hair, but she pulled most of it out. One of the gardeners saved this and sent it to me."

I nodded. "That is all you have of her, is it not? That and the teapot?"

"The Biltmores planned to toss the teapot in the dustbin because of that one chip. So my girl asked if she could buy it. 'The forget-me-nots will remind you of me, Ma,' was what she said. When Selina saw it on my shelf, she snatched it and ran off. That demon broke off the nob on the lid. She told me she planned to break it to dust, one piece at a time! I offered her sweets and all my money to get it back. But she didn't care. That one enjoyed being cruel—and she knew she was tearing my heart right out of my chest. It was all I had of my girl! That and the curl. That's when I decided to do something. See, I couldn't stomach it no more, miss."

"She told you what they did to Larissa, right?" I wanted to be clear about this.

"No, miss. Worse. She bragged to me. Said as how they stood there and spit on Larissa while my baby screamed and cried and begged them to get her out. Of course, once she was hauled out of that well, no one would believe what happened. They wouldn't take my daughter's word against theirs. Not that she made much sense, see? I heard as how she jabbered and jabbered, but couldn't talk sensible like. Selina told me about how Larissa had bare patches on her scalp from pulling out her hair. And her arm? Well, the bone stuck clean through the skin."

"And then what?" Mr. Waverly asked. "How did she die?"

"They said it was suicide." Cook's eyes fluttered. They were closed when she asked, "You suppose a girl who used her right hand for everything could tie a hangman's knot when her right arm was bad broke? I don't. No, sir. I suspect she had help."

That thought shook me to the core. "Oh, Lord."

"But I found that ribbon by the bed where the girl died. Why did you leave it there?" Mr. Waverly's face was tense with confusion.

"I dropped the ribbon by accident. I planned to give it back to that little French girl, because she's a luv. Poor child. She set great store by that piece of finery. As for Miss Miller, I wouldn't have let her take the blame for long. I wrote this out, so you'd know what's what." Cook pulled a piece of wrapping paper from between the pages of her Bible. On it, in a shaky hand, were the words, "I killt Selina Biltmore," and her signature.

A shiver ripped through the woman as if she'd been taken over by a chilling wind. "Selina said she watched Larissa die. Told me that she and her brothers were there in the barn. Said my daughter kicked and squirmed. That's what makes me saddest. My child died without comfort, see? She wouldn't come home to me 'cause she didn't want to be a burden. I would have taken her! Oh, God above! Why didn't she run home to me?"

Cook closed her eyes and sighed. Mephisto looked up at her and meowed. With one last shudder, Cook slumped to one side. Mephisto leaped neatly from her lap to mine. Cook would have fallen onto the floor if Mr. Waverly had not caught her. He pressed his fingers to her throat. After a bit, he shook his head. "She's gone."

Chapter 47

Despite my belief that Parthena Jones never meant to kill me, Mr. Waverly instructed the constable to take her to jail for the time being. "You can speak on her behalf before the magistrate," he told me.

Caje secured a hearse for Belinda Connelly's mortal remains. I comforted Emma as she and Caje and I watched quietly while they carried Cook from her tiny room. "She's with her daughter now. I believe that with all my heart, even if she did kill herself," I said.

Williams went and fetched Miss Miller, who had been staying at Lucy's house while we carried out my plan. "How can I thank you enough, Miss Eyre—I mean, Mrs. Rochester?" she asked me. "You have saved me and the girls. However did you guess it was Cook?"

"There were so many signs," I said. "Although most of them were inconspicuous. Cook lied about the scratches on her arms. She had access to laudanum and could easily dose the girls. When I found a piece of the teapot in Selina's drawer, I realized the girl had taken Cook's prize possession. Signora

Delgatto told me that Selina had pushed a governess down the well—and I started to wonder how Cook's governess daughter died. Finally, there was powder sprinkled around Selina's bed. At first, I assumed it to be the bath powder that she favored. But it never smelled of camellias. Cook was always baking. It would make sense that flour might have fallen from her person onto the floor in the Senior dormitory while she and Selina struggled."

Lucy and Mr. Douglas volunteered to stay at the school until Mrs. Thurston awakened. "Someone needs to tell the superintendent what she missed and that Miss Miller has been exonerated," Lucy said. "Bruce can do that while I help Miss Miller with the children. You go back to my house with your husband. I imagine you could use a good night's sleep. Adèle will be so thrilled to hear she is going home with you!"

Lying in each other's arms, Edward and I talked until the sun peeped around the gold velvet curtains in Lucy Brayton's guest bedroom. My ribs still ached, but thanks to the wrapping, the pain was bearable.

"So you destroyed the letters you found, the ones that were from the King?"

"Yes. All but one," I said and explained how I had been interrupted while burning them. "There was no good reason to keep the letters. Selina is dead. Her family has nothing to gain. Surely we can both spare some pity for a man forced to wed a woman under duress."

"Indeed. I hated my father for his devotion to Thornfield above all else," Edward said. "I mocked how he took his responsibilities as a country squire so seriously. But along the way here, I was forced to see my tenants in their own homes, struggling to go about their lives. They deserve better from me."

"Mr. Carter also encouraged me to visit our local families. I did not realize the ways in which a squire's wife could help. We've been so happy, just the two of us, and I pray we always shall be . . . but it is wrong of us to enjoy the benefits of your position without earning them. I can learn to ride. I can take baskets around. Mr. Carter can teach me simple remedies. I can report back to you when a family needs help."

"We can make the rounds together." As he spoke, a new excitement tinged his words. How odd that we would come to this new place in our lives, that a threatening note would change so much for the better.

"Rebuilding Thornfield takes on a new meaning to me," my husband said. "As the manor house for the countryside, it was the hub for all activities. I had forgotten how many found employment brewing beer for our parties, making washing balls for our laundry, weaving fabric for our linens, raising doves for our dovecote, and helping harvest and preserve the bounty from the fields and orchards. When I was young, my parents opened the place up for Christmas, gave parties after foxhunting, raised a cup at Michaelmas, and in lean times opened the house for merriment that fed the locals for weeks. I thought of those events as entertainment for my parents and older brother, Rowland. Now I understand a deeper purpose. They brought opportunities to our tenants. Individually, each merriment was a small thing, but taken together, they created a mechanism for keeping my father informed about how his tenants were doing and providing the locals with extra provisions and coinage. I believe it is my duty to reach out. I hope you will not find it too tedious."

I squirmed a bit, thinking of how much I'd enjoyed our solitude. But how could I return to our old ways knowing that all around us our tenants suffered? This was a road I'd not intended to travel, but my feet were well along the path. I could not turn back. Instead, I would accept certain discomforts as rent paid for all the blessings come my way.

"I shall be proud to take on the role of lady of the manor. Adèle will enjoy welcoming visitors and having an audience. Eventually, we'll find a new school for her. Perhaps one in

Millcote. But one that is close by so she can come home whenever she wants. I especially want her around for the
holidays."

"Adèle talks about Ned as if he were old enough to converse
with her or offer an opinion on her choice of hair ribbons."
Edward chuckled. "Wait until she sees how dependent he is!"

I smiled, thinking of her lavish affection. She had thrown
herself at me, clutched me tightly, and declared I was *"très
courageuse"* for facing Selina's killer. But when she learned I had
climbed a tree, she stared at me in frank astonishment.

"Wasn't that amusing, Edward? Did you hear what Adèle
said? 'Mademoiselle, you know how to climb trees? *C'est vraiment incroyable!*'"

"She is quite correct. I also find you incredible. Let me show
you . . ."

Edward, Adèle, and I enjoyed Lucy's hospitality for several
more days. Most importantly, our hostess took the three of us
to Hatchards, where we spent an entire morning selecting all
sorts of wonderful books. At Edward's insistence, Lucy took
Adèle and me to her mantua-maker. "I know you like your
wardrobe to be simple," my friend said. "But simple and elegant are often one and the same. Let me show you."

We also visited her milliner and ordered several new
bonnets.

On our last day, Polly packed my things and Edward took
off with John on errands concerning our solicitor. I sought out
my "sister" Lucy. After dinner last evening, Lucy had presented
Adèle with a lovely set of full-color paper dolls. My little
French friend seated herself in the middle of the parlor and
presided over an entire family of attractive flat people with
elaborate wardrobes.

"When can we get *le chat*?" Adèle had asked me the same
question every day since Cook died. Mrs. Thurston had

mentioned to Lucy that she didn't want the animal, and once Adèle heard that *le chat* was destined to be "an orphan," she insisted we take Mephisto home with us. Given the mice that shared Ferndean with us, I thought this rather a good idea.

"Soon," I said. "Do you know where Mrs. Brayton is?"

"I believe she is in her bedroom," Adèle said. "A letter came for her. All the way from India."

I found Lucy with one hand on an open letter. In the other was a damp handkerchief. Her red and puffy eyes told me she'd been crying.

"Is your husband all right? Have you had news from him?"

A week ago, I would have held myself apart from her. But after all we'd been through together, that invisible wall had crumbled. Seeing her distress, I pulled an ottoman next to her chair so I could be by her side. Literally and figuratively. While she struggled to gather her thoughts, I took one of her hands in mine. The flesh was hot and damp to the touch.

"Lucy? Are you unwell? Do I need to call a surgeon?"

"No," she said.

But I knew a remedy. I rang for Polly. "Gin, please. Two tumblers."

After pouring us both a glass of courage, I begged Lucy to speak to me.

"Three years ago, my husband and I quarreled badly. That was when I quit India and came home to London; he stayed in Bombay. After my departure, a young widow attracted his attention, and . . ." She paused. "He sought comfort from her."

"Oh, Lucy. Oh, dear friend. I am so, so sorry!" I threw my arms around her neck and held her in my embrace. Doing so, I inhaled the rich fragrance she favored, the sweet smell of gardenias.

"I have long since forgiven him, Jane. We both said horrid things to each other in our quarrel. I did not take into account the strains on him, and he did not appreciate my position, either. But Augie and I had made our amends to each other even before I returned to nurse him through his malaria; it has left our marriage stronger."

After a sip of gin, Lucy continued. "Meanwhile, the widow had returned to Brussels. But it appears that she was with child and later delivered of a son. She died of complications from childbirth two months ago."

"And Augie's infidelity still rankles? He must still have been in communication with her if he has heard of her death."

"Yes and no. Her solicitor contacted Augie after she expired. The boy is definitely his."

"How hurt you must have been! And how hard it must be for you to receive a reminder of his dalliance!"

"You think these are tears of sorrow? We still have much to learn about each other, don't we? These are tears of joy. Joy! Augie has just written to ask me if I would be willing to raise the child. Of course I would! I shall write him back right away. Is that not wonderful? The child is currently with a nurse, so I shall send her funds so that they can travel to London. Oh, Jane, we shall have a son! God be praised, I am to be a mother!"

Chapter 48

Ferndean Manor, Yorkshire
November 11, 1820

"Miss Jane! Master Edward! We have a visitor!"

Mrs. Fairfax's voice carried to where Edward and I sat in the parlor, chatting with each other and enjoying a few rare moments of quiet. The household had hummed with activity since we had returned to Ferndean. I had just handed Ned to Hester after rocking him to sleep in my arms. How I enjoyed the solid feel of him and his sweet baby face. He had grown so much during the two weeks that Edward and I had been gone. And now, nearly another month later, our son had begun to master the art of crawling and had started to grab for anything that caught his fancy.

Since coming home with us, Adèle had blossomed. The French girl proved very helpful with the baby, especially in that interval when his wet nurse Hester had stayed home with her own daughter. Mr. Carter told us, "Her child's better now, but it was a near thing. All the children in Hester's family had been weakened by the croup. Your sending along fresh eggs and chickens to replenish their flock helped tremendously."

Whenever I watched Adèle plant kisses on Ned, I thought

my heart might burst with happiness. After she coddled her new friend, whom she called *"mon ange,"* Adèle would return to teasing Mephisto with a feather tied to a string.

As Cook had explained, Mephisto loved children. It seemed he also loved me, transferring his affection from his previous owner and attaching himself to me so completely that Edward swore Mephisto had become my familiar. Each time he purred in my ear, I thought of Belinda and her daughter Larissa. I prayed they had been reunited. I was also moved to count my blessings, starting with the joy of motherhood.

I wasn't surprised when our visitor turned out to be Bruce Douglas. Edward and I greeted him warmly.

"I have come to talk with you about the missing jewelry," he said, after paying attention to Adèle and admiring Ned. "And a bit more afterward, if you can put me up for the night."

I asked Adèle to go and help Mrs. Fairfax prepare refreshments.

"What have you learned?" Edward leaned forward and squinted up at Mr. Douglas. My husband was wearing a pair of spectacles with smoked lenses. I thought them rather dashing. His vision continued to improve as we administered hot compresses to his eye.

Mr. Douglas pulled up a garden chair. "May I review the facts of your case? I think you will come to the same conclusion that I have."

I could not see the point, but I trusted Bruce Douglas, so I said, "Of course. Shall we wait until Mrs. Fairfax brings us tea?"

"Please. It was a long ride here."

Serving tea would also give me a chance to prepare myself. I'd already determined the jewels gone forever, but hearing my suspicions confirmed would reopen a tender spot.

Mrs. Fairfax carried in the tray. After I poured, Mr. Douglas asked me to close my eyes and walk all of us through the events of the day I left for London. I left nothing out that I could recall. Mrs. Fairfax assisted me where I stumbled.

When I opened my eyes, Mr. Douglas shared what he'd learned. "That guard Glebe was a complete dolt, but his observations had merit. You were the only woman in the mail coach so commonly dressed. This raises the question, in a crowded area full of wealthy travelers, why target you?"

I thought this over. As did Edward and Mrs. Fairfax. But we had no answers.

"None of my contacts received any stolen goods that matched the description of your jewels. A professional might have taken the pieces to Amsterdam, where diamond specialists could have divided up the gems, recombined them, and sold them without fear they'd be recognized. But none of my sources has heard of such a happening. They have no reason to lie. That leads me to believe it was not a professional thief but an amateur who stole them from you, Mrs. Rochester."

I realized where this was heading, and my stomach reacted by twisting into a knot. Mrs. Fairfax sat in silence, an expression of bewilderment on her face.

"You think it was a person well aware of my wife, her mode of dress, her travel plans, and where she carried the jewels." Edward spoke very quietly. "Is that right, Mr. Douglas?"

"Yes, I am sorry to say that I think it was someone acquainted with Mrs. Rochester's peculiar circumstances."

"But wouldn't an amateur have immediately taken the jewels to the first unscrupulous merchant he could?" I asked.

"Not necessarily. You suffered a black eye, and you said that you gave the thief one as well. Glebe's report said as much. Mr. Waverly himself followed up after he met you. The constabulary in London knew to look for a man with a black eye who was trying to sell a diamond circlet with matching necklace and earrings."

"But he could have sold the jewelry in another town. A town where no one knew our man had a black eye." Edward gently set his empty cup on its saucer. A muscle flickered along his jaw, a sign that tension was building inside him. Mrs. Fairfax offered to prepare more tea. I thought that a good idea and said so.

"No. London was the place to sell them. Why go to all the trouble of stealing them only to exchange them for a mere pittance of their value? London would be the place to find a jeweler who had good custom, one comfortable with high society, who could therefore offer top dollar for the lot. In London, one might remain anonymous. London would have been the best place—the only place—to offer such an opportunity. But my sources tell me that nothing of the kind has gone on offer." Mr. Douglas did not look jubilant; indeed, he recognized the gravity of his implications, and the regret showed on his face. He was leading us down a path where we did not want to go.

"Which might mean that your sources are wrong. Or that the thief hasn't had the chance to convert the gems," I reasoned.

"And why wouldn't the thief have had time to find a jeweler?" Edward wondered.

I thought he knew why but wanted to hear my opinion. "Because the thief needed time to heal before he traveled to London. Perhaps there has been a reason that kept him away. Some pressing matter, such as his employment or his family. Remember, I was attacked on the Great North Road, still a good distance from the city."

Mr. Douglas smiled at me. "Mr. Rochester, your wife is exceedingly skilled at this art of rational thinking."

"But how could anyone know what I was carrying—and how I was carrying it—and forgo my portmanteau, unless . . ." I paused. "Do you have the drawing I made? The one of the thief?"

Mr. Douglas withdrew it from his pocket. "I showed this

to John as he took my horse. He said he went to detain the man we're looking for."

I looked over my sketch with a curious mixture of anger and sadness, the twin by-products of betrayed confidence. "What do we do now?"

"I have the authority to take the culprit with me. If that is what you wish. You can certainly bring the thief before the Assizes."

I rose and walked to the door. "Hester? Could you come here, please?"

Perhaps I should have waited so that Edward and I could discuss the matter further, but I couldn't help myself. I needed to know if my suspicions were accurate. I wanted to hurry this along, because waiting for the blow only increased the pain.

"Yes, miss?"

Mrs. Fairfax set down the tea tray. Seeing the expression on our faces, she asked if she might leave us alone.

"Please keep Adèle and Ned occupied. Do not let them in here," I instructed the housekeeper before turning to Hester. "You have brothers, right? Three or four?"

She froze and stared at me with huge eyes.

"One of them looks like this?" I held up the sketch I'd drawn.

Her eyes traveled from me to Edward and back to me. She fell to her knees, sobbing, her face pressed to the carpet. "Please, oh, please, miss. He shouldn't have. He was wrong. And it's my fault, too. I didn't mean to! I just told him about the jewels and how pretty they was. His children had nothing to eat. Nothing! So he thought if he took them . . . but then he couldn't sell them . . . and we're both going to hang! I know we are!"

"Hush," I said. I lifted the woman to her feet and sat her in a straight-backed chair while Edward and Mr. Douglas went out to the barn. They came back shortly with John, who was holding a shotgun on one of the Muttoone brothers.

"Josiah! I'm sorry! I'm so, so sorry!" Hester wailed.

After one look, I knew. He had been my assailant.

He stood there in the midst of the parlor, head bowed and thick tongued, stumbling an apology. Over and over, he apologized. Most touching, he begged that we forgive Hester. "It weren't her idea. She mentioned it, and I took it on meself."

"Where are they?" Edward asked gruffly.

"Under your h-horse's t-tack in the stable." The young man could barely talk for stuttering.

Edward dispatched John to find the gems and Leah to fetch her husband, James. After a brief conference, Mr. Douglas and Edward decided to detain Hester and Josiah in the small room we used as a larder until we could talk the matter out. James was given the shotgun and told to stand watch.

While I listened, Mr. Douglas and Edward discussed various legal remedies. We called in Mrs. Fairfax, who was naturally curious about what had happened—and positively horrified when she heard. Eventually, Edward laid the decision at my feet. "What do you think I should do? He broke the law. He hurt you. That is what makes me angriest."

I was angry, too. However, I was also ashamed. "How many children in their family have died? How long were they hungry? What did we do to help them?"

That was all I asked. It was enough. Edward gave the siblings a stern dressing-down and then told them to quit the place.

"Seems to me they got off lightly," Mr. Douglas said.

"Not really," I said. "They have lost their income. They will have to confess this transgression to their families."

"Their children will not suffer," Edward said. "I shall see to it."

The three of us sat up late that evening, talking until we were exhausted. "I believe your response was correct," Mr. Douglas said. "You showed compassion and mercy."

"Actually," Edward said as he swirled amber brandy in a

snifter while we sat before the fire, "my wife showed compassion and mercy. I bowed to her wishes."

I stirred the coals, watching them fade until they were nothing more than gray and white ashes. "Their crime was in response to our neglect. We should have done more for them."

"And we will, my darling. I promise you."

That night I dreamed I stood in the garden and stared up at the stars. As a child, I promised myself that my mother and father looked down on me. It was fanciful and reassuring, but it gave me no comfort now. I wanted to see my son grow into a man. I wanted to be at Adèle's side when she wore a bridal veil. I wanted to stand beside Lucy and Augie Brayton's son when he matriculated at Eton.

I breathed in the sweet fragrance of violets and turned to see my friend Helen beside me. "Did you cry out for help? Was it your voice I heard?"

Of course. She smiled at me. *We are never really parted from those we love. The stars disappear in the harsh light of day, but still they shine. They might be invisible, but they are there.*

The next morning my husband woke me up with a kiss. We took our time getting dressed.

"I had the strangest dream." I took my husband by the hand.

"What about, my darling?" He kissed my palm, and we walked side by side down the hallway. Edward stopped and poked his head into the kitchen. "Mrs. Fairfax? Would you bring our tea out into the parlor?"

"I am trying to remember. It was about my old childhood friend, Helen. Helen Burns. She came to me. I can't recall what she said. Give me a minute."

I was backing into my chair when something stopped me. A flash of purple caught my eye. I turned and stared at it, there on my seat.

One perfect violet.

Author's Note

It is easy to confirm that *Jane Eyre* was first published in 1847; however, pinning down the exact year in which Charlotte Brontë's classic was set proves more challenging. Allusions to publications by Keats and Byron suggest a timeframe between 1814 and 1820. There are other hints as well.

The book that intrigues eight-year-old Jane, Thomas Bewick's *A History of British Birds*, was published in two volumes, between 1797 and 1804. Since the rest of the tale (up until the concluding chapter) takes effect over the next ten years of Jane's life, we are now looking at an "autobiography" set somewhere around the year 1815.

In any event, I chose the year 1820 for this continuation of Jane's narrative because the death of George III and the ascension of his son made for such a fascinating period in history. Few men have ever been as thoroughly blessed and as totally despicable as King George IV, George Augustus Frederick of the House of Hanover. It is against the backdrop of this sovereign's immorality, selfishness, and irresponsibility that Jane's character truly shines. Although King George IV was endowed with every advantage, and Jane Eyre a fictional orphan with none, there is no question in my mind which of these two characters has stood the test of time.

To learn more about this era, please visit my website, www.JoannaSlan.com, for a listing of resources.